Victorian Women and
the Theatre of Trance

Victorian Women and the Theatre of Trance

Mediums, Spiritualists and Mesmerists in Performance

AMY LEHMAN

McFarland & Company, Inc., Publishers
Jefferson, North Carolina, and London

Portions of Chapter 6 appeared first as an article in the
Summer 2002 issue of *Nineteenth Century Theatre and Film*.
Reprinted by permission of Manchester University Press.

LIBRARY OF CONGRESS CATALOGUING-IN-PUBLICATION DATA

Lehman, Amy.
   Victorian women and the theatre of trance : mediums,
spiritualists and mesmerists in performance / Amy Lehman.
     p.   cm.
   Includes bibliographical references and index.

   ISBN 978-0-7864-3479-4
   softcover : 50# alkaline paper

   1. Women and spiritualism — United States — History —19th
century. 2. Women mediums — United States — History —19th
century. 3. Mesmerism — United States — History —19th century.
4. Theater — United States — History —19th century. 5. Women
and spiritualism — Great Britain — History —19th century.
6. Women mediums — Great Britain — History —19th century.
7. Mesmerism — Great Britain — History —19th century.
8. Theater — Great Britain — History —19th century. I. Title.
BF1275.W65L45   2009
793.8 — dc22   2009026561

British Library cataloguing data are available

©2009 Amy Lehman. All rights reserved

*No part of this book may be reproduced or transmitted in any form
or by any means, electronic or mechanical, including photocopying
or recording, or by any information storage and retrieval system,
without permission in writing from the publisher.*

On the cover: Cora Scott Hatch, around 1857; frame and
background ©2009 Shutterstock

Manufactured in the United States of America

McFarland & Company, Inc., Publishers
  Box 611, Jefferson, North Carolina 28640
    www.mcfarlandpub.com

To Lyle and Margaret Lehman

Table of Contents

Acknowledgments ix
Introduction 1

1 — Victorian Theatre and Theatricality in Victorian Culture   9
2 — The Victorian Woman as Actress and the Roles She Played   17
3 — Mesmer and Charcot: The Trance Performance as Medical Show   31
4 — The Performances of Elizabeth O'Key: The Medical Theatre of Mesmerism   39
5 — "Double Consciousness" in Acting Theory and Trance State   55
6 — "Call Me Gypsy": Anna Cora Mowatt's Trance Performances   63
7 — The Rise of Spiritualism and the Fox Sisters   79
8 — Séance as Theatre   88
9 — Spirit Travels to Distant Times and Places   102
10 — Cora L. V. Richmond: Spiritualist Trance Star   115
11 — The Performance of "Ouina" and the Racial "Other"   127
12 — Spiritualism Crosses Over to England: Florence Cook and the Materialization Séance   142
13 — "Katie King" and Robert Dale Owen   160
14 — Materialization, Ectoplasm and Realism   168

Epilogue 178
Chapter Notes 181
Bibliography 191
Index 199

Acknowledgments

Thanks to my sister Cynthia Kester
for all kinds of support.

Thanks to friends and colleagues
who have encouraged me over the years,
including Karla, Juli, and Gretchen; Joan and Robin;
and to Laurie for the gift of my first computer.

Thanks to Lelsey Kordecki for reading and
responding generously to an early draft.

Introduction

> Theater is a license for a remarkable exercise in group imagination.
> — Bert O. States, *Great Reckonings in Little Rooms:
> On the Phenomenology of Theater*[1]

Spiritualists in the nineteenth century spoke reverently of a place they called the "Borderland," a shadowy threshold where the living communed with the dead, and where those left behind in the material realm could receive comfort or advice from another world. A place of limitless possibilities, the "Borderland" was also a theatre where fantastic dramas of revelation and recognition were performed. Here the actor was a trance medium, and the characters discarnate spirits of wise souls from the past or cheeky spooks having a lark with their earthly audience. The audience itself was as varied as the characters who appeared. Spectators might be amused skeptics or ardent believers. They came hoping for news of loved ones who had passed on, or just wanting entertainment or escapism. This Victorian theatre of spirits was produced through trance performances and séances, often conducted by women. These riveting embodiments of a bizarre range of spirits had significant potential as a means of self-expression for Victorian women. Female trance performance had antecedents in the earliest known rituals of shamans and oracles, and Victorian séances and ancient rituals also shared a fundamental dynamic with theatre — all were essentially "a remarkable exercise in group imagination."

Performances of faith or performances of theatre have always been imaginative contracts which succeed and flourish only with the participation of their spectators. Their audiences must willingly suspend disbelief, and accept, if only for the duration of the performance, what is seen and heard as genuine. Trance mediumship and the Spiritualist movement it engendered are often dismissed as simple fakery. Spirit manifestations are seen as no more than deliberate attempts by clever charlatans to prey on people rendered vulnerable by loss or by their desperate desire for guidance from an otherworldly power. Too much of the time, this was probably true. Fraud has doubtless played a role in many performances of shamans, oracles and trance mediums throughout history. But the interpretation of all such phenomena as mere trickery is reductive, and a dead end to attempts to understand and derive meaning from them. A fuller account should be taken of a range of possible explanations and influences, and credit given to the powerful creativity of the individuals involved. Whether or not they were "real," trance performances must have offered something of value to their performers as well as their spectators, particularly in the forms they took in the nineteenth century Victorian theatre of spirits.

In trance performances, as in legitimate theatre, the motivations and desires of the performers and audiences were complex. Naiveté alone cannot explain the passionate emotions and belief aroused by the impersonations and enactments of séances — happenings which in other contexts might seem transparently absurd. A clearer and more highly faceted lens through which to view séance phenomena, mediumship and trance performance, particularly in the Victorian era, is that of theatre; including the theories and practice of acting, audience and reception dynamics, and the effects of theatrical spectacle. Nineteenth century trance performances and the women who enacted them may best be explored in the context of the popular theatre, and in the intense theatricality of the times.

Because theatricality informed so many aspects of Victorian culture, fascinating performances occurred not only on the stages of theatres, but in lecture halls, auditoria and private parlors where mediums or trance speakers assumed the characters of different spirits: of the recently departed, of exotic Indian chiefs, pirates, and gypsies, or of historical figures like George Washington or Benjamin Franklin. The female trance performer attracted special attention, since by assuming the voice and behavior of these spirit "others," an ordinary woman might transcend her normal social role for the first time and speak publicly and authoritatively, not only about the glorious Spiritualist afterlife, but about more earthly (and controversial) issues such as abolition, women's rights or the position of Native Americans.

A woman performing in a trance state in the Victorian era might be found in a number of different contexts: as a professional medium, a Spiritualist trance speaker, or as the medical subject of scientific experiments on the effects of mesmerism or hypnotism. In all of these cases, she appeared to enter into an altered state of consciousness in which she could access and manifest esoteric wisdom, spiritual entities, or even normally hidden aspects of her own personality.

Controversy often centered on the participation of women, since assumptions about women's mutability and their ability to "act" heightened anxiety about their social and moral stability already called into question by cultural stereotypes. The Victorian obsession with women performing as Spiritualist mediums, trance speakers, or medical exhibitions on the effects of mesmerism (especially in Britain and America) culminated in the English novel *Trilby* written by Gerald Du Maurier in 1896. The wildly popular work of fiction and its stage versions portrayed the young heroine Trilby, who became a successful singer in a trance, as the helpless victim of Svengali, the manipulative male who controlled her performances for his own purposes. Although it did so in a superficial and sensational way, the story of Trilby and Svengali touched the sorest point of women's trance performances for the Victorians, and a central question of this study: Were Victorian women empowered or victimized by the theatre of trance in which they performed?

Organization

This book discusses the experiences of these women as part of a narrative of Victorian theatre, looking at them in terms of dramatic role playing, and considering the contexts in which the women performed as varieties of dramatic spectacle. Insights and interpretive techniques from theatre and performance studies guide an exploration of why and how these performances occurred. Discussions of the larger picture alternate with more specific case studies.

The introduction surveys the origins and theories of female trance performance in ancient times. The opening chapters discuss the Victorians' love of theatre and drama, and developments in acting, stage spectacle and realism. They also deal with the centrality of images of women and the feminine to a cultural obsession with theatricality and acting, and look at some of the "roles" women were assigned both on stage and off. Next, a chapter about how mesmerism laid the groundwork for trance performance in the Victorian era is followed by the first case study, which focuses on a young woman named Elizabeth O'Key. O'Key's entertaining displays of singing, dancing, and jokes in a state of mesmeric trance drew crowds of spectators to medical exhibits in London in the 1830s. A chapter exploring "double-consciousness" as the common ground of the trance state and acting, and its therapeutic implications, precedes the next case study, of actress Anna Cora Mowatt. Mowatt manifested the cheeky character of "Gypsy" when she began to use mesmerism to relieve symptoms of what was most likely tuberculosis in the late 1830s. The rise of Spiritualism, initially in America in 1848 then spreading to Britain in the 1850s and 1860s, and the wealth of trance performances it unleashed, is discussed next. An exploration of the similarities between Spiritualist séances and Victorian theatre, and the performance possibilities of "spirit travel," is followed by a case study of Cora L. V. Richmond, the most successful Spiritualist trance speaker of the nineteenth century. The performance of "racial others" like Cora Richmond's Indian spirit "Ouina" are featured in the next section, before the focus shifts to Britain, where a new phase of trance performance, the "materialisation séance," became popular in the 1870s. The next case study is of British medium Florence Cook and her spirit embodiments of Katie King. Katie was such a popular character on the Spiritualist stage that she was played by several different mediums, and the next chapter focuses on her notorious manifestations in Philadelphia in 1874. The final chapter discusses materialist mediums such as Eusapia Palladino and Madame D'Esperance, and the advent of the ectoplasmic séance, the *ne plus ultra* of "realism" in the theatre of trance at the end of the Victorian period. The epilogue examines the decline of materialization séances, which paralleled the declining success of spectacular realism in the theatre.

By using theatre as a way to focus on women trance performers and their experiences, which have largely remained obscure footnotes in nineteenth century social history, this study hopes to show how the trance state, allied to the transformative possibilities of theatre, provided significant opportunities for Victorian women, to speak, act, and create outside the boundaries of their normally restricted social and psychological roles.

Ritual Origins of Female Trance Performance

Although this book deals specifically with the Victorian era, connections among women, theatre and trance have a long history, which can be better understood by first looking at some of the earliest historical examples of trance performances. Theatre historians speculate that the first performers may in fact have been mediums acting in a trance. Many theories of the origins of theatre link it to rituals performed by priests, shamans or prophets whose ability to mediate between this world and the next by communicating the will of the gods, often through impersonating them, to the living, made them revered and influential figures in many ancient cultures. Theatre in China, for instance, may have arisen from priests embodying spirits of the gods or of the dead. Indonesian shadow puppet theatre was influenced by the tricks mediums used to represent spirits with light and shadow.

In Western culture, the best known example of an early trance performer may be the Delphic oracle of ancient Greece, who was always a woman. Her powerful performances took place not in the open air theatres of Athens or Epidauros, where women were not allowed to act at all, but in the temple of Apollo at Delphi, where the pythia or priestess impersonated Apollo himself. Seated over a tripod in the temple at Delphi, the pythia went into a trance state which seemingly allowed the god to speak through her in the first person, answering questions put to him by suppliants. The answers were written down, sometimes in verse, by male priests, but it was the female pythia alone who received the initial communication or inspiration, and she alone who many believed embodied the god. Historians suggest different explanations for the apparent trances. Some posit possession, or self-induced hypnosis. E. R. Dodds wrote that the "god entered into her [the oracle] and used her vocal organs as if they were his own, exactly as the so-called 'control' does in modern spirit-mediumship."[2] Dodd was "fairly certain that the Pythia's trance was auto-suggestively induced, like mediumistic trance today."[3] Other scholars suggest that the pythia was fully conscious and calculating in what she did; like an actress deliberately orchestrating her own performance, the pythia "would certainly make the consultation a dramatic ritual."[4]

A similar range of explanations would be suggested for nineteenth century trance phenomena, and the resulting debates resemble those in our own time about the origins and meaning of the characters and behaviors manifested in states of hypnosis or in dissociative identity disorder, commonly called multiple personality disorder. Whatever its origins, in ancient Greece, at least, this apparent ability to manifest the god in a trance gave the Delphic oracle considerable political and religious influence. The Delphic oracle famously advised the Athenians during the Persian and Peloponnesian wars, while also giving advice on more intimate domestic matters.[5] Inscriptions from suppliants found on small stone tablets at Delphi include questions about whom to marry, and when or if a child might be born. The concerns with family and everyday life are similar to those of men and women who consulted mediums in later centuries. Shamans, oracles and mediums were alluring then for the same reasons mediums, psychics and channelers continue to attract followers well into the twenty-first century.

E. T. Kirby describes the process by which shamanic trance impersonations, which originally occurred in specifically ritualistic contexts like that of the Delphic oracle, developed into purely theatrical spectacle.[6] He asserts that "the delusionary or hallucinatory experience ... of shamanistic performance ... may be considered a basic aspect of primal theatre."[7] Other theories suggest that Greek tragedy in particular arose from the performance of ritual dithyrambs for Dionysus, while the frenzied behavior of Dionysus, and Bacchus' female followers, the maenads, is compared to the trance possession of the Delphic oracle.[8]

The violence of the maenads and reports of the exhaustion of the oracle after a successful trance performance suggest the dynamic of catharsis, which is key to the earliest definitions of tragedy from Aristotle's *Poetics*. Catharsis is also clearly present in many ritual performances. Although the precise meaning of "catharsis" as used by Aristotle is still debated (who is meant to experience catharsis, for instance: the audience or the performer?), the word is essentially associated with release and purging, and has undeniable therapeutic implications. Interesting connections between performing or acting out strong emotions and a cathartic or therapeutic effect persist in modern psychiatric theories, and have obvious significance for female trance performance, as the case studies will show.

The notion of an altered state of consciousness is also crucial to most theories of ritual and performance. Even historians who deny any supernatural phenomena (William Ridgeway, for instance, posits that drama evolved from funeral ceremonies conducted by mediums in a trance to honor the heroic dead, not from contact with spirits or gods)[9] concede that some alteration of consciousness was the usual pre-condition for the priest or priestess' performance, providing the liminal state necessary for these phenomena to occur. The concept of liminality in ritual and performance was developed most notably by Victor Turner in *Ritual and Theatre*. The term "liminal," which comes from the Greek word for "doorway," describes a state that is betwixt and between, full of possibility and potential creativity. Turner compares the three part structure of ritual (a *liminal* phenomenon) to that of theatre (a *liminoid* phenomenon). Part one is a period of stasis, part two is the passage through a liminal phase, and part three is a return to stasis with a difference.[10] Turner discusses primarily initiation rites — rituals in which some change of status is to be effected by the performance, such as the passage from childhood to adulthood, or of the living to the afterworld. The liminal phase is the crucial, creative and liberating moment. In the liminal phase, one is temporarily freed from the restrictions of the former state but has not yet taken on the restrictions of the future state. This is an altered state of consciousness in which one is neither sleeping nor waking. When one is "not herself" she has a freedom of speech and behavior not found in other states. It is comparable to the state of an actor who takes on a role and "becomes" another self, at least for the duration of the performance. It is this altered state which seems to be the key to people's fascination with trance, and to some extent with theatre and acting as well, so it is no surprise that we find the two linked historically and theoretically.

Modern theatre scholars interested in the liminal or transformative potential of theatre have theorized how performance can both subvert and reify stereotyped gender and social roles, and some of their ideas provide useful tools for analyzing trance mediumship. This study's analysis of Victorian women performing in trance draws on the insights of current scholars like Judith Butler and Laurence Senelick, who posit that gender is a concept or an identity created by *performance*: that, for example, there is no essential biological femininity, but that, "female-ness" is produced by *acting* "female." Because acting, then, can create a social reality, performance has the potential power to subvert stereotypes. Conversely, repeated enactments may make stereotypes even stronger.[11]

This tension between playing the stereotype and subverting it is part of the drama of the female trance performance. And the fact that the acting and the role playing take place when the performer is in an altered state of consciousness gives them even more power, since the performer can disclaim personal responsibility for any words or behaviors that transgress normal social, gender or psychological roles. It is not surprising that some form of trance performance has attracted women throughout history. Given the increased rigidity of social roles in the period, the lure of trance mediumship for Victorian women was potentially very powerful, though the degree to which its benefits, as well as its risks, were realized would vary greatly.

1

Victorian Theatre and Theatricality in Victorian Culture

Theatricality in Victorian Life and Culture

The term "theatrical" can be ambiguous, and sometimes overburdened, but I use it here in a broad and fairly straightforward way to refer to elements related to, or sharing characteristics with, aspects of the legitimate theatre; including actors and audiences, role playing and impersonation, and setting and spectacle. I also use the terms "theatrical" or "theatricality" to suggest an "interpretive model for describing psychological identity" and "social ceremonies,"[1] as well as a mode of perceiving oneself in the world.

Victorian society was theatrical in that many of its members saw their world as a stage and themselves as actors. The play in which they found themselves was a great Dickensian drama overflowing with colorful characters, strong sentiment, love stories and narrow escapes. The popular theatre was a great unifying obsession for many Victorians, cutting across class, gender and national boundaries. Whether exalting in its emotionalism and spectacle, or deploring its corrupting influence, few people were indifferent to the theatre, particularly to actors and acting.

People whose imaginations were fired in the theatre sometimes tried to recreate the drama at home. Perhaps because theatrical conventions and dramatic roles already reflected much of what they felt and understood about their own lives, it was a short step to bring theatre and play acting into the domestic sphere. Amateur theatricals, which had developed as home entertainment in the eighteenth century, enjoyed even greater popularity in the nineteenth century. Tableaux vivants and charades were popular parlor games in Europe, England and America. Particularly for middle or upper class women, putting on performances at home could be a way to participate more privately in a thrilling world of play acting without endangering their respectable status, as participation in a public, or professional activity might do. The involvement of women in home theatricals, in which they impersonated fictional characters just for the entertainment of family and friends, would also set a precedent for women's activity as mediums, when they performed spirits in séances for the same sorts of private audiences.

More daring men and women of a higher class, might try to go public, although not of course, as professionals. For their own amusement, socialites in Paris in the 1830s staged comic "well-made plays" by Eugene Scribe for invited audiences of as many as four hundred people. In London in the 1820s and 1830s it was not unknown for private theatres to be hired by wealthy amateurs who wanted to get a taste of performing on stage, with a very few of these perhaps wanting to launch a professional career, though this seemed to have happened only rarely. The real attraction for amateur actors was to experience, even briefly, the thrill of being on stage and the center of attention. The desire for celebrity was as powerful for the Victorians as it is for us today.

The charisma of star performers was key to nineteenth century theatre, and this was the era in which actors first became international celebrities. Visual extravagance and any appeal to the senses was also crucial. The Victorians' appetite for theatricality, in the sense of vivid and usually visually delineated emotion, extended to every mode of communication and form of art in their culture, and was seemingly insatiable. The theatrical nature of Dickens' fiction, for instance, has been much discussed. Theatre and cultural historian Martin Meisel has argued that drama, fiction and painting shared strong narrative conventions related to the images they were expected to convey, which had to simultaneously satisfy two apparently contradictory functions: to represent "reality," and to "realize the ideal."[2] A novel, picture or play, for instance, had to provide both the specificity and immediacy of reality that an audience could empathize with, and the more universal quality of expressing or "realizing" a broader cultural or moral ideal, such as "True Motherhood" or "Gentlemanliness." The best actors were able to achieve a performance that conveyed both the reality, and the ideal essence of their characters. George Henry Lewes, an early theorist of acting, gave famous French tragedienne Rachel the highest possible praise when he described her Phèdre as "inexpressibly affecting and intensely true. As an ideal representation of real emotion, it belonged the highest art."[3] Successful theatre gave audiences individualized characters and intimate situations with which they could identity, along with a larger world of essential human emotions and values.

The popular and ubiquitous Melodrama in particular was often successful in satisfying both these of these requirements. Many melodramas portrayed working or middle class people in familiar circumstances and places (girls selling flowers at Waterloo station in London, for instance), while suggesting that particular characters simultaneously stood for symbolic types and situations such as "Youthful Innocence" (the virginal heroine) menaced by "Sinister Evil" (the Black haired and Black-hearted Villain). Images like these were pervasive on the popular stage, and also seemed to provide examples of how to view the world and delineate social and moral roles outside the theatre. Some of the confluences between social and stage roles for women, which will be discussed in the next chapter, were especially powerful.

Performers themselves, as well as the ideas or universal types they represented, fascinated Victorians. Actors and mediums seemed to play with fundamental concepts of character and truth, working out, in their enactments of reality, the dictum that "seeing is believing." Empiricism and the scientific method had a growing influence on philosophy, science and even art in the nineteenth century. People in many fields seemed increasingly to rely on sensory data, especially visual phenomena, to explain the world. The credo that knowledge could be obtained by what was observed through the senses was key for materialist and positivist philosophers, and also for pseudo-scientists like physiognomists and phrenologists. Phrenologists, for instance, insisted that physical bumps on the head were true indicators of personality and predictors of human nature. The spectators at a melodrama relied in a similar way on the character's outward appearance as a reliable indicator of the character's true inner self. The implication for people in the every day social drama of Victorian life was the same — what you perceived through the senses — sight, hearing, touch — was a reliable indicator of truth and reality. Even believers in the spirits would expect "physical proofs" — voices, movements, the playing of musical instruments by unseen hands, and material phenomena such as "apports," or the sudden appearance of objects such as flowers or jewels in the séance room. Philosophical notions about the ideal and the real, as well as about materialism and the senses provided the basis, as they trickled down into popular understanding and beliefs, for some of the major theatrical trends of the time, discussed below.

The Supernatural Made Visible

Early nineteenth century audiences loved Romantic and gothic drama, which offered graphic portrayals of the supernatural on stage. These plays satisfied an appetite for physical and sensory (real) demonstrations of even presumably non-physical (ideal) elements. One of the first gothic melodramas, *The Castle Spectre* (1797) included a spectacular ghost scene. The blood curdling effect when the apparition of the heroine's murdered mother appears was described in the stage directions:

> The folding doors unclose, and the Oratory is seen illuminated. In its centre stands a tall female figure, her white and flowing garments spotted with blood; her veil is thrown back, and discovers a pale and melancholy countenence; her eyes are lifted upwards, her arms extended towards heaven, and a large wound appears upon her bosom....[4]

Other notable gothic plays included dramatizations of Mary Shelley's *Frankenstein*, which appeared in English theatres in 1823. In 1824, Weber's opera *Die Frieschutz* was made into four melodramas and two burlesques (the irrefutable sign of popular success), in productions brimming with terrifying sights like ghouls, serpents, wheels of fire, skeleton stags, thunder, lightning, a river of blood and the spectral figure of the "dreaded Black Huntsman."[5]

Successful vampire plays were staged in 1820, 1834, 1852, and 1862, years before Bram Stoker's *Dracula* was dramatized in the 1890s. A version of *Dr. Jekyll and Mr. Hyde* first appeared in theatres in 1887, and when it was performed in London in 1888, the actor Richard Mansfield was so convincing in his terrifying transformation of the mild Jekyll to the fiend Hyde (performed in full view of the audience) that he was suspected of being connected with the Jack the Ripper murders which were terrorizing the city at the same time.

Victorian plays also frequently included vision scenes, in which characters saw ghost-like enactments of people and events distant in time or space. Two of the most frequently produced plays of the mid Victorian period featured famous vision scenes, as well as mesmerizing lead roles for the actors. *The Corsican Brothers* dealt with a pair of twins with strange psychic powers. *The Bells*, in which Henry Irving played a man haunted by the apparition of an old Jew he had killed years before, became a standard hit for the charismatic actor. Audiences were riveted by Irving's portrayal of growing terror as manifestations of the phantom appeared more and more real to him.

Spectacle, Sensation and Barnum's Museum

Sensation of any kind, whether gothic or just weird and freakish, could draw large crowds. The most popular theatrical displays in New York City at mid century were at Barnum's museum on Broadway. The "museum," housed several floors of large exhibit halls and galleries, where bizarre spectacles combined the Victorians' love of enlightenment with entertainment. At Barnum's one could see a mind boggling variety of oddities including a giant, Siamese twins, Joyce Heth (the oldest living woman), Tom Thumb (the well loved dwarf), and the so-called "Feejee mermaid." A group advertised as the "Shaking Quakers," composed of former Shakers from the Canterbury, New Hampshire, Shaker community, did a dancing, twirling and singing act supposedly based on the unrestrained religious rituals which had given the "Shakers" their name. There were magic shows and even a gypsy fortune teller who could be booked for private consultations. Barnum's Museum also included a large and well equipped theatre for the performance of what Barnum insisted be moral plays (like the temperance melodrama *The Drunkard*) or farces suitable for the whole family. Barnum booked appearances by some of the most popular shows of the time, including T. D. Rice's black face "Jim Crow" act, minstrel shows, the operatic diva Jenny Lind, and a run of *Uncle Tom's Cabin*. The child actor Cordelia Howard was a stand-out as Little Eva in the play, and Barnum capitalized on the popularity of infant prodigies when he produced plays featuring child stars the Bateman sisters, Kate and Ellen.

The Growth of Realism

The trend which best reflected the materialist tendencies of the age was Realism. When the first "spirit bodies" began to appear in trance performances in the 1870s, Realism was gaining ground in the legitimate theatre, especially in terms of visual spectacle, design and production practices. Early Victorian scene painters of the Romantic theatre had attempted to convey the sublime and ineffable atmospheric effects in Nature as realistically as possible. By the 1830s, attempts were being made to make the interiors of rooms and houses more realistic through the use of the box set — a room with the 4th wall removed. Widespread use of the box set and movement towards use of solid three-dimensional scenery instead of illusionistic painted flats and drops was somewhat slow to catch on, since flats and drops were easier, quicker to change, and less expensive for most theatres. But by the 1890s, the realistic box set was being fully exploited in larger professional theatres, especially by American producer director David Belasco. Belasco's almost obsessively detailed real settings, and similar scenic lavishness in Augustin Daly's productions, exemplified the trend for meticulously furnished interior settings on Broadway as well as on the London stage. Belasco's realism culminated, in the early twentieth century, with a production for which he purchased the entire contents of a boarding-house room to place onstage as a set for a 1909 play *The Easiest Way*—the ultimate in "slice of life" theatre.

For much of the second half of the nineteenth century, melodramas and the carefully plotted "well-made play" were still the most popular types of drama, and although they were not particularly "realistic" in terms of plot or character, they depended heavily on visual realism for excitement and an emotional charge. Dion Boucicault's melodramas were marketed on the strength of sensational but realistic effects like the exploding steam boat in *The Octoroon*, or the train bearing down on an innocent victim tied to the tracks in *After Dark*.

The need for detailed realism in staging became more pressing as the realism of social dramas like Henrik Ibsen's and the new naturalistic drama gained ground. In his preface to the naturalistic play *Miss Julie* (1888), playwright August Strindberg condemned the use of sagging old canvas flats in production. Strindberg had written *Miss Julie* in part to prove that he could write a play which satisfied Emile Zola, whose manifesto of Naturalism called for objectivity, frankness, determinism and amorality in theatre. Production values were especially crucial to support the naturalist philosophy that characters were determined by their environment. As Strindberg observed, every time a supposedly solid wall made of canvas shuddered when an actor entered through its equally flimsy door, the illusion of reality was destroyed, and the audience distracted. Strindberg insisted upon scenery that was solid as possible, and upon real, not painted props such as books and dishes onstage. The tendency towards scenic naturalism approached the absurd in André Antoine's Théâtre Libre, where the radical young director hung real beef carcasses on stage for a play called *The Butchers*.

Few productions took naturalism in settings so far. But realism in terms of characters and acting style began to make inroads in some of the avant garde new plays of Henrik Ibsen, for instance. Especially striking were Ibsen's Nora, Hedda and Mrs. Alving, modern heroines who shocked audiences in the last decades of the century. In London, actor manager Henry Irving's personal charisma and emotional naturalism, despite the overt theatricality (and idiosyncrasy) of his mannerisms made him a celebrity at the Lyceum theatre. His pre-eminence as an actor manager, alongside actress Ellen Terry, was representative of a burgeoning star system, which by the end of the century would make international celebrities of actresses as varied in style as Sarah Bernhardt, renowned for her immense sensational charisma, and Eleanora Duse, praised for the profound truthfulness of her acting.

Nonetheless, by the last quarter of the century, the theatrical balance had begun to tip towards setting and spectacle over characters and acting. Even the most celebrated actor in London or New York could not depend solely on his acting prowess, or the power of language to win over audiences and satisfy fans. Theatre manager E. T. Smith, who headed Astley's theatre in London, which produced popular "equestrian dramas" featuring daredevil horseback riding and stunts more or less integrated into its melodramas, had voiced this opinion in testimony before a parliamentary committee investigating professional theatre in 1866. Justifying his own productions, which were as much circus as legitimate drama, he declared "for a person to bring out a merely talking drama, without any action in it, or sensational effects, is useless; the people will not go to that theatre; they will go where there is scenic effect, and mechanical effects to please the eye." At the end of the century, producer and director Max Beerbohm concurred, "Our public cares not at all for the sound of word, and will not tolerate poetry on stage unless it gets also gorgeous and solid scenery...."[6] Henry Irving, the most successful actor manager in late Victorian Britain, seldom ventured onstage in any other than sumptuous settings with the most lavish and realistic visual effects.

American theatre was if anything even more obsessed with realistic spectacle, demonstrated by the productions of David Belasco. Belasco insisted on solid physical realizations and even living creatures when possible. In an 1881 production of a play called *The Curse of Cain*, Belasco "indulged to the full his liking for literalism" in the scene of the gypsy camp by "providing for the public edification a braying donkey, neighing horses, cackling hens, crowing cocks, quacking ducks, and a rooting grunting pig."[7] Not even Shakespeare was excepted from this literalist treatment. In a production of *A Midsummer Night's Dream* featuring real trees and flowers on stage, live rabbits and other forest animals gamboled among the plants and foliage. So much for "the word creates the décor."

The insistence on literalism also extended to the portrayal of the still popular supernatural plays. Belasco's 1877 production of a play called *The Dead Secret* was essentially a ghost story which relied on "the most primitive and venerable machinery of supernaturalism," and embodied every effect including "luminous hands, bouquets fresh from Elysian fields," as well as that favorite device of séances, music played by "spiritual fingers upon material guitars."[8] Henry Irving's 1878 production of the ghostly melodrama *Vanderdecken*, a play about the Flying Dutchman, succeeded "on the strength of its weirdness and the admirable scenery applied to it," including a prologue in which "by the means of a magic-lantern a vision of the phantom ship is exhibited in the background."

Staging and scenic technology, like magician's tricks, were developed to achieve specific effects involving the portrayal of the supernatural in performances throughout the course of the century. Two of these were the "Corsican trap" and the "Vampire trap," both named for the plays in which they were featured. The Corsican trap or "ghost glide," as it was called, was a long trap or opening in the stage floor parallel to the proscenium which allowed the actor to move slowly across the stage, appearing to gradually sink into solid ground. The vampire trap was a spring-leaved trap which could be set into either a wall or the stage floor, letting the actor appear to make a sudden supernatural entrance, and then depart through a solid surface. One of the most popular effects was "Pepper's ghost." It was named for Professor John Henry Pepper of London's Royal Polytechnic Institute, who helped develop the technique in 1862. The illusion produced looked somewhat like a holograph, and was created with carefully angled mirrors and lighting to reflect an image from off stage onto the stage in a ghostly manner. It could also be used to supernaturally transform one image to another, like an ordinary man into a monster. Versions of "Pepper's ghost" are still used today (in Disney theme parks, for instance) for stage and haunted house illusions.

There were, as mentioned above, philosophical bases for these theatrical trends, and these also had important ramifications for trance performances. Both on and off the stage, Victorians grappled with the assumption that "seeing is believing" in literal and visceral ways that can be difficult to grasp and easy to mock in a "postmodern" world. Mediums' attempts to provide physical evidence for the spirits became more and more absurd as the century progressed, as did the efforts of scenic and special effects artists in the Victorian theatre to show "reality" on stage. In the last decades of the nineteenth century, some séance mediums began to produce an actual substance called "ectoplasm" which they claimed was a material manifestation or actual "physical body" for the spirit they were contacting. The concept of a physical spirit was an insurmountable oxymoron for even some of the most hard core Spiritualists, when mediums trying to satisfy audience demands for physical proofs found themselves obliged to produce *matter* as evidence of *spirit*. The production of "ectoplasm," discussed in the concluding sections of this book, was perhaps the grossest manifestation of this conundrum.

Subtle and far reaching questions about appearance and reality were raised by trance performers throughout the century, as the number of journals, essays, and books (fiction and non fiction) lavished on the subject of mesmerism and Spiritualism shows. And many of the questions raised about truth, appearance and acting revolved around the issue of women's theatricality, and her innate, uncanny talent for playing a role both on and off the stage.

2

The Victorian Woman as Actress and the Roles She Played

The Fearful Power of Women Acting

A classical scholar in 1918 writing about the ancient Delphic oracle commented on the long history of women performing in trances: "It has been observed at all times and in all countries that women are especially prone to orgiastic religious seizure, and with such moods prophecy and magic have been associated."[1] The author would have been familiar with the proliferation of female mediums in the nineteenth century, and his tone reveals a typical Victorian attitude about the volatility of the female psyche (and a typical Victorian confidence in the validity of applying contemporary theories equally to all times and places.) It was a common assumption that women were prone to uncontrollable emotional, spiritual or erotic fits, which might be linked to occult powers or phenomena. And because women in Victorian society were charged with providing stability and standards in the home, and passing on traditional values to their families, this potential unreliability, this mutability and irrationality, had serious implications. A society already beset by major social, scientific and cultural upheavals was even more at risk if the "hand that rocked the cradle" was unsteady.

There were many reasons for Victorians to feel that times were turbulent, and that they badly needed the woman's steady hand at home to ground them. Major movements in population were part of the problem. In nineteenth century Britain and America, people moved from rural to urban areas to work in the factories spawned by the Industrial revolution, radically increasing the size of many cities. Between 1801 and 1851 the population of London grew from 900,000 to 3,000,000, and by 1901 had reached 6,000,000.[2] The attendant problems of overcrowding, crime, pollution, poor sanitation and poverty bedeviled major British and American cities throughout the century. Technology speeded up communications and transportation with telegraphs and railroads, and the pace of every day life increased. Not just material conditions were changing. The emergence of scientific and philosophical theories such as Darwinism and positivism indirectly created anxiety, as traditional ideas about religion, the social order, and gender roles began to be questioned. Belief in the survival of the soul and the afterlife, which were at the crux of Spiritualism's appeal, had been called into question to a greater extent than ever before. J. Arthur Hill argues that "particularly after the biological advance associated with Darwin and his followers ... the belief in a real individual survival faded almost away for most scientific men and even for the thinking layman and priest...."[3]

Women's assigned roles as moral compasses and keepers of domestic purity were touted in pulpits and periodicals. At the same time, women themselves were beginning to agitate for change. American women's rights activists held their first convention in Seneca Falls, New York, in 1848, the same year that the Fox sisters in Hydesville, New York, heralded the advent of Spiritualism with their infamous rappings. Even as some attempted to extend social and political rights and opportunities for women, others pushed even harder to confine them to the domestic and private sphere, and the powerful myth of the "Angel in the House" was born. The phrase, the title of a popular sentimental poem sequence written 1854–1863 by Coventry Patmore, crystallized the conventional Victorians' notion of the place of women. This notion coexisted with the less overt but equally powerful notion that women had a dark destructive side. This demonic side was symbolized in art by representations of women as seductresses, temptresses like Salome, or supernatural beings like fairies or mermaids. Nina Auerbach writes of the dark side of the Victorian myth of Womanhood her book *Woman and the Demon*. "While right-thinking Victorians were elevating woman into an angel, their art slithered with images of a mermaid. Angels were thought to be meekly self-sacrificial by nature: in this cautiously diluted form they were pious emblems of a good woman's submergence in her family. Mermaids, on the other hand, submerge themselves not to negate their power, but to conceal it."[4] The simultaneous but conflicting inclinations to see Woman as both the Angelic linchpin of domestic bliss and its demonic destroyer gave Victorian attitudes towards women a decidedly schizophrenic cast.

Women's unstable qualities were believed to be exacerbated when they engaged in activities which involved performance or spirituality, which capitalized on their inherent intuition and emotionalism. Mediumship, of course, combined elements of both. Like public speaking (including preaching) or acting, it required exposure before an audience, however small. Female mediums were subject to some of the same criticism aimed at actresses for displaying themselves in public. Some mediums tried to retain their propriety by insisting that they were not *professionals*, who acted in front of the public, but *private* mediums only, performing for small circles of invited guests, and never for money.

The very scarcity of women (other than actresses) in the public sphere drew attention to them. To see any woman, other than a professional actress, on a public stage, was a sensation. Catherine Booth, wife of Salvation Army founder William Booth, commented on the drawing power of women Salvation army speakers in late nineteenth century London. She explained that "generations of the suppression of woman, and the consequent prejudice and curiosity with respect to her public performances, conspire immensely towards her attracting the people."[5]

Clearly any woman who engaged in public performance was an interesting figure, partaking of the allure of actors and theatre in general, which were at the time "charged with an extraordinary symbolic increment."[6] Actresses especially, associated as they were with erotic self display (and prostitution well into the nineteenth century), represented some of the most titillating potential of their sex. Charismatic performers, rather than fine dramatic literature, characterized the theatre of the time. Even the plays of Shakespeare, still the most frequently performed playwright in the nineteenth century, often functioned primarily as vehicles for star actors. The contemporary phenomena of celebrity worship has it roots in the massive public appeal of starring actors like Henry Irving and his costar Ellen Terry in Britain, the Booths (Junius Brutus, Edwin and John Wilkes) and Anna Cora Mowatt in America, and tragediennes Rachel and Sarah Bernhardt in France. All of these performers were internationally famous. While Bernhardt was not typical of working actresses of the nineteenth century, her success marks the apex of popularity to which a performer might aspire. She is significant as a symbol of the riveting power of the actress, and responses to her tell us a lot about the way acting, especially female acting, entranced the Victorians.

The notion of a mesmerizing or hypnotic power is implicit in descriptions of many actresses of the time, including Bernhardt. Sigmund Freud, for instance, wrote of watching Bernhardt perform in Paris in 1885. He was barely cognizant of the play in which she appeared, but was riveted by her performance and the sense of intimacy created by her voice and presence.

> I can't say anything about the piece itself.... But how that Sarah plays! After the first words of her lovely vibrant voice, I felt I had known her for years. Nothing she could have said would have surprised me; I believed at once everything she said ... I have never seen a more comical figure than Sarah in the second act, where she appears in a simple dress, and yet one soon stops laughing, for every inch of that figure lives and bewitches. Then her flattering and imploring and embracing.... A curious being: I can imagine that she needn't be any different in life than on the stage.[7]

If a student of human nature like Freud was rendered almost inarticulate by the sheer presence of the actress, it is not surprising that nineteenth century theatre reviewers had difficulty analyzing their appeal. Reviewers often resorted to ambiguous references to the bewitching nature of other actresses's presence. J. Ranken Towse said of Mary Anderson: "It was by the spell of her personal charms that she instantly made her way into the hearts of the American public."[8] William Winter referred both to the "massive reality" of Charlotte Cushman's presence and the inescapable "spell of her imperial power."[9] Such phrases show the influence of the Romantic concept of the sublime, that powerful, irrational and ineffable quality that was both overwhelming in its emotional effect and nearly impossible to put in words. Actress Mary Garden's ability to enchant was said by one critic to stem from her mutability; she was said to be endowed with "multiple personalities" and a "gift of versatility."[10] Fanny Kemble, of the famous English acting family, who was also extremely popular in America, was said to "have the power, which the very greatest geniuses of the stage possess, not only of enchaining the attention, but compelling an unconscious imitation of her looks in those of her hearers."[11]

Kemble seemed to mesmerize her audience. However, she also seemed to become "mesmerized" herself while performing. Fanny Kemble wrote about slipping into a trance-like state when acting, describing what she experienced when playing the role of Juliet:

> ... I began to forget myself ... for ought I knew, I was Juliet; the passion I was uttering sending hot waves of blushes all over my neck and shoulders, while the poetry sounded like music to me as I spoke it, with no consciousness of anything before me, utterly transported into the imaginary existence of the play. After this I did not return into myself til all was over....[12]

For Kemble, performance, like a mesmeric trance, had an effect on her that was both emotional and physical. Accounts like these could have only reinforced suspicions about the uncontrollable, even "orgiastic" nature of female performance.

Critiques of actors and actresses also tended to place a premium on the personal magnetism of the performer while discounting any consciously acquired skill or technique on their part. The tragedian Edmund Kean, for instance, arguably the most celebrated actor of his time, was often thought to be completely spontaneous. His performances were ascribed to his emotional personality and genius rather than conscious preparation or technique. Audiences seemed to like to imagine that the actor was simply an elemental force of nature, no different "in life than on the stage," as Freud said of Sarah Bernhardt. A much repeated observation of Samuel Taylor Coleridge compared watching Kean act to "watching Shakespeare performed by flashes of lightning." This quote is often taken to refer to the unreliability of inspiration in performance. It may refer more accurately, however, to the deliberate technique of "points-making" which was a fundamental technique of Romantic acting. Actors like Kean focused on the character's big emotional climaxes rather than striving to portray a more consistent or "realistic" psychological trajectory or Stanislavkian through line. At the dramatic height of a speech or scene, an actor might literally strike a pose, like an actor in Kabuki theatre, holding it long enough for the audience to appreciate and respond. So the impression of performing by "flashes of lightning" may in fact have been due to technique rather than inspiration.

The nineteenth century acting technique of making points was encouraged by the dramaturgy of the melodramas which dominated the stage. The style was in fact difficult to *avoid* in many popular plays. Actress and author Anna Cora Mowatt describes the popular play *The Lady of Lyons* (one of her own star vehicles) in a short story about an actress. The fictional actress, Stella, talks of the moments in the text designed to win a round of applause (literally "clap-traps").

> The author had planned a series of prominent points, all as unmistakable as sign posts on a turnpike; a succession of dramatic traps, in which the hands of the audience are invariably taken captive. These Stella could not miss. It was only in the fifth act that she rose above her author, and filled out and perfected his incomplete portraiture.[13]

That Kean may have persisted in such as style of acting even when playing Shakespeare shows the extent to which nineteenth century theatre was more of an actor's than an author's game. Kean did not deny that he was going for the big emotional effects — most actors of the time were. He did claim, however, that he carefully planned and rehearsed these moments. Still, his appeal to audiences was fed by the Romantic mythos that he, like other great artists, was an inspired genius whose talents were a gift from the Muse, not the result of hard work and training.

Other compelling evidence for the Victorians' obsession with actors, and their conception of women as actresses, in is the numerous appearances of actors and acting in novels. For many people, reading fiction became as popular a pastime as theatre going in the nineteenth century. Novels, like productions of plays, were readily available and appealing to the imagination, although theatre would have had the edge, obviously, for the class of audience which was still largely illiterate. Actors and acting show up frequently in fiction, although the theatre was often treated with suspicion or regarded with ambivalence, as in Jane Austen's *Mansfield Park*, where the morally corrupting influence of amateur dramatic performances is shown. In Thackeray's *Vanity Fair*, the heroine Becky Sharp, though not an actress by profession, uses her talent for acting and mimicry to deceive and manipulate others. She takes part in amateur theatricals, at one point playing the role of Clytemnestra, who murders her husband, the Greek general Agamemonon upon his return from the Trojan War. Clytemnestra is a classic example of a woman's dangerous power to deceive: she lures her hero husband to his death by pretending to be a most loyal and welcoming wife. The theme of the inherent theatricality and deceptiveness of women showed up in more sensational fiction too: in Britain in *Lady Audley's Secret* by Mary Elizabeth Braddon, adapted for the stage several times.

American author Louisa May Alcott, writing under the pseudonym A. M. Barnard for magazines, produced serial stories and novellas which featured unscrupulous women playing the roles of helpless ingénues to deceive those close to them. She wrote them at a time when she badly needed the money, and she had a sure fire sense of what would sell, although she kept it secret in her lifetime that, as the author of *Little Women*, she had also penned sensational and gothic potboilers. One of her stories which exemplifies the Victorian male's fear of women's unsettling ability to hide their evil motivations behind a smoke screen of feminine wiles is *Behind a Mask, or A Woman's Power*. In this novella the heroine Jean Muir "resorts to all sorts of coqueteries and subterfuges including the feigning of an attempted suicide"; she is "a woman filled with anger directed principally against the male lords of creation. But she is primarily an actress."[14] It is as an actress that this femme fatale is most fascinating and frightening, particularly since her animus is directed primarily at men. In the guise of an innocent young governess, she sets about ruining the wealthy Coventry family as revenge for past wrongs they have done her. She "lies or cries at will, feigns timidity or imperiousness to suit her needs"[15] and in short, uses "all the dramatic skills known to the theater." And after a successfully performed fainting fit, she looks over her shoulder "with a gesture like Rachel's."[16]

Alcott was not the first writer to invoke the image of Rachel in her fiction. The celebrated French tragedienne Rachel thrilled and sometimes terrified audiences with her performances of heroines like Medea and Phaedra. Her very name invoked the ambivalent power of the actress, and her fame, like Sarah Bernhardt's, transcended national boundaries. The American actress and author Olive Logan, who wrote about women's experiences in the theatre in the nineteenth century, vividly recounted the effect of Rachel's acting on an American audience at mid century. When Rachel in the role of the "the spectral Camille glided from the side-scene in 'les Horaces,' and that low, weird, wonderful voice smote the ear and heart of the listener, we knew that Rachel was, without a rival, the greatest living actress."[17]

In her novel *Villette*, Charlotte Brontë models the character of the stunning actress called Vashti on Rachel. Vashti's performance overwhelms the heroine, a reserved school teacher named Lucy Snowe, who is both attracted and repelled by the performer's emotional excess. Vashti seems inhuman, even possessed, as she captivates her audience. Lucy describes how

> For awhile — a long while — I thought it was only a woman, though an unique woman, who moved in might and grace before this multitude. By — and — by I recognized my mistake. Behold! I found upon her something neither of woman nor of man: in each of her eyes sat a devil. These evil forces bore her through the tragedy, kept up her feeble strength — for she was but a frail creature.... They tuned her voice to the note of torment. They writhed her regal face to a demoniac mask. Hate and Murder and Madness incarnate, she stood.[18]

The actress's power is based on an expression of emotion so intense that it seems to overwhelm the consciousness. Lucy struggles to articulate Vashti's effect, resorting, as did critics in their reviews of Rachel, to the notion of "magnetism" to explain it:

> The strong magnetism of genius drew my heart out of its wonted orbit.... I had seen acting before, but never anything which astonished Hope and hushed Desire; which outstripped Impulse and paled Conception; which, instead of merely irritating imagination with the thought of what might be done, at the same time fevering the nerves because it was not done, disclosed like a deep, swollen, winter river, thundering in cataract, and bearing the soul, like a leaf, on the steep and steely sweep of its descent.[19]

Lucy gets a chance to experience the power of acting herself when she is asked to perform in a play being put on at the school where she teaches. When she is asked to fill in for an ailing student, she is at first reluctant. Lucy is modest, a conventional, even "cold" woman (her last name, after all, is "Snowe"). She is not eager to expose herself to the gaze of a curious audience. But when ultimately persuaded to take on the role of the (male) villain, she is astonished and disturbed by the pleasure she finds in performing:

> What I felt that night, and what I did, I no more expected to feel and do, than to be lifted in a trance to the seventh heaven. Cold, reluctant, apprehensive, I had accepted a part to please another: ere long, warming, becoming interested, taking courage, I acted to please myself. Yet the next day, when I thought it over, I quite disapproved of these amateur performances; and ... I took a firm resolution never to be drawn into a similar affair. A keen relish for dramatic expression had revealed itself as part of my nature; to cherish and exercise this new-found faculty might gift me with a world of delight, but it would not do for a mere looker-on at life....[20]

Lucy equates the thrill of performing with an alternate state of consciousness or trance state, seeming to sense that the pleasure of both states is the freedom from a conventional reality which they offer. She feels the power of playing with an alien identity. But she is afraid, or feels that she does not have the right to pursue either the power or the pleasure of impersonation, and views it as a dangerous and seductive temptation. Lucy cannot escape herself, and she makes a conscious choice to remain an anonymous (and safe) spectator, a "mere looker-on" at other performers in life. Unlike the trance mediums who would find a way to play other selves successfully, the fictional Lucy cannot go so far.

Gwendolyn Brooks, the heroine of George Eliot's novel *Daniel Deronda*, also has a compelling experience acting in amateur theatricals. Eliot's fictional portrayals of women who performed were influenced by her friendship with the real life English star Helen Faucit. Faucit was regarded as the "English *Rachel*," and Eliot's husband, George Henry Lewes, was also taken by Faucit's "ineffable charm," which he described in an essay of dramatic criticism. Both Eliot and Lewes seemed to regard the actress as a "subject of almost scientific interest."[21] Heroines who acted also appeared novels by less well known female writers, Florence Marryat (who was also a medium) and Alma Ellerslie.

Perhaps female characters in novels were so often portrayed acting since, not only were professional actresses a source of endless interest, but Victorian readers suspected that women in real life were acting much of the time as well. Women were believed capable of assuming other roles or personalities much more easily than men, since it was thought they were inherently more psychologically volatile. A deeply rooted belief in the connection between acting and feminity underlay these attitudes. The conviction that indeed theatre as a whole was "feminine" in essence was articulated by one of the greatest actress of the age, Sarah Bernhardt. She said

> I think that the dramatic art is essentially feminine. To paint one's face, to hide one's real feelings, to try to please and to endeavor to attract attention, these are all faults for which we blame women and for which great indulgence is shown. These same defects seem odious in a man.[22]

Bernhardt's observation suggests that women can both get what they want and please others by acting, and that they are both blamed and indulged for their tendency to do so. It also suggests that acting is both a "natural" or essential part of femininity and a tactic that can be cunningly utilized to simultaneously disguise and satisfy their desires. The ability to act made women attractive and fascinating, but also potentially dangerous. This thinking would have been considered both rational and justified to many Victorian thinkers. The image of Woman as uncannily mutable and deceptive, did not spring fully formed from the heads of paranoid Victorian intellectuals. It was grounded in theories of eighteenth-century philosophers such as Jean Jacques Rousseau, who legitimized the essential connection between acting and women through assertions and arguments like those made in his *Letter to M. d'Alembert on the Theatre* written in 1758. Rousseau characterized women as inherently theatrical since they could so easily pretend to be what they were not. He claimed, as had Bernhardt, that women used their feminine arts to disguise their thoughts and desires, and to gain by manipulation and deception what they wanted. But Rousseau took this conceit a step further, proposing that since a woman was already an "actress," for her to act on stage meant putting on yet another layer of disguise, making her twice an actress and twice as untrustworthy. The professional actress commanded an unnerving degree of power by means of her personal attractions and the emotions she portrayed on stage. The most dangerous and irrational of these emotions was Love, which Rousseau regarded as the central obsession of theatre and the indisputable "realm of women." Such a theatre, concentrated on the portrayal of love performed by women, might, Rousseau warned, dangerously "extend the empire of the fair sex." It would "make women and girls the preceptors of the public," giving them "the same power over the audience that they have over their own lovers."[23]

Like Rousseau, French philosopher and theatre theorist Denis Diderot also sensed that the performances of women could be dangerous, again for murky reasons having to do with irrational emotions. Diderot suggested that because women's passions were much more violent than men's, men had to be vigilant about keeping them under control.

As pervasive as these notions remained well into the nineteenth century, not everyone, certainly not women who actually experienced for themselves the power of performing, would have agreed that women who acted on stage or off were volatile, unstable and in urgent need of strong masculine oversight. Women's acting could be constructive and liberating rather than, as it was feared to be, destructive and malevolent. Its greatest benefit was perhaps the escape it offered from some of the psychological and social limitations which confined Victorian women. This potential freedom, and hence the appeal of performing, extended to women of all different classes, since "even for those outside it the stage incarnated fantasies, providing vicarious release in the notion that here was an area of special dispensation from the normal categories, moral and social, that defined woman's place."[24]

This argument from Martha Vicinius's study of the changing roles for Victorian women articulates the strong "symbolic appeal" that acting had for people in the nineteenth century. Although she had no formal connections with the theatre or actors, Florence Nightingale, who struggled in her personal and public life with the limitations placed on Victorian women, wrote about the power theatre and acting had on women's imaginations. In *Cassandra*, her polemic on the constraints imposed on Victorian women, she argues that regardless of how appealing it was for a young woman to experience "extraordinary events, isolation, misfortunes, which many wish for" vicariously through fiction or drama,[25] this was *not* the reason she was readily attracted to the life of the actress. Acting was an appealing option not because of the emotional high of performing, but because it represented an opportunity for genuine and substantial creative work. A woman might want to be an actress

> not for the sake of admiration, not for the sake of fame; but because she [the Actress] studies, in the evening she embodies those studies: she has the means of testing and correcting them by practice, and of resuming her studies in the morning, to improve the weak parts, remedy the failures, and in the evening try the corrections again.[26]

On a practical level, acting was one of the few careers available for women at this time. An acting career could offer economic as well as creative possibilities, in addition to a dispensation from the normal categories that limited women. As Faye Dudden put it, while "'acting female' is what traditionalists and reactionaries prescribe for women ... an 'acting female'— a woman who plays roles—reveals the possibility of escaping that imperative."[27]

Performance, then, whether as an actress in the theatre, or in the context of enacting a role in a trance state, could be a powerful means of escaping from normal restrictions on behavior and feelings. In a mesmeric trance, or as a medium in a séance, a woman could express negative, violent, or otherwise unacceptable thoughts and feelings with relative impunity. She could find a release from, or a coping mechanism for, the psychological and imaginative limitations imposed on her. But whatever the context in which she performed, she still had to deal with the specific parameters and expectations of the social and the stage roles which pervaded Victorian culture, reifying male constructs of femininity both on and off the stage. Feminine stereotypes were inevitably present in any Victorian performance dynamic. For this reason, women's trance performances should be seen less as a clean escape from the prescriptive social and stage roles than a way to *co-opt* and *subvert* them. Because they were a significant factor, the major categories of women's stage roles in the nineteenth century are a useful place to begin an examination of trance performances through the lens of Victorian theatre.

The Roles She Played: Angel, Demon or Madwoman

Stage roles for Victorian women were often variants of one of several widely known cultural stereotypes. At opposite ends of a spectrum were the pure and virtuous "Angel in the House," who sanctified the domestic sphere; and the seductive "femme fatale" who, in a perversion of the Angel's role, deserted and broke up homes and families. The femme fatale might appear in a slightly more sympathetic versions as the "fallen woman" whose moral or social transgressions were expunged only by death or at the very least permanent exile from decent society. A third influential stereotype and stage role was the Madwoman, best represented by Shakespeare's Ophelia. This role type was often seen in melodramas in the form of heroines like Crazy Jane and Lucy Ashton. Crazy Jane and Lucy (better known in her operatic incarnation as Lucia di Lammermoor) embodied popular notions about the fragility of female identity, and women's susceptibility to altered states of consciousness. These qualities fascinated early nineteenth century audiences, and would also prepare them to interpret and understand the speech and behavior of the mediums and trance speakers they would later encounter in séances and Spiritualist lectures. These common stage characters, and the plots in which they were featured, which were immediately recognizable to Victorian audiences, also provided narrative models for the spirits and stories that would be manifested in trance performances.

The heroine of *Crazy Jane*, which had a successful run at the Surrey Theatre in London in 1829, was, like Ophelia, an iconic madwoman of the Victorian stage. Both characters modeled how an ideal woman should behave, and when her fragile equilibrium was threatened, what her consequent madness — her loss of conscious control and slide into an alternate state — might look like. Similar images and situations formed part of the allure of trance performances, as case studies in chapters to come will show. The popular visual image of Ophelia distractedly strewing flowers was a literal illustration of female madness. It is echoed in the engraving on the title page of an 1830s version of *Crazy Jane*. The drawing, "taken in the theatre by a Mr. R. Cruikshank," shows an Ophelia-like Jane in a wild woodland setting, near a stream like Ophelia's "willow brook." Jane wears a tattered white dress, and is wreathed in a long leafy garland. Leaves and branches seem to start out from her disheveled hair, and her eyes are huge dark blanks. The resemblance between Jane and the iconic Ophelia are not merely visual. Both heroines have conflicting duties to father and lover, and both are driven mad by the struggle to reconcile two incompatible ideals of womanly virtue. When the villain threatens Jane that he will kill her father unless she agrees to marry him, which would dishonor her and the memory of her dead lover, her dilemma is inescapable. Whatever Jane's decision, she must fail in one of two competing ideal roles: either that of the loving maiden eternally faithful to the memory of her dead lover, or that of the loyal daughter who will sacrifice everything to save her father. Jane chooses honor and loyalty to her lover, and in an act deemed "heroic" she rejects the evil Lord Raymond. But the cost of her choice is terrible. Her father disowns her for her refusal to save him, calling his daughter pitiless and "unnatural," and blasting her with this curse, reminiscent of Lear's invective against his daughters:

> May conscience lash thee with her scorpion scourge
> From door to door to beg for mouldy bread
> Thy beauty blasted and thy reason fled!

At this Jane "utters a piercing shriek, as if deprived of her reason." As the scene ends, she shrieks again and "tearing the bridal flowers from her hair" rushes off in a frenzy (II. vi.).[28] Jane is portrayed sympathetically, with some acknowledgment of the difficult choice and double standard she faces. But in spite of the sympathetic tone, the overriding message of the play is that madness is the only natural, and indeed the only *possible* response to the dilemma in which Jane finds herself. As a good and obedient daughter, she can only redeem herself for her failure to save her father by falling into the madness he has wished upon her.

Lucy Ashton from *The Bride of Lammermoor*, another ubiquitous stage role in the early Victorian period, is also torn between loyalty to family and loyalty to a lover. Lucy loves Ravenswood, a longtime enemy of her family. When her family forces her to break off her betrothal and become engaged to a man she does not love, she fears she will go mad. She says "grant that I may retain my sense in this awful trial. Already my weak brain begins to waver."[29] Her fears are realized when Ravenswood confronts her with her "wilful and deliberate perjury"—her denial of their love and vows to one another. She is at first speechless from shock, but in one mad outburst before she dies, she attempts to give voice to the conflict and isolation she has felt:

> Ravenswood, you know not what I have endured all united against me—
> your long silence—my letters intercepted—no friend to aid—no succour—
> no resource—they have broken my heart, but never, never could they
> change my love [V.i.].[30]

Victorian Shakespearean commentator Anna Jameson describes similar conflict, and the forced separation from a lover as the cause of Ophelia's madness: "The conflicts of duty and affection, hope and fear, which successively agitated Ophelia's gentle bosom, were of themselves sufficient to dissever the delicate coherence of a woman's reason."[31] She links madness with femininity, further arguing that in the mad Ophelia,

> the feminine character appears resolved into its very elementary principles — as modesty, grace, tenderness. Without these a woman is no woman, but a thing which, luckily, wants a name yet; with these, though every other faculty were passive or deficient, she might still be herself.[32]

This passage implies that female identity is defined by the possession of specific qualities, and without these qualities a woman is not merely deficient but she is nothing — a cipher. Elsewhere in her analysis Jameson suggests that a woman could only demonstrate her defining qualities of love, tenderness, etc., in her duty towards others, particularly men. It would follow, then, that a conflict in duty would also constitute a conflict or a fracturing of identity or consciousness itself, i.e., madness — as it does in the case of Ophelia.

Not only audiences and critics saw Ophelia a "document in madness." Medical doctors agreed. George Farren, a doctor who submitted Shakespeare's characters to scientific/medical analysis, wrote of Ophelia's mad scene: "It is impossible to conceive of any thing more perfect than the picture of disease given by Shakespeare in this scene of Ophelia's . Every medical professor who is familiar with cases of insanity will freely acknowledge its truth."[33]

The medical and scientific professions did indeed appropriate the figure of Ophelia as an icon for madness, and as a sort of diagnostic measuring stick in the early nineteenth century. Elaine Showalter asserts that illustrations of Ophelia, notably a series of pictures produced by Delacroix between 1830 and 1850, inspired by Harriet Smithson's portrayal, "played a major role in the theoretical construction of female insanity.[34] Doctors sometimes went beyond merely using Ophelia as a model of insanity to imposing her image on female asylum inmates. Showalter cites the perhaps extreme case of Dr. Hugh Welch Diamond, who worked at the Surrey and Bethlehem Asylums in England in the 1850s. Dr. Diamond dressed patients in long black robes (a costume associated with Ophelia) with garlands of flowers in their hair. He posed them with weeds or flowers in their hands, and photographed them. Dr. Diamond's manipulation of the madwomen under his care, and his attempts to make them conform to or "perform" his ideal of madness, foreshadow the work of French physician Jean-Martin Charcot at the asylum of Salpetriere in the 1870s and 1880s. Charcot's mesmerized patients were also coached for the cameras, and sometimes instructed to perform as Shakespearian heroines while in a trance.

Fascination with Ophelia, the role that embodied the Victorian conflation of madness and femininity, demonstrates what power these familiar stage roles could have, and how they interacted with Victorian's perceptions of women's *social roles*. In turn, the expectations formed by social roles, that women were inherently unstable, irrational, ethereal beings, laid the foundation or expectation that women would take on the roles of mediums or trance subjects. If a woman sensed that she was assumed to be a potential madwoman or hysteric simply by virtue of her gender, might she not capitalize on the mutability or oracular and prophetic powers attributed to the mad? Or at least seize the opportunity to let her hair down a little? In some ways this is the choice that mediums and trance performers might have made — to play the hand that was dealt them and use, rather than resist, the given role.

This is not to suggest that going mad simply in and of itself was a freeing option for any woman. Insanity, obviously could lead to a tremendous loss of control. A diagnosis of madness and confinement to an asylum by relatives or guardians was a genuine threat for some women who kicked the traces of Victorian conventions — including those who dabbled in mediumship or Spiritualism, or publicly espoused radical social causes like women's suffrage. This was almost the fate of Georgina Weldon, an English medium, operatic performer and playwright. She narrowly escaped being committed to an insane asylum by her husband. She managed to use the theatrical aspects of her unconventional tendencies, to fight in court, and win several dramatic law suits involving her professional and personal rights. She also turned the asylum episode into a play in which she starred, titled *How I Escaped the Mad Doctors*.[35] Weldon turned potential victimization to her own profit.

Her example shows that Victorian women were not always simply the victims of their roles. They could in certain situations put to good use those qualities ascribed to them. They might take the opportunity to capitalize on their assumed "acting" skills. Or they might use their presumed ability to enter into altered states of consciousness to sidestep culpability for outrageous or radical speech and behavior, case studies in some of the following chapters will show. But first, an exploration of how Victorian trance performance arose from experiments and exhibits of mesmerism, which began with Anton Mesmer in the late eighteenth century, and peaked with Dr. Jean-Martin Charcot's mesmeric theatre at the asylum of Salpetriere at the end of the nineteenth century.

3

Mesmer and Charcot: The Trance Performance as Medical Show

Anton Mesmer

The founder of mesmerism was a showman with the flair of a P. T. Barnum, and he exploited its theatricality from the very beginning. Mesmerism was named for Viennese doctor Franz Anton Mesmer who popularized the practice of "animal magnetism," as it was first known, in the last decades of the eighteenth century. In 1775 Mesmer described in his "Letter to a Foreign Physician" a mysterious "universal fluidium" which provided the matrix for the force he identified as animal magnetism. He was elaborating on and recasting ideas advocated by alchemists and scientists for centuries about the vital forces which permeated and linked all living things. Mesmer's work borrowed extensively from the sixteenth century scientist/magician Paracelsus who claimed that magnets could control this vital substance or "fluidium" which connected everything in the universe, from the stars and planets to the human body. Mesmer claimed that magnets could be used to re-direct the fluidium's patterns of movement, channeling and harnessing its energy flows, particularly where blockages might be causing problems in the human body.[1]

Although looking back to medieval traditions in science, Mesmer's insistence on the concrete physical reality of the invisible but potent fluidium would prove to be very much in the mainstream of nineteenth century scientific materialism. Nineteenth century science increasingly emphasized matter as the basis of reality, and a reliance on sense perceptions of matter as the basis for judging or knowing truth. Sight, for example, was thought to give the most immediate access to reality.[2]

Because nineteenth century scientific theory was based on sensory observation of material reality, science began to seem more accessible to non-specialists, and certain pseudo-scientific trends like mesmerism, and its forerunners physiognomy and phrenology, became widely popular, as both a kind of "do it at home" science and as a form of entertainment similar to the medicine show. Although mesmerism, like phrenology, was never fully accepted as a science, it reached a large public and was popularized by lecture/performances in the early Victorian period. As Terry Parssinen observes in his article "Mesmeric Performers," the line between scientific (or pseudo-scientific) lecture and entertainment was thin, and "mesmeric performers of the 1830s and early 1840s drew on the rich traditions of scientific lecturing, lay healing and popular entertainment."[3] In these early traveling mesmeric shows the mesmerist was always a man, and the subject (either a volunteer from the audience or the mesmerist's assistant) was usually a young woman: a power-gender relationship that would be repeated in the work of Dr. John Elliotson in the 1830s and Dr. Charcot in the 1880s with their female trance subjects.

Anton Mesmer's first healing sessions took place in the dramatic setting of his luxurious house on the Landstrasse in Vienna. Patients entered a room furnished with a large tub or "baquet," which was filled with magnetized water. By grasping iron rods extending from the water, patients could be brought to a state of mesmeric "crisis." In the crisis, which resembled a fit or convulsion of some kind, the flow of energies in their bodies could supposedly be disrupted and re-channeled into more healthful patterns. Mesmer would eventually claim that he could redirect energy through bodies by making passes with his hands or merely gazing at them.

The rooms for the healing sessions were as carefully arranged as stage settings, and the atmosphere appealed to every sense. The rooms were opulently decorated, richly carpeted and hung with velvet curtains to reduce distracting noise from outside. Mirrors hung on the walls (to increase the effects of the magnetic forces), and the air was delicately perfumed. Music played on the pianoforte or glass harmonica, an instrument which had a uniquely eerie and otherworldly sound, added to the soothing and mysterious atmosphere.

Mesmer demonstrated the savvy of a theatrical producer and the charisma of a star. His entrances into the rooms set up for the healing sessions were carefully timed for maximum effect. When a calm, celestial mood had been established, with the lights dimmed and the curiosity of his patients at its height, Mesmer would enter, costumed in a purple silk robe and carrying a magnetized wand. The force of Mesmer's personality and physical presence were frequently remarked upon and were a significant factor in the success of his healing sessions. Robert Darnton, in his account of the craze for mesmerism in pre–Revolutionary France, indicates that mesmerism was very much dependent on the force of personality of the individual who practiced it. Mesmer "exerted an influence on his age that testifies to the power of the personality hidden in his robes and rituals, the power that we appropriately acknowledge in expressions such as a "mesmerized" audience or a "magnetic" personality.[4]

Darnton notes that the vocabulary of mesmerism can be used to describe the effects of personality on an audience. Indeed this is how it was used in the nineteenth century, as shown by the theatre critics and theorists who, struggling to describe or account for the ineffable charisma and power of certain performers, found the vocabulary and theory of mesmerism useful (as in descriptions of Sarah Bernhardt and Rachel mentioned previously). Significantly, the vocabulary of mesmerism was used more frequently to describe female performers than male performers: women onstage seemed to acquire both the hypnotizing charm of Svengali and as the allure of Trilby.

Such a woman was one of Mesmer's patients, a young pianist named Marie-Thérese von Paradise. This young woman, blind from birth, was a musical prodigy who was being patronized and supported by the Austrian Empress. She was a performing celebrity in her own right before she achieved notoriety via her connection with Mesmer, to whom she came for treatment in the 1770s. She soon moved in with him (initially with her parents' blessing). Mesmer cured her of her blindness, but the cure had a deleterious effect on her musical abilities and she became unable to perform. When her father came to take her away from Mesmer's care, she resisted and a scene ensued. Rumors of impropriety arose, which prompted an investigation of Mesmer's practice. Local authorities concluded that "animal magnetism" was a public menace. In 1779, no longer welcome in Vienna, Mesmer moved to Paris hoping to find a more receptive atmosphere for his work.

Paris was more than ready to receive Mesmer and his theories. France in the 1780s and 1790s was enjoying a craze for a variety of pseudo-scientific and occult practices (like alchemy, phrenology, etc.) which were rich sources of entertainment and debate. Mesmerism became popular immediately. It was discussed in journals, and taken up in songs, cartoons, and a farce called *Les Illuminés*.

Mesmerism was not just a form of entertainment or subject for gossip, however. Mesmer worked seemingly miraculous cures, although he practiced only on patients who believed completely in him and his theories, since the element of personal influence and suggestibility was crucial. Other practitioners of mesmerism emerged in the 1780s, notably an aristocratic follower of Mesmer named Puységur. Puységur stressed even more strongly than Mesmer the necessity of belief in the magnetizer (rather than belief in the physical reality of the magnetic "fluidium").

Puységur practiced mesmerism on the peasants on his country estate, and had striking success with a young man named Victor Race. Race had long suffered from an apparently incurable respiratory ailment. Puységur was able to relieve Race's symptoms by mesmerizing him. Moreover, Puységur observed and recorded the emergence, in the trance state, of alternate personalities, radically different from the personality of the young man in his normal waking state. Normally, Victor Race was shy, diffident, and inarticulate. Under mesmerism he became sharp, well-spoken, and able to make suggestions about his own treatment. He also appeared to display some telepathic ability to read Puységur's thoughts. His experiences illustrate the principle, proposed by a twentieth-century scholar on the subject, that in a mesmeric trance "the constraints that the self has imposed upon the self may be thrown off; the mind may be put in touch with aspects that are otherwise hidden."[5]

The case of Victor Race demonstrates several important ideas which would be developed throughout the nineteenth century as understanding of hypnosis and the psychology of the unconscious increased. Race showed that a subject could express normally repressed thoughts or feelings in a trance state. Psychologist Pierre Janet, late in the nineteenth century, asserted that an even wider array of repressed material might be released in the trance state:

> A system of ideas, emotions and behaviors could split off from the personality and exist with a certain degree of autonomy in the unconscious. This dissociated material could be brought into consciousness through the use of hypnosis.[6]

Janet's description provides a likely explanation for what happened in the trance state not only to Victor Race, but also to some of the trance performers under discussion here, who shared with Race what appeared to be psychic powers (such as foretelling future events) and the ability to diagnose and suggest helpful treatment for their own physical problems.

In 1784, at the height of mesmerism's popularity in France, Louis XVI appointed a royal commission to investigate. The commission concluded that the idea that cures could be effected by the manipulation of a "universal fluidium" was an "ancient fallacy."[7] But even the findings of the royal commission did not prevent the spread of mesmerism to other European capitals in the 1790s. In Germany, Friedrich Wilhelm II was treated with the magnetic cure. Although he did not live long after, the influence of mesmerism grew, especially among Romantic artists and intellectuals.

As Maria Tatar notes, the mesmeric trance came to be associated with higher vision, insight, and inspiration among Romantic thinkers. Trance states were linked to the creative process in the works of E. T. A. Hoffman and Heinrich von Kleist.[8] The character Ottilie in Goethe's *Elective Affinities* achieves a kind of second sight while in a trance state, and Friedrich Schlegel himself dabbled in mesmerism. In 1819 Schlegel attempted, while mesmerized, to communicate with a distant companion. Mesmerism in Germany was also subject to satire, as it had been in France. A farce called *The New Age*, by the popular and prolific playwright August von Kotzebue (1761–1819), appeared on stage for a brief time, satirizing physicians who practiced "animal magnetism." In France, Eugene Scribe wrote a play called *Irene, ou le magnetisme*. Theatrical satires of mesmerism in England were represented by popular playwright Elizabeth Inchbald's *Animal Magnetism* (ca. 1788).

Mesmerism as a medical practice became widely know in England through the work of Dr. John Elliotson in the 1820s and 1830s, as will be discussed in detail later. Elliotson was part of a circle of prominent professional, literary and artistic friends such as Charles Dickens, and actor William Charles Macready, who also dabbled in mesmerism. It was Charles Dickens who brought a copy of Scribe's mesmeric farce *Irene* to London in 1847 after seeing a production in Paris. Dickens got up an amateur production of *Animal Magnetism* in the same year, and himself played the doctor.

Dickens, the most theatrical of Victorian novelists, was personally drawn into the practice of mesmerism in the 1840s. He discovered that he had the power to put others in a trance when in 1844 he became friends with a woman named Madame De la Rue, who he began to mesmerize for therapeutic reasons. Madame De la Rue suffered from a variety of ailments that were similar to those which afflicted Dr. Elliotson's patients — convulsions of the limbs, headaches, insomnia, and neurasthenic symptoms including catalepsy.[9] With Monsieur De La Rue's permission, Dickens was able to put Madame into a mesmeric trance and help relieve her symptoms.

Dickens relied on standard mesmeric techniques of inducing states of sleep-waking (mesmeric sleep) and mesmeric trance in his subject; in which the "patient" prompted by the doctor/mesmerist could explore fears, fantasies, and dreams through verbalized free association. The mesmeric sleep functioned to alleviate pain and exhaustion; while the purpose of the "waking" trance was to allow the subject and the mesmerist to "discover and come to terms with the underlying causes of the disorder and illness."[10] For several months Dickens and the De la Rues were in almost daily contact: Dickens mesmerized Madame frequently, even when they were separated. Although Monsieur De la Rue was understanding of the close therapeutic bonds between his wife and Dickens, and treated Dickens as a trusted doctor and advisor, Dickens's wife Catherine grew jealous of her husband's obsession with the sick woman, possibly sensing the erotic potential of the mesmerist/subject relationship. Partly due to her pressure the relationship was ended.

Dickens' life and fiction reveal other connections between theatre and mesmerism. For instance, he wrote a play called *The Frozen Deep* which included a character who became clairvoyant in a trance state, and the character Lady Dedlock from *Bleak House* is a kind of "prima donna of the mesmeric stage." Taken as a whole, Dickens' incorporation of mesmerism into his theatrical as well as his literary work exemplifies the theatrical possibilities of the practice. These possibilities were realized at the end of the nineteenth century when French doctor, Jean-Martin Charcot, staged his mesmeric exhibits of women in trance at the asylum of Salpetriere.

Dr. Charcot as "Svengali" and the Prima Donnas of Mesmeric Trance

When Sigmund Freud wrote his impressions of Sarah Bernhardt, cited earlier, he had come to France to study with the famous Dr. Jean-Martin Charcot at the psychiatric asylum of Salpetriere, where in 1885 Charcot was experimenting with the use of mesmerism on female patients. In trances induced for diagnostic and therapeutic purposes, the women, mostly categorized as "hysterics," displayed fascinating powers of performance, re-enacting scenes from their traumatic life experiences or "suggestions" from the doctors. Dr. Charcot was in some ways the real-life precursor of the fictional character Svengali, the mesmerist who controls the singing talent of the innocent young woman Trilby, in the 1894 novel. Trilby, alongside the performing hysterics at Salpetriere, emerged as the Madwoman in stage melodramas had, from the seemingly disparate realms of popular art and medical science to become emblematic of Victorian attitudes towards women's performance.

In *Trilby*, written and illustrated by Gerald Du Maurier, Svengali discovers that a young woman living the Bohemian life of an artist's model in Paris has a genius for singing while in a mesmeric trance. Svengali, who is apparently the only one who can induce and control her trances, becomes her teacher, her master and ultimately her destroyer. The heroine's transformations from a charming but simple girl happily living a Bohemian life among her artist friends, to an operatic diva, and back again were the key to the character's appeal. Her perpetual changes were not just *what* she did, but *who* she was—transformation was her "maddening essence." *Trilby* was one of the most sensational and widely read novels ever written, with phenomenal sales in Britain and America. The image of Trilby performing in a trance was further disseminated by its numerous stage adaptations. There was a mania for all things related to the story, and Trilby's image was see everywhere, even in advertising campaigns for everything from ice cream to hats.

The first stage version of the play appeared in Boston on March 4, 1895.

Three months later a parody, "Thrilby," was produced at the Garrick theatre in New York. Running at the same time was a circus version, where a bareback rider dressed as Trilby rode under the whip of a ringmaster dressed as Svengali. There are many reasons for Trilby's appeal. As one scholar has suggested, the story's "mixture of romance, sentimentality, occultism and anti–Semitism appealed to the widest possible audience."[11] Recent scholarship has focused on cultural fascination with and fear of the "otherness" of the figure of Svengali, particularly for English and American audiences for whom Svengali embodied stereotypes of the foreigner, the Jew and the quack mesmerist. Daniel Pick suggests rightly the Victorian perception of mesmerism as a disturbing means of control, one that might be used by sexual predators disguised as doctors as well as unscrupulous demagogues and politicians.[12] But it was not only the mesmerist who was an object of anxiety. The mesmeric subject, usually a woman, might exhibit powers even more uncanny and disturbing than Trilby's singing ability. *Trilby* tapped into a potent combination of cultural anxieties, not only about mesmerism but about women behaving irrationally or performing in public. Fear of women's innate mutability extended, as we have seen, to suspicion of actresses, and also to mad or hysterical women. Dr. Charcot and other Victorian medical doctors described hysterical women as "impressionable, capricious, malleable, seductive, untruthful" and "recalcitrant" and considered the hysteria a distinctly feminine as well as theatrical type of madness, in which the sufferer "recriminates with bitterness, gives herself over to scenes, tears, and extravagances" and "makes a show of her passion."[13]

When the relationship between male mesmerist and female performer was immortalized with publication of *Trilby* in 1894, Dr. Jean-Martin Charcot had already been directing his medical theatre at Salpetriere since the 1870s. He had begun the exhibitions of mesmerism as part of a series of lectures on the symptoms and treatment of hysteria, which as conceived of and diagnosed in the nineteenth century was by definition a female malady. Charcot had been criticized for his use of mesmerism on women in the medical arena because his experiments were so theatrical. Staged like plays in the space used as a theatre for exhibitions of medical experiments at Salpetriere, the patients were actresses and Charcot was the impresario.

Charcot had initiated his experiments by deliberately inducing, by means of mesmerism, or as it was beginning to be called "hypnotism" a state of artificial hysteria in them. He referred to this as "experimental neurosis."[14] A favorite demonstration at Salpetriere involved a pretty young woman named Augustine who, in this trance state, acted out the rape which had precipitated her hysterical symptoms. These and other re-enactments of traumatic events from the patients' lives may have had some therapeutic or cathartic value for them. Other experiments seem less likely to have had any benefit for the sufferers. In these cases, female patients were hypnotized and asked by the doctors to perform imaginary acts of violence which included stabbing or shooting the doctors and attendants. One patient named Blanche Wittman was described as "carrying out imaginary crimes with a dramatic flair equal to Sarah Bernhardt." This made her "much in demand for medicological demonstrations."[15] The women were also photographed, as madwomen had been in England earlier in the century, ostensibly to create helpful visual "documents of madness" for diagnostic purposes.

The audiences for these performances were not limited to doctors and scientists, however. Literary and theatrical celebrities attended performances, and it was even said that the real Sarah Bernhardt used the women as models for some of her roles, that she "mimicked the great doctor's patients or perhaps one should say the great director's actresses."[16]

Like many of his contemporaries, Freud was initially impressed by Charcot, and almost as charmed by the doctor's charisma and presence as he had been by Sarah Bernhardt's. Freud would later become skeptical about mesmerism, although his work with hypnotherapy stemmed from mesmerism, and would be an important step in the development of his theories of psychoanalysis. While many doctors questioned the legitimacy of mesmerism itself, and particularly its medical use, its theatricality and appeal to the popular imagination were undeniable. Public fascination with mesmeric performance is evidenced by detailed reports that were published on the exhibits of Dr. John Elliotson in London in the 1830s.

Dr. Elliotson's experiments with mesmerism fall in time between the shows of Mesmer at the beginning of the century and the theatre of Charcot at the end, and are not as well known as either. However, the intriguing performances given by Elizabeth O'Key in the context of Elliotson's medical exhibits of mesmerism are perhaps best case study of this phenomenon, and the subject of the next chapter.

4

The Performances of Elizabeth O'Key: The Medical Theatre of Mesmerism

In the spring and summer of 1838, in the lecture theatre of University College London Hospital, an extraordinary series of highly theatrical performances took place. A sixteen-year-old housemaid named Elizabeth O'Key, who had been admitted to the hospital suffering from epilepsy, underwent the new experimental treatment involving mesmerism. In the hypnotic or "mesmerized" state the normally subdued girl sang, danced, told jokes and generally entertained the fascinated audiences who had gathered to see the lecture/demonstrations of the effects of mesmerism. Dr. John Elliotson, a respected if unconventional physician and teacher, played the "Svengali" to O'Key's "Trilby," conducting the experimental sessions, mesmerizing her and attempting to direct her performances.

Although the context for the event was scientific, the goal to study the physical effects of mesmerism, the demonstrations were clearly a variant of Victorian theatre. The medical exhibit revolved around a single virtuoso star and depended more on her skill and charisma than on a script. O'Key's display of herself in the trance state was comparable to that of popular "emotional" actresses of the period,[1] who claimed that their ability to rivet audiences came from losing themselves in a character, not from conscious technique. Like actor Edmund Kean, O'Key was striking because of the volatility of her behavior and emotions, and her personal "magnetism." Her unpredictable, apparently unstudied qualities were, like Kean's, admired by observers familiar with the Romantic ideals of untrained genius and spontaneous artistic inspiration.

Even the structure of the sessions followed the formula of an evening in the theatre in the early nineteenth century, which usually began with the performance of a tragedy, alternating with song or dance interludes, and followed by comedy and then a farce or pantomime. The shows at the hospital usually began with the drama of serious interactions with

Dr. Elliotson which then began to be interspersed with interludes of singing, dancing and wisecracks from O'Key. O'Key's performances tapped into the Victorian public's fascination with the figure of the woman in an altered state of consciousness, and also fit the stage formula for the madwoman.

It is difficult to say whether she (along with her sister Jane, who was admitted around the same time and received similar treatment) was "mad" in any clinical sense of the word. The teenaged girls had been admitted after being diagnosed with epilepsy, which was still an area of confusion in medical science in 1830. Epilepsy was often confused with hysteria, and epileptics were routinely confined to asylums alongside the insane.[2] Definitions of both epilepsy and hysteria were vague. There were "boundary disputes" among depression, hysteria, hypochondria and insanity. Hysteria and epilepsy came under the general classification of neuroses or functional nervous disorders (as opposed to clearly somatic disorders).[3] "Hysteria" was used to label a variety of emotional or mental disturbances suffered by women, since the term was "still the archetypal feminine functional nervous disorder in the nineteenth century."[4] Hysteria and epilepsy were often confused because both were characterized by convulsions, the origins of which might be physical or psychological (although by the end of the century Dr. Charcot would insist on distinguishing between the two disorders).[5]

Whether truly "epileptic" or "hysterical" in any medical sense of the word, the "fits" or convulsions for which the O'Key sisters came to be treated would have laid them open to the general charge of madness in the popular sense of the word, i.e., in the sense that many Victorian women were labeled mad because of their deviant or unacceptable behavior or ideas. The attitudes of doctors and audiences towards O'Key also reveal how madness and hysteria were linked to perceptions of women and theatricality, foreshadowing Dr. Charcot's infamous exhibitions of madwomen at the asylum of Salpetriere in Paris in the 1880s.

When Dr. John Elliotson undertook treatment of the young women in 1838, mesmerism was a relatively new practice in England. Mesmerism had been slower to take hold in England than it had been on the continent, partly because it had come from France, and the English still regarded French innovations of any kind with suspicion in the early nineteenth century in the aftermath of the French Revolution and Napoleonic wars. Dr. Elliotson's work with mesmerism at the University College Hospital was considered dubious by many physicians and scientists, although he himself was highly respected.

Elliotson was born in 1791, the son of a London businessman. He had his medical training in Edinburgh and at Guy's Hospital in London. When he first became interested in mesmerism, he had risen to the post of first Professor of the Principles and Practices of Medicine at the University of London. Elliotson was an enthusiastic supporter of phrenology and the first president of the Phrenological Society of London. His interest in phrenology dovetailed with his interests as a diagnostician. Elliotson was also innovative in his use of drugs, and is credited with introducing the stethoscope into common practice in England. He was an advocate of reform in medical education, and an excellent teacher and lecturer. His efforts at reform were supported by Thomas Wakley, founder of the influential medical journal *The Lancet*. Elliotson and Wakley eventually parted company on the subject of mesmerism, and much of the debate over Elliotson's mesmeric exhibitions took place in the pages of *The Lancet*.

There had been some experimentation and a few treatises written about mesmerism in England before Elliotson became actively involved in 1837, but it was the work of Baron Potet de Sennevoy, a French investigator and practitioner of "animal magnetism," that first captured Elliotson's attention. Elliotson invited the Baron, who had come to England to spread the new doctrine, to perform clinical demonstrations of mesmerism at the University College London Hospital. Articles in the popular press and in *The Lancet*, which at this point was reporting on the practice but withholding judgment, heightened public interest in the subject.

In 1837 Dr. Elliotson, his assistant Mr. Wood, and the Baron began using mesmerism in the hospital to treat women suffering from various nervous complaints or hysteria. The intention was to use mesmerism as a therapy for the patients, but the experimental treatments soon became more about showing the effects of mesmerism than treating the patients medically. The most notorious of these treatment/performances would be that of Elizabeth O'Key, the sixteen-year-old maid who was first admitted to the wards on April 4, 1837. Little is known about O'Key, and unfortunately there are no accounts in her own words of what she experienced in the hospital. Most of the information about Elliotson's work comes from his own lecture notes, or from reports by the sub-editor of *The Lancet* who attended the demonstrations. Both the lecture notes and reports were published in the journal. Thus events must be interpreted in light of the fact that evidence comes primarily from only one point of view: that of the male doctors and professional men whose scientific background, education, social position, and gender gave them specific and limited expectations about the nature of the phenomena they would observe. The issue of interpretation is inherent in most theatre history research, since audience expectations play a crucial part in the performance, reception, and reporting of any theatrical event. A similar dynamic exists whenever a person or group of persons is brought before an audience to display specific kinds of behavior — whether the performance is by an actress on the stage or by a patient in the lecture hall, diagnosed as "epileptic" or "hysterical" as Elizabeth O'Key was.

The following discussion of the reports published in *The Lancet* keeps in mind that what *The Lancet* writer observed was filtered by his expectations. What the writer chose to report, emphasizing or repressing certain details, was influenced by his assumptions about what the readers of *The Lancet* expected and what might or might not properly be reported in a scholarly/scientific journal.

Two facts that are known about Elizabeth O'Key are crucial. First, she deliberately applied to be admitted to the University College Hospital specifically because she had heard about the Baron's work there and wished to be treated by mesmerism. Secondly, both she and her sister had previously been involved with an evangelical preacher named Edward Irving, whose followers exhibited a particular talent for speaking in tongues. Irving, a talented and charismatic orator, had become very popular in London in the early 1830s when members of his congregation, mostly women, began speaking in tongues and prophesying about the millennium during his services.[6] Elizabeth and her sister Jane had both participated in some capacity in Irving's large public meetings which featured ritualistic demonstrations of glossolalia. Even before they became patients of Dr. Elliotson, therefore, they were "experienced in a specialized form of public performance" and had already been "engaged in a kind of mental-spiritual concentration and role-playing."[7] In some sense, then, Elizabeth O'Key chose the theatrical situation and a performance dynamic when she applied to become a patient and the subject of the experimental exhibitions being conducted at the hospital. These facts raise the question of whether she might have been just a fraud or a publicity seeker. Was she genuinely in an altered state of consciousness, induced either by religious ecstasy or mesmerism, when she spoke in tongues for Irving's followers, or sang, danced and told jokes for the doctors and students at the university medical college? Or did she fake the state of ecstasy or trance? The question is nearly impossible to answer. The authenticity or "truthfulness" of O'Key's performances in the religious or medical arenas is even more difficult to determine at this distance than it was for observers at the time. What remains true, however, is the significance of the performances. Whether O'Key was pretending to be mesmerized or not, and whether her behaviors in the supposed trance state were conscious or unconscious, they provide a vivid example of the potential power of trance performance.

Before Dr. Elliotson held a public demonstration of his experimental mesmerism of Elizabeth O'Key, he lectured on his treatment of another young woman who had suffered epileptic attacks. This "Clinical Lecture on Animal Magnetism" was published in the September 9, 1837, issue of *The Lancet*.[8] Elliotson used mesmerism to artificially induce the epileptic attacks and/or alternate state of consciousness in the young woman, evidently for the purpose of finding out how mesmerism might be used to manipulate the symptoms of the illness. When she was first mesmerized by means of "passes" Elliotson made over her face with his hands, the girl displayed a state of somnambulism which Elliotson called "sleep-waking." In this state the girl could not see, hear or feel pain, but she talked constantly, in a "witty" and "rambling" manner, and displayed "a great spirit of mimicry." When these "fits" were over, she would rub her eyes, appear to wake up, and "resume her natural character, which was that of a quiet, modest girl."[9] In subsequent mesmeric fits the girl displayed an even wider variety of behaviors and volatile changes of mood that were regarded as inappropriate. She "sang, whistled, danced, was rude, noisy, laughing or miserable by turns." Elliotson's report emphasizes the girl's talent for mimicry, and he mentions the occurrence of this trait in several other female somnambulists, including one who, oddly enough, could imitate the sounds of the violin and piano while in a "sleep-waking" state.[10]

The girl's mimicry seemed harmless enough, although her imitation of other patients in the wards seems to have been somewhat cruel. Some of her behavior, however, was more threatening. For example, sometimes during the passes that were performed to bring her out of the trance state, she became "exceedingly abusive," swearing and displaying some kind of sexual impropriety that Elliotson seems to have been reluctant to detail explicitly. In his carefully chosen words, she became "sometimes rather affectionate."[11] Elliotson's reluctance to characterize her behavior as erotic or sexual in this context was prudent; he was already in some danger of being accused of immorality for practicing mesmerism in the first place, since the practice was regarded by some as no more than a devious new method for men to take sexual advantage of young women.[12]

This first report set the stage for the even more spectacular performances of the O'Key sisters, and indicates what was considered "normal" behavior for a young lower class woman — the norm from which O'Key would deviate when she performed under the spell of mesmerism. On May 10, 1838, *The Lancet* published a detailed account of what they called an "Exhibit of the effects of animal magnetism" on Elizabeth O'Key. The "exhibit," which was held in the lecture hall of the University College Hospital, was attended by two hundred people, probably almost exclusively men. Many of them were medical doctors and students, interspersed with other professionals and interested observers. Some audience members were described as "carriage company"—an upper class crowd looking for entertainment. These spectators "arrived by turns and saw the phenomena by bits,"[13] treating the exhibit as they might have done an evening in the theatre, popping in to catch the last act or a comic afterpiece, as audiences often did in the late eighteenth and early nineteenth century London theatre.

Elliotson began the exhibit with a lecture on the general principles of mesmerism as Elizabeth O'Key, who was to demonstrate some of his points, sat passively by. Her silent, motionless presence effectively aroused the interest of the audience; it was noted that several curious spectators used opera glasses to gaze at her more closely. *The Lancet*'s description of O'Key's physical appearance stressed her diminutive size and apparent fragility. The description also implied assumptions about her character, suggesting that she was a blank slate, with no distinctive personality or presence:

> Her figure was somewhat womanish, but her face and head were those of a child. No particular character was indicated by her features, or by any expression of feeling that could be observed in them.[14]

The ambiguity of the impression created by this initial description is interesting in that there seems to be some doubt about whether O'Key is a woman or a child. The adjective "womanish" applied to her body suggests maturity, while the mention of the childlike face and head suggests that she is quite young, at least in terms of her character or intellect.

The blank quality vanished as soon as O'Key was mesmerized, which was done quickly and easily by a few passes before her face. Her empty expression instantly changed to one of "mingled archness and simplicity" and the personality that emerged was vivid but still ambiguous, partly innocent and partly aware.[15] This initial change was so striking that it convinced many observers who were on the lookout for fraudulence that O'Key had entered a genuine state of trance, and that a genuine shift of consciousness had occurred. And if O'Key were merely pretending to be mesmerized, the reporter for *The Lancet* implied, she had performed a consummate feat of acting:

> The question of deception was at once met by a conviction, derived from appearances, that the most accomplished actor that ever trod the stage could not have presented the change with a truer show of reality.[16]

The reporter indicated several times that the general consensus of the observers was that O'Key was exhibiting real behavior, and not "acting." Part of the insistence that her trance and behavior were "real" and not an act was probably based on the assumption that a young, inexperienced lower class girl could not have had the skill or intelligence necessary to fake the rapid and radical transitions of character and feeling that O'Key showed. This assumption was clearly not shared by the reporter, who, as the exhibits continue, makes increasing reference to O'Key's "artistic skills" and seems ready to believe that O'Key did indeed possess the talent necessary to mimic the trance state and carry out an elaborate fraud on the doctors and spectators.

In the "sleep-waking" phase of her performances, O'Key interacted with the fascinated audience, speaking with what was, again ambiguously, described as "innocent familiarity" to such distinguished spectators as the Marquis of Anglesea. Her "familiarity" was both verbal and physical. She complimented the Marquis several times on his "white trowsers," and when Elliotson's passes put her into a deeper state of unconsciousness for a few minutes, she fell asleep in the arms or laps of the nearest gentlemen. O'Key was particularly familiar with Elliotson. He experimented with her to show that she could imitate the gestures he made without being able to see him (her view was blocked by a large wooden frame that was held in front of her face). When he tried the same experiment without the use of the wood to block her view, she called him a "silly man." Throughout the demonstrations, O'Key did not show, in the trance state, the respect, timidity, and deference for Elliotson and the other doctors that characterized her attitude in the normal waking state. At first Elliotson encouraged this playful, informal dynamic, teasing her with the elaborate tricks he played on her to demonstrate her gullibility and susceptibility when mesmerized. In the first exhibit, for instance, he told her that she could not see him because he had crawled into the boot of a certain gentleman in the audience. She went to the man and said "Oh! come out ... don't live in that nasty hole." She had begun to put her hand up the gentleman's trouser leg before Elliotson hastily put her back into a deep sleep with a few passes of his hand. Incidents like these suggest to a twenty-first-century reader an atmosphere of eroticism or sexual playfulness. But even if such a thought occurred to the reporter of the events, he did not comment on it, perhaps reluctant to suggest such an indelicate interpretation to his readers. The previously mentioned marquis, at any rate, was discomfited by O'Key's attentions to the gentlemen in the audience. He left the theatre before the end of the first exhibition, saying that he found the atmosphere "too warm."[17]

There were other points when O'Key got out of control, abandoning Elliotson's orchestrated program of scientific demonstration and launching into "acts" of her own. These often involved singing or dancing. Once, as Elliotson was magnetizing her pupils to show how they dilated or contracted according to the passes he made in front of her eyes, she began to sing a song with the words "buy a black sheep." The report in *The Lancet* describes what followed:

She sang one verse, adding, "I don't remember any more, but I'll sing Jim Crow." The mill-board was here placed before her face for some experiment which we cannot recollect, when she said to the board, "Oh you nasty boy. What a dirty black fellow you are." She then sang a verse of "Sound the Loud Timbrel," and on coming to the line, "Jehovah shall triumph," said to the board, "Will you triumph, you dirty beast. I'm sure you won't, misce, crutis, crece croo," — words which were unintelligible.[18]

It would be interesting to know if her singing and gibberish here resembled anything she did in her performances as a tongues-speaking disciple of the evangelist Irving. The words that Irving's followers spoke in their ecstatic state were supposedly from real languages unknown to the speaker in their normal state of consciousness. The words uttered here by O'Key might be a corrupted Latin, and perhaps in this instance she was drawing on a previous successful experience in public performance.

Also intriguing in this context is her reference to the stereotypical Negro character Jim Crow. Just a year earlier, the American vaudeville performer T. D. Rice had brought his popular "Jim Crow" act to the Surrey Theatre in London, starting a vogue for minstrel shows in England. Rice would have appealed to the working class audiences in London as he did to those in America. In New York City, Rice was a regular performer at the Bowery, a theatre near the notorious Five Points district of the city, where slums abounded and gangs ruled. Rice and his Jim Crow song and dance were a particular favorite of the "Bowery B'hoys," rowdy working class single men, mostly apprentices and journeymen, living in boarding houses, with little likelihood of advancement.[19] O'Key could have seen one of Rice's London performances, and the popularity of the song can explain her familiarity with it. Her performance of "Jim Crow" is interesting not so much for what it shows of her awareness of the current popular theatre, but for what it may indicate about her own attitude, conscious or not, towards her performances. Did she associate herself with Jim Crow, a marginalized character performing in an acceptably controlled context for white, primarily upper- and middle-class audiences? Like T. D. Rice, her success depended in some measure on the exaggeration or caricature of features attributed to a marginalized member of society. As Rice caricatured the "Negro" in his performances, O'Key caricatured "Woman," playing up her unstable, sly, childlike or manipulative qualities. Contemporary scholars of performance might view O'Key's playing of gender and ethnic stereotypes as potentially subversive. Laurence Senelick, for instance, has suggested that the very act of playing a gender stereotype on stage can call it into question. "Gender roles performed by 'performers' never merely replicate those in everyday life; they are more sharply defined and more emphatically presented, the inherent iconicity offering both an ideal and a critique."[20] One might say that O'Key's playing of the madwoman was both an ideal and a critique of that social and gender role. The notion that the performance may offer an "ideal" could just as well suggest the possibility that playing the role *reinforces* (rather than critiques) the stereotype, especially if one believes that gender is already only an "act" or social role that is reified by repetition: that is, "woman" or female exists only in as much as person act female both on and off the stage. In any case it would be difficult to prove, even if it were likely, that the London audience at a spectacle in 1838 would respond in the same way as a twenty-first century performance studies scholar to the playing of a gender and ethnic stereotypes in this unconventional performance. This is not to say, however, that the performances would not have been disturbing and powerful for the Victorian audience, as responses to O'Key indicate that they were.

O'Key's performance of the Jim Crow song appears even more significant in light of her references to someone she called "the Negro," who was apparently a sort of spirit guide or advisor with whom she occasionally consulted and conversed. "The Negro" came to O'Key while she was in the trance state and played the role of advocate or defender for her. In one instance, O'Key was asked to lift a heavy weight to demonstrate her increased strength while in a mesmeric trance. She told Elliotson that her "Negro" had advised her not to do so, because although she would be physically capable of lifting up to eighty pounds while mesmerized, she would hurt her ribs if she did. Previously when O'Key had suffered an attack of "pleuritis," she had told the doctors that the "Negro" had told her that the inflammation was a result of her ribs being sprained from lifting heavy weights. These episodes indicate that O'Key may have felt it necessary to create or tap into a protective personality to see to her best interests, which often seemed to be overlooked in the mesmeric demonstrations. But why would O'Key choose (consciously or not) a figure so socially powerless for a protector, and what does her invocation of the Negro in this context indicate about the psychological dynamic of her performances in general?

Because the male doctors who ought to have done so were not adequately protecting her health, having allowed scientific experimentation to take precedence over healing, one could speculate that O'Key felt that only a character as liminal and socially powerless as herself could empathize with and be an advocate for her. Perhaps, in fact, the Negro appealed to her precisely because he was a liminal figure. Like herself, especially when she was under the spell of mesmerism, the Negro was outside the bounds of society. The view of O'Key as a liminal figure is reinforced by the structure of her performances, which correspond to Victor Turner's model for the social drama or rite of passage, with O'Key's movement through the stages of separation (from a normal state of consciousness), liminality (where abnormal behavior occurred) and reintegration (return to a normal state of consciousness).[21] O'Key's actions under mesmerism provide a clear example of the ludic and subversive possibilities available to the subject in the liminal phase. It makes sense that in this phase other liminal and playful entities like the Negro/Jim Crow figure might emerge, possessed of a potency they lacked in a "normal" state.

Because of the freedom from restraint offered by mesmerism, O'Key could manipulate her own performances, creating characters and "bits" which co-opted the stereotypes and expectations of her audience. She was able to assert and express herself with unusual freedom, through characters which were either aspects of her own personality, or as the Negro seemed to be, separate, autonomous entities.

Near the end of this first performance, another patient, a girl younger than O'Key, was brought in from the hospital wards. Attempts were made to mesmerize the newcomer, but O'Key was unwilling to give stage to her rival. When the child was placed in the chair O'Key had occupied, O'Key "whistled and sang in a sweet tone, once with very artist-like variations, evincing symptoms of a ripe faculty of music." She concluded with a reprise of "Jim Crow," and was on the point of dancing, offering to "wheel about and turn about" in the words of the song, when she was stopped, "to the manifest disappointment of many spectators."[22] At this point, the reporter is explicitly characterizing O'Key as a performing artist. Subsequent reports increasingly stress her performance skills, which come to be seen as identical with her ability to fool Dr. Elliotson and his gullible colleagues. The authenticity of her mesmeric trances is called into question, and debate arises over whether or not O'Key or other patients might be capable of faking or "acting" the behavior which is coming to be expected of subjects in a trance state. Assumptions about the nature of women could be used to argue either side of the question: on the one hand a woman would not be intelligent or skillful enough to fool highly trained male doctors; on the other hand, with a woman's ability to deceive and transform herself (i.e., to act) she would be able to successfully mimic the trance state.

In either case, O'Key's trance performances were apparently riveting. The new child who was brought in was not as satisfactory or entertaining a subject as O'Key. She could not be mesmerized, but merely yawned when repeated passes were made before her face. Dr. Elliotson tried to show the child how to magnetize O'Key, who remained unaffected by her little costar and treated her with amused contempt. O'Key said to the child, "Suppose, my little dear, I was to knock you off your perch. I say, Dr. Elliotson, 'spose I was to knock you off your perch; how funny you'd look. But I won't do that; I wouldn't hurt you."[23] Clearly, the mesmerized O'Key was capable of both playing with the idea of metaphorically "knocking Dr. Elliotson off his perch," making a fool of him, and of controlling this impulse in herself. This suggests the tenuousness of Elliotson's control over the situation. Although he appeared to be directing the performances, he was not completely in control. It was O'Key who manipulated the doctors at certain points. As she did so, she found temporary freedom from conventional restraints on her behavior and language, freedom provided by the extraordinary combination of mesmerism and performance.

This particular performance ended in such a way that O'Key seemed to be in charge, only conceding an appearance of control to Dr. Elliotson. At first Elliotson could not awake her from the deep sleep which constituted the third stage of the mesmeric trance. Elliotson conjectured that the restlessness of the growing audience might be distracting her. Elliotson's assistant Mr. Wood also tried unsuccessfully to awaken her, then he asked her in a whisper to tell him when she would come out of the trance — evidently in an attempt to demonstrate her clairvoyant abilities. She replied, "In five minutes."

"Shall you awaken yourself?"—"No." "How then?" "You must wake me." "In what way?"—"By rubbing my neck."[24]

Not surprisingly, in five minutes O'Key awoke as she had predicted, in her "natural state" of downcast timidity. As she was escorted from the theatre, she received compliments and congratulations from members of the audience, shaking hands with some of them as if she were an actress greeting fans after an exhausting and triumphant performance.

Dr. Elliotson's next public exhibit of mesmerism took place on June 2, again before an audience of distinguished guests and celebrities. (The poet Thomas Moore was present and appeared fascinated by the proceedings.) The report of June 2 also mentions the inconvenience of the hospital theatre, which had no permanent seating for spectators, many of whom were forced to stand or perch on a shelf in one corner for the whole three hours. The reporter suggested that everyone might have been more comfortably accommodated nearby in the theatre of the University of London.

Elliotson began this demonstration as he had the first, with a lecture on mesmerism. Elizabeth O'Key and her sister Jane, who had also shown a predilection for performing while mesmerized, were to be the major attraction. For openers, however, Elliotson brought on several other patients, two young men, a woman and a girl, to show the different effects of mesmerism on different subjects. Mesmerism had no effect at all on one of the men, who merely "smiled" at the process, while the other man simply dropped into a "real" sleep. The woman and the girl were easily mesmerized, but displayed none of the entertaining permutations of personality and behavior which characterized the O'Key sisters in the trance state.

This second mesmeric exhibition demonstrates to what extent the interpretations about the O'Key's performances were colored by (1) assumptions about what was "natural" behavior for them and (2) the conviction that any deviation from that norm must be the result of deliberate deception (performance), some kind of madness, or an alternate state of consciousness (a mesmerized state). Both Jane and Elizabeth were assumed to be dull and spiritless in their natural state. Any show of initiative, energy or vivacity was attributed either to fits of "delirium" or to the effects of mesmerism. Jane was said to be

> so constantly in the state of delirium that to the spectator it appears to be her natural condition, and from a natural state it is only distinguishable at first by the extraordinary ease, sociability, and simplicity of manner, her occasional misuse of words, and an extreme conscientiousness and quickness of remark.[25]

Her articulateness, intellectual quickness, and social ease are considered abnormal, as are strong displays of feeling or resentment against her doctors. For instance, the reporter of *The Lancet* felt it worth remarking that Jane O'Key showed a particular hatred for a certain Mr. Mayo, a medical man who "never appears to have done her any harm, but evidently takes great good-tempered pleasure in performing innocent experiments on her."[26] The nature of these "experiments" is unknown, but it is implied that her feelings were irrational and without cause, whereas in fact one wonders if her dislike of Mr. Mayo did not arise from an understandable irritation at the constant tricks and experiments to which the girls were subjected, both in the public demonstrations and in the wards of the hospital.

In this second public performance Elizabeth O'Key again showed her penchant for singing, which, along with her facetious remarks to the audience, proved to be a big hit. When she was first put into a trance she seemed to be unaware of the large audience that had assembled. When Dr. Elliotson pointed them out to her, she cried, "Where the d—l did you all come from?" which provoked great laughter. Soon after, she began to skip around and sing:

> I went into a tailor's shop,
> To buy a suit of clothes,
> But where the money came from,
> G — A — — knows.[27]

This was greeted with even greater laughter. Elliotson evidently wanted to get back to what he considered the real business of the show, which her playfulness was making impossible. Saying that he "must stupify [sic] her" (i.e., bring her into a deeper, more passive stage of trance), he did so easily, and she instantly passed from the state of "excessive merriment to that of perfect quiet."[28]

At other times during this demonstration Elliotson seemed to be concerned not only with getting back to his agenda of scientific experimentation, but with preserving the propriety of the situation, which O'Key's subversive acts were constantly on the verge of derailing. Her subtle resistance to him provides the dramatic conflict and action in these performances. At one point when Elliotson awakened O'Key from deep sleep into the lighter phase of trance, she indignantly denied having been asleep at all. The report states that

> Dr. Elliotson having assured her that she had been asleep, she replied, "Oh, Dr. Elliotson, you're mad; you're quite a baby; I haven't been to sleep; I wouldn't go to sleep in daylight; I'm going to make a parson now," twirling her handkerchief; and before she could be prevented (a prelate and many reverend gentlemen being present) she had twisted it into a head and cassock, when Dr. Elliotson stupified her with a pass.[29]

The mesmeric trances also allowed O'Key to express attitudes or opinions about a variety of subjects which would have been inappropriate or unacceptable for her in her "normal" state. In the June 2 demonstration, while she was in a trance she and Elliotson got into a discussion about whether she had been good or naughty, which gave her the opportunity to complain about several things, first of all her diet. She told Elliotson that she had a good appetite, but was not getting enough to eat, and added, "you've stuck me at half-diet, I suspect." He replied that she shouldn't want any more than the bread, milk and tea that she was getting, and that when he had let her have meat, she had become violent.[30] She denied that she had been violent, and told him if he let her have more to eat she would clean the ward for the nurse. Elliotson then asked her if she would go to church, and she answered:

> "I don't know. I don't much like the Gospel glipers (drivers). They're too cross, and they're always scolding one into goodness. Besides, it's of no use women going to church, for the parson only talks to the men; he says 'When the wicked *man* turneth away from wickedness he shall save his soul alive.' I wish he'd save my sole [sic], and then I wouldn't have such a hole in it," she

added, turning up her foot to show the worn condition of the bottom of her shoe; "though I don't see why the women shouldn't be preached to, for they are quite as great scoundrels as the men."[31]

O'Key's attitude seems flippant, but it may indicate a deeper disenchantment with the role of religion in her own life, and the church's inability to address her specific concerns. The fact that she had once been involved with the radical evangelist Edward Irving reinforces the probability that she had been disappointed by the traditional church. (Apparently, women played a prominent part in Irving's church.) The parson O'Key mocks here, however, speaks only to men, and his message does not comfort, or even apply to, her. Her trance performance allowed her to express her rebellion and dissatisfaction with impunity.

Part of the speech quoted also shows O'Key in the character of entertainer or joker, making a bad pun with "soul" and the "sole" of her shoe. There is no indication in the report of how the audience reacted to this particular exchange, but Elliotson seemed, again, to have grown uncomfortable with the conversation. Without addressing her objections to the parson, he dismissed her speech with "Well, but you must go to church, and mind you behave well there," and put her into a deep sleep. O'Key was apparently not to be put off so easily, though. She awoke again in a few moments and immediately resumed her remarks about the church, saying that she did not like Mr. Stebbings, the parson. Elliotson answered, "I'm sure he's a remarkably good man. He is one of the best men I know. You must see he's a good man by his looks," to which she replied, "I don't know that. Perhaps he's a hypocrite. Don't you know that you should not take a man by his looks," at which point Elliotson, outwitted, put her to sleep again.[32]

It is ironic that O'Key should have advised Elliotson not to judge merely by appearances, since in fact that is primarily how he judged her in the course of his experiments. The content of her speech did not appear to interest him at all. Instead he focused almost exclusively on the physical effects of mesmerism on her, ignoring her observations about herself and her own treatment (in the case of diet, or lifting the weights, for example), and the ramifications these might have had in the matters of diagnosis and treatment. The bulk of his experiments involved exploring how her senses and movement were affected by the trance state; he focused on her body while her voice remained unheard.

Public demonstrations of mesmerism with Elizabeth O'Key as the principal performer continued into the fall. Her crowd-pleasing antics also continued, and seemed increasingly to function as a way for her to vent hostility. For instance, during one performance she acted out a small scene, a sort of divertissement or routine on the subject of "affected young ladies." She impersonated several different young ladies, caricaturing their behavior. She then turned directly to the audience and said, "Now what would I do with such a fine lady? Why, kick her a — to be sure."[33] O'Key may have had some specific young lady in mind, perhaps someone she had worked for, or she may have been expressing a more generalized class resentment. In any case, it must have been very satisfying to her to be able to utter such words and perform such acts in front of an attentive audience of gentlemen.

As the reporter for *The Lancet* saw more of Elizabeth O'Key he became more skeptical about the effects of Dr. Elliotson's mesmerism and more impressed with O'Key's acting skills. Finally, in an article published on September 15, 1838, he definitively dismissed the validity of the mesmeric experiments, while devoting much of the article to discussing O'Key's performances. Although there is a trace of tongue-in-cheek exaggeration in his tone, perhaps to make Elliotson appear all the more foolish, he also expressed genuine admiration for O'Key's resourcefulness and artistry. He noted that

> the talent which she possesses in greatest perfection is imitation; the talent possessed by few of representing feelings and states of the mind vividly, so as to impress spectators with their reality. In this O'Key is excelled by few actresses on the stage.[34]

In this reporter's opinion, O'Key could not only "act" all the stages of mesmerism, but she could create a stage persona and exert a charisma which was almost inexplicably powerful. "Elizabeth is a genius in her line," the reporter asserted; "this is betrayed by her dark, piercing eye, her wonderful performance, and the power she exercises over all who have come much in contact with her."[35] Although the reporter was deliberately debunking mesmerism, he resorted to the concept of a mysterious power, possibly emanating from the eyes (as Mesmer had claimed it could), to describe O'Key's influence. Even as the scientific value of mesmerism was rejected, its function as a metaphor for a performance dynamic persisted. And in this case it was the mesmerized Trilby figure (O'Key), who ultimately exerted a greater control over the dynamic than the controlling Svengali figure (Elliotson).

The reporter also remarked upon the entertainment value of O'Key's jokes, sarcasm, wit and familiarity, and seemed to sense, if not elucidate, the carnivalesque feeling of freedom and release which pervaded O'Key's performances:

> Her improvisations at the mesmeric sittings, the witticisms, the sarcasms, the snatches of song, which she spouted so prodigiously, were, not infrequently, worthy of the licensed fool of the old comedy.[36]

The image is appropriate: Elizabeth O'Key as the fool for the medical and scientific establishment, entertaining, mocking, and making light of their authority. But also like the fools of classical comedy, church or court, she did little, ultimately, to undermine the men, institutions, or status quo. Instead of inciting any kind of institutional change, the trance performances at most empowered O'Key on an emotional and psychological level. For her, the dynamic provided a liminal space where subversive possibilities might be played out and where "unnaceptable" or "unnatural" feelings, behavior and attitudes might be expressed.

There is an intriguing hint that O'Key might even have parlayed the talent that emerged in this dynamic into a career: the reporter of *The Lancet* concluded his discussion of her case by suggesting that the proper venue for her performances was not the scientific lecture hall but the stage. He asserted that

> some of the minor theatres may find it no bad speculation to get up a mesmeric farce, in which O'Key, with a little training, would appear with advantage.[37]

There is no evidence that O'Key ever went on the stage after leaving the care of Dr. Elliotson, although various "mesmeric farces" were apparently gotten up in this period. O'Key had begun the process of co-opting the power of the trance performance for herself by taking advantage of the potential freedom offered by mesmerism. It would take Anna Cora Mowatt, an American actress in the next decade, to manipulate the dynamic with more success than O'Key had been able to do.

5

"Double Consciousness" in Acting Theory and Trance State

Responses to O'Key's performances show the fascination exerted on an audience by the heady combination of theatre and mesmerism. Elizabeth O'Key was, for some observers, as much an actress as the subject of a medical or mesmeric experiment. Her performances reinforce the fine line, and the difficulty for audiences in determining the distinction, between "acting" and behavior in a trance state. The subject or actress herself, as well as her audience, sometimes conflated the two. Moreover, acting and trance activity were often explained in terms of the same psychological phenomena in the nineteenth century; the argument was made by theorists of both mesmeric phenomena and of acting that some kind of double or alternate consciousness was a necessary pre condition for both. One of the earliest uses of the term "double-consciousness" in the nineteenth century was in 1817, in the title of an article, "A Double-Consciousness, or a Duality of Person in the Same Individual," by a Samuel L. Mitchell, published in a medical journal. It referred to the case of a young woman named Mary Reynolds who exhibited two distinct personalities which alternated in her for 15 or 16 years.[1] The same case was mentioned in an 1860 article which appeared in the journal *Harper's*. In Mary Reynold's case, the dual personalities were not just different, but opposite and conflicting. The first was "sedate, sober and pensive," while the second was "gay, cheerful, extravagantly fond of society, of fun and practical jokes."[2] The polarization of personalities in Reynolds, which could only be expressed when the subject was in an alternate state, resembles a later case described by Dr. John Elliotson.

Elliotson had remained fascinated with the general question of what he called the "dual or intermittent state of consciousness" long after he was forced to abandon his experiments with O'Key at University College Hospital in London in the 1830s. He published on the subject well into the second half of the century. He wrote an essay titled "Dual Consciousness" which appeared in an 1877 issue of the *Cornhill* magazine in which he described cases of otherwise "normal" subjects who exhibited two distinct "mental lives" or personalities. He cited several cases to illustrate the "relation between the phenomena of dual consciousness and somnambulism"; and also cited examples of otherwise "normal" individuals with more than one distinct personality or "mental life." One of these was a woman he calls Felida X, in whom a vivacious personality emerged when she dropped out of her usual state of consciousness.[3] Both cases are reminiscent of that of Anna Cora Mowatt (the subject of the next chapter) in whom the colorful and cheeky "Gypsy" emerged when she was in mesmeric trance. Epes Sargent, the friend of Mowatt who introduced her to mesmerism and later wrote extensively about spiritualism, declared succinctly that "the human mind is so constituted that it may manifest discrete, or entirely separate, state of consciousness."[4]

When Victorian thinkers made connections between acting and different levels of consciousness or states of being, they were building on a long tradition of attempts to theorize about the process of acting. Early acting theories posited a flow of "spirits" like the so called "fluidium" of Mesmer, which operated through the actor. "The spirit moves the actor, who, in the authenticity of his transport, moves the audience."[5] Thus the image of Proteus, the Greek god who transforms himself swiftly from one shape to another, reoccurs in acting theory. In the seventeenth century the great Shakespearean actor Richard Burbage was called "a delightful Proteus," and "the Protean metaphor implied that the actor possesses not only the power of self-alteration, but also the more mysterious Delphic power of self-abdication in favor of the role."[6] A theory that depended on self alteration (or self abdication if it applied to women!) was appealing for some Victorians. Ideas of self-help, and one's ability to change or reform were popular. The notion of "self-abidication" with its connotation of sacrifice for a higher goal or greater good, would have been particularly applicable as an ideal for women in the nineteenth century. Reviews as well as the personal accounts of actresses often stressed that the emotional abandonment of oneself to a role was fundamental to the process of acting. As mentioned previously, this idea was so prevalent that a category called the "emotional school of acting" was created to describe actresses like Fanny Kemble, Helena Faucit, Clara Morris and Anna Cora Mowatt, who were known for throwing themselves passionately and apparently spontaneously into a role, to the point of forgetting themselves completely.

Fanny Kemble's descriptions of losing her normal sense of self and achieving an almost trance like state in performance constitute some of the best evidence of this phenomenon. Her description of being completely swept up in the playing of Juliet (cited in Chapter One) is one example. Another is Kemble's account of her experience in the role of Belvidera in *Venice Preserv'd*, a seventeenth-century melodrama which still provided a popular vehicle for actresses in the nineteenth century. Kemble wrote:

> In the last scene where poor Belvidera's brain gives way under her despair, and she fancies herself digging for her husband in the earth, and that she at last recovers and seizes him, I intended to utter a piercing scream; this I had not of course rehearsed, not being able to scream deliberately in cold blood, so that I hardly knew, myself, what manner of utterance I should find for my madness. But when the evening came, I uttered shriek after shriek without stopping, and rushing off the stage ran all round the back of the scenes, and was pursuing my way, perfectly unconscious of what I was doing, down the stairs that led out into the street, when I was captured and brought back to my dressing room and to my senses.[7]

Here the emotional abandonment to the role goes beyond acting into what could be described as hysteria, in which the actress's normal sense of self is overtaken by another consciousness. Vocabulary common to descriptions of hysterics, trance performers and stage actors suggests conflation of these roles — the subjects "lose themselves," are "possessed" or "taken over" and furthermore might "entrance" or "mesmerize" those who watched them.

In the early years of Spiritualism, some doctors explained trance phenomena as a kind of hysteria, or mental illness. One, Dr. Frederic R. Marvin, even coined a name for the disorder, "mediomania," which he describes in detail in a pamphlet published in 1874 titled "The Philosophy of Spiritualism and the Pathology and Treatment of Mediomania."[8] In fact, J. Arthur Hill in *Spiritualism: Its History, Phenomena and Doctrine* wrote that "it is possible that many 'mediums' who give trance addresses and supposed clairvoyance at spiritualist meetings are people in whom there is a dissociation of consciousness, and that there is not external spirit agency at all."[9] Frederic H. Myers, an influential psychical researcher late in the century, linked his study of mediumship to emerging ideas about the unconscious. His thinking differed from that of other investigators in that he viewed the trance state not necessarily as a form of mental illness, and the unconscious or "subliminal self" not just as "the receptacle of forgotten and repressed ideas," but as sources of creativity, inspiration and even genius, and a way for human beings to gain access to "worlds beyond themselves."[10]

Actress and Spiritualist performer Emma Hardinge Britten, whose comments elsewhere also leave open the possibility that she believed mediumship could have psychological rather than supernatural origins, spoke of her own sense of double-consciousness, feeling as if she were two different individuals, when in a state of trance. She described her anxiety as she prepared for one of her first public appearances as a trance speaker.

> Conducted finally to the platform, my last clear remembrance was of listening to a lovely quartette (sic) beautifully performed by the Troy Harmonists, and then I had a dim perception that I was myself standing outside of myself, by the side of my dear father—dead—when I was only a little child—but whose noble form I could plainly see close by me, gesticulating to, and addressing somehow, my second self, which was imitating him, and repeating all the thrilling words he was uttering ... then, as ever afterwards in the countless platform addresses I have given, I have seemed, and still seem, to be two individuals—one whose lips are uttering a succession of sentences, sometimes familiar to me, still oftener new and strange, but always unpremeditated by my second self; in fact, I am rather an onlooker and occasional listener than the originator of the spoken words.[11]

The kind of double consciousness that Britten describes here was more common, certainly among actresses, than the total loss of self that Kemble claimed to have experienced when acting Belvidera—although the latter makes a great theatrical anecdote. In a more analytical passage, Kemble herself discusses acting less as an hysterical possession and more as a double consciousness.

> The curious part of acting, to me, is the sort of double process which the mind carries on at once, the combined operation of one's faculties, so to speak, in diametrically opposite directions; for instance, in that very last scene of Mrs. Beverley; while I was half dead with crying in the midst of the *real* grief, created by an entirely *unreal* cause, I perceived that my tears were falling like rain all over my silk dress, and spoiling it; and I calculated and measured most accurately the space that my father would require to fall in, and moved myself and my train in the midst of the anguish I was to feign, and absolutely did endure.[12]

William Archer cites this passage as a classic example of the double consciousness of acting. Archer, an avid student of theatre and keen observer of performers, took a scientific approach to developing a theory of acting by submitting questions to working actors about their processes and experiences. The results were written up in *Masks and Faces*, which focused on the question of whether or not an actor had to actually feel an emotion in order to play it effectively. Archer's study was originally conceived as a response to the famous *Paradox of Acting* written by Denis Diderot. Diderot had proposed, after investigating actors of his time, that in fact a cool rationality and absence of passion was necessary for actors to successfully impersonate the emotions of the characters they played. The question of whether to be effective (which meant provoking emotion in the audience), an actor had to actually *feel* the emotions he played had been central to discussions of acting since.

Archer observed that many theorists and actors in the nineteenth century took issue with what they perceived as the extreme polarization of "sensibility" and rational control Diderot posited. Indeed the whole notion of being lost in a role or performing only in a state of inspired emotion was insulting to some artists, who felt that such a theory diminished the role of skill and effort. It was evidently common for people to "overrate a fine actor's genius, and underrate his trained skill."[13] (Edmund Kean, whose audiences were in the grip of a Romantic fervor earlier in the century, had been hounded by the assumption that his acting was all inspiration and no work.) It was particularly easy for Victorian audiences to underrate the skill of actresses. Some actresses, however, appeared to capitalize on the assumptions made about their sensibilities, in a sense co-opting the qualities so commonly ascribed to them, and perpetuating the notion that it was their own passionate inspiration or sensibility which was the root of their acting. Of course not all observers inevitably assumed that women's performances, either as legitimate actresses or as trance performers, were always the product of uncontrolled emotion, hysteria or some form of double-consciousness. The reporter who referred to Elizabeth O'Key an "a genius in her line," though he intended by doing so to characterize her as a fraud, by recognizing her skill and artistry paid a back handed compliment to her as an actress.[14]

Archer addressed the apparent paradox of the feeling aroused by the "non-feeling" actor by suggesting that it was not an either-or — that both objectivity and emotion (sense and sensibility) were present in an actor during performance, either as two different levels of consciousness, or as alternating or double states. Archer's theories centered on this duality, and he insisted that the "real paradox of acting resolves itself into the paradox of dual consciousness."[15]

For Archer, the existence of states of dual consciousness were self evident. He called the "double action of the brain" "a matter of universal experience" and thought that acting was a process in which one routinely found "special forms of this multiple activity."[16] His insights about the commonality of co-consciousness are supported by modern theories of clinical hypnosis.[17] And Archer's study records the experience of several performers who describe their ability to maintain several different levels of awareness or activity at once. The actor Forbes-Robertson referred explicitly to the functioning of different "strata of mind" during performances.[18] Henry Irving, the successful late Victorian actor-manager and the first member of the theatrical profession to be knighted in England, spoke of the necessity of a "double consciousness" for actors, "in which all the emotions proper to the occasion may have full sway, while the actor is all the time on the alert for every detail of his method."[19]

George Henry Lewes, whom Archer called "the most highly trained thinker who ever applied himself to the study of theatrical art in England,"[20] developed an analysis of acting which reinforced the theory of the differing levels of consciousness present in the performer and made use of the most recent theories of physiology and psychology of the times. It is also probable that the widely read Lewes was familiar with Dr. John Elliotson's writing about dual consciousness, like the essay cited above which appeared in the *Cornhill* magazine in 1877. Lewes's major profession was journalism, but he had studied medicine (though he never got his MD), and was self educated in philosophy, the sciences (namely physiology, anatomy, and biology) and literature. He also wrote plays, and was a successful drama critic. Lewes enjoyed performing in an amateur theatrical group with his friend Charles Dickens, and seems to have come by his love of acting naturally; his grandfather had been a successful actor, playing the Harlequin in pantomimes at Drury Lane. Lewes's almost clinical approach to observing and theorizing about acting is indicative of how, "to a large extent in Victorian intellectual life, science set the standard against which all other categories of truth and knowledge had to be judged; its method was pronounced to be the panacea for all intellectual problems."[21] The Victorian predisposition to turn to scientific methods to explain even artistic questions would extend to the investigation of Spiritualist and trance phenomena as well.

Lewes' acting theory, rather than arguing the existence of different states of consciousness existing *simultaneously*, posited a state of rapidly *alternating* levels of consciousness. Lewes drew on his wide knowledge of popular theatre for a theatrical metaphor based on a sensational performer of his time named Andrew Ducrow. Ducrow performed on horseback in the popular equestrian melodramas, and Lewes compared what happened in the mind of the actor with Ducrow balancing control of several different horses: "When Ducrow rode six horses at once he pressed the reins of each alternately, now checking, now redirecting. Attention in like manner shifts from one series to another."[22]

Lewes' physiological ideas also reflect electrical analogies, as in his "laws of discharge and arrest" which he applies to the actor's expression of waves of emotion which gradually subside, a technique especially notable in Edmund Kean and the French tragedienne Rachel. Lewes wrote of Kean, for instance:

> Although fond, far too fond, of abrupt transitions — passing from vehemence to familiarity, and mingling strong lights and shadows with Caravaggio force of unreality — nevertheless his instinct taught him what few actors are taught — that strong emotion, after discharging itself in one massive current, continues for a time expressing itself in feebler currents. The waves are not

stilled when the storm has passed away. There remains the ground-swell troubling the deeps.[23]

In its reference to electrical impulses, Lewes' theory of acting closely resembles some theories of mesmerism, and harkens back to one of the earliest interpretations of the phenomenon, first called "animal magnetism," as the operation of electric-like currents conducted from the magnetizer to the subject.

As we have seen in the discussion of the power of actresses, the vocabulary of acting, references to the "spell binding" or "mesmerizing" quality of the actress show up frequently in nineteenth century theatrical reviews. Not surprisingly, then, the technique of acting would also be analyzed as a process of "hypnotism," not just of the audience, but of the actor himself, who might thereby achieve the alternate states of consciousness which had been posited in performance.

German writer and director Max Martersteig (1853–1926), in the wake of work being done with mesmerism and hypnosis by Charcot, Freud and Bernhiem at the turn of the century, proposed that actors spontaneously "hypnotized" themselves by concentrating on the imaginary character or "other" consciousness, while simultaneously maintaining some part of normal consciousness to control the performance.[24] "Martersteig's transfiguration theory made specific use of the premise that hypnotic suggestion can release creative energies 'without voluntary participation.' The hypnotic instrument is the play itself, which begins to work its magic on the actor's 'cerebral system' from the very first reading."[25] For Martersteig, the term hypnosis seemed to refer to a state in which the actor's concentration on the imaginary character became a kind of "idée fixée" to which he surrendered,[26] not unlike the way a trance medium might surrender to a spirit personality.

Obviously self hypnotism per se never became a widely used technique for actors. The hypnotic or trance state theory does have staying power, however, in relation to the idea of role playing, for instance in contemporary psychiatric theory. The strongest connections between role playing of actors and the double or alternate consciousness of psychiatric patients lie in the realm of the modern diagnosis and treatment of Dissociative Identity Disorder or D.I.D. There are many similarities, at least on the surface, in the descriptions of the experiences of trance mediums and the manifestations of different personalities in cases of D.I.D.— probably because both apparently depend on an altered state of consciousness. There are also long standing difficulties and disagreements among experts about how to precisely define or explain these states. However there are some generally agreed upon characteristics within the scholarship about the altered states of consciousness in D.I.D. and their connection to a state of clinical hypnosis which may provided a basis upon which to draw comparisons to the performances of trance mediums.

1. Hypnosis is generally *classified* (if not precisely *defined*), as "an alteration of consciousness."[27]
2. Subjects do not always need a doctor or hypnotist in order to enter the hypnotic state, i.e., *self-hypnosis* is possible and was recognized by doctors as early as the mid nineteenth century.
3. Trance can be considered a more inclusive category of hypnosis in that "Trance is an older and broader concept than hypnosis and subsumes a variety of different psychological phenomena."[28]
4. Hypnosis may be generally seen as a means of communicating with the unconscious, and is characterized by dissociation (defined as "any functional disconnection between elements of a person's psyche irrespective of what the psychological or physiological mechanism of that disconnection may turn out to be"[29] (i.e., the trance state, mental illness, etc.) and
5. The *purpose* of the dissociation or "splitting" into discrete consciousnesses or personalities is to "create alternative self-structures and psychological realities within which or by virtue of which emotional survival is facilitated."[30]

It is the last of these characteristics — the function or purpose of the manifestation (the "creation" of alternate personalities as a kind of emotional coping mechanism) which is most revealing for our examination of the roles played not just in by legitimate actresses in the theatre, but in trance performances.

The next chapter is a case study which focuses on the notion of trance as a coping mechanism in the manifestations of the character "Gypsy" by Anna Cora Mowatt. The therapeutic effects of Anna's performances of Gypsy reveal the connections among performance, trance and psychology, which may be linked, as this chapter suggest, by a common state of double consciousness. Anna's experiences with Gypsy may also lend support to the interesting argument that "performance and psychoanalysis are offspring of the same ancestor: the placebo effect" and that "the two have been artificially sundered to protect the scientific legitimacy of psychoanalysis in its flight from its origins in hypnotic performance."[31]

6

"Call Me Gypsy": Anna Cora Mowatt's Trance Performances

Anna Cora Mowatt came to prominence as a playwright in 1845 when her comedy *Fashion* successfully premiered at the Park Theatre in New York. *Fashion*, considered the first American comedy of manners, brought Mowatt instant fame as a playwright. Her meteoric rise as an actress began soon thereafter with her performance of Paulina in the romantic melodrama *The Lady of Lyons* at the same theatre, and within the next few years she would become a star in both America and England. Only three years earlier, however, Mowatt had been desperately ill. Having taken the first few tentative steps towards a theatrical career by performing in a series of staged readings in Boston, she had begun to suffer from symptoms associated with consumption — severe lung congestion and hemorrhages, and a high fever. Conventional treatment had not helped, and her doctor was not optimistic about her prospects for recovery. A family friend, Epes Sargent, suggested that she try the new experimental therapy called mesmerism, and recommended William Francis Channing, a medical student and mesmeric healer. Anna Mowatt and her husband James knew little about the new treatment and were at first reluctant. But when Channing explained the potential of mesmerism, James, desperate to help his wife, agreed to let Channing try the experiment on Anna Mowatt.[1]

Mesmerism had rapidly gained adherents as a form of therapy for a variety of emotional and physical problems, including consumption, when it was introduced into America in the 1830s. Anna Mowatt's very first trance, induced by Channing, resulted in immediate alleviation of her symptoms, and subsequent trances resulted in continued improvement. When Channing had to be out of town, Epes Sargent agreed to take over the sessions himself.

Sargent soon began to notice something peculiar about Mowatt when she was in the trance state, or "somnambulic" as he called it. A different personality began to emerge, one which was more assertive, confident, and physically stronger than Mowatt in her normal state. The mesmerized personality had a superior intellect, nerves and reflexes, and spoke in the third person of

Mowatt as an inferior self. Sargent decided to question the somnambulic Mowatt about this "puzzle" of the seemingly "higher" personality.

> "You always speak of your lower self in the third person, and you never speak of your present self in the first, and you object to being addressed by either your Christian or your surname. How shall I call you?" "Call me gypsy," she replied. "Then I suppose we must give a corresponding name to your waking self. Since she does many things you disapprove of, suppose we call her simpleton?" At this she clapped her hands in glee, and said, "Nothing could be more apt." So the distinctions were adopted, and the two names were ever after seriously used, though not when she was in her normal state.[2]

Over the next few years, Mowatt would continue, in her periodic trances, to be transformed into the colorful, impudent character of Gypsy. Although Mowatt claimed never to remember anything she had said or done while she was mesmerized, her husband James Mowatt, Epes Sargent, and a few close friends would describe her alternate "Gypsy" personality as the antithesis of the lady-like Mrs. Mowatt, who, in her "normal" state, embodied the feminine ideals of her age.

Historians have discussed Mowatt's significance as a playwright (*Fashion* was followed by *Armand, or the Peer and the Peasant* in 1847) and a popular actress of the "emotional school" in the mid nineteenth century.[3] Her role in raising the social status of the theatrical profession has also been acknowledged. In order to succeed, Mowatt had to overcome serious illness, social ostracism and the enormous stress of playing conflicting roles in her public and private lives. The mesmeric trances, and the emergence of "Gypsy" constituted important coping mechanisms, which helped her remain healthy enough to work, and provided a crucial outlet for elements of her personality which were denied expression in her conventional stage and social roles. Gypsy was the "alternative self structure" posited by hypnotherapists by which her "emotional survival" was facilitated.

As we have seen in previous chapters, historically one popular view of the mesmeric trance has been that it was an excuse for a male practitioner to exploit a female subject/performer, while other studies have shown the potential helpfulness of mesmerism for women. Alex Owen has discussed how women might benefit from trance states (such as those experienced by nineteenth century mediums) by "gaining another voice," and with it an unusual opportunity to express themselves freely.[4] Moreover, "women's involvement with spiritualism was at one level all about gender expectations, sexual politics, and the subversion of existing power relations between men and women."[5] Owen's point may also apply to Mowatt's involvement with mesmerism, since Mowatt, like the spiritualists discussed by Owen, relied on a trance state.

Mowatt's experiences show that mesmerism was a powerful resource for her in her struggle to embody the paradox that later generations might call the "Lady Actress."[6]

As an actress in the Victorian era, Mowatt's place in society was problematic since while audiences were fascinated by actors and actresses, and often made celebrities of them, the public also regarded performers with deep suspicion, and considered them socially marginal. An actress, therefore, "was able to anticipate professional rewards which few other women in the age enjoyed, but only at considerable sacrifice of intangibles precious to nineteenth century woman — personal esteem and social acceptability."[7] The problem was exacerbated in early nineteenth century America when life in the young country was characterized by a "sharp increase in confusion of social roles" in general. Historian Carroll Smith-Rosenberg has argued that role conflict for women in particular in the nineteenth century was intense and contributed to the complex of emotional and physical problems that doctors loosely grouped under the term "hysteria."[8] William Egginton, in *How the World Became a Stage: Presence, Theatricality and the Question of Modernity*, describes this role conflict as "the tensions that develop between the various scriptings, between the ideals adopted and the possibilities of enacting those ideals" and continues that it is these conflicts and tensions which are "the core of the problems clinical psychologists seek to treat."[9] In the absence of an available clinical psychologist, it seems that some Victorian women found their own relief, ironically, through performance — if not on stage, then in a trance state or as a medium.

Actresses were especially vulnerable to social and psychological role conflict, and Mowatt's risk was greater than most, since she actually had some social standing to lose. Whereas traditionally most actors had come from lower class or acting families, Mowatt came from a prominent family. She was born Anna Cora Ogden in 1819 to an old New York family of impeccable social pedigree. Her father was a respectable businessman and the son of an Episcopal clergyman. Her mother's grandfather, Francis Lewis, had signed the Declaration of Independence. And her first husband, James Mowatt (whom she married at the age of 15), was quite wealthy until he lost his fortune in the economic crash of 1837. This financial catastrophe, and James's ill health were the factors that initially propelled Anna onto the stage. She had always had a flair for drama and amateur theatricals, and in 1841 she decided to undertake a series of staged readings, primarily of poetry, at the Boston Museum to earn money.

She was well received by audiences and the press. The critic of the *Boston Atlas* noted sympathetically that "Mrs. Mowatt resorts to this employment of her talents and acquirements with a view of rendering them productive of pecuniary emolument, in consequence of reverses to which her family has been subjected."[10] The subtext of the *Atlas* article was clear. Mowatt was a lady in distress and her performances were anomalous; she was driven to desperate measures to save her family. The critic only implied what everyone already knew — that it was inappropriate for a lady like Mowatt to perform in public for any other reason.

In antebellum America in particular, the theatre was no place for a lady — whether on or off the stage. As Richard Butsch has argued in *The Making of American Audiences*, "Antebellum theater was not exclusively male, but it was clearly a 'masculine space.'"[11] Rowdy working class audiences and the association with prostitution were strong deterrents for respectable women.[12] Nonetheless, acting could have a strong appeal for women, as we have seen, providing not just a living, but a chance for self-expression and an escape from restricted social roles. Even when the heroines she played on stage were themselves conventional (as they usually were in the popular melodramas of the day) the emotional release of acting and the chance to weave a spell over a large audience were very attractive, and Mowatt felt this keenly. As Mowatt acknowledged when looking back on her career, "The power of swaying the emotions of a crowd is one of the most thrilling sensations I ever experienced."[13]

In spite of her obvious love for acting, however, Mowatt was careful in her autobiography to make the case that acting was her only viable means of supporting her invalid husband and three adopted children. She knew that her popularity with the public depended on her appearing to be, above all else, a dutiful woman, wife and mother. This was tricky, since success depended on seeming to embody the very *ideal* of the feminine, and acting or performing in public was by definition *unfeminine*. Catherine Burroughs pinpoints the difficulty in her book about women and the Romantic theatre, observing that "the ability to perform femininity correctly was essential to women's comfortable survival in both private and public settings,"[14] and that to be successful, an actress had to "move between public and private spaces without wavering in her skillful gender performance."[15] Mowatt's autobiography is itself an attempt to negotiate this space, and reveals that her success in achieving a degree of respectability for herself (and others in the theatre) was due in part to the way she crafted her public image. She never challenged the superiority of stereotypes of femininity like duty to husband and family, but instead argued that all her decisions were informed by her desire to satisfy their dictates.

This flawless performance of femininity was costly. To maintain it, "unfeminine" aspects of behavior and personality had to be hidden. The fact that Gypsy appeared just at the point when Mowatt's struggle with her social roles became most acute suggests that Gypsy may have represented repressed aspects of her psyche.[16] An examination of the events leading up to the appearance of Gypsy, and of her specific words and actions, bears out this interpretation.

Mowatt wrote that her first public performances as a dramatic reader in 1841 took an enormous toll on her physically and mentally. But it was not the act of performing itself which was stressful — Mowatt actually loved being on stage. It was the reaction of some of her closest friends which hurt her. Although she claims that both of the men closest to her (her husband and father) supported her efforts, the rejection of other family and friends caused her suffering for which she was "wholly unprepared."

> Some beloved relatives, and some who had been my nearest, dearest friends — friends from my early childhood, who were associated in my mind with all the sweetest, happiest hours of my life, — now turned from me. They were shocked at my temerity in appearing before the public. They even affected not to believe in Mr. Mowatt's total loss of means. They tacitly proscribed me from the circle of their acquaintance. When we passed in the street, instead of the outstretched hands and loving greeting to which I had ever been accustomed, I met the cold eye and averted face that shunned recognition....[17]

As the performances continued, Mowatt recalled, "My health gave way"[18] and "The continued coldness of some of my dearest friends preyed upon my mind, and threw me into a state of morbid nervous excitement. I was attacked with fever and hemorrhages of the lungs. For several months I was considered by my physician, Dr. C——— to be in a state which rendered recovery very improbable...."[19] When several attempts at traditional treatment failed, Dr. Channing, who had been introduced to the Mowatts by Epes Sargent, suggested mesmerism.

Mowatt and her husband were justified in being dubious, at first, about mesmerism, since in 1841 mesmerism was not fully accepted as a science or legitimate medical therapy, and like the other so-called "pseudo sciences" physiognomy and phrenology, never would be. However, by mid century mesmerism would reach a wide public as a form of lay healing/medicine show entertainment.[20] Popular interest in mesmerism and other occult phenomena would spike in 1847 in America with the notorious "Rochester rappings" of the Fox sisters in Hydesville, New York. In Mowatt's lifetime, mesmerism would become associated with Spiritualism, a practice dependent on communication with the dead or other supernatural entities, usually via a medium in a mesmeric trance. Spiritualism with its emphasis on personal revelation and lack of institutional authority or doctrine, became the ultimate "self-help" religion of America in the nineteenth century, part of a trend towards "programs for personal rejuvenation."[21] This seems, in part, how Anna Cora Mowatt eventually came to regard mesmerism.

But first there were serious reservations to be overcome. Mowatt writes that her husband

> had never seen a mesmeric subject — never heard a case fully described. He [Mr. Mowatt] strongly objected to my being made the subject of an experiment. An argument ensued which I did not hear. It ended in Dr. C — — —'s assurance that I might be greatly benefited by mesmeric treatment, but could not be injured. Mr. Mowatt finally assented to the doctor's proposition. I was suffering too much to express an opinion or even to have one.[22]

Dr. Channing and James Mowatt decided upon the treatment. Anna Mowatt herself, she is at pains to make clear in her autobiography, was not responsible for trying the therapy. Her insistence that it was not her idea to try mesmerism was a way for her to disclaim responsibility for subsequent words and actions that emerged with the Gypsy persona, as she also disclaimed responsibility for her career as an actor by arguing in her autobiography that financial necessity forced her onto the stage.[23]

But while Mowatt admitted freely that the mesmeric trances became, for some time, vital for her physical and emotional health, she was not a passive prisoner of the trances. Although she did not analyze specifically how mesmerism worked, control of the state itself was very important to her. She proved to be what was referred to as an "independent somnambulist."[24] Initially, she needed the help of a mesmerist to reach the trance state, but once there, she was not controlled by him, like a helpless Trilby at the hands of a conniving Svengali. Mowatt would have resisted such a relationship, and indeed she was at first uneasy with mesmerism. "I soon grew impatient," she said, "at this apparent surrender of free will — one of Heaven's choicest gifts to men."[25] It is not surprising that Mowatt was concerned. The possibility of the exploitation of innocent females by unscrupulous male mesmerists was hotly debated throughout the century.[26] Mowatt was reassured, however, by the knowledge that she could not be mesmerized unless she wished to be, nor could she be forced to do anything against her will while mesmerized. She could, she stated, "at any time, defeat the will of the mesmerizer, unless I chose to submit."[27] As an added safeguard, Mowatt eventually devised a way to control her own return to consciousness, so that she could end the trance state independently of the mesmerist whenever she wished, thus achieving an even greater degree of control over the mesmeric process than was usual. Epes Sargent recorded the incident in his essay on Mowatt in *The Scientific Basis of Spiritualism.*

> While somnabulic she wished me to give her the power of passing from her abnormal state, and to effect this directed me to magnetize her ring, so that in my absence she could, by pulling it off, pass into her usual condition.[28]

This "abnormal state" was so called not simply because it was an alternate state of consciousness but because the characteristics Mowatt displayed as the Gypsy were "abnormal" for Mowatt in her usual conscious state. As previously noted, the personality which Mowatt named Gypsy was, according to Sargent, "in every respect a superior one, intellectually, morally and I may add physically."[29] Gypsy was wise, assertive, strong and courageous. She was "exalted," "full of vivacity and glee" but also calm, more in control of her emotions and less prone to "hysterical" reactions than Mowatt in her normal state. "Awake she [Mowatt] would scream if a caterpillar got on her dress," Sargent noted, but "somnambulic she would manifest the greatest tenderness for every living thing, taking up even a wounded snake from the road and placing it where it would be safe from passing wheels."[30]

Another striking feature of Anna Cora Mowatt and her Gypsy persona is the paradox which juxtaposed a woman anxious for respectability with the disreputable figure of the gypsy. The connection is more meaningful if we remember that actors, like gypsies, were in Mowatt's time still on the margins of social respectability. Even today, actors may sometimes be compared to gypsies — actors with a touring show are still occasionally called "gypsies." The word "gypsy" itself can suggest not just geographic rootlessness but "homelessness" or alienation in a social or psychological sense. Actors, and even more so actresses, have been traditionally associated with a kind of dislocation and instability arising not only from their peripatetic lifestyle but from the changes in identity implied in playing many different roles. And in the early nineteenth century, both actresses and gypsies were regarded as morally dubious.

Anna Cora Mowatt could not have been unaware of these prevailing Victorian images and attitudes. She was certainly aware of other aspects of the Gypsy image — the Romantic figure of freedom, a sort of lawless child of nature. Mowatt had capitalized on this stereotype in the first play she ever wrote, a verse drama called "The Gypsy Wanderer, or, The Stolen Child" which she produced for a home theatrical for her family and friends when she was still a teenager.[31] The sentimental plot involves a pathetic child (played by Mowatt's little sister Julia) who is kidnapped by gypsies and is finally reunited with her grieving mother, played by Mowatt herself. The play is conventional but foreshadows the heightened emotion that would characterize much of Mowatt's later writing and acting style.

The most famous portrayal of a gypsy on the stage in those years was Charlotte Cushman's impersonation of the old gypsy fortune teller Meg Merrilies in the successful dramatization of Sir Walter Scott's *Guy Mannering*. Cushman was a powerful actress (some called her "masculine"), and the first great American tragedienne. In addition to her finest role, Lady Macbeth, she was known for playing male characters, or what were known as "breeches roles," like Romeo, Hamlet, and Claude Melnotte in *The Lady of Lyons*. She had first played the weird Meg Merrilies at the Park Theatre where Mowatt would later have both her acting and playwriting debuts. Cushman first played Meg Merrilies in 1837, the same year that the financial collapse ruined James Mowatt and propelled Anna Cora Mowatt into professional theatre. Charlotte Cushman's old gypsy woman was eerie, more supernatural than human, and unforgettable. A typical review referred to the character as a crazed "sibyl, a pythoness, before whose oracular utterance the boldest might have trembled." Ladies in the audience had to cover their faces during the agonizing death scene, which even one of her co-stars later described as too intensely affecting to watch.[32] Fellow actress Mary Anderson wrote of Cushman's performance:

> When, in the moonlight of the scene, she dashed from her tent on to the stage, covered with the gray, shadowy garments of the gypsy sibyl, her appearance was ghost-like and startling in the extreme. In her mad rushes on and off the stage she was like a cyclone. During her prophecy ... she stood like one great withered tree, her arms stretched out, her white locks flying, her eyes blazing under their shaggy brows. She was not like a creature of this world, but like some mad majestic wanderer from the spirit-land.[33]

Anna Cora Mowatt never played Meg Merrilies, or any Gypsy on stage, but judging by the character's appearances in her life, she was drawn to its wildness and ambiguity, as well as to its marginal social status.[34]

Scholar Deborah Epstein Nord has made the connection between women writers and the figure of the gypsy, which signified in women's literature of the period "social marginality, nomadism, alienation, and lawlessness."[35] Nord cites the appearance of gypsy figures in Charlotte Brontë's *Jane Eyre* (1847), Emily Brontë's *Wuthering Heights* (1847), and George Eliot's *The Mill on the Floss* (1860) and *The Spanish Gypsy* (1868), suggesting that for these women writers the gypsy expressed "a deep sense of unconventional, indeed aberrant femininity."[36] She posits "to imagine oneself a gypsy is to escape, in some sense, from conventional femininity: it is also to claim kinship with those who mirror and explain one's anomalousness."[37] Particularly relevant for Mowatt's case is the suggestion that "in the case of social stigmazation, perhaps, the girl child ... imagines a bond with an alien and exotic people that enables her to reinvent feminine identity."[38] This helps explain the appearance of the gypsy in Mowatt's imagination or psyche at the moment when anxiety stemming from conflicting feminine roles was most intense. Gypsy provided an opportunity for Mowatt to develop an alternate identity.

Gypsy liked to talk, and one of the most striking features of her discourse was her ability to give detailed and specific suggestions for Mowatt's treatment. Gypsy gave advice to Mowatt's doctors and caretakers about how to alleviate the anxiety Mowatt felt because of her illness, and how to help her cope with the disorientation which she felt on waking from the long periods of trance state (sometimes several weeks) which were necessary to relieve her physical symptoms. When Gypsy's instructions were followed, Mowatt's health improved. Epes Sargent reported, "Mrs. Mowatt, though of a remarkably sensitive constitution and not weighing a hundred pounds when I first knew her, was much benefited by the treatment she prescribed for herself while somnambulic, and attained a weight of one hundred and fifty pounds."[39] Gypsy exhibited a degree of self-poise, intelligence, and self-control which would have been regarded as striking in a man and even more so in a woman. Gypsy "seemed to look down upon all the contents of her normal memory as from a superior position,"[40] and she demonstrated this by referring to Mowatt as the "Simpleton." Even when Sargent tested Mowatt's physical reflexes and senses in the trance state (for example, putting hot or cold food in her mouth to see if she could distinguish the different temperatures), Gypsy did not submit passively to the experiment. Instead, Sargent noted, she was "supremely and independently conscious all the time, and would reason upon the phenomena, describe them, philosophize upon them, and oppose my own opinions with an ability far transcending that which she exhibited in her normal state."[41]

Her resistance to male authority is apparently what led Sargent to refer to Gypsy, with some acerbity, as a "dictator." Especially unsettling to Sargent was the fact that Gypsy would

> ... predict crises in her disease with wonderful accuracy, and take all responsibility both from mesmerizer and physician as to prescribing for her case. Indeed the physician's office soon became a sinecure. She in her abnormal state, was always her own physician, and her own despotic ruler, showing absolute confidence in all her prescriptions.[42]

Mowatt's usurpation of the male doctor's prerogative to prescribe and treat the female body clearly made Sargent nervous. Gypsy threatened to make her own mesmerist, not to mention the entire male medical establishment, expendable.

In one of the more sensational episodes of clairvoyance, Gypsy once predicted that Mowatt would have a severe hemorrhage of the lungs in six months. And indeed Mowatt did — on the very day and hour indicated.[43] There are several possible explanations for this incident. It could have been a powerful example of auto-suggestion or self-hypnosis. It could have been genuine clairvoyance. It could have been a deliberate and sensational "performance" — as indeed the whole Gypsy persona could have been. In any case, Mowatt's apparent clairvoyance is perhaps the aspect of her behavior most vulnerable to the charge of fraud or "acting." Interpreting Gypsy as just a role Mowatt played, however, raises even more vexing questions. In the case of the physical symptoms, for instance, one has to ask if Mowatt would have been capable of inducing a lung hemorrhage in herself. And if so, why would she do so?

Certainly an actress as savvy about theatrical effects as Mowatt would have known what a dramatic impact her sensational prediction and physical crisis might have on her "audience" of doctors and husband. In judging the nature of acts performed in a supposed trance state, and the validity of the trance itself, the potential effect on the audience and what the trance subject has to gain from the transaction must be taken into consideration. (As indeed the reception of any piece of theatre is linked to the expectations of the audience.)

Some nineteenth century physicians, as discussed in the precious chapter, compared the words and actions of mesmerized subjects to those produced in a state of hysteria (a poorly understood state which was thought by doctors at the time to be similar to the trance state); these should be interpreted with care. The Victorian medical establishment was in fact skeptical of hysterics for the very reason that they considered hysteria innately theatrical in its manifestations:

> The theatrical character of the disorder increased doctors' distrust of hysterical patients. Desirous of attention, it seems at almost any price, hysterics appeared to be playing to their audience, almost enjoying their symptoms.[44]

In Mowatt's case, of course, there was additional reason to be suspicious because she was an actress, and the sincerity of actors was always an issue.[45] The question arises, was Mowatt acting the whole trance phenomenon and the character of Gypsy? Did she "play" to her audience's expectations that mesmerism would produce otherwise inexplicable incidents of foresight, clairvoyance and a colorful exotic personality? It is hard to say what those around her expected besides relief of her physical distress (Mr. Mowatt hardly knew enough about mesmerism to hope for even that much), and on that count the trances were a "success." The fact that Gypsy's appearances might also be interpreted as successful theatre does not make them by that definition alone fraudulent. To regard Gypsy, or role playing in itself, as mere fakery is too reductive. Mowatt's Gypsy, or the abilities and traits which constituted Gypsy were not necessarily false or deceitful. There is no proof that Mowatt deliberately fooled her audience by "acting" the role of mesmeric subject and/or Gypsy. In fact Sargent explicitly defends Mowatt against the potential charge of trickery:

> Those who discredit these phenomenon will say there was deception. I cannot look back to the most trifling incident that would justify the suspicion; and yet I was so unduly skeptical that I was always on the lookout for something that might raise a question of the reality of what I witnessed.[46]

Authentic or not, Mowatt's trances did attract the notice of some prominent men interested in mesmerism. Sargent records that

> among the persons I remember to have introduced to Mrs. Mowatt while she was somnambulic were N.P. Willis, Dr. Mott, and Dr. William E. Channing, the great Unitarian divine. Willis, whom Goethe would have classed among his "demonic men," was deeply interested, and kept up an animated conversation for an hour or more with the somnambule.[47]

Although it may have been personally rewarding to Mowatt to be the focus of attention from prominent men, the public performance of Gypsy for profit was apparently never considered. (Nor would it have been necessary, since Mowatt was able to have a very successful performance career without treating her public to the role of Gypsy.)

For the purposes of this discussion then, the significant question is not whether or not gypsy was "real" (as opposed to a character played by a talented actress) but why she appeared and how she functioned for Mowatt. Gypsy was more than a source of medical advice for Mowatt. Gypsy also apparently gave her the ability to discourse on theological and philosophical topics. Sargent noticed the strong spiritual side of Gypsy: "She would claim to see and talk with spirits; but finding me incredulous on the subject, did not urge it. She spoke always of that circle of the spirit-world proximate to this world as containing beings subject to the same laws of progress that we find here."[48] Gypsy, not Mowatt, had this special knowledge and perception. These insights may have been more compelling to her listeners coming from a mysterious mesmeric personality then they would have had coming from a mere actress and "Simpleton" as Gypsy referred to Mowatt.

The fact that Gypsy did not "urge" or press her claim to communicate with spirits on the skeptical Sargent can be read in two ways: either Mowatt was a skillful enough performer to know not to push her effects or strain the credulity of her audience too far, or Gypsy had sense enough not to press esoteric spiritual ideas on one who was not ready to receive them. These spiritual ideas, it soon became evident, included the tenets of Swedenborgian philosophy, of which Mowatt claimed to have no knowledge at all in her waking state. Her own husband was at first skeptical about this aspect of her trance communications. But when he began to read Swedenborg for himself, he became convinced that the knowledge transmitted from the spirits via Gypsy was valid and true. He and Mowatt became confirmed Swedenborgians, and remained so for the rest of their lives.[49] Mowatt's autobiography makes clear the comfort that she gained from this religious philosophy in later years.[50] This was another benefit indirectly due to mesmerism, and of course Gypsy.

In addition to displaying intellectual and spiritual abilities, Gypsy was assertive enough to oppose the male authorities around her in a way that sometimes startled them. The following anecdote in which Sargent is scolded for a mistake he has made in treating Mowatt illustrates Gypsy's attitude towards her male mesmerist, and the complex relationship among Gypsy, Mowatt and Sargent.

> On one occasion, by her own direction when somnambulic, she was kept so two weeks, without returning once to her normal state. As we resided quite near each other on Broadway, I had frequent opportunities of visiting her. Her last recollections in her normal state were of seeing Broadway heaped with snow; while a rose-bush on a stand in her parlor had on it a bud yet green. When, a fortnight afterwards, I suddenly removed the mesmeric influence, brought her back to her natural state, and led her, first to the window, so that she saw the bud had become a flower, she — having no consciousness whatever of the lapse of time, supposing that she had been "asleep" not more than an hour or two — became wildly agitated and almost frantic. I saw that I had made a mistake in not preparing her for the change. This I could easily have done by giving her what she called an "ordination" to carry the remembrance of the experiences of the last fourteen days into her waking state. This I accomplished at last.... After a somewhat profound state of coma, the well-known change in her countenance and the unconscious, child-like smile, admonitory of the coming of her second and higher self, to whom while somnambulic she had given the name of the "gipsy," appeared, and, after a breath of relief, she took my hand and said, "You should have known better than to wake her so suddenly. You should have guessed that the changes to which you were to introduce her would bewilder and astound her. Now put your hands on her head and ordain that she shall be reconciled to the change, and take it as a matter of course." I obeyed the direction, and the "simpleton," as the normal self was called, returned and accepted the situation as if nothing remarkable had occurred.[51]

Gypsy comes across as quick thinking, decisive, and more intelligent than either Sargent or Mowatt, the "simpleton." This story, taken together with the incident described earlier in which her insistent self-diagnosis and prescription provoked Sargent to call her a "dictator" who made the physician's office a "sinecure," demonstrates the subtle subversiveness of Gypsy. Gypsy's presence obviated the need for male authorities to diagnose and treat Mowatt. From Gypsy's point of view, men were necessary only to carry out orders, not to give them.

Clearly then, unlike the other roles Mowatt played (and very successfully) in her normal state, Gypsy was not a construct of idealized femininity. As such she may have provided relief from those restrictive roles. This hypothesis suggests that Gypsy can be most usefully understood as an alternate or suppressed self (rather than a supernatural entity, as most mesmerists and the Spiritualists would have defined her). Gypsy functioned for Mowatt as the repository of her more intellectual and aggressive traits, one might say her repressed "masculine" traits. In fact, Sargent and even Mowatt herself, true to the conditioning of their time, probably stressed Gypsy's "superiority" so often *because* she was more "masculine" than Mowatt herself.

Sargent did not, of course, have theories of modern psychology to explain Gypsy as a dissociated part of Mowatt's psyche who appeared as a result of hypnosis or P.I.D. But Sargent's comments on the phenomenon of what he calls "discrete degrees of consciousness" which occur in "somnambules" (a category he elsewhere elides with that of mesmerized subject) indicate an intuitive grasp of what might today be characterized as aspects of "repression," and foreshadow modern descriptions of states or personalities that manifest in altered states of consciousness.

> The wonderful fact of discrete degrees of consciousness is fully proved in somnambulism. This consciousness may be above that of the normal state or below it. The case is on record of a pious clergyman who, when somnambulic would manifest kleptomania. He would steal and secrete articles without any rational purpose. The somnabulists who walk on the roofs of houses, or jump out of windows, have a certain consciousness, though it may be disordered by delusion. Dr. Pritchard says, "A somnambulator is nothing but a dreamer who is able to act his dreams." Insensible to external phenomena, his functions are still obedient to an inward consciousness. But as there are many degrees of somnambulic consciousness, Pritchard's definition is a very limited and misleading one.[52]

Sargent goes on to defend Mowatt's trance experiences, stressing that she, unlike the unfortunate clergyman, showed no signs of immorality in the trance state. But because Sargent seemed most concerned with proving the general propriety and usefulness of mesmerism, he neglected to ask why

Mowatt, when mesmerized, would manifest the very specific and striking personality of Gypsy. Sargent's term "discrete degrees of consciousness" suggests that trance personas like Gypsy may not be supernatural entities, but split off aspects of the trance subject, and thus supports the theory that Gypsy was an aspect of Mowatt's personality. The phrase is also reminiscent of the "dual consciousness" suggested by some theories of acting as well as the "double personalities" described by observers of mesmerism in the nineteenth century.

> In some rare but remarkable cases both of natural and of mesmeric somnambulism, the subject developed personality and intellectual qualities different from and sometimes superior to those of the waking life, and to these cases terms such as "double personality" were sometimes applied.... There were even cases ... in which the subjects, when somnambulic, gave themselves new names or spoke of their normal selves as alien personalities.[53]

However, Sargent's examples of the clergyman who turns kleptomaniac and the sleepwalkers who walk on roofs in a trance state are telling for the obvious inference that he fails to draw: that actions or traits that come out in the trance personality are often those which are taboo or forbidden to the subject in their normal state. And although Sargent calls it "misleading," Pritichard's characterization of trance subjects as "dreamers able to act their dreams" may come close to the mark. If dreams include repressed fantasies or unconscious wishes, then mesmerized subjects often do seem to "act their dreams." We might assume that Mowatt, in the guise of Gypsy, did as well.

As an eyewitness, Sargent's interpretation of Mowatt's mesmeric experiences must be taken into account, although he is unable to offer a definitive explanation of the phenomenon. Mowatt herself did not attempt to pin down exactly what Gypsy was or how she came to be, but she did believe that the effects of mesmerism were vital to her well-being.

Modern theories of the therapeutic function of hypnosis can also shed light on Mowatt's experiences, although first of all, it is interesting to note that some contemporary scientists share their nineteenth century counterparts' skepticism about mesmerism/hypnotism, and apparently for the same reasons. For instance, one theory, advocated by T. R. Sarbin and his associates, in the late twentieth century, is that what appears to be a hypnotized state is simply an act in which the subject "strives to take the role of the hypnotized person."[54] This "role" could include the playing of an alternate personality like Gypsy. In a similar vein, the neo-behaviorists explain the subject's behavior in terms of suggestibility, or having learned through experience the responses appropriate for a hypnotized person. The "sociocognitive theory" posits that "responsive hypnotic subjects retain control of their behavior and guide it strategically in order to meet implicit role demands as these become regnant in the hypnotic test situation."[55] These theories bring to mind the notion of the subject's desire to satisfy her audience's expectations. The volitional control of behavior suggests these trance experiences are a kind of acting or performance. However, the notion of a completely conscious attempt to "act" the part of Gypsy and fool those around her, as discussed earlier, seems too reductive an explanation for Mowatt's experiences. Furthermore, the sociocognitive theory apparently does not take into account the possibility of some alteration or difference of consciousness — which may be some part of the performance process even for legitimate stage actors and actresses.

A modern psychiatric theory which can be more helpful in analyzing Mowatt's Gypsy (and other phenomena and personalities described as occurring during mesmerism in the nineteenth century) is the "neo-dissociation theory" first suggested by Pierre Janet. The aspect of this theory most relevant to this discussion is still largely unexamined:

> Secondary personality induced by hypnosis has attracted very little scientific research. It is the general opinion, however, that such a secondary personality results from subconscious dissociation reaction evoked by hypnosis, *which cannot be accounted for by the conscious acting of the subject* [italics mine].[56]

The neo-dissociation theory would certainly support the view that Gypsy was not an merely an "act" on Mowatt's part, but part of a more complex psychological phenomenon.

Even more interesting is that some modern neo-dissociation theory suggests that the secondary personality manifested under hypnosis may be "healthier" and more "complete" than (one might say "superior" to) the primary personality. The process of producing the secondary personality may in itself be beneficial:

> It appears that producing multiple personalities in healthy subjects in deep trance is a healthy, progressive procedure, dealing with the unconscious knowledge in a creative way.... In connection with spontaneous secondary personalities it can be clearly observed that the characteristics of secondary personalities very much reflect the features rejected by the present personality. Producing multiple personalities might be a sort of psychic mechanism that the subject can utilize when striving progressively for greater adaptation and satisfaction. On the other hand, the ability to create secondary personalities spontaneously might be a regressive defence mechanism against an insurpassable intrapsychic conflict.[57]

The last reference to the "intrapysychic conflict" is a reminder that indeed the Gypsy personality may be regarded as a product of Mowatt's role conflict; that the "psychical process known as splitting — spaltung — which can result in the co-existence within the psyche of different distinct personalities ... was the result of conflict."[58]

Modern research into the therapeutic potential of hypnotism also supports the idea that mesmerism might have relieved physical symptoms (especially the lung hemorrhages) of Mowatt's tuberculosis:

> That hypnotism may be especially effective in the treatment of psychosomatic disorders receives a certain support from recent successes in the treatment of external and internal hemorrhages, burns, stress symptoms, allergies, and other problems linked to automatic and immune system functioning.[59]

Mesmerism was crucial in helping Mowatt cope with the ill health which almost ended her career before it began. It provided an outlet for the unfeminine aspects of her personality which she had to repress, an outlet which helped relieve her physical and psychological suffering. The mesmeric trance gave Mowatt Gypsy, through whom she could oversee her own medical treatment, contradict and instruct those around her, and deliver opinions on esoteric religious and philosophical matters without offense. No offense was taken, because Gypsy, not Mowatt, was responsible for any subversive behavior. Gypsy exemplified the crucial "double-consciousness effect which permitted one part of the personality to speak and the other to represent the disclaimer."[60]

Trance performance opened up to Mowatt an alternate consciousness and personality which allowed her to speak and act more freely, and thus to push the limits of the social and gender roles she played. Though it seems ironic, mesmerism's power was embodied, for the well-born Mowatt, in the marginal and socially inferior figure of the Gypsy. And this in fact appeared to be the case for many of the women who embodied alternate personalities in the form of spirit performances which created and perpetuated the Spiritualist movement that emerged in the mid nineteenth century.

7

The Rise of Spiritualism and the Fox Sisters

At mid century, trance performance blossomed in a new and even more fruitful context, that of Spiritualism, which was founded on the belief that persons in trance states could contact spirits from beyond the physical realm. The role possibilities for trance performers expanded infinitely to include the spirits of every being who had ever lived and some who never had been incarnated, but still wanted to reach through to the living to relay information and inspiration about the after life. The voices, personalities and later even "bodies" of these spirits were manifested by trance performers who began to be referred to as "mediums," through performances or sittings referred to as "séances." The séance came to be a particular kind of trance performance in which a small group of people, generally in a darkened room, sat around a table with their hands touching, while the medium went into a trance and made contact with spirits, some related to those at the table. Séances, which came to be a regular practice of Spiritualist believers, were also put on as amateur theatricals for some interested in their dramatic and entertaining aspects. The structure and performance of the séance as a form of theatre will be discussed in the next chapter.

The Spiritualist movement, which some refer to as a "religion," began, most historians agree, in Hydesville, New York, with the notorious "rappings" of the Fox sisters in 1848. Hydesville, a tiny town near Rochester, was located in an area of the country known as the "Burned Over district," so called for the waves of fiery religious revivals which had swept through upstate New York and New England in the eighteenth and early nineteenth centuries. The rappings and revelations of the Fox sisters would come to seem, for some, just the latest manifestation of these spiritual revivals. Catherine (aged 11 or 12) and Margaretta (aged 14), known as Kate and Maggie Fox, were living with their parents in an isolated farmhouse when the family began to be troubled by mysterious loud rappings and knockings throughout the house. The Foxes were at first unable to discover a cause for the disturbances, until Kate and Maggie stumbled upon a way to contact the source of the noises. On March

31, 1848, Kate got the knocking to respond to her by snapping her fingers and calling out, "Here Mr. Splitfoot, do as I do!" By questioning the spirit and receiving replies in the form of raps — one for "yes" and two for "no" — the Foxes were able to communicate with, and verify the intelligence of the spirit, who could correctly answer all kinds of questions about the family and neighbors. The restless spirit was found to be that of a peddler who had been murdered and buried in the cellar of the Fox house. The cellar was later dug up, and according to some reports, the remains of a body were found, confirming the spirit's story. The spirit rappings continued, and eventually whole messages were communicated by having someone point out or say the letters of the alphabet, pausing at each letter to let the spirit rap at the correct one; in this way words and sentences were spelled out. The phenomena seemed to occur only when one of the girls was present, although other family members or curious neighbors who began to come to the house to witness the spooky phenomena for themselves might also pose questions and indicate the letters of the alphabet to obtain answers. Other spirits began to identify themselves and tell their stories through Kate and Maggie Fox, and Hydesville became the center of attention and what we might now call a "media blitz," with crowds coming from miles around to see the "spook house." Tired of the crowds and sensation seekers, the Foxes moved to the nearby farm of their son, David. But even there they were not left in peace, but were followed by the "spirits," as well as the earthly crowds. Kate and Maggie traveled to the home of their older sister, Mrs. Leah Fish, in Rochester, New York, that summer. Leah, a widow, made a genteel living for herself and her daughter Lizzie teaching piano lessons. She was a capable businesswoman and a good manager, and took charge of her younger sisters right away, as well as of their subsequent careers, at least in the early years. In Rochester, Kate and Maggie began to give private demonstrations of spirit communications. Word of their talent spread beyond friends and family, and the spirits suggested they go public. The first public performance on November 14, 1849, featured just Maggie and Leah, who had begun to develop mediumistic abilities herself. Part demonstration of the mysterious spirit knockings, part investigation to expose a fraud, the event was held at Rochester's largest and finest theatre, the Corinthian Hall. In spite of controversy and several more shows and investigations, the spirits triumphed, and audiences wanting to see and willing to pay for them grew. Kate and Maggie, along with Leah, won influential supporters and patrons, including newspaper publisher Horace Greeley, who helped convince them to move to New York city in June 1850. These friends then provided respectable lodgings where the sisters could devote themselves to holding séances, or "sittings" as they were often referred to, for New York's elite.

When Kate and Maggie Fox with their sister Leah came to New York they were put up for a while at Barnum's Hotel (owned not by the great show man P. T. Barnum, but by his cousin). P. T. Barnum's Museum on Broadway, which had opened with great fanfare in 1842, was going strong when Kate and Maggie Fox arrived in the city. Its bizarre exhibits of curiosities and human oddities were part of the popular and sensational theatrical entertainments that had New York City primed for the Fox sisters' performances. Maggie and Kate's careers as trance speakers were clearly made feasible by the particular kind of sensation making theatre so popular at Barnum's museum. Maggie and Kate were much sought after for their uncanny abilities to connect to the spirit world. Many people were eager, even desperate, to talk to spirits, and realized immediately the significance of these communications and what they might reveal about heaven or the afterlife. Trance séances became a sensation. As other mediums emerged in the next few years, spirit impersonations grew more elaborate, and phenomena moved beyond basic communication by knockings to the point where mediums seemed to actually embody, speak and perform as the spirit entities. A new kind of theatre, the séance, had been born, and the Fox sisters were its first celebrities.

Spirit rappings spread rapidly throughout upstate New York and New England, like the fires of revivalism which had come before. Soon there were mediums and trance performers everywhere, many of these young women. Some thought of the manifestations as more like a disease, an uncanny contagion with the Hydesville rappings as the source. It was estimated that by 1851 every town, city and hamlet in New York State had at least one medium.[1] Even those who were not particularly religious or prone to believe in the supernatural were affected. In Berlin, New York, a young woman named Marietta Davis fell into a nine day trance and upon awakening said she had been in heaven, where she had met the spirits of many old friends, as well as Jesus himself. The Reverend J. L. Scott, who published her story in 1854, wrote that up until then she had not been "of open religious habits, being disinclined to religious conversation...." However, he continued, "during the revival of 1847–8, her mind ... was religiously exercised." And then, she was swayed not by the testimony of others, but by personal experience in the form of her own compelling contact with the spirits during her extended trance.[2]

Many practitioners of spirit communication came to believe in Spiritualism as a religion, although it had no set theology or rituals (aside, perhaps, from the form of the trance state or séance itself). The majority of messages communicated by the "spirits" were Christian, biblical, and Protestant in nature. Because Spiritualism worked by direct revelation to individuals (sometimes from Jesus himself), and not through the mediation and interpretation of a priesthood or any other earthly authority, it appealed to ordinary devout Americans who were weary of theological squabbles, and of trying to adhere to complicated and equivocal theological doctrines of Protestant sects which differed minutely in matters of theology. Uriah Clarke expressed the relief provided by this new belief, writing, "Spiritualism is no sectarianism; it delivers the soul from all false trammels, and bids every conscience be free in the light of heaven."[3]

Spiritualist believers did not organize under a single central authority, or require adherence to any set of doctrines. They even resisted founding any kind of national convention until 1893. Instead they grouped themselves into informal organized "circles," usually under the influence of a gifted and charismatic medium like Cora Hatch. The strength of the movement came from the powerful individual performances of trance speaking and mediumship, and followers gravitated to Spiritualistic "stars" in the same way nineteenth century theatre audiences followed celebrity actors. Not all Spiritualists became practicing mediums, nor did every medium necessarily become a Spiritualist believer; but every person, regardless of background or faith, was considered to have the potential — at least some degree of ability — to contact spirits for themselves.[4]

Definitions of Spiritualism were flexible. Some nineteenth century commentators considered Spiritualism a science, or at least a "pseudo science" like physiognomy or phrenology, which were grounded in the materialistic belief that physical features of the face or the shape of a person's head could reveal the truth about their character. Spiritualism also offered sensory evidence of the truth — in this case the of soul's survival after death — rather than requiring faith in the unseen. Still, Spiritualism was more of a folk practice than a scientific or even theoretical system. It owed what intellectual content it had to the ideas of Swedenborg, an eighteenth-century Swedish philosopher, as they were channeled through the writings of Andrew Jackson Davis, an American known as the "Poughkeepsie Seer." Davis's early works were basically transcriptions of trance lectures through which he claimed to have received various inspirational and prophetic revelations from the spirits. The publication of his book *The Principles of Nature, Her Divine Revelation, and a Voice to Mankind* in 1847 was "one of two events that precipitated spiritualism out of the swirling religious atmosphere of the time" (the "Rochester rappings" were the other).[5]

The peculiar phenomenological and theatrical appeal of Spiritualism, in addition to its attractiveness as a philosophy or religion, is described by John Buescher in his book *The Other Side of Salvation*. Spiritualism was, he notes,

... bound up with individuals' intimate experiences of the uncanny, the entertaining, the weird, the gothic, the romantic, and the bizarre. It was attentive to phenomena: materializations, disembodied voices, psychic displacements, physical levitations, and sensory contact with the individual spirits of the dead.[6]

The popular appetite for the spooky and the supernatural described above had been nurtured in theatrical audiences by the gothic melodramas so popular in the first decades of the century. But even more compelling than its spooky theatrics was Spiritualism's promise of contact with lost loved ones, and its glimpse into a wondrous afterlife in the "Summerland" as the Spiritualist heaven was called. "No matter how weird or uncanny the séance was, it was now an exciting revelation of ultimate benignity and happiness, rather than ultimate terror, punishment or oblivion."[7]

Within a few years of the advent of the spirits in Hydesville, New York, hundreds of professional and amateur trance speakers and mediums were performing. One of the most successful and long lived stars of the nineteenth century Spiritualist stage was Cora L.V. Richmond, also known by her maiden name Cora Scott and her other married names of Hatch, Tappan, and Daniels. At the height of her career as a Spiritualist platform speaker, Cora Richmond was a well paid celebrity in both America and England. She will be the subject of the next chapter's case study.

Cora Richmond's biographer, H. D. Barrett, saw Spiritualism as a turning point in history, ushered in by the work of young women like Cora and the Fox sisters. This view of the movement's historical importance was not uncommon at the time. In an essay titled *Our Times* which appeared in the October 1873 issue of the Spiritualist periodical *Brittan's Quarterly Journal*, the editor S. B. Brittan echoed the sentiments of many believers in Spiritualism when he declared, "We must regard the period in which we live as the most remarkable in the history of the world." They saw the mid nineteenth century as a watershed in human development — not for the work of Darwin on the physical evolution of the species, but for the spiritual advances being brought about by the flood of "revelations" received through mediums and trance speakers. Things were happening quickly, Brittan observed:

> We live in an age of rapid transitions. The constant changes present us with more than kaleidoscope variety. Without the aid of Darwin, we perceive that, not long ago, we were in chrysalis — in the soul's state, in respect to our intellectual development; today imagination takes wings and we revel in a higher and more illuminated atmosphere; what or where we shall be tomorrow the day will determine.[8]

Brittan added that "in this strange and tremendous transition the injustice of the distinctions of caste and color are swept unregretted away by the oblivious tide...."[9] He might have added that some unjust gender distinctions were also being swept away. None of these changes would be easy, he cautioned, especially for those men like himself who had formerly held all the power. But the transformation would be worth it: "Sad as this change must be, and is, for those who have kept the world's guardianship so long; yet great is the joy of the freed and new-breathing millions, who, while they were bowed down, made little or no complaint."[10] Brittan went on to employ an analogy from theatre to describe the new "roles" opening up for people everywhere: "The Nineteenth century has opened a great theater of human activities, wherein every 'live man ... may have a place and a part before a very large and liberal audience.'"[11]

One of the notable changes Spiritualists observed in the new era was the increasing importance of women. Female mediums played a prominent part in the Spiritualist movement, as did "feminine" qualities such as intuition, sympathy, and sensitivity to non rational influences. Much was made of the fact that it was two *young girls*, the Fox sisters, who were the first to receive the spirit communications that ushered in the new era of regular communion with the spirit world.

H. D. Barrett saw the feminine component of Spiritualism as a necessary cosmic corrective to the gender inequality of the ages, which by the nineteenth century had swung too far towards the masculine. The work of female spiritualists made women's contributions and "feminine influence" more prominent in society as a whole. When Cora's work had begun, at mid century, he argued,

> The pendulum of thought had oscillated far to one side, and the mystic rap at Hydesville was the call to halt, a signal for it to turn in the opposite direction, but only so far as to evenly balance between the male and female influence in life.[12]

The spectacle of a young, fragile, poorly educated girl fearlessly speaking with authority granted her by the Spirits must have been irresistible.

> Think of it, readers, if you can imagine the picture,—a child of twelve years of age standing before crowds of people, discoursing to them upon the most abstruse questions in ethics, philosophy, science, and theology, in a scholarly, dignified manner! What did it all mean?[13]

The question is rhetorical—Barrett makes clear what he thinks it means through his rhapsodic (not to say hagiographic) introduction to Cora Richmond's biography, in which he portrays her as a sort of "Little Eva" of Spiritualism; an innocent, beautiful child whose purity sheds light on the murky plight of oppressed women, as Little Eva in *Uncle Tom's Cabin* (published a few years earlier) had shed light on the plight of the oppressed slaves. With its dramatization, *Uncle Tom's Cabin* became one of the most frequently performed stage plays of the nineteenth century, reaching mass audiences and adding fuel to the fires of Abolitionist sentiment in the decade before the Civil War. (Abraham Lincoln is supposed to have said when her first met the author, Harriet Beecher Stowe, "So you are the little lady that started the big war.") When Barrett wrote of Cora Richmond, "A little girl was the first apostle chosen to do the work designed by the spirit world,"[14] he was tapping into the widespread image of a martyred child as savior, as well as into the contemporary zeitgeist regarding the growing influence of the feminine

As Ann Douglas put it in *The Feminization of American Culture*, "Beneath the conjunction of femininity and Christianity" Spiritualism demonstrated a "probably unacknowledged assumption that the modern age in some sense would belong to the woman...."[15] Eugene Taylor makes a similar point in *Shadow Culture,* writing of the "feminine" aspects of many nineteenth century American mystical communities associated with Spiritualism which, inspired by the trance experiences of their charismatic leaders, represented a kind of "feminine" alternative to more conventional and rational "masculine" institutions. "As a repressed and often persecuted aspect of a society dominated by masculine forms, the early mystical communities in some ways represented a feminine psychology of the collective unconscious expressed on a national scale."[16]

Nonetheless, contends Mary Farrell Bednarowski, although Spiritualism was innately feminist, "the movement never produced a very coherent theoretical basis" for feminism.[17] Moreover, while "Spiritualism questioned with great energy the fact that women were excluded from so many avenues to power" it "never went so far as to question society's description of what a woman should be and what that description might have to do with her exclusion."[18] Spiritualist belief and practice, rather than radically disrupting gender status quo, might just as often exploit the ideals of femininity for its own ends.

There was no question that female trance performers could capitalize on their feminine attractions to win over audiences. A reviewer of the popular Miss Jay in 1855 admired her tasteful dress, brooch and hair before commenting on her

> intelligent, good-looking face, a most excellent voice, and a very graceful delivery. While listening to her I was more and more reconciled to the idea

of intonation so just and expressive, that it more than compensates for the want of volume in the voice, and goes far to dispel our old and rusty prejudices.[19]

Though female trance performers were often able to charm male audience members, and "reconcile" them to the idea of women appearing in public, this by no means solved the problem of their ambiguous social status. The kind of ostracism Mowatt had felt in the 1840s had not disappeared in the first decade of Spiritualism, and even the most famous and successful trance speakers suffered from it. The originators of the movement, Kate and Maggie Fox, as professional mediums, for instance, became household names by the middle of the nineteenth century. But their fame faded to obscurity in their later years, and their personal lives were haunted by trouble. Their older sister Leah, who at first actively managed them, was ultimately both happier and more prosperous, perhaps because her life ultimately took a slightly more conventional and less risky path. Although she managed their careers at first, personally she was able to give up professional mediumship after marrying a well-off New Yorker named Daniel Underhill, who gave her financial support but also allowed her to pursue her own interests, which included becoming a supporter and writer about Spiritualism.

Kate and Maggie were both married briefly, but both struggled with alcoholism, which became severe and crippling towards the end of their lives. Kate married an Englishman named Jenckens, and continued to perform as a medium in England for a few years. She returned to America after he died, leaving her without support.

Maggie Fox's disastrous love affair with the famous arctic explorer Elisha Kent Kane, with whom she had a long, drawn out and stormy romance, shows that mediums, like actresses were still not accepted into respectable Victorian society. Fame and visibility were still two of the least desirable qualities for respectable women, and the difficulty of their ambiguous social position was not compensated for by their celebrity or ability to earn their own living. Maggie's relationship with Elisha Kent Kane was complicated by her reluctance to accede to Kane's demand that she give up mediumship, and by Kane's own unwillingness to reveal to his family the extent of his relationship with a "common rapper." When Kane set off on a rescue expedition to find the well known arctic explorer and hero Sir John Franklin, Maggie gave up séances to wait for his return. She felt bored, isolated and miserable in the quiet retired life she tried to lead in his absence, which lasted much longer than anticipated. This was not surprising given the stimulation of her life up to this point, to which she, as well as Kate, must have grown somewhat addicted. When Kane finally returned after a long and harrowing journey in which he and his crew had been all but given up for dead, Maggie was at first ecstatic, then bitterly disappointed when Kane told her that he was still unwilling to marry her in the face of his family's objections. They quarreled, reconciled, and seemed unable to either give up or resolve their relationship. There is some evidence to suggest that Kane secretly married Maggie Fox not long before his untimely death, and she used his name for the rest of her life. But the Kane family refused to recognize the union. Maggie was desperate financially, and after trying unsuccessfully to sue the Kane family for the money she believed Elisha had left her in his will, she returned to mediumship to support herself. Medium Frances Green McDougall, in solidarity with her fellow "rapper" or to profit from the public's fascination the scandal, published a "trance novel" in 1866 titled *The Love Life of Dr. Kane*. It was told to her by Kane's spirit to explain "his great devotion to young spirit medium Margaret Fox, whom he had secretly married."[20]

By the 1880s, Maggie, like her sister Kate who was now widowed after losing her English husband Jenckens, had become a full-blown alcoholic. In 1888, the sisters confessed that they had faked the ghostly rappings which precipitated the age of spirit contact. They claimed to have produced knocking sounds by manipulating and cracking the joints in their feet and knees. For a while they made money giving lectures about this "deathblow" to Spiritualism. However, before she died, Maggie recanted the confession, and Kate began conveying spirit messages to close friends once again. Ultimately, trance mediumship brought the sisters neither wealth nor happiness. Both died in penurious circumstances, essentially drinking themselves to death.[21]

8

Séance as Theatre

Mesmeric exhibitions had been a form of medical theatre for O'Key, and Mowatt had impersonated the vivid character of Gypsy in a state of trance, but Spiritualism widened the forms that trance performance might take to include both the public trance lecture and the séance. The Fox sisters, for example, did trance performances in both contexts, although they more often held private séances than public lectures. The trance speaker performed in a rented public hall or theatre, for an often sizeable audience, who had probably paid to see the show, just as they would have for other lecturers and platform speakers who traveled from town to town in the nineteenth century giving talks on a variety of entertaining and educational topics. The only difference was that the trance speaker, in an altered state of consciousness, spoke (most often, apparently, without preparation) in the voice and character of a discarnate spirit, and usually had no memory of what she said when the lecture was over. In the séance, a medium contacted spirits for a select audience of sitters usually in a private home or rooms, but the experience was just as much a form of theatre as the public lecture.

Medium Frances Green's account of one séance describes it in unmistakably theatrical terms. She comments on how difficult it is for séance audiences to give an accurate report, or review of the performance:

> As there is no programme of the performances, and therefore the spectators do not know what is coming till it is nearly or quite past, and at the same time the actors, themselves, do not remember any thing of what has happened, when they return to the normal state, these representations seem to go by with a kind of meteoric splendor, which arrests the attention, and thrills the heart for a little while; and then it is extremely difficult to give any thing of a definite idea of what has passed.[1]

The séance audience, like the melodrama audience, found its powers of rational analysis, and certainly its objectivity, overwhelmed by the effects of representations which could so "arrest the attention" and "thrill the heart." George Henry Lewes, in his discussion of acting, had noted the same response from audiences in theatre when they observed a great actor like Edmund Kean. "The ordinary spectator is moved, but is incapable of discriminating the source of his emotion...."[2] In the case of trances, even the performer herself, often unconscious of what she said or did in the trance state, was poorly equipped to give an accurate account of the experience.

For the séance (as for drama) to be effective, the audience, and sometimes the performer as well, was supposed to be overcome by emotion. The category of "emotional actresses" who could only perform under the influence of profound feeling illustrates this expectation on the performer's side. As for the séance spectators, to be overcome with feeling would not have been a strange or even unwelcome experience, since attendance at popular theatre of the time would have prepared them for this response. It was the fundamental function of the Victorian theatre as a whole, and of actors in particular to elicit, irresistibly, the deepest feeling. George Taylor's argument about early Victorian actors holds true for actors well through the nineteenth century; the "purpose of their playing" was to "communicate feeling, what they called 'passions,' by which were meant not only affective states of mind such as anger, fear or desire, but all mental activities, such as sensation, perception and recognition."[3] Acting techniques might vary, with different means employed to convey or depict a character's feelings and thoughts, but the actor's fundamental goal of provoking the audience's feelings remained the same. Although an immediate and intense emotional response does not completely preclude the possibility of subsequent rational analysis, it does, as Frances Green's comments show, complicate it.

Theories about the interaction of theatre audiences with actors can also shed light on the dynamics of the séance. Just as the most seemingly objective observers of a séance would have been prepared by experiences in the theatre to be bathed in emotion, they would also have been, like theatre audiences, biased in their expectations about what they would see by a whole host of preconceptions and past experiences. Theatre and performance theorists suggest that the predispositions of individual spectators (and of the group as a whole) not only affect their response, but actually help create the *meaning* of a performance. This theory has its roots in "reception theory," an outgrowth of "reader response criticism" that argues that the reader of any text is influenced by a horizon of expectations which, interacting with the text itself, creates meaning.[4] The séance observer's horizon of expectations has been created in part by the conventions of Victorian theatre itself. In this sense the séance spectator is not merely a "target of theatrical manipulation," but more actively and substantially a "co-producer of the performance."[5] This view helps one see spectators of séance phenomena not as gullible dupes but as crucial participants in the process of creating the meaning of the performance. The spectator shares responsibility for and mutually defines and interprets what happens during the performance, even, to some degree, if that performance is based on trickery or fraud.

Certain types of performances including "rituals of trance and possession" have been categorized as "closed performances." These are performances which "predict specific addressees; requiring definite kinds of competence for their 'correct' interpretation."[6] The "ideal spectators" of closed performances are those who have the skill to read the performance conventions, including the ability to recognize the genre of the performance and to understand what elements to expect based on this type (that is, the "rules of the genre"). In the case of trance performances, a significant factor in the spectator's response would be not only the correct anticipation of what was supposed to happen in a séance, but their own strong desire to see and believe the phenomena that were "supposed to" occur (related to the strong willingness to "suspend disbelief" discussed previously.) It is not difficult to see why nineteenth century spectators would have been quick to believe in trance manifestations, since so many mediums impersonated or claimed to have been taken over by the spirits of deceased relatives and friends of their sitters. Early deaths and high infant mortality rates clearly made ready audiences for these impersonations, and it is no surprise that Spiritualist activity increased after the great losses of life of the Civil War and, after a decline at the turn of the century, spiked again briefly during World War I. The stakes could hardly be higher for the medium's audience. Whereas for the theatre audience the ability to suspend disbelief could earn you a few hours of diverting entertainment, in a séance, the reward was reunion with the dead, as well as evidence of life after death. The strong motivation to believe in the reality of the trance impersonation of a lost loved one helps explain why so many individuals were convinced by performances that seem to us today to be so transparently fraudulent.

With such ideal spectators, primed by both their desire to believe and their familiarity with the conventions, of Victorian theatre which were shared by séances, these performances could indeed work very well, "provided that the spectator truly corresponds to the one imagined and reacts in the predicted manner." However, "it is very different when a 'closed' performance [such as a trance séance] is attended by spectators very different from the model desired."[7] This helps explain the wide divergence in reactions to trance séances, even among spectators of the same séance, as well as the careful vetting and selection that often occurred before the admission of spectators to a séance. It was understood by the medium that a less than ideal spectator might spell disaster for the performance, or at least compromise its "success" in terms of genuine spirit contact.

How then, were there so many "ideal spectators" for Victorian séances?

As we have seen, conventions of theatre prepared them, as well as the prevalence of sudden loss of loved ones. Given their popularity and ubiquity, it appears that trance performances could and did "succeed" on more than one level. Even if they did not satisfy the audience as authentic contact with spirits, they succeeded simply on the level of theatrical entertainment. Even when a non-ideal spectator attended and presumably did not buy the reality of performance *as genuine manifestation of spirits*, they might still "enjoy the event as pure spectacle," and count it a success *as theatrical entertainment*.[8]

Although Victorian investigators did not use the vocabulary of "reception theory" to explain spiritualist phenomena, it is clear that they understood and were utilizing its basic concepts. Frank Podmore, for instance, a psychical investigator and author on the subject, argued that it was the desire and will of the spectator to believe in spiritualistic phenomena which made for successful séances. His research of the early years of séance phenomena led him to conclude that "the real secret of the ready credence accorded for more than two decades to these dark séances lay in the overwhelming predisposition to belief on the part of the assistants."[9]

Podmore's tests of audience perceptions of trance activity show further details about the influence of audience expectations. Podmore describes a test of basic table turning, in which sitters around a table, with their hands touching, feel the table move with no evident effort exerted by anyone in the room. Podmore writes:

> When no expectations were formed of any probable result, and the attention of those sitting around the table was diverted by conversation or otherwise, the table did not move at all. Again, no results followed when half the sitters expected the rotation to take place in one direction and half in another. But when expectation was allowed free play, and especially if the direction of the probable movement was indicated beforehand, the table began to rotate after a few minutes, although no one of the sitters was conscious of exercising any effort at all....[10]

Podmore's experiment tested the influence of the audience's beliefs. The beliefs or motives of the performer or medium herself, of course, also had a significant impact on the performance. The medium's religious or theological views clearly affected the kinds of spirits they manifested and what these spirits said. Podmore cites the case of a clergyman turned trance performer who becomes the medium for the spirit of one of his deceased parishioners. This particular parishioner had left the congregation before he died, going off to attend a rival Wesleyan chapel. It must have been very satisfying, then, for the minister—*cum*—medium when the spirit expressed sincere regret for this desertion, and for not having listened to his spiritual advisor more faithfully in life![11]

These anecdotes and the skeptical, sometimes cynical tone of Podmore's reports also reveal something about his own expectations as a researcher. Reports of Spiritualist or trance phenomena were complicated by the agendas of their authors, who often had a strong stake in either *defending* or conversely *debunking* the authenticity of the phenomena they described. Confirmed believers in Spiritualism, for instance, might present their subjects as saints, glossing over or omitting instances of failure or possible fraud. Autobiographies as well as biographies of mediums present the same challenges as those of actresses, since they too may be written as part of an attempt to construct a respectable identity, conforming to idealized cultural images.[12]

"Scientific" reports of experiments with trance states might be written in the service of a specific medical or psychological hypothesis. Such was the case of the investigations conducted by Dr. Elliotson with Elizabeth O'Key in the 1830s, meant to demonstrate the therapeutic value of mesmerism, or Dr. Jean-Martin Charcot's experiments with hypnotism at the asylum of Salpetriere near Paris in the 1880s.

Séances and trance performances are also difficult to judge based on artefacts like texts which record words, but are less successful at conveying movements, gestures, facial expressions or intonations. A verbatim transcription of the words of a séance or trance performance, like the script of a play, does not adequately convey the full impact of the event. Nonetheless, common elements of the structure, style and impact of trance performances begin to emerge from details in the hundreds of descriptions published in books, journals and pamphlets.

Many of these records describe several categories of spirit phenomena. The earliest type were the loud percussive noises or "rappings" like those produced at the Fox family home in 1848. Knocks or raps were heard when the Fox sisters, Kate and Margaret, were nearby, purportedly coming from an "intelligence" later identified as the spirit of a peddler who had been murdered and buried in the house's cellar. As previously mentioned, many people took these phenomena seriously as evidence of the intrusion of the spiritual into the physical world, and attempts to contact spirits, and gain evidence of their presence via "table turning" or "table tipping" spread quickly in homes throughout upstate New York and New England. Within a year the early leaders of the American women's rights movements were writing the Declaration of Rights to be read at the Seneca Falls convention of 1848 on a table around which they had previously attempted to consult the spirits.[13] Although Spiritualist beliefs and ideas rapidly gained adherents as attractive and liberating alternatives to the more rigid theology of conventional religions, séances and trance performances appealed to the more casual participant as well, offering an opportunity for a new and exciting home entertainment. "Table Turning" became a popular parlor game in some homes, like amateur theatricals or tableaux vivantes.

As interest in séances increased, "how to" handbooks (similar to those written for home theatricals) were published. These stressed the necessity of creating the right mood and setting to encourage the spirits to appear. Lights, music, costume and even the receptivity of the audience were taken into consideration in these instructional manuals. In the *Plain Guide to Spiritualism* written in 1853 Uriah Clarke advises those interested to form a mediumistic circle of anywhere from 3 to 20 people, with equal numbers of men and women. He urges each individual to

> seek to put yourselves in sympathy with those whom you communicate (sic); elevate your thoughts and emotions to the plane they occupy, and invoking the dominant influences, then let each person freely yield, willing to be an instrument for the manifestations of the spirits under the guidance of the supreme Spirit whose government is over all.[14]

Clarke's advice reinforces the "willing suspension of disbelief" that must occur for the séance to be successful. Sitters at a séance, like their counterparts in theatres, had to invest emotionally and imaginatively in the performance in order to experience its pleasures and rewards. Clarke's advice also suggests that not only the audience, but the actor — the one who embodies the spirit, must be sensitive, sympathetic, and yielding to their influence. Like actresses of the "emotional" school popular in the 1850s, mediums also had to give themselves up completely to the role, and allow the emotions and consciousness of the character to supersede their own, in order to act effectively.

Another "how to" piece on forming a spirit circle appeared in an 1887 edition of the periodical *Two Worlds*. "How to Investigate Spiritualism, or Rules for the Spirit Circle" was written by Emma Hardinge Britten, a successful professional medium and prolific author on the subject.[15] Britten had begun her career as a legitimate actress on the London stage, and later moved to New York City where she discovered her mediumistic skill. As one acquainted with the optimum conditions of performance for both theatre and séances, her advice could serve for both. She suggested, for instance, that a sitting should not normally exceed two hours. Theatres were moving towards shorter performances as well throughout the century. The long hours in the theatre, with programs that might include two full-length plays (a tragedy or melodrama followed by a comedy, sometimes capped off by a pantomime or farce) common early in the century had virtually ceased to be by the 1880s. Audiences had less tolerance for sitting in a theatre for more than 2–3 hours, and performances which got out early enough for theatre goers to catch the last train home to the suburbs were becoming the norm.

The comfort and safety of theatre audiences were also becoming more important. Health and safety regulations were being instituted in public theatres (especially in the wake of disastrous theatre fires throughout the century), and Hardinge mentions a similar concern for the sitters at a séance. The space in which the séance was conducted, Hardinge insisted, should be well-ventilated and never overheated. Britten advised that strong lights be avoided, which may have reflected the increasing tendency to darken auditoriums for legitimate theatrical performances, especially as the developments in gas, and later electricity, made it easier to focus and control lights. Britten was probably also thinking of the so-called "dark séances" common at the time, in which both sitters and medium sat in a completely darkened room. The darkness, Spiritualists insisted, helped create conditions receptive to the spirits while skeptics noted the obvious — that lack of light would make it easier to perform the "tricks" which mediums were accused of using to produce their manifestations.

These manifestations might include the loud rappings on walls or floors, or the tipping or levitation of heavy tables or other furniture previously mentioned. But there was more — Spirits might also sing, or play musical instruments (the trumpet, guitar, and tambourine were popular). They could grasp hands with the sitters, and pinch, poke or slap them. They could make objects ("apports") such as fresh flowers or letters appear and drop into the middle of a table or room.

When the séance consisted mainly of phenomena like these, the medium seemed to function more as an impresario, or producer of spectacular effects (visual and aural) than an actor. Precautions were often taken to insure that the medium was not somehow producing the effects herself by trickery or with the help of a concealed confederate, or that the "bodies" felt moving around the séance room were those of the spirit, not of the medium. Mediums were sometimes bound hand and foot, placed in carefully guarded "spirit cabinets" which they could not leave without being seen. To manipulate the sights and sounds that occurred in a séance room, a medium in such cases would have to be an escape artist.

The similarities between mediums and stage magicians did not go unnoticed. The famous magic escape acts of Harry Houdini, who was able to free himself from handcuffs, chains and straitjackets, owed much to techniques developed by professional mediums who preceded him. These included the Davenport brothers who toured successfully for years producing phenomena in America, Britain and Europe. As early as the 1860s, magicians were reproducing some of the same effects commonly seen in séances. Clearly the history of Spiritualism and magic shows were intertwined.

A Scottish magician, John Henry Anderson, known as the "Wizard of the North," toured the United States in 1860 and took advantage of audiences' interest in that year's presidential campaign by having spirits communicate through him the results of the Lincoln-Douglas presidential race. Robert Heller, an English magician and pianist, also toured the United States and "tipped tables, racked chairs, and made words appear on his bare arm, written in blood...."[16]

The celebrated French magician Robert Houdin, from whom Houdini (christened Erich Weiss) borrowed his stage name, wrote a book about the secrets of magicians in 1868 which listed among the categories of conjuring tricks those used in the "Medium Business — Spiritualism, or pretended evocation of spirits, table-turning, -rapping, -talking, and -writing, mysterious cabinets, etc."[17]

Houdini himself in his book *A Magician Among the Spirits* wrote detailed accounts of how technical effects, such as an escape from chains or handcuffs, could be reproduced by natural means. Such techniques could have been used by mediums who were tied up or confined in "spirit cabinets" during séances to prove that they themselves could not be producing any of the ghostly phenomena. When the British Society for Psychical Research was formed in 1882, professional magicians and conjurers were hired to help investigate some cases.

Mediums in this case, as mentioned above, were more the stage managers of technical effects than actresses playing roles. But audiences of séances, like theatre audiences, ultimately required more than tricks and special effects. The greater power of the performer or medium lay in her ability to embody characters. It was characters, not just effects, that people wanted to see in séances. And if the spirits of deceased friends or relatives were not forthcoming, the famous, exotic or just the entertaining might do.

The medium Lizzie Doten obliged by manifesting the spirit of celebrated poet Edgar Allan Poe several years after his death. Through her he communicated a new poem on the subject of Life after Death. The editor of the April 1861 issue of *The Spiritual Magazine* in which the poem was published called it "wonderful as a reproduction of the singular music and alliteration of Poe's style" whether or not it was authentic Poe. The first stanza read:

> From the throne of life eternal,
> From the home of love supernal.
> Where the angel feet make music over all the starry floor —
> Mortals, I have come to meet you,
> Come with words of peace to greet you,
> And to tell you of the glory that is mine for evermore....[18]

Cora Richmond's spirit guide, the Indian maiden Ouina, also wrote poetry published in Spiritualist periodicals, as well as children's stories, which came out in the anthology *Ouina's Canoe*. When asked once by an intellectual lady poet why the spirits did not produce such fine poetry through her as well, Cora's spirits reputedly replied, with perhaps unintentional levity, "We do not create brains, we only use them."[19]

Musical pieces from the spirits of great composers like Beethoven or Mozart, might be performed via the medium, or the medium might play the piano or violin in the style of a great departed musician. Madame Llancaré played the piano blindfolded while entranced by Mozart and Mendelssohn.[20] Medium Lenore Piper (one possible model for the spiritualist heroine in Henry James' *The Bostonians*) was controlled at times by the spirits of artistic geniuses J. S. Bach, Sarah Siddons, H. W. Longfellow, and — the odd man out — Commodore Vanderbilt (a genius, perhaps, at the art of making money.)[21]

It was not only the classical musicians or artists who came through, though. Mediums and spirits were no snobs. In New York City at a séance held in Barnum's hotel for a distinguished audience including William Lloyd Garrison, William Cullen Bryant and Horace Greeley, the recently deceased Spiritualist and folk music impresario Jesse Hutchinson of the popular Hutchinson Family Singers appeared to perform. The spirit of Jesse levitated a guitar and tambourine and played the hit tune "The Old Granite State."[22]

A report of an 1854 séance in Buffalo, New York, in a private circle led by one male and one female medium, tells of the performance of the spirit of a recently deceased local musician. He began by leading the sitters in a musical version of *The Lord's Prayer*, followed by 15 other sacred hymns. At that point, perhaps tired of all the solemnity, the circle requested some secular songs, and the spirit obliged with patriotic and popular tunes including "Hail Columbia," "The Star Spangled Banner," "Yankee Doodle," "The Old Oaken Bucket" and "Lily Dale."[23]

Spirit performances sometimes seemed to be an odd mixture of vaudeville acts more than anything else. In 1884, a female medium in the course of a single trance performance manifested 31 different spirits altogether. Among them, as reported in the periodical *Banner of Light*, were Captain Hodges, a "firm, erect military man"; Alice, a "tall queenly Soprano"; Helen, who sang "Sweet Beulahland"; Little Wolf, "a perfect Indian brave"; and Mrs. McCarthy, an "Irish lady whose vocabulary amused without offending genteel taste."

The variety of spirit personalities produced by a single trance subject could be impressive. The distance between the medium's "normal" behavior and the odd or excessive acts she performed in the trance state was in itself fascinating. A lengthy account of a séance held at a later date by the same circle which enjoyed the concert described above, shows this.

This performance was held at the home of the female medium's father. It began again with music and singing, but then the Spirit hushed the circle and said, "Keep perfectly quiet and we will show you some things which you have never seen. We will make some dance who never have danced before." Suspense mounted as the circle sat in "breathless silence, awaiting the denouement."[24]

The spirit then called upon a Mr. L. to play a dance tune on his flute and "Miss B. [the medium], who was as dead to all appearance as Lazarus was, and who had never attempted to dance a step in her life, commenced beating the tune with her hands and feet. This she continued more and more vigorously till the music seemed to lift her from her chair, and she took the floor and danced a full hour...."[25]

So carried away was the medium by her trance state and the presence of the spirits that she was transformed, miraculously, into a performing diva before the eyes of friends and family who would never have suspected her capable of such a display. The woman who had never danced before seemed to have a superhuman energy, and an unaccustomed boldness with the opposite sex, as the account suggests. She "seized upon" a young gentleman who was also in a trance state, and "drew him out upon the floor. They danced together till he was entirely exhausted, when she led him to his seat, and resumed the floor alone." The reporter interpolates with breathless admiration that "although I have seen much dancing in many countries, I can say in all sincerity, that I never before saw such perfection in the 'poetry of motion' as I did in the somnambulic performance of this most extraordinary girl."

> The ecstatic review of continues, noting in detail how the prima donna commenced the concluding scene, which, for its intense interest, defies description by human language. With her eyes still fast shut, she went to a far corner of the room, where the guitar had been placed, took it under her arm, and commenced thrumming the strings as if she had been an experienced performer, notwithstanding that she could not, in her normal state, produce a musical note on any kind of an instrument, after continuing this for a few minutes, she took a position in the corner of the room where the guitar stood, leaned her back against the wall, and commenced chanting an anthem which the Spirit who used her organs evidently composed extemporaneously. The music was solemn and sublime — the voice which uttered it seemed like the chant of a whole choir of angels, so far did it exceed anything she could possibly do herself in the normal state.[26]

Spiritualist books and magazines are rife with descriptions of otherwise subdued women performing roles which would have been unthinkable to them in their "normal" states. As Laurence Moore noted, female mediums were particularly attracted to performing spirits who represented an "otherwise forbidden male social role," and it was not unusual for female mediums in the midst of a trance performance to turn into "swearing sailors, strong Indian braves, or oversexed male suitors." Another example of such manly behavior was observed in a medium who, transformed into a rough and sporting fellow, appeared to be "hunting and calling her dog, and loading her gun, and taking her swig of whiskey, all of which were done to perfection.'"[27]

In a series of manifestations in 1851, a Mrs. Eliza Wilcox of Upper Canada Village embodied a cast of spirit characters which included Samuel Ceasar, a colored man 5 years dead, who gave "an astonishing demonstration with Mr. Wilcox's violin." Another character was Frank, an illiterate boy who in life had been extremely athletic, strong, and fond of "running, leaping, lifting and like games," feats by which he was identified when they were exhibited through the medium. She also performed Caleb Cory, a sea captain from Fall River, Massachusetts who had been lost and presumed dead in a great storm in 1815. His manifestations were "peculiar and astounding. He caused numerous sounds and motions closely resembling those of sea-faring life — such as taking in and making sail, raising and lowering boats, tearing up and repairing decks, handling and nailing down plank, etc. He even imitated the sculling of a boat, by giving the table the same sort of motion."[28]

Crusty or ornery old gentleman seemed to be favorites with some female mediums. Emma Hardinge Britten's work on Spiritualism in America includes an account of a fine young female medium from Augusta, Maine, "through whom the spirits give some curious demonstrations, manifesting among other things the spirit of an old Revolutionary soldier, who, in unabated opposition to King George of England, refuses to rap time to the tune of 'God Save the King,' but beats time to the air of 'Yankee Doodle' with amazing force and alacrity."[29]

The most devout and demure woman, under the influence of trance performance, might suddenly become a rambunctious, swearing old codger. An article with the delightful title "Strange Developments in a Family of Episcopalians" recounts how a Mrs. Ford near Hartford, Connecticut, who normally "had a great horror of profane language," began when under the control of spirits to utter oaths and curses. Apparently her outburst was contagious, as shortly after hearing her Mr. Ford began to curse too. A doctor was consulted and declared her insane (although there is no mention of whether Mr. Ford was also diagnosed insane). But this didn't stop Mrs. Ford, who continued her profane screaming fits, alternating them with the singing of "the most beautiful and difficult airs in music, of which airs she had no previous knowledge" and with "clear and intelligible" utterances of most heavenly strains in thought."[30]

The variety of roles that might be performed by the same medium was remarkable. A French girl in the course of a single trance could produce

> a young whimsical woman of slightly defective pronunciation, or "Phillipe," or "Mr. Tetard, chewing tobacco or drinking ordinary wine" or "Abbe Gerard, who intends to deliver a sermon but whose head is thick and mouth sticky because of the preceding incarnation," or again an obscene fellow, a baby, or a little girl of three years.[31]

Spirits were no respecters of class when it came to choosing (or being chosen by) their mediums. Laura Edmonds, the daughter of New York Supreme Court Justice J. W. Edmonds, was recorded to have been entranced by the spirit of a 12-year-old newsboy who had died of cholera in 1854. Edmonds (1816–1874), a lawyer, scholar, and New York state legislator, was one of the first serious investigators of spirit phenomena in the wake of the Fox sisters' manifestations. Judge Edmonds was convinced of the identity of the spirit his daughter manifested, a boy named Tim Peters, by the detailed knowledge it had of Tim's life and circumstances. The spirit of Tim told how his father had been "intemperate" and died when run over by a rail car. "Tim" was also familiar with the haunts of news boys, like upper Nassau street, and most convincingly, "his shrewdness, his slang terms, and his manner of speaking were particularly characteristic of the class of boys to which he said he belonged ... he spoke of men and boys with whom he had been thrown in contact, in a manner so natural as to carry conviction that he was what he said he was." Moreover, "there was a keen shrewdness of thought, a reckless devil-may-care manner, and a love of fun about him that can be seen in combination only in them.... He sometimes swore, but immediately checked himself, and said that his mother (who was with him) told him he must not talk so...."[32]

The judge must have considered the spirit especially convincing, since his respectable and sheltered daughter could not possibly have had knowledge of the kind of life, men and language with which the spirit Tim was familiar, or swear and exhibit the recklessness that characterized Tim. Moreover, the judge's own daughter could not be a fraud. Edmonds' colleagues in the New York State supreme court and legislature were less understanding. He was forced to resign as chief justice after he published his first book on Spiritualism.

Emma Hardinge noted diplomatically that in some cases what appeared to be spirit possession, i.e., the effects of a "*supra mundane* psychology," might be more nearly the effects of "*mundane* psychology." She referred to the "magnetic contagion of the times" and even suggested that the real effect of a spirit might be not so much to *possess* the medium but to "*externalize character*, and develop into sudden prominence the hidden traits, perhaps scarcely known to their possessor" (italics mine).[33] This interpretation resembles some modern psychiatric explanations for what occurs in hypnosis, when a normally repressed social role comes to the fore.

True to their theatrical potential, Spiritualist phenomena were portrayed in legitimate stage plays or variety shows. As mesmerism had become the subject of theatrical farces in the early years of the century, Spiritualism was taken on by the English pantomime, a long time vehicle for the timely satire of social oddities. In the 1861 article "Spiritualism and the Pantomimes" which appeared in a spiritualist periodical, the author, a believer himself, takes the ribbing of Spirits and Spiritualists in good humor. Resigned to the fact that any phenomena which attracts so much of the public's attention is fair game for the traditional English pantomime, he writes, "Spiritualism has in 1861 found itself in that special form of attractiveness which makes a subject fit for the pantomimes." He mentions several theatres — the Princess, the Lyceum, and Drury Lane among them — where "tables and chairs and men are rapped, and moved and raised and floated about the stage" to the delight and applause of the audiences. He quotes some of the terrible puns (a hallmark of pantomime dialogue) from the Drury Lane pantomime *Peter Wilkins*. "If I am intruding perhaps you'll tell me so" one character remarks. Peter hears rappings and exclaims

> What sounds are those? Don't frighten a poor chap!
> One who's so poor he's hardly worth a rap.

The author expresses his hope that, amidst all the jollity, audiences may learn something, and observes with a touch of irony that audiences might find the Spirits and their phenomena somewhat less amusing when experienced alone in the dark at night, rather than in a crowded, well lit theatre.[34]

Not all spirit phenomena were comic, and manifestations could at times take a dark turn, with unhappy spirits appearing more as characters from a tragic melodrama than as formulaic comic types. John S. Adams wrote of the experiences of his wife, a medium, in manifesting a series of spirits for Dr. A. B. Child of Boston. The first was a "high and holy" spirit who identified herself as "Love" and claimed to have come to help Dr. Child along with his spiritual development, so that he might "ripen in beauty and purity."[35] Part of Child's development would include helping another spirit progress, and the medium Mrs. Adams told the doctor that soon "a poor, undeveloped, dark spirit" would come to him for guidance. The spirit visitant when she manifested seemed to be in the throes of deep emotional suffering, embodied with intense physicality by the medium: "The unhappy visitant sighed heavily, clasped her hands at one moment, at the next, placed them on her breast as if some deep sorrow weighed heavily there. Her face was strongly marked with the outlines of agony. The body was contorted, the head at times bowed upon the breast, her hands firmly clasped and elevated...."[36] This picture of suffering would have been familiar to an audience accustomed to the conventionalized portrayal of emotions in the theatre. The depiction could have been recognizable from an eighteenth or nineteenth century acting handbook or illustrated manual which recommended universal poses and gestures of the arms and hands, to convey the various states such as "Grief" and move the audience.

Medium Samantha Mettler combined serious and comic acts in her performances. She did dance and pantomime, and enacted dramatic scenes of life among the spirits. In these last she was sometimes joined by spectators who also fell into trances, and impersonated additional characters in these spontaneous playlets.

Audience involvement could be part of the fun for stage acts of mesmerism. Miss Chandos Leigh Hunt mesmerized audiences, as well as performing in trance herself, as part of her shows. In what sounds like a performance by a modern stage hypnotist, she sometimes made spectators do absurd thing in trance to make the audience laugh. On one occasion, a little gender play was part of the subversive fun when an

> innocent looking youth was the star of the show. He prowled up and down like an animal in the zoo, agreed that his name was Mary Jones, and sang a sweet ditty. One of the women ... responded with a song entitled "The Slave Girl's Love."[37]

The motives of trance performers were as varied as the characters they played. One of these motives, was of course profit, while another was the subversive fun of playing "forbidden roles." Other mediums who embodied spirits through séances, speeches or automatic writing, did so evidently in an effort to gain wider experience and knowledge of their world — which might include traveling far distances in time and space, as we shall see in the next chapter.

9

Spirit Travels to Distant Times and Places

As acting in the legitimate theatre might give an actress the opportunity to vicariously experience other feelings, personalities or worlds, the trance's altered or dual consciousness made this possible also for Spiritualist mediums and lecturers. As the enormously successful trance performer Cora Richmond observed, it was only when she was "separated in consciousness" from her body that she was she able to visit other people and places.[1] Trance performing opened up horizons for mediums literally, by giving them opportunities to travel for speaking engagements, as well as metaphorically, by enabling them to visit distant times and places in spirit.

Even on the earthly plane Spiritualists tended to be a cosmopolitan lot; mediums and ideas circulated freely among America, England, and Europe. Cora Richmond was equally at home in Britain and America, and toured both extensively. Medium and Spiritualist historian Emma Hardinge Britten was born in England and acted in London theatres before moving to New York to start a career as a Spiritualist speaker and writer. Later in her life she traveled widely throughout Europe, Asia, Australia and New Zealand, studying and writing about spiritualist phenomena.

Both women traveled in spirit as well as in the flesh. Their embodiments of and contacts with entities from distant times and places gave them, and other mediums like them, an imaginative access to other worlds that was impossible by any other means. Spirits purportedly traveled freely through history as well as ranging the earth from pole to pole, and sometimes even further, to other planets and galaxies. Cora Richmond produced adventurous narratives as Ouina, the native Indian girl who told the dramatic story of her life and death on the mid Atlantic shores of pre colonial America. Emma Hardinge Britten communicated with a variety of historical entities, including the spirit of lost arctic explorer Sir John Franklin in the 1850s.

As a spirit speaking through a medium Mrs. Elizabeth Sweet declared, "The spirit is a great and unceasing traveler," proving this with detailed reports of journeys through outer space. The effusive accounts of these celestial and interplanetary travels resemble those of Victorian explorers on first sighting the spectacular vistas of exotic earthly destinations. "Vast and grand are all things pertaining to this fair country" the medium relayed from a spirit sightseeing trip on a distant planet. "My vision cannot compass its unlimited boundaries; my eye cannot scale its lofty mountains.... As I stand and look upward, countless myriads of worlds are revolving around their orbits in the illimitable regions of space."[2] Spirit travel was also, like more mundane Victorian travel, an opportunity to indulge in Romantic descriptions of the sublime.

It was also an opportunity to explore the world historically, geologically, and anthropologically. In London in 1875 an extensive account of travels through Egypt, India, Greece, Persia, and the Holy Land was compiled and published by an H. Nisbet. One of the journeys described was a long trip from Judea to Persia, which included a trek through the wilderness, attacks by wild beasts, a side trip to legendary Mt. Ararat to see the site of the Biblical deluge, and a stunning view of a summer sunset over the Red Sea. It continued with a chase by sea robbers, but the intrepid travelers were not discouraged. Upon landing they "resolved to travel homewards by way of Egypt" in order to "have an opportunity of seeing the ancient temples and other buildings of the far famed land." Like most Victorian travel writing, Nisbet's work was a mixed bag, with elements of autobiography, amateur anthropology, and journalistic, scientific and adventure writing. The table of contents alone ran to 7 pages of tiny print listing sub-headings such as *Theology of the Egyptians, Grecian Idolatry and Myths, Languages and Races of Mankind, Marriage Customs of the Persians, Storm and Sea fight on the Persian Gulf, Voyage on the Red Sea,* and *Indian Temples.* The voluminous narrative work was reprinted at least once, and was reviewed in the *Spectator* of May 8, 1888. "Though there is much to interest the reader in the travels and adventures" the review concluded, "and the descriptions of people and places, it has a strong 'Arabian nights' flavor about it which gives it a likeness to an opium eater's dream." This seems a measured assessment, given the true source of the work, whose full title was *Hafed, Prince of Persia: His Experiences in Earth-Life and Spirit-Life, being Spirit Communications received through Mr. David Duguid, the Glasgow Trance-painting Medium.* The travels described had happened in ancient times, and the spirit of Hafed also turned out to be one of the three Magi who visited the Christ child at Bethlehem.

Hafed's narrative is one of the more extreme examples of spirit travels through time, and represents the Victorians' intense interest in classical and biblical history. But spirits could also travel in real time, through space to exotic destinations. As polar exploration and interest in the far reaches of the

Arctic and Antarctica increased at mid century, spirits from these regions also began to appear in séances and trance performances. One tragic expedition in particular which seemed to capture the attention of mediums and the public alike was that of Sir John Franklin, from whose spirit Emma Hardinge Britten and other mediums received communications in the 1850s. British scientist and explorer Franklin and a crew of 134 men under the auspices of the royal British navy left England in May of 1845 headed for North America to search for the Northwest passage. Franklin had led two previous expeditions to the frozen Northwest and had already mapped portions of the region. In one of these journeys he had lost half his men, mostly to starvation. This time he was much better prepared. The two ships he commanded were the best equipped ever to attempt an arctic voyage. They had the latest technology including steam engines, enough tinned food to last 3 years, and a library of 1,000 books. Ill luck hounded Franklin and his men nonetheless, and after the ships were trapped in frozen ice, the crew set off overland with sledges to try to make their way back south to inhabited regions. Years later, Inuit natives told eerie tales of encountering desperate white men in their travels, and of coming on a deserted encampment with the frozen corpses of men who had died in their tents or close by. Franklin and his men never returned, and it was years before evidence was found to show exactly what had happened to them. The British and American navies both mounted rescue operations after 1848, in addition to private search expeditions funded by Franklin's widow, Lady Jane. Lady Jane herself consulted mediums hoping for news of her husband, and when Franklin's death was confirmed in 1854, she continued to try to discover as much as possible about his last days in the Arctic.

Emma Hardinge Britten was appearing in Boston when she first encountered the spirit of Sir John Franklin. According to her autobiography, she arrived backstage at Allston Hall one afternoon to give a trance lecture, and was told that the subject she was requested to lecture on, which had been chosen by a committee and kept secret from her until that moment, was "give a description of the arctic regions and the fate of Sir John Franklin."[3] She went out onto the platform, and found a number of bouquets of flowers from friends and admirers waiting for her on the table beside her chair. She was moved to look in the bottom of the pile for a modest nosegay of violets, which she held in her hand during the entire lecture. While she was entranced, spirits revealed to her and to the audience that "violets were the favorite flowers of the martyred Franklin and were apropos to the tragic theme of the address."[4] It was only after the lecture that Emma noticed a card with a name and address attached to the violets, expressing warm wishes from a Mrs. Sisson whom she had never met or heard of. She found out that the woman was a celebrated

Boston Spiritualist. When she met Mrs. Sisson coincidentally a few days later, the woman greeted her warmly and said, "Sir John told me to be ready, for you would be sure to come." Sir John Franklin's spirit had instructed Mrs. Sisson to have the bouquet of violets sent to the lecture hall, and evidently also influenced the committee to choose his fate as the subject for Emma to lecture on that day. Sir John, it turned out, was Mrs. Sisson's dear friend and spirit guide. He had told her that he wanted Emma Hardinge to be his contact for the public lecture because her father, who had passed away when she was a child, had also been a sea captain and "devoted explorer." Both the father, Captain Hardinge, and Emma's brother, a sailor who had also passed away, were now both in Sir Franklin's "spirit bands of exploration."

This incident was not Sir Franklin's only means of making himself known from the other world. Mrs. Sisson's husband was what was called a "drawing medium," capable of producing sketches that came directly from the spirits. Through him, Franklin's spirit drew detailed "maps" of the arctic regions, which the medium himself had never seen. As Emma said, "This man, who so far as I could judge, had never read a line concerning this awful land of ice and desolation, had drawn an immense portfolio full of chalk drawings, all being charts of different scenes, places, and passages of those regions."[5] These maps were pronounced to be accurate by men who had actually been to the Arctic, including the celebrated explorer Elisha Kent Kane. Kane would himself be lost for several years while on an arctic expedition, but miraculously make his way home. Kane was more intimately connected with the Spiritualist movement through his involvement with Maggie Fox. He said in fact that it was Emma Hardinge who first urged him to meet the famous medium.

A remark by medium Ellen Ward in her book *Angels Messages* sheds light on why Spiritualists were so fascinated by arctic explorers. Ellen Ward identified with the intrepid adventurers into the fantastic unexplored regions of the earth, as one who was herself exploring a vast and marvelous country — the spirit world of eternal knowledge. She saw herself as striking out to follow Christ into the unknown world to which he had ascended at death. Even mediums with less exalted spiritual aspirations could have understood the thrills and the perils of beginning such a voyage of discovery.

> With what wonder did the world look after Sir John Franklin, when he set sail for the North around the world. So I will now set sail from the time Christ's apostles saw him ascend out of their sight. Now in order to know the Son better, we must first know the Father. I shall not repeat the church catechism, nor try to define God, but launch out in the broad bosom of eternity, that immense sea which rolls before us all, and as we view all those mighty domains, we know they have an owner.[6]

British writer Harriet Martineau had dabbled with mesmerism, and was also interested in a more mundane but still serious concern with the ethics and function of world travel and travel writing, which she discussed in two books, *How to Observe: Morals and Manners* (1838) and *Eastern Life, Present and Past* (1848). Martineau's advice about the responsibilities of travel writing might have been written about spirit travels in time and space. The kind of political and social critique Martineau suggests could also be a function of the travels made in the course of trance performances. Martineau claimed that the most important quality of travel writing was that it be instructive. Rather than strive for slavish accuracy the travel writer should convey the *essence* of truth. Any individual account, she wrote, might not be "abstractly and absolutely true," but "when all thinkers say freely what is to them true, we shall know of abstract and absolute truth more than we have ever known yet."[7] Martineau was not suggesting that the observation and recording of the details of other people and cultures should be haphazard or subjective, but that the immediate and temporal goal of fact finding should not subsume the ultimate goal to illuminate and disseminate essential truths about humanity. The emphasis on essential truths rather than meticulously accurate details was also a characteristic of Spirit communication.

There are other ways in which travel writing and Spiritualism seemed to offer similar opportunities for Victorian women. The expansive and liberal function of travel writing which Martineau articulated resembles that of spirit travel narratives in that both allowed Victorian women to simultaneously *critique* and *define* their society. British author Fanny Trollope's account of her life in America in the 1830s, for instance, yields a critique of conditions in Britain as well as America. The writing of American Isabella Bird, who traveled extensively in the American west as well as outside of the United States, can be read in much the same way. Scholars of Victorian travel writing, like historians of Spiritualism, have suggested that for women these acts of traveling, and writing or speaking about their experiences implied a subtextual "transgression" or "deviance." Real or spirit travel allowed women to venture outside the domestic sphere, and in recording their adventures to express political or social views more freely.[8]

Deviant and transgressive elements come across in Spiritualist travel narratives about alien societies — literally alien in the case of tales of life on other planets — and in descriptions of the afterlife. Many accounts of the progress of the soul after death were influenced by the cosmology of eighteenth-century mystic Emmanuel Swedenborg. His work was mediated through the widely read works of American Andrew Jackson Davies the "Poughkeepsie seer" whose writing had become a foundation of Spiritualist philosophy. In exhaustive accounts of his travels and experiences as a spirit, Swedenborg described in detail a series of heavenly spheres, in which Heaven and the planets could be found. Henry James would later describe these voluminous and somewhat indigestible works as "singularly void of literary fascination"[9]— a description which could apply to much Spiritualist writing. However, even the most mundane manifestations or tedious communiqués from the other world were of urgent interest to Spiritualist believers who were anxious to get a head's up on what to expect when they crossed over. As one spirit reminded a medium, Man is "always desirous to gain some knowledge of the coast he is nearing, of the journey he is sure to take, of the place he is to inhabit, and of the best way he can reach it."[10] Other spirits concurred, noting that

> the man who is lacking in practical knowledge, when he arrives in the spirit world, is as helpless as the person who, entering a strange country, can not understand the language of the people among whom he has entered.[11]

Clearly there was a need, in Spiritualist literature, for the kind of "instructive" travel writing that Harriet Martineau had advocated for those on the earthly plane. A simple "how to" of how to get from here to there was described in an account of a trip from Earth to Heaven by the spirit of Henry J. Raymond. He reported moving first through Earth's atmosphere, walking on air, and waiting to sail out into the cosmos for Heaven for the right "current" or channel in which to make the ascent. His first stop was on a planet which was "one of the magnetic chain which belts the spirit world ... of a color and material like opal."[12] Even the most intrepid spirit traveler had to rest from time to time, and luckily there were excellent accommodations to be found even in the afterlife. Henry Raymond was pleased to find, on his opalescent planet, a magnificent hotel and resort for travelers that looked like a palace of alabaster, and provided every necessity and luxury imaginable.[13] And as it turned out, the Spirit economy was not so different from a market economy on earth; since even in the other world "the effort to supply want or demand produces a system of exchange or barter...."[14]

In addition to spectacular landscapes and scenery, the spirit world also had thriving cities. An ethereal city called Spring Garden, described by the spirit of Margaret Fuller through an unidentified medium, was a sort of Athens of the afterlife, a center of art, learning and magnificent public spaces and architecture. It was arranged with wide avenues in concentric circles around a large central pleasure park, where booths with delicious food and drinks could be found, and where one could get around via entertaining modes of transportation such as "elegantly formed sleds on galvanic runners, which glide over the ground with swiftness most exhilarating to the senses."[15] Another strange and beautiful vehicle in the other world seemed to resemble an animal ride on a merry go round; "Our phaeton" as it was called, "was a small, white, swan-shaped carriage, ornamented with golden designs, and propelled by a galvanic battery in the graceful swan head."[16] Whatever their appearance, these vehicles were phenomenally speedy, "fast as lightning" or "quick as thought." As Robert Cox has suggested in his work on nineteenth century Spiritualism, this instantaneous achievement of movement to and from remote locations, by spirits or by the astral bodies of living people, fulfilled the Victorians' urgent desire for the "erasure of distance and social isolation" that had been "sparked by developments in wire, steam and rail."[17]

Another woman named Ella Grace visited other worlds in her own spirit form through the power of her mediumship. She described one tiny planet and its charming inhabitants as a sort of lilliputian utopia. The small but perfectly proportioned inhabitants lived in miniature houses exquisitely furnished, where they had all the modern conveniences, shrunk to suit them. They spent mornings in the open air fishing, walking and eating strawberries with sugar for breakfast. They took a stroll to the river, then a pleasant boat ride to an island where a spacious library, lecture hall and art gallery were located. In the afternoon they attended a poetry reading, and in the evening

> after supper the whole town went riding in the cunningest little carriages drawn by the cutest little ponies. The latter seemed to be made to be petted, so docile and affectionate were they, and they seemed the most interesting and delightful animals that I ever came across. Everything about the world pleased and interested me, and I wish that I could convey to others something of the pleasant impression these little people and their surroundings made upon me.[18]

For some, such a place might have seemed as banal and precious as its description, but for Ella Grace it was a pleasurable little heaven to which as a medium she could travel in spirit whenever she liked.

Some spirit travels were most valuable for those at home as a means of catching up with loved ones who had gone ahead. The medium Mrs. Lizzie Green was able to bring reassuring news from the spirit world to parents of adult children who had passed over. The medium's amanuensis and publisher, Mr. Helleberg, was told that his *spirit* son was going to marry the *spirit* daughter of a family friend. The marriage was to be performed in the afterlife by the reverend Mr. Swedenborg himself, and family and friends on the earthly plane could also participate, celebrating simultaneously as mediums passed along every detail of the wedding ceremony to them as it occurred.

9— Spirit Travels to Distant Times and Places

Two mediums were present on the earth side to relay details of the proceedings from beyond. The happy father wrote how

> a private clairvoyant fell in a trance and described not only the clothing of the bride and bridegroom, but many other spirits present. The bride's dress was pure, sparkling white, frosted with gold dust, with long train full of the finest lace, and a very beautiful veil, frosted also, and adorned with a handsome wreath on her head of white flowers set with three beautiful diamonds on her forehead. She had also a diamond brooch and necklace, with a splendid ring on her finger, and slippers on her feet to match.[19]

This trance performance allowed parents who had lost beloved children to be able to celebrate a wedding with them in spirit life, without being deprived of a single detail of the festivities. The earthly parents were also able to enjoy reports of the "honeymoon tour" undertaken by the newlywed spirit couple and their party of spirit friends and relatives. Portions of this "travel journal" were also published in Mr. Helleberg's book.

> March 9, 1882. Our party of tourists, after having been carefully selected in accordance with their ability to utilize the magnetic currents that connect the planets in our solar system, and their adaptability to the electric and magnetic condition of Mars, whither we were bound, started on the journey at, according to your time, midnight, February 23. We proceeded without any incident of note until we reached Maluka Plains, where we met a party of excursionists on a visit to Our planet earth.... We were surprised to find that these excursionists were acquainted with our guide and leader, Mr. Swedenborg, for he had frequently visited the most interesting points of our stellar system.... The party we met were on a tour of scientific exploration, and gladly availed themselves of information imparted by Swedenborg....[20]

The medium had the gratitude of the earthly parents and friends as well as the professional satisfaction of a job well done when the spirit complimented her at the conclusion of these communications. The spirit graciously noted that "we would be ungrateful beyond measure not to speak in acknowledgement of the virtues and noble qualities of the medium, through whose superbly developed medial powers we have been enabled to speak to the world." Spirit thanks also went to Mr. Helleberg as the scribe and publisher of the medium's trance communications: "To you Mr. Helleberg, I return the thanks and the thanks of those cooperating with me, for the patience, earnestness and honesty which have characterized your association with us in this work. Our blessings rest upon you, and be assured that your greatest reward will be in the happy land which your aged footsteps are nearing."[21]

It was typical of a Victorian honeymoon tour, like that described above, to combine pleasure with education. Visits to the planets Mars, Venus or Jupiter allowed for the observation of strange people and customs which constituted subjects of anthropological and ethnographic interest to spirit travelers. The spirit of the Persian magi Hafed, cited above, declared that the inhabitants of some other planets were superior in every way to people on earth. Some were physically larger, and some smaller, but all were well formed in terms of physiognomy, and "more open in countenance, so that each one can read the character of his neighbor."[22] Hafed used his interplanetary travelogue as an opportunity to critique the moral state of life on earth, saying, "It would be well with the earth were its peoples in such a condition. In the worlds I refer to, there is no transgression of God's law, and consequently there is no suffering."[23]

Late in the century, a French psychic investigator named Flournoy reported on a subject named Hélène Smith who provided fascinating details of her travels to Mars in a trance state. She described houses, villages, and carriages without either horses or wheels. Some of her observations she drew, including Martian landscapes and a flying machine which looked like a "carriage lamp with a dust lamp stuck through the glass." But her most interesting revelations were linguistic. She was able to both speak and write in the Martian language, which bore a striking similarity to French in terms of its sounds, construction, and alphabet. Flournoy concluded that the Martian travelogue originated solely in Smith's imagination, and was "subconsciously elaborated in her somnambulistic state."[24]

An unidentified spirit communicating through medium Mrs. Ellen Ward also told of the superiority of other worlds. She visited three planets, each with a distinct race and culture. On the third planet lived people with "large limbs and muscles" who enjoyed a climate that was temperate and "genial" year round. They were vegetarians. They were highly educated and possessed a "better system of astronomy than we do." And while they had "no religion, such as Christians call religion" they had "a very high order of morals." In this utopia there were "no wars, no courts nor prison houses, and murder was unheard of...." Furthermore, "the women have very little or no pain at childbirth. The families are large, with eight and ten children."[25]

In a book published a few years later, the spirit of Madame Frederika Ehrenborg had some remarkably similar observations to make about the planet Mars through the medium Mrs. Lizzie Green. In fact the similarity of the passages can only be explained by plagiarism, or by the fact that the same spirit communicated exactly the same descriptions in the same words to two different mediums several years apart. This latter explanation would have been favored by those not willing to admit to any kind of fraud. It was a common Spiritualist belief that the same spirit might manifest itself through several different mediums. Whether these passages in the two different books originated with the spirits, the female media, or the persons who took down and published the spirit communications (in both cases men) the woman's point of view regarding child bearing, child rearing, and family life was considered significant enough to emphasize and present at some length.

The spirit of Madame Ehrenborg described how, in addition to the superiority of the many elements of government, society, and the arts on Mars, legislative policies there provided for the most advanced pre-natal, as well as post-natal care for women and infants. In a kind of socialist utopian dream scape, expectant mothers were brought together to be nurtured in convenient, beautiful locations. They were housed in buildings of the finest architecture, surrounded by art and "kept under the most elevating influences, both of body and mind." Inspiring lectures and ennobling music helped produce in the mothers "the desired condition of harmony, which had a corresponding effect on the little one concealed from mortal view." Then, at a "proper time after parturition ... the mother was discharged and restored to freedom, and the new born baby was taken care of, raised and maintained by the fostering care of the government."[26] Even with its overtones of "Big Brother" style social controls, one can see how such as system might have appealed, at least in theory, to some Victorian women. Childbirth could be dangerous for women in the nineteenth century, and infant mortality rates were high. The idea of a benevolent and powerful support system to ease the burden could have been wonderful, and the prospect of being quickly "restored to freedom" after bearing children who were then carefully raised with every advantage, nothing short of miraculous. A later statement from this book is an even more explicit example of the spirit travelogue as social critique:

> On Mars the doctrine of discrimination on the score of sex was never taught, but the equality of the sexes has always been recognized. This indiscrimination has always been operative in employments and in the choosing of persons to fill official station [sic].[27]

Travels in History

The kind of political or social critique made possible by the embodiment of spirits who could travel to distant places in the universe, as seen above, was also possible when the trance performer manifested the spirits of famous and respected figures from history. It was still considered largely inappropriate for respectable Victorian women, who were supposed to focus on their domestic and maternal duties, to speak or work publicly for political issues. This is one of the reasons, as other historians of Spiritualism have pointed out, that female Spiritualists often claimed to be just the channels, not the initiators, of political speeches or acts. And who better to claim as their inspiration or guide than a revered (or at least recognized) male political figure from the past. Thus the proliferation of mediums claiming to be in touch with the spirits of George Washington, Benjamin Franklin, Abraham Lincoln, or similar entities who could give legitimacy and authority to their voices.

Spiritualists had a cosmic theory for the fact that prominent men from the past seemed so frequently to communicate with mediums in times of trouble. They believed that after death most spirits (except for the most recalcitrant and unsalvageable villains) would continue to learn, grow, and increase in wisdom and their desire to help their fellow men. A kind of spiritual evolution would continue in Heaven, which was seen as a series of learning experiences and levels of existence through which one continued to progress even after death. The evolving spirits were compelled to share their insights with those in the earthly life, through mediums and trance speakers. Some of these spirits expressed opinions or gave advice on issues ranging from capital punishment to the interpretation of Biblical revelations and theology. The spirit of Swedenborg might appear to challenge conventional views on hell, and prophets such as Moses, or even Jesus himself, might communicate on questions of the afterlife.

Messages from these spirits could be quite specific and pointed. On August 31, 1882, medium Mrs. Lizzie S. Green received a written communication from the spirit of Thomas Paine (directed to the psychical investigator Carl Gustav Helleberg,) which began with:

> I am here to-day, sir, to say a few words in opposition to capital punishment. What is the argument in its favor? One citizen has taken the life of another citizen, and you say he has thereby forfeited his right to live. From whence do you get this doctrine? Does it belong to and is it a reflex of your boasted Christian civilization? The Mosaic law demanded an eye for an eye and a tooth for a tooth, but is this the doctrine of Jesus, the assumed founder of Christianity?[28]

Spirits sometimes made practical interventions by inspiring the invention and development of new earthly science or technologies. The telegraph, for instance, was supposedly inspired by communications from the spirit of Benjamin Franklin, who continued his experiments with electricity, and his love of new inventions in the after life.[29] Spiritualism was itself sometimes referred to as the "spiritual telegraph" in a conscious comparison to the parallel developments in earthly communication technology. Medium Amanda Jones explicitly claimed that her primary function as a medium was to receive from the spirits and pass along inspiration for new inventions. Doing just that, in 1873 she patented a new system for vacuum canning, thoughtfully given to her by the spirits.[30]

It was common for both male and female mediums to manifest the spirits of the founding fathers to counsel their fellow citizens on matters of vital contemporary concern. Many of these performances occurred in America in the years preceding the Civil War. The spirit of George Washington came via medium John Edmonds, for instance, to rebuke his countrymen for forgetting the principles of liberty on which the nation had been founded. Judge Edmonds, a respected lawyer and state legislator, was chief justice of the New York State Supreme Court when he began serious research of psychical phenomena in the 1850s. He wrote a book recounting his experiences, in which the spirit of George Washington was portrayed as a noble, confident presence who had appeared with an aspect of "great firmness, as if he could stand unmoved amid a conflict of worlds" to speak on the principles of American freedom, and the current controversy regarding slavery:

> Bound up as my heart even yet is in the continuance of its freedom; looking on its institutions as the great fountain of freedom that was yet to flow over the whole earth, I ask myself "Where now is the spirit that made us free?" and from dark and dismal depths alone a voice answers, "Here buried beneath the load of oppression and selfishness which has grown up and overwhelmed us."[31]

Many other spirits also expressed their opposition to slavery in the mid nineteenth century. Sometimes these spirits came from the recent past, appearing shortly after their deaths to mediums. California medium Fannie Green, for instance, "was often entranced by the spirit of deceased California senator Edward Baker and delivered trance lectures from him, in which his opposition to slavery, it was noted, had intensified since his death."[32]

The experiences and roles made accessible through these different types of trance performances liberated the female medium, as well as her audience, from the boundaries of space, time and history. They operated in a number of different ways: to feed an appetite for scientific inquiry or social critique, to reunite families separated by death, to provide transport to a personal Utopia, or to lay out a road map to Heaven. A reality for Spiritualist believers, spirit travel and indeed the whole phenomena of trance performance could, moreover, serve even for those who doubted the spirits as a compelling metaphor for the exploration of the Unconscious. William F. Barrett discussed the potential for access to some hidden part of the self in *On the Threshold of the Unseen*, as he explained his objection to the use of the word "medium." He said:

A "medium" is too often taken to imply an intermediary between the spirit-world and our own, whereas, many so-called Spiritualistic communications are nothing but the unconscious revelation of the medium's own thoughts, or latent memory, or "subliminal self."[33]

Whether the revelations came from spirits or from the unconscious, the power unleashed by their performance could be life changing, as the story of Cora Richmond, the century's most famous trance performer, will show.

10

Cora L. V. Richmond: Spiritualist Trance Star

Cora L. V. Richmond was born Cora Lynn Victoria Scott on April 21, 1840, in Alleghany County, New York, not far from the home of the Fox sisters in Hydesville. Cora grew up at time when passions were brewing over the issue of slavery, and the cause of abolition was beginning to sweep through the north, especially New England and western New York where she lived, the so-called "Burned Over district" with its turbulent history of religious and social reform movements. She came by her radical reformist tendencies naturally. Cora Scott's father David, a miller by profession, was a free-thinking follower of the Reverend Adin Ballou who preached and taught a form of "Practical Christian Socialism." Ballou founded a Christian Socialist utopian community called Hopedale near Milford, Massachusetts, in 1841. Experimental communities like Hopedale, or the transcendentalists' Brook Farm, were springing up all over America in the mid nineteenth century, and Cora's father David Scott moved his family to Hopedale in 1850, when Cora was 10 years old.

Cora Scott's youth and early experiences with spirit communication were recorded in H. D. Barrett's biography written in 1895. Barrett's work is unabashedly hagiographic, designed to construct a saintly persona for his idealized subject. Barrett had an interest in constructing such an image for the woman who co-founded the National Spiritualist Association which he headed. To validate Spiritualism's most important and popular practitioner would reinforce the legitimacy of the movement as a whole. Even given Barrett's agenda, however, some clues about the real Cora can be derived by reading critically, and between the lines of the quotes and anecdotes which he chooses to illustrate her life's story.

Cora was reputedly an emotional child, with frequent mood swings. She was a good scholar when she tried, and a fellow student remembered that she seemed "to take her lessons in without studying."[1] This skill would have come in handy if Cora was, as some skeptics would later suggest, indeed able to quickly read and retain vast amounts of written material on numerous subjects, which she could later present as "spiritual revelations" during her trance performances. She may in fact have had an extraordinary, even photographic memory, and have been extremely well read, although she stopped going to school at the age of 12, soon after the first manifestations of her ability to communicate with spirits began in 1851.

Cora successfully participated in "little theatricals" at school. One school mate remembers "her recitations of pathetic sacred poetry ... her rendering of the little poem 'We Are Seven,' so touchingly spoken as to invest the sweet lines with a significance unfelt before, even by those familiar with its words."[2] It is interesting to note that even this recollection of a childhood acquaintance emphasizes the affective power of her *performance* over the somewhat ordinary content of *what she performed*, a familiar and sweet but possibly trite little poem.

In 1851, Cora's father David Scott moved his family again, from Hopedale, Massachusetts, to form a new branch of the Christian socialist colony in Waterloo, Wisconsin. It was there that Cora, age 11, first began to exhibit mediumistic abilities.[3] The first manifestations were reportedly spontaneous messages from her deceased aunt (her mother's sister) via slate writing. Slate writing was a common mode of spirit communication, involving the mysterious appearance of writing, with a pencil or piece of chalk, on a piece of slate that had not been touched by the medium herself or by anyone else. Almost immediately after the first contact with her aunt, Cora also began to receive messages from the spirit of A. A. Ballou, the recently deceased son of the Reverend Ballou who had founded Hopedale. The younger Ballou had been the spiritual heir and shining hope of the religious community, and his recent death had been a devastating loss. Through Cora, the young man could continue his spiritual ministry after death. A. A. Ballou became the most important and frequent spirit manifestation for Cora in the early years.

The younger Ballou's spirit also communicated to his father Reverend Ballou through a "writing medium" named Elizabeth Alice Reed, who lived at the Hopedale community in Massachusetts, and through at least one other medium as well, named Mary Bowers. The elder Ballou was convinced enough of the truth of the manifestations of all three women to write a book about these and other spirit phenomena. Reverend Ballou's book included the caveat that even if some spirit phenomena appeared to reinforce views irreconcilable with Christian beliefs, no inference contrary to Christian doctrine should ever be drawn from them. He believed that not every spirit which came through was reliable or good, and that "*low* and very *imperfect* departed spirits sometimes manifest themselves."[4] Sometimes what appeared to be spirit phenomena were not the result of spirit activity at all, but were caused by the will or mind of the medium which Ballou referred to as an "undeparted spirit" rather than a "departed spirit."[5] Ballou also acknowledged that he personally had felt a strong desire for proof of his son's survival after death, though he did not go so far as to say that this desire made him more credulous.[6]

Ballou, as others did, posited an explanation for mediumship which implied a kind of double consciousness at work in the medium. Whereas ordinary people, he suggested, inhabited only one sphere — the material sphere — a few special individuals could also move into an "internal spiritual sphere." These people might then

> pass and repass from one of these spheres to the other, so as to partially blend their two consciousnesses into one. Dreamers, somnambulists, mesmeric subjects, clairvoyants, seers and what are called spirit mediums, are of this general description. They are more susceptible, receptive, and retentive of spiritual magnetism than the generality of people.[7]

As Cora's mediumship developed she began to embody and speak as other spirits, in addition to that of A. A. Ballou. One of the most significant was the spirit of a German doctor and surgeon. This spirit, intelligent, sophisticated, and skillful, spoke three languages (reputedly unknown to Cora herself) and controlled her for an hour each day in order to heal and treat people who came to her for help. She seems to have impressed many with her healing powers in the early years of her mediumship. A lady who recalled first meeting Cora in the 1850s on a pleasure boat cruise on Lake Erie remembered how the young medium was "most wonderfully controlled by a German Physician, in a dignified manner, prescribing for an invalid lady of the company."[8] At some point Cora's mother and aunt also became mediums, though neither became as famous as Cora. David Scott soon had his daughter appearing as a trance platform speaker in Wisconsin. Managing his daughter's paying career as a medium evidently superseded his dream of founding a new Hopedale in Wisconsin. Scott had demonstrated an interest in utopian schemes and progressive religion even before Cora's birth, and it is difficult to guess to what extent his motives in promoting her as a Spiritualist speaker were idealistic, and to what extent mercenary.

His control over her career was short-lived in any case. David Scott was dead by 1853, and Cora and her family moved back to Buffalo, New York. There she joined a Spiritualist society and became a regular trance speaker, and the major support of her widowed mother. Buffalo was relatively open to Spiritualists at the time. The Fox sisters had made appearances there not long before, and there were other mediums also working in the city. Cora teamed up with another young woman named Sarah Brooks to hold joint séances. In these performances, one of them would go into a trance and speak in a foreign language while the other one translated. Both could capitalize on the striking impression created by their youth and good looks, as well as linguistic feats nearly unbelievable from girls of their age and education.[9]

In August 1856, at the age of 17, Cora married the first of her four husbands, Benjamin Franklin Hatch. Hatch was over 50, and had been a practicing mesmerist or "magnetic physician" in New York City. The couple moved to the city shortly after their marriage, where Hatch began to manage her career, taking on the role previously filled by her father David Scott. Hatch rented halls or theatres for her performances, made necessary travel arrangements, and dealt with publicity and ticket sales.

Cora's fame, and the demand for her trance performances on the Spiritualist platform grew. A review of a performance at the height of her fame depicts how audiences saw her, and how she could charm them before ever speaking a word:

> Her attire was simplicity itself— plain and tasteful, and an entire absence of all unnecessary ornamentation — the exquisite taste with which one or two flowers were made to nestle amongst her light brown hair, the ever bright smile on her lips, the strange indefinable something that thrills you when her eye falls on you — all unite in producing such a favorable impression that many of her audience are psychologised [sic] before she rises to speak.[10]

Everything about her self presentation reassured the spectator that she was innocent and authentic, dressed as she was, simply, without affectation or the need to conceal herself in a fancy costume. She was also well-bred, showing "exquisite taste" in the arrangement of flowers in her hair; and endowed with an irresistible personal magnetism that could thrill with just a look. Another observer was equally impressed with her, but for different reasons. He dismissed the nonsense about spirits, but praised her skill in public speaking, saying, "To pass a candid opinion it is really to be deplored that this gifted lady ascribes her orations to spirit influence, as she really possesses abilities which she may reasonably be proud of."[11] What this observation did not take into account was the double bind of the talented Victorian woman, who was generally expected to hide her light under a domestic bushel, or at least shine only for those at home. Even with a gift for public speaking, a young woman wishing to remain respectable would have been less successful, less likely to attract large audiences for her serious, wide ranging lectures if she had *not* attributed them to the spirits, and presented herself merely as the humble conduit for their wisdom.

Cora was also remarkable for never resorting to physical phenomena or the materializations that became a popular sensation in the 1870s. She did not rap on walls or move tables or cause musical instruments to be played by unseen hands in the course of her trances. The only instrument she used was herself; enacting the spirits with her own voice and body. In her performances, spirit beings never showed up as independent entities, appearing from thin air or developing from ectoplasm extruded from her person or clothing. Her performances would always remain a matter of acting rather than creating special effects, although she never criticized the materialization séance, and was said to be "a firm advocate for its truth, and the firmest of friends to her co-workers in the cause, the phenomenal mediums."[12] Physical manifestations were flashy but complicated and difficult to sustain over a career of mediumship; and Cora's reliance on her talent for speaking and characterization, compared to mediums who depended on more problematic spirit materializations, may have contributed to the longevity of her career.

Audiences for Cora's platform lectures grew, and she was a favorite of Spiritualists. They supported her even when scandal threatened, and defended her vociferously in the Spiritualist press when, two years into her marriage, she sued her husband for divorce in the fall of 1858. The tawdry public proceedings, begun in the fall of 1858, involved shocking accusations and counter suits which went on intermittently until 1864. Because Cora was famous and Spiritualist gossip was highly newsworthy, the story was reported on with varying degrees of glee, outrage and disgust in the popular press; as well as in the numerous Spiritualist publications then in print. The charges Cora brought against her husband in the initial suit included both "sexual and financial misconduct."[13] Some of the documents still exist, and contain conflicting descriptions and interpretations of events that may have occurred during the brief marriage.

In the initial action, Cora accused her husband of deliberately deceiving her before they were married by leading her to believe that he had a thriving and financially successful medical practice which would more than enable him to fully support her and her widowed mother. He had also claimed to be well established in respectable New York society, with friends and acquaintances with whom it would be suitable for her to associate. Only after they had married and moved to New York did she find out that both the practice and the social circle were virtually non-existent. Moreover, he made no attempt to find any kind of work, but expected her to support him. It was only by his explicit "request and solicitation," she stated, that she began to give Spiritualist lectures in public again, in New York City, Boston and the surrounding areas.

It appears likely that Cora had hoped by marrying Hatch to be able to give up public trance performances, at least for the time being. Despite the celebrity and acclaim, the work could be difficult and sometimes demoralizing. An account of her experience in Lynn, Massachusetts, just a year before she filed for divorce reveals a devastating instance of public humiliation.

Cora had been hired for an exhibition of trance speaking at the Lyceum Hall in Lynn, Massachusetts, on November 17, 1857. The procedure on such occasions was to allow the audience or a sub committee of the audience to choose the topic to be lectured on. Topics were often scientific or philosophical, like "The Physical Basis of Life," "The Laws of Material Change," "Astronomy," or "Atoms and Molecules and Natural Crystals and their Composition." Cora, with the help of the spirits, had successfully lectured on difficult or abstruse topics before, but this it time was different. The audience was not ideal. Instead of being full of supporters and admirers, which seems to have usually been the case, it was composed of hostile skeptics and anti–Spiritualists. They evidently came in with the attitude that they would under no circumstances be gulled by this "delusion" and they were aggressively proud of their refusal to be made fools of, as, they supposed the rest of the world had been.

A letter written to a Boston newspaper by a committee formed from the Lynn audience opens with these words:

> The above named trance medium [Mrs. Cora Hatch] has recently visited Lynn, where, as in most other places, the most extravagant claims in regard to her eloquence, logic and scientific attainments were put forth by her friends and circulated all over the city. But Lynn, though always awake to new and startling views, on any and all subjects, and with a considerable portion of its population ready to adopt the new and the strange is, nevertheless, just the worst place in the world for a person of vast pretensions, who has not some solid foundation on which to build those pretensions. It proved to be such in an eminent degree to Mrs. Hatch on her late recent visit to this city. Every one of her claims to more than ordinary human powers or knowledge was utterly annihilated on Tuesday evening last. Never was there a more complete defeat than that suffered by Mrs. Hatch on that occasion.[14]

The letter goes on to describe how, in the first evening's lecture, Cora spoke in a very vague and general way on a topic only loosely related to the one given her, and went on for so long that no time was left for questions. The next night, the audience, who had felt cheated by the previous night's demonstration, decided to start off with a tough scientific test, pitting her against a "scientific gentleman present" to discuss "THE PYTHAGOREAN PROPOSITION."

> Upon the announcement of the subject the blood rushed to Mrs. Hatch's face til it seemed ready to force its way through the pours [sic] of the skin. She stammered and asked what proposition of Pythagoras the committee

wished her to discuss. Their reply was that the very learned spirits ought to know without inquiry of the committee. She was left to her own resources, and commenced a rhapsody on what she was pleased to term the Pytha*goran* philosophy.[15]

Cora hesitated. She spoke in a "bungling" manner and when her debate opponent said that she had completely mistaken the question, the audience "laughed at the lady's blunder." When the medium tried to cover by replying that she had not misunderstood, but preferred to discuss the philosophy rather than the mathematics of Pythagoras, "the confusion of countenance with which she uttered this transparent falsehood was noticed by the whole rational part of the audience."[16] A public school teacher and the local reverend then stood up and said that the medium did not know what she was talking about. "Confusion" and a disturbance followed, and Dr. Hatch stepped in. He began to "abuse and insult" in a coarse manner and with foul language the men attempting to expose his wife. Two more mathematical questions were quickly posed, and answered incorrectly by the spirits, and the contest was over. The Hatches left the auditorium in defeat.

Although this disaster seems to have been a rarity, and the majority of Cora's performances over a long and successful career were received with enthusiasm and gratitude, such an incident must have been unnerving for the young medium at the time. If she had not wanted to continue lecturing after her marriage, she might have felt misused, and resentful not only of the audience but of the husband who continued to put her in situations where public humiliation was always a possibility. If Cora had hoped for a normal, middle class Victorian life with a husband to support her financially and morally, and provide her with her own respectable home, this incident, and the marriage portrayed in the divorce documents would have been a bitter disappointment to her.

In addition to the financial problems, the divorce documents reveal sexual issues. Most serious of these was the suggestion that Dr. Hatch might have seduced female clients in his previous practice as a mesmerist. That an unscrupulous man might entrance a woman in order to take advantage of her had long been the biggest fear surrounding mesmerism. Cora claimed that her husband had not only told her of his infidelity to his former wife, but boasted that his "power and influence over females was such that he could have illicit intercourse with them, saying that 'had he access, no married woman could withstand his powers of seduction.'"[17]

Cora also claimed that her husband's excessive conjugal demands on her were injurious to her health. She may have been referring to the risks posed by pregnancy, miscarriage or abortion. There is no conclusive evidence that she was ever pregnant during her marriage to Hatch, although a letter exists in which she refers to an illness that might have been related. In all her subsequent marriages, Cora only had one child, who died in infancy, and her health may not have permitted her to bear other children. She suffered from "severe hemorrhages of the lungs" when traveling in Britain in the 1870s.[18] The symptom resembles those experienced by Anna Cora Mowatt when she was suffering from the illness (probably tuberculosis) which nearly derailed her acting career. Cora apparently never gave up trance lecturing completely throughout her subsequent three marriages, although she seems to have taken time off during her second marriage to Colonel Tappan, before and after the birth of her child. Except for a few letters from her, there is scant information in her own words about her personal life. But after the divorce scandal, her carefully tended public image, at least, attributed to her the ideal qualities that the Victorian public required of their female celebrities.

The Indian maiden Ouina, who was the most famous spirit role in Cora's repertoire, will be discussed in the next chapter. But she is only one of a number of spirits which Cora played in the course of her career. One of as many as 12 or more spirits, each with their own special field of knowledge, might be called on to discourse on a topic chosen by audiences at her trance lectures. Which spirit manifested depended on the situation, and the subject that was to be lectured on. Cora's transformation into these diverse characters was a theatrical highlight of the lecture. Her biographer Barrett wrote:

> The marked personalities of each of these controls is worthy of especial note, because of the diversity of the work which they had to perform. This diversity was so great as to completely change the personality of the medium at the various times when these divers controls were in possession of her organism.[19]

Cora would usually begin the performance with a prayer. (One skeptic, outraged at the blasphemy, declared this to be the most "offensive part" of her "performance."[20]) She would then make contact with the spirit who was to entrance her and speak through her. She claimed to be able to see the spirits as they came to her, but not to remember the content of what was spoken through her, or what she did, during her public lectures. A contemporary account describes her appearance in the trance state:

> Her eyes are rolled upward, a slight nervous tremor is observable through her whole frame, then an expression of mingled pleasure and surprise flits across her countenance, lips quiver, and the tears start in her large blue eyes, and then, with a spasmodic jerk, her faces resumes a natural expression, but all glowing with a new animation appears to be intently gazing at the spirits who are entrancing her.[21]

Her beauty and elegant simplicity, combined with the uncanny style of performance described above, and the voluble eloquence of the spirit lectures was difficult to resist. Though fragile in appearance, the trance state imbued her with a physical and mental strength she lacked otherwise, enabling her to answer questions "one after another with knowledge, fearlessness and force of logic as well as scientific statement."[22] The contrast between the woman in her normal state and the powerful, keen woman who emerged in the trance state was a large part of her fascination (as it was for Elizabeth O'Key and Anna Mowatt).

Cora's reception in cities and towns throughout Britain as well as America was a measure of her popularity. A witness of her arrival for a lecture in a small Yorkshire town described the crush at the door of the town hall where she was to perform. The local police had to be called in to control the crowd, and passages in the hall were so packed that Cora had difficulty making her way to the stage platform. Some of the crowd must have come just to jeer or disrupt the performance, but Cora was able to win them over. The witness was able to report with admiration that "the charming magnetism of our medium lulled that great surging mass, swaying it from resistance to acquiescence until the souls of the people were so stirred that with one accord ... cheer after cheer resounded through the Yeadon Town Hall."[23]

There are many stories of Cora winning over skeptics or detractors. Popular writer Nathaniel Parker Willis, who was left cold by the Fox sisters, claimed that he was so entranced by one of Cora's performances that he forgave her for transgressing the biblical injunction against women speaking in public. An even tougher critic, the "notorious Tammany ruffian" Captain Rynders, who expected to find her a "humbug" was won over by her skill and beauty, and declared himself to have the "highest possible regard for the lady's talent."[24] Henry James heard Cora give a trance lecture in 1863, and evidently used her as inspiration in his novel *The Bostonians* (1886). The novel is about a young, innocent but charismatic medium named Verena Tarrant, whose Svengali-like father is grooming her to follow in the footsteps of a famous and successful medium named Ada Foyt. Critics have noticed the similarity between James' descriptions of Foyt in the novel and photos and descriptions of Cora Scott. The "surprised look" and copious "ringlets" are seen in publicity photos of Cora Scott which would have been widespread in Massachusetts where she often lectured, and in Boston during the time James was working on his novel.[25]

Trance performers often lectured on controversial social or political issues. Like many other Spiritualists, Cora was a committed abolitionist. After the Civil War, she married a colonel in the Union army, W. Daniels, and moved with him to Washington, D.C., and later to New Orleans where Daniels was working out his commission during Reconstruction. Both were strong advocates for the freed slaves, and in addition to lecturing in Washington, Cora also wrote for the pro-freedmen press. Cora's biographer suggests that she and other Spiritualists did have some affect on national legislation during and after the war. "It is no secret," he wrote, "that certain efforts were made to incorporate into national law some of the hints and suggestions received from spiritual séances."[26] In January 1866 Cora described her activities to her friend, Spiritualist and former Quaker Amy Post, in Rochester, New York.

> Washington has rec'vd several new ideas through the humble instrumentality of the writer as [sic] I think many hearts [?] will have cause to remember the lectures which have been given foretelling the future — and war — until the nation shall be willing to do justice to *all*.[27]

Other passages in this letter demonstrate the close connections among Spiritualists and those working for the rights of former slaves. As Cora was writing her letter, she was sitting with a mutual friend, Sojourner Truth, who (unable to read or write herself) had asked Cora to write to Amy Post to find out how her daughter and grandchildren, who lived near Rochester, were doing. Cora described Sojourner Truth with admiration.

> I cannot tell you the pleasure it gives me to write for her, and to hear her talk — her words are like pearls cast from the crown of Truth — the world will long remember her when other names are forgotten. She is now one of the attendant managers in the hospital of the Freedman's aid society in this city and is doing a good and great work in behalf of those suffering people —... But she says "Where's Frederick — that his voice in not heard in this trying hour" — he is needed to instruct his people — and lead them on to Freedom. ["]There are important events transpiring here now and I am so glad I came to Washington. I have spoken twice to the color'd people in their churches — and am to give another [speech] this evening. They listen with profound attention and hearts full of interest — They feel that a great change is to come for them — but not through the government — it is distinctly understood that they are to *fight* for Freedom![28]

She then described a parlor entertainment she had given which represented the history of the "color'd race":

> A few friends were invited to witness some Tableaux which our household gave for their entertainment — among the most interesting scenes were the "Past — Present — & Future" which represented the three conditions of the color'd race. First as slaves — 2nd as soldiers & Freed men — 3rd as Free men & women — black and white all together. It was a glorious hit to these Washington "conservatives" and the color'd people were invited into the parlor and *shared equally* our hospitality.[29]

In August 1866, Cora and Colonel Daniels traveled to Rochester on a lecture tour, and stayed with Amy and Isaac Post. Later that year, Colonel Daniels wrote to the Posts to ask for financial assistance to enable him to leave his work so he could stay home with Cora to care for her. Cora was expecting a child, and gave birth to a baby girl soon after. In November Cora herself wrote again to the Posts, mentioning the "sunbeam" who had come to stay with them. "We are full of hope and joy and our darling 'Etta' sends her love and a kiss from her rosebud lips to you both."[30]

At the time Amy Post received this letter, she also received a request for money from Margaret Fox Kane, then using the married name she insisted she had a right to. Maggie asked to borrow $9 so she could travel to Rochester for a speaking engagement, promising to pay Amy back from the money she would make from the lecture.[31] Maggie's difficulties were a sad contrast to the happiness that comes through in Cora's letters.

Another letter from Cora to Amy Post, written in February 1867, shows Cora's continuing interest in the intersection of Spiritualism and politics. She wrote that Washington Spiritualists were divided on the question of translating their personal beliefs into political action. Those in the conservative camp only wanted to engage speakers who would "eschew politics entirely," and consequently had small audiences and weak lectures. The more radical camp, to which Cora belonged, were determined to do what they could in Washington in terms of "influencing Congress and bringing order out of chaos." Cora ends this letter, however, with words assuring her friend that no matter how absorbing or important her political work was, it would not detract from her domestic duties. Her maternal role, she insisted, made her happy, and now took precedence over her role as a Spiritualist:

> But I am so much of a mother that I am almost wholly absorbed in my babe and so much a wife that Husband and Rosebud are ever uppermost in my thoughts. I still am willing to be the instrument of any good that can be accomplished without injury to those sacred duties which claim everything.— Darling will finish this and tell you somewhat of politics baby is calling and I must close with love to your entire household....[32]

Her words sound genuinely happy, as if she might be able to achieve contentment in a fragile balance between her public and private life.

By July of 1867, the family had moved to New Orleans, where their political and social work was harder going due to the hostility of the population — or the white population at any rate. Cora attributed the people's resistance to change to the lingering effects of "Catholicism and slavery," writing, "It will be a long time before we shall see the shadows removed from the Southern people." On the positive side, she wrote, "The colored people are by far the best population to work upon, and there we shall begin." She added in closing, "We think of you the more because 'our kind' of society here is very limited."[33] By "our kind" it is not clear whether Cora meant Spiritualists or social liberals, although in fact the two were often the same.[34] It is possible she was referring to whites, since although New Orleans appears to have had one of the strongest communities of black spiritualists in the south prior to the war,[35] white southerners were less likely to welcome the practice, suspicious in part of its northern abolitionist associations.

This brief period of rewarding work and happy family life was not long lived. Within a few months of this letter, Cora, her husband Colonel Daniels, and her baby girl contracted yellow fever. Cora survived but Daniels and the child died. Although Cora married twice more, she never had another child. She seems to have spent even more time on social and political causes in the following years. After two failed marriages and the death of a child, work in the form of political activity and trance speaking, as well as being the most obvious means of financial support available to her, must have also been a comfort and welcome distraction. Women often had personal reasons, many times involving loss, for turning to Spiritualism. Cora's friend Amy Post, for instance, had turned to the spirits for comfort after the death of a child.

Cora became a speaker and fund raiser for the Louisiana Homestead Association to help poor families (both black and white) in the Reconstruction south. She frequently lectured (often controlled by Ouina) on the plight of the native American Indians. From 1868 to 1870 she served as vice president of the American Anti-Slavery Association, which had begun to focus its efforts on Indian rights. In 1869 Cora married once again, this time Colonel Samuel F. Tappan, a fellow advocate and worker for Indians' rights, and she continued her public trance performances.

Cora continued to work for the rights of freed men and native Americans throughout the 1870s, as well as continuing her trance lectures. She became minister of the First Society of Spiritualists of Chicago and in 1877 divorced her third husband Colonel Tappan, and married William Richmond, a member of her congregation. She was still politically active in 1887 when she met with the governor of Illinois to plead for the lives of the Haymarket anarchists. In 1893 she gave a paper on Spiritualism at the Columbian Exposition in Chicago and, after many years of resisting the organization and centralization of the movement, helped found the first National Spiritualist Association, becoming its first vice president. Cora lived another 28 years after the publication of H. D. Barrett's biography of her in 1895. She died at her home in Chicago in 1923. To the end, she used her trance performances and the celebrity they brought her in the service of the marginalized or voiceless.

11

The Performance of "Ouina" and the Racial "Other"

Mediums holding private séances most often contacted spirits with personal connections to the sitters—friends and relatives who had passed to the other side. Public trance speakers on the Spiritualist circuit were more likely to manifest heroes or celebrities from the past (like Washington) who would be recognized by a large number of the audience. The colorful spirits of Indians, blacks, and gypsies embodied by Cora Richmond, Mowatt, and O'Key represent yet another category of manifestations—the socially marginalized or exotic (which sometimes overlapped with the celebrity or hero type in the case of spirits like Pocahontas). Because the Indian, the Black and the Gypsy were also recognizable and popular dramatic types, the appearances of these spirits could mean a better chance of commercial success for the medium or trance performer, since an audience for exotic characters like these had already been developed in the legitimate theatre of the day.

Still, the motives for trance performers were not always purely mercenary, and there were more complex reasons for the embodiment of Indian and black spirits. Many mediums and Spiritualist speakers, especially the women, exhibited a high degree of compassion and empathy for spirits of marginalized figures. There was an affinity between the female medium and the spirits of those who in their earthly incarnations, had also experienced a lack of legitimate power or a right to be heard. This makes sense from the dramatic or performative point of view. Most actors believe that at least some degree of identification or sympathy with the character they play is necessary for an effective performance. Victorian women, still largely barred from the mainstream of social and political power, could have instinctively understood the alienation and marginalization of the spirits they manifested. This affinity could only be increased by the knowledge that the manifestation of such spirits in trance allowed them to capitalize on the mutability, talent for acting, and sensitivity to occult influences which they were already assumed to possess.

The sensitivity of women spiritualists to the oppressed can also be seen as an extension of the generally "democratic" nature of Spiritualist philosophy and practice, which in turn was seen as part of a larger tide of change in the era. As Spiritualist editor S. B. Brittan said in the essay quoted earlier, the nineteenth century was "an age of Rapid Transitions" in which the "distinctions of caste and color are swept away" to the joy of those who, while oppressed and bowed down had "made little or no complaint."[1] Among the formerly "bowed down" who now found a voice were, of course, the native American Indians. The number of them manifested in trance performances, and the commonly repeated themes of their communications, were proof of this. A further reason for "playing Indian" may have been that it was, for Americans, "one way to solidify and express 'new national ideals,' to revel and rebel...."[2] This mix of revelry and rebellion comes through in the combination of radical rhetoric and energetic native dance and song in these performances.

Pocahontas, Tecumseh, King Philip, and Red Jacket were some of the most frequently manifested Indian spirits. They had celebrity appeal, and often served as the medium's primary "spirit guide," filling her with urgent wisdom to impart to her hearers. Cora Richmond's Ouina, for instance, was regarded by some as a prophet of the new "religion" of Spiritualism. Wendell C. Warner, a politician, diplomat and spiritualist lecturer, compared Cora Hatch and her Indian spirit Ouina to Jesus, writing, "What Christ is to the Christian, what Mahomet is to the followers of Islam, what Buddha is to the dwellers in the Orient, what Luther was to the reformation, was Mrs. Richmond, Ouina and the guides to me."[3]

Cora Richmond and "Ouina"

In her many years as a Spiritualist trance speaker, Cora Richmond was controlled by several different spirits. In addition to the German doctor who practiced healing, these included the spirits of recently deceased public figures like the late President Andrew Jackson, Benjamin Rush and Theodore Parker. But the most theatrical character Cora manifested, and the one which brought her the most celebrity, was the Indian maiden Ouina. Ouina began to appear to her around 1851, and soon became the most important of her "spirit guides."

An entire chapter of Cora Richmond's biography is devoted to Ouina's short but dramatic time on earth, and her story is as romanticized as Cora's own life. Ouina's biography and some of her "writings" were also published in 1882 as "Ouina's Canoe and Christmas Offering, Filled with Flowers for the Darlings of the Earth." Ouina was the brave, self-sacrificing Indian girl of American mythology, a type of Pocahontas. Cora first began to manifest Ouina at a time when the figure of Pocahontas was becoming firmly entrenched in the consciousness of the American people as a national, native heroine. Ouina's adventurous story shared features of the Pocahontas legend, which was being dramatized in the legitimate theatre. When Ouina first began to make her appearances on the Spiritualist stage, heroic Indians of both sexes were already familiar figures in popular melodramas.

The story of the original Pocahontas, the Indian Princess who rescued Captain John Smith, had been retold countless times since the earliest days of American nationhood; it was popular enough, for instance, to have been included in Noah Webster's first reader. When the seventeenth-century English explorer Smith was captured by Pocahontas's father's tribe, she threw herself between the white man and the Indian braves gathered to kill him, and bravely saved his life. In many versions of the story, the two fell in love. The legend was dramatized for the stage as early as 1808, in a version by J. N. Barker titled *The Indian Princess or La Belle Sauvage*, which played successfully in American theatres, as well as in at least one theatre in London. Another successful version was *The Indian Prophecy* (1827) by George Washington Parke Custis, in which the heroine was typically beautiful, brave and resourceful, and attuned to the natural world in a way impossible for white men to be — she was described as a "nimble fawn." The only Pocahontas play written by a woman, *The Forest Princess* by Charlotte M. S. Barnes, was published in 1844 and was probably inspired by the popular hit *Metamora* (1829).[4]

As in other Indian dramas of the period, the embattled native hero of *Metamora* was a "clear manifestation of the contemporary American psyche and situation."[5] American citizens were conflicted about harsh new government policies directed at native Americans, and expressed their ambivalence about the treatment of the native Americans in the growing use of the "noble savage" as a symbol of American Nationalism. This ironic symbolism was reflected by the new dramas featuring Indian heroes, and reinforced when the first great American tragedian, himself a focal point of rabid nationalism, took on the title role in *Metamora*. The play, by John Augustus Stone, was written specifically for Edwin Forrest, who had offered a prize for the best American drama — with the best role for him. The noble savage Metamora fit the bill, and it became one of Forrest's most successful roles. Edwin Forrest was infamously the focus of conflict between American and British patriots in the Astor Place riot of May 1847. The incident started when a violent fight broke out between Forrest's supporters and the supporters of rival British tragedian William Charles Macready during an appearance by Macready at the Astor place theatre. The eruption of hostilities was the culmination of a bitter feud between the two actors which had gone on for several years, fueled by xenophobia and class hatred. When Forrest supporters, the rowdy and rabidly anti–British "Bowery B'hoys" disrupted Macready's performance, a riot broke out which virtually destroyed the interior of the theatre before moving out into the street. In the open plaza in front of the theatre, paving stones were pried from the ground and used as missiles. Ultimately troupes had to be called in to subdue the fighting, but not before 22 people were killed and hundreds injured.

The upsurge in the number and popularity of Indian plays produced in American theatres followed the passage of President Andrew Jackson's Indian Removal Act of 1830. Jackson's bill made it legal for white settlers to confiscate Indian land, and forced the Indians themselves to migrate further and further west. "Public outcry against the inhumanity and injustice of the bill was loud and long," and the Supreme Court upheld the Indians' rights in a lawsuit brought against the U.S. by the Cherokee nation. Despite public protest, President Jackson refused to back down or implement the court's ruling.[6]

Years of conflict between whites and Indians followed, and by the end of the 1840s, just as Spiritualist manifestations were beginning, most Eastern Indian tribes had been pushed west of the Mississippi River. As early as 1846, Indians were being regarded with a kind of nostalgia, like a race of exotic animals close to extinction, suitable for preserving in lavish picture books like those of Audobon's. A book was published in Philadelphia in 1846 titled *History of the Indian Tribes of North America, with Biographical Sketches and Anecdotes of the Principle Chiefs. Embellished with One Hundred and Twenty Carefully Colored Portraits*.... It was favorably reviewed in a British periodical, by an author who wrote admiringly, "Perhaps never has savage life worn a form so inviting and poetical as in the annals of Indian tribes."[7] Included in the book is a portrait of Pocahontas in her "civilized" dress. It was also in this period that portrayals of Pocahontas began to appear in reliefs and paintings in the U.S. capitol.

Both Cora Richmond's Indian spirit Ouina and the idealized Pocahontas of myth and drama were variants of the Ideal Woman. Rarely, a play might include a nod to gender equity, as in *Pocahontas: A Historical Drama* written in 1837 by Robert Dale Owen (son of the English social reformer Robert Owen), which portrayed a heroine who believed that women should "stand beside/Not crouch behind" the men who love them.[8] Owen was unusually sympathetic to women, which may have rendered him more susceptible to their influence, or more likely to be duped by them and their spirit manifestations, as the infamous case of his experiences with "Katie King" will show in the next chapter.

In most cases, despite her "savage" origins, the Indian maiden exemplified the qualities of conventional white heroines, willing to sacrifice herself for others. Sometimes, like Pocahontas, she married a white man. Less often she bore his children — although audiences loved the classic story of the civilized white man falling in love with the pure Indian maiden, they were more squeamish about any portrayals of the fruits of miscegenation. The Indian heroine was willing to give up everything, including her life, for love — particularly for love of the white race. The title character of the play *Oolaita or The Indian Heroine* is an instinctive "Christian": merciful and generous, bravely confronting her own savage tribe to save innocent whites.

Cora Richmond's Indian maiden Ouina fit this model of martyrdom. Her story, as told through Cora, was thrilling and romantic enough to have been immensely appealing, even if it hadn't been related by a spirit. When "Ouina" as she came to be called, first appeared to Cora, the spirit referred to herself as "Shenandoah" which was the name of her birth place, her tribe and her father; she also answered to the diminutive "Shannie." Ouina/Shannie claimed to have been born in the mid fifteenth century on the coast of what is now Virginia. Her mother, Cliona, was the daughter of a Spanish sea captain and the only survivor of a shipwreck. Cliona was rescued by the "king" of the local Indian tribe, Shenandoah, after having washed up on the beach during the storm that killed her father and his shipmates. When the Indian leader brought the strange girl back to the village, "she was looked upon as a visitor from another world; and the children of the forest stood ready to fall down in worship at her feet."[9] King Shenandoah took the Spanish girl for his wife. Cliona became beloved amongst the Indians, and was credited with improving their lives by her gentle and civilizing influence. She sometimes missed her European home. To comfort herself, she sang Spanish songs, though like a dutiful wife she hid her sorrow from her husband. Cliona died giving birth to her baby girl Ouina, who was then cared for by her doting father. In her idyllic girlhood, Ouina/Shannie gamboled about the forest like a Disney heroine.

> She wandered at will among the forest trees, and sent her light birch canoe flying over the waters ... she seemed to have the power to talk with the birds in the trees and with the animals that roamed through the valley ... she loved the beautiful in life and was sportive as a fawn, but she never had the heart to kill even an insect.[10]

At the age of 15, about the same age at which Cora had become a professional medium, Ouina had a vision. Her mother's spirit warned her that the tribe faced peril from both an Indian chief from the west who would conquer them, and from "white people" from the east, who, "in a cloud like a white bird borne on the wind and flying over the sea," would decimate the remains of the tribe.[11] The prophecy eerily suggests the Native American ghost dance rituals and visions which foresaw the destruction of Indian culture in America, as the inexorable westward movement of white settlers throughout the nineteenth century pushed tribes out of their lands. Warnings of the destruction of their own race, like that received by Ouina, were also reminiscent of the millennial frenzy of groups like the Millerites, who had predicted the end of the world for October 22, 1844. For Cora, Ouina's vision put a personal face on the persecution of native Americans, fuelling the medium's fight for Indian rights for the rest of her career.

Like many melodrama heroines who were too good for this earth, Ouina's story had a tragic ending. After meditating on his daughter's grim prophecy for 7 days and nights, her father decided that she had been possessed by an evil spirit to foretell the destruction of the tribe. Ouina had to be sacrificed. She was tied to a tree to be shot by arrows, then burnt. A young Indian brave who tried to save her died in the attempt. But miraculously she was spirited away by "angels" before a single shot was fired, and presumably took up her spirit life, as she was never seen on earth again.[12]

Cora might have connected Ouina's persecution to the plight of some female mediums who were accused of being in league with the devil, subjected to legal action, or confined to insane asylums. English medium Georgina Weldon actually wrote a play about her narrow escape from a husband and "mad doctors" who tried to have her committed. To be a medium was a risky proposition in the early days. Mrs. Helen O. Richmond, who saw Cora and Sarah Brooks give one of their joint séances in Cleveland in the 1850s, wrote of the courage of the two young trance performers. She described how Cora and Sarah, "dressed in Indian costumes, made by direction of the spirits—would be controlled by Indian girls.... It was a brave thing to do in those days, when to be a spiritualist was to be ostracized, and to be a medium, given over body & soul to the tender mercies of the evil one...."[13]

Indians were commonly associated with demonic or supernatural power, and were thought, as a race, to possess natural spiritual abilities. In an article titled "Gleanings in the Corn Fields of Spiritualism" (*The Spiritual Magazine* of May 1861) William Howitt noted that American Indians had always had "...their prophets, or medicine men: their dreams and séances; their firm persuasion of the visitations of good and evil spirits. They have wonderful accounts of prophecies which heralded the white man for ages...."[14] Such prophecies, and spirit outcry against whites' treatment of Indians, were a common feature of Spiritualist trance performances.

On August 4, 1882, the spirit of Tecumseh, leading a band of Indians, communicated the following through medium Mrs. Lizzie S. Green:

> We come to speak to palefaces at Washington. Me talk for my people — the redfaces in the hunting-grounds in the Far West where the sun goes down. Poor redfaces, nearly all gone. Paleface kill many and drive them from their old and much loved hunting-grounds. You tell them to go on reservations, and the big father at Washington take good care of them. They Go. Big chief at big city send paleface agents to give them blankets, ponies, guns, and bread to eat. Paleface agent start big store in wigwam and cheat redface, and give him fire-water to make him mad and crazy. When my people see how they are cheated they get mad and put on war paint and kill much. Big paleface chief say to blue-coat warriors, go and kill redface and make them come back and let paleface agent swindle much more.

The Indian spirits in this particular communication offered a solution for this problem, which coincided with enlightened white thinking in general, and probably with the attitudes of the medium personally. Instead of persecuting them, the Indian spirits suggested, the whites should help them to assimilate by educating their children, giving them "paleface" clothing and big homes and teaching them to raise crops for food and to sell. In this way, the Indians might be coaxed to leave their "hunting grounds" peacefully, and learn to "love paleface and paleface ways."[15]

The portrayals of Indian spirits not only elicited public attention for their plight, but also marked their status as tragic Heroes in the great National drama being played out throughout the nineteenth century. One such heroic character appeared in the performances of an eighteen year old female medium who was contacted and controlled by a spirit who identified himself as the son of the fabled Indian Chief Black Hawk. In the Aristotelian tradition of tragic heroes, the Indian leader had undergone both reversal and recognition, coming through suffering to enlightenment and ultimately forgiveness for his white oppressors. He describes his protective and instructive relationship with whites. His words via the medium were recorded complete with "native" patois and grammar:

> Me one that watches over his bones buried under your house. Me been in the spirit land one thousand and fifty moons. Me mean you no harm, though me come from a low sphere, and me am offensive to the pale-faced angels. Yet me love the spot where me passed me happy youthful days on the then wild hunting grounds. Me cherish no bad feelings towards the white skin, who in days of yore wronged me red brothers of their homes. The Great Spirit teaches I to forgive. And me now would eradicate, with tears of blood, all wrong, and have peace and happiness in the stead of penury and despair....
>
> Me can hear the hum of strife. Like the buffalo's cry it falls on me ear, and as he turns his dying eye on I, me strive to staunch the wound me has made. Me friend, me can tell you of naked woes which me did suffer. Me was once a proud chief. Me had only to rub the golden god of me wishes and slaves

rose up at me bidding. Even now a pang arises in me soul, as me am tortured with forgotten memories. Me tell you more some time. Me no understand English well. Old Black Hawk — me say old, because me Son the Famous Black Hawk.[16]

Several elements of this speech are revealing of white Christian attitudes and beliefs about Indians. The spirit's statement that he comes from a "low sphere" and may be "offensive to pale faced angels" echoes the words of William Blake's little African boy in the poem — "My skin is black / but O my soul is white."[17] Even as the Indians deplore their treatment, they acknowledge their own racial and religious inferiority to the race that has wronged them. Reassuringly for whites, the afterlife is also segregated — and whites need not fear that Indians will try to claim equality with them. Many Spiritualists did argue that there were in fact "separate spheres" in the afterlife for the different races. The justification for this segregation was ostensibly that spirits would not want to mix socially in Heaven, any more than they had on Earth; and that such natural divisions of divine space would be more familiar and comfortable for everyone, helping all spirits to feel at Home when they had passed over.

The issue of reconciliation with, or Native Americans' forgiveness of, the white race is often spoken of, or implied, in the words of these Indian spirits. Indian spirits collectively seemed to take on the burden of absolving the white race of the crimes committed against them in nineteenth century America, even as those crimes were going on. The "abundance of forgiveness" offered by Indian spirits in an afterlife gave whites, in the words of Robert Cox, "a sort of antinomian ticket out of collective guilt."[18]

Ambivalence pervades the manifestations of Indian spirits by other mediums as well. A medium named Jane M. Jackson, for instance, in an article written for *Banner of Light* ("The Indians" in the October 3, 1868, edition) sturdily defends Indian rights, citing an 1854 treaty. At the same time, she condescends to them, urging whites to treat them kindly, give them land, and teach them how to cultivate it so that they can become "civilized" and "industrious." She describes with pride and affection her own spirit guide, the paternal and powerful King Philip, and speaks of

> his noble qualities, forgiveness of injuries, faithful care, his wisdom, love and protection. I thank God that he permits this good chief to return and control mediums. I ask his advice with the same reverence and confidence that I would an earthly parent, and obey him the same. No act or thought of mine escapes his watchful care. He sees what I need and obtains it for me. Dearly do I love the name he has bestowed upon me, "White Flower." As my chief controller I reverence him, but I do not love the less other Indians who watch over me. It would be unjust to them to do so. I am deeply grateful to

all my red brothers and sisters, and words could not express my love and gratitude to the "medicine man" who ever watches over me, the child of his adoption.[19]

In this case, as in many others, the Indian spirit is a character who is both real and ideal. He is King Philip, the specific historical individual who actually lived; but also the "Good Father." In this regard, many spirit manifestations shared a key quality with the stage characters they resembled. They satisfied, in Martin Meisel's formulation, the audience's appetite for representations of the real, idiosyncratic and individual which at the same time symbolize a larger, "universal" type, like the "Good Father" or the "Ideal Woman."

King Philip is also a "medicine man," a role which Indians could continue to play in the afterworld. Some Indian spirits were still eager to practice their healing powers, even advertising their services, through their mediums, in Spiritualist periodicals of the day. This "notice" appeared in *Mind and Matter*:

> Me, Red Cloud, speak for Blackfoot, the great medicine Chief from happy hunting grounds. He say he love white chiefs and squaws. He travel like the wind. He go to circles. Him big chief. Blackfoot want much work to do. Him want to show him healing power. Make sick people well. Go quick. Send right away. No wampum for three moon.[20]

In the paper's layout, this ad appears on the same page with offers for services from other mediums and trance healers, such as the one promising to send special magnetized paper, which could heal or develop the recipient as a medium, for only 3 3-cent stamps for 3 months.

Sometimes an Indian spirit functioned as a kind of personal body guard for his medium. Emma Hardinge Britten, for instance, felt comforted by the presence of an Indian spirit called Arrowhead, who she described in her autobiography. "He seemed always impressed to come to me upon momentous occasions or before periods of apprehended danger. Sometimes he would stand over me, waving his war hatchet above my head, as if in the attitude of protection. Sometimes he would dash his tomahawk in the air, as if in the act of striking an enemy."[21]

An 1855 report from the *New England Spiritualist* tells of a female medium who channeled the spirits of two boys named John and Jim whose spirit guide was a wise and protective Indian. The boys had been very poor, but good and charitable boys, in life, and were greatly enjoying the spirit world. John said through the medium that he had learned that "the way to feel good was to do good" and he continued his work as a spirit, by softening the hearts of people who had contact with the little beggar children. The fatherly spirit of John's Indian guide also tells the spirit boy that one way for him to help his mother, who is still living, is to influence those around her on earth to be kind to her.[22]

Not all Indian spirits were so serious. Some seemed more interested in entertaining, than counseling those to whom they appeared, as seen in this account of 6 Indian spirits (coming through 3 female mediums) in a circle at Roxbury. This rollicking band

> gave us the songs in their peculiar style of singing, in the pure Indian dialect, (of which the mediums knew nothing while in their normal states) while one of the mediums accompanied their singing by dancing (as we suppose) in their native style, which was her (the medium's) first lesson in the art.[23]

The popular medium Lizzie Green's trance performances of Indians show a wide range of tones. In some cases the spirit messages were meant for a specific person, and the characters she was called to manifest were individual, eccentric and almost Dickensian: "In the earlier stages of my mediumship and still sometimes I was frequently controlled to personate the peculiar and characteristic idiosyncrasies of spirits during earth life, and to delineate their sickness and death." At other times she received spirit communications with a more universal significance: "prophetic warnings" and "revelations" as well as "panoramic visions of past events of those both in and out of the body, and of events to transpire in the future of earth life."[24]

In some of her more casual or playful séances, attended by "leading citizens" in Cincinnati in the 1880s, Lizzie Green was reported to have been guided by

> a rough and gruff Indian spirit, who called himself "Chip," and referred to his "medy" and the power he had to invoke and exercise in keeping her in profound trance condition. Ever and anon, a smart, witty and talkative Indian maiden who called herself "Winnie" by the permission and condescension of "Chip" would take possession of the medium, and talk most freely and interestingly to each and all of the members of the circle.[25]

Another spirit Lizzie Green performed was the Indian "Swanee," who while imposing to look at, was also cheerful and accommodating. Swanee was described as being "indispensable" by one of the mediums he contacted, apparently because he was more fun to have around than the more common run of grave and tedious spirits who appeared only to lugubriously "chant Te duems, and converse of naught but heaven and beatification." Instead, Swanee made a "jolly boon companion and a merry welcome guest" who enjoyed hunting, especially with a man named Clark Dye. When the spirit and the man went hunting together, Swanee sportingly made use of his clairvoyant skills to help Dye locate the birds they sought to shoot.[26] The tone and content of Indian communications in trance performance ranged, as this shows, from the sublime to the ridiculous. The same was true for the trance performances involving black spirits, although given the urgent and divisive nature of slavery, most spirit communications on the subject were more serious.

Slavery and Blacks in Spirit Performances

The plight of the slaves before the war and the freed men after was never far from the minds of Spiritualists. How then, did this affect the trance and mediumistic manifestations of the blacks at the center of this massive upheaval? Guilt seems to have been an undercurrent in many trance performances. Spirits sometimes came through mediums to reassure them that they, at least, were intervening for the slaves on earth by comforting them and softening the hearts of their masters. These spirits urged the slaves to remain patient and docile, to expect justice not in this life but the next, counseling them to "pray on, hope on, poor slave; thy bondage is of earth, not heaven; thy poor bleeding heart will be freer and brighter, and far happier in the spirit home than the one who calls thee slave, and lashes thee with many stripes of suffering."[27]

The legacy of slavery and the ravages of the Civil War were frequent topics of spirit communications. Medium Fanny Green described a spiritual journey she took to Heaven before the Civil War, where she encountered the spirits of brave negroes who were being rewarded for having fought for "their country" (the United States) during the American Revolution. Green blamed the founding fathers for not having recognized the contributions and rights of negroes at the time. She also, like many others, interpreted the catastrophic Civil War as a kind of historical karma for the sins of the nation at its birth, in not freeing the slaves. What the founding fathers had "claimed for themselves," she declared, "they denied to others; and for this immeasurable wrong they are now paying the penalty, in outflowing rivers of blood—in broken hearts and desolated homes."[28] Her words clearly echo the declaration in Lincoln's second inaugural address that the war was a penance for the national sin of slavery. Some Spiritualists believed that it was the spirits who had revealed this truth to Lincoln, and also claimed that the president's Emancipation Proclamation was inspired by spirits who were contacted when Mary Lincoln brought a medium to the White House for séances in the 1860s.

Spirit rhetoric energized the Abolitionist movement before the war, and led many abolitionists to became fervent Spiritualists. A Spiritualist periodical claimed "we number two or three millions of Spiritualists in the United States; and I suppose without an exception, every elector among us has quietly gone into the anti-slavery ranks, whatever may have been his previous party attachments"—a claim, the article argued, borne out by the results of the 1860 election. The article titled *The Death Blow of American Slavery from Spiritualism*, added, "Spiritualism is doing a mighty work here just now" but "without getting the credit for it. I allude to the dissolution of our Union, on the slavery question."[29]

Spiritualists continued to call on the activism that had been engendered by the abolitionist movement before the Civil War to inspire reform after the war. In 1882, the medium Lizzie Green received communications from both William Lloyd Garrison and William Wilberforce urging listeners to reinvigorate themselves with the zeal for reform which had won the battle against slavery, and focus their efforts now on other corrupt institutions and governmental practices. Garrison declared that the spirits were gathering to help in this new and important work, which included "reform in the currency, reform in the civil service, a complete overhauling and reconstruction of government, the overthrow of rum, and the enfranchisement of women."[30]

Wilberforce, in his spirit communication, compares the former bondage of negroes to the current enslavement of the working classes, warning that only through immediate and radical change will the "civilized world" avoid another apocalypse like the Civil War. "You are now fastening upon yourselves a slavery more appalling and degrading than African slavery ever was," he rages, "the slavery to which I refer now is the slavery of labor to capital." With the force of a biblical prophet, or a Cassandra of ancient times, he paints a terrible picture of the future:

> Unless a spirit of justice and fair dealing shall speedily characterize the treatment of the poor toilers by their wealthy employers a mighty crash will come, and outburst of indignation in revolution that will render the bloody scenes of the past of trivial moment in comparison. The elements are generating, the storm clouds are surely gathering, and at a moment when least expected they will burst upon the country and the world in proportions only equaled by the fierceness of the conflict and its bloody issuers. Let those whom it concerns beware. I beseech them, beware in time.[31]

The apocalypse of the Civil War and the legacy of slavery remained the rod by which all future national crises would be measured, and a constant goad to the consciences of liberal Americans. Even Spiritualists who fought mightily for abolition and worked for freed men's rights were not immune to a general sense of white guilt and fear; like an undercurrent it was often present below the surface of Spiritualist discourse and performance. Many spirits seemed to be manifested for the purposes of subtly reassuring whites that negroes, like Indians, upon achieving the serene vantage point of the after life, would bear them no ill will, and would be eager to forgive their former oppressors.

One spirit performed through a female medium, told the story of his earthly life as a slave. He had been tormented and abused by his brutish owner, until he wished to die, and in a mad fury he had murdered the man and been beaten to death in retaliation. In the spirit land, he was being taught to repent his sins and become worthy of moving to a more advanced sphere of existence. While grateful for the joys of the beautiful heaven in which he found himself, the former slave still harbored bitterness about his treatment on earth, and hatred for the former master. But, he recounted, "the spirits who taught me lessons of love and truth told me these feelings were wrong — that I could never become pure and good, or a fit inhabitant of those spheres of beauty, unless I forgave those who had been my former enemies." The spirits turned to the power of theatrical vision to convince him, and presented him with a vivid scene of the tortured agonies of the spirit of his former master, who was still imprisoned in his own blind rage and sin. The spectacle was effective. Like good theatre, it deeply moved the former slave, and aroused such pity in him that, he recalled, he "hourly prayed that the suffering of my tormentor might cease. He was to be pitied while I was in such a lovely place."[32] Like the Indian spirits manifested by mediums for the enlightenment of their oppressors, the negro spirits also become the instruments of revelation and salvation for white men.

Equally reassuring was the former slave spirit's declaration that white spirits would not have to mix with blacks in the afterlife, any more so than they would with Indians. He was told by his heavenly guides, recounted the black spirit, "that I should be permitted to inhabit a country where there were none but those of my race and kindred, if I was so-minded."[33] This plan bears an odd resemblance to schemes on earth to move former slaves to their own colony in Liberia, and would have been seen by many liberally minded people, including Spiritualists, as an acceptable and even compassionate solution to the problem of what to do with the freed men.. The segregation of spirits into separate spheres seems difficult to reconcile with Spiritualist ideals of equality—and to frequent Spiritualist references to the "democratizing" tendency of the afterlife. This paradox may have been easier to accept for some Spiritualists since the separation was regarded by the spirits themselves, as medium Elizabeth Sweet was told, as something that was based on internal affinities, not extrinsic features; and that segregation was something that was chosen, not forced upon spirits in the afterlife. (Even today the belief that "separate but equal" is possible continues to have staying power for some.) Any self-selected divisions could be attributed to the Romantic notion of sublime spiritual affinities and it had nothing to do with base material or physical matters. "Kindred sparks may be lodged in the most uncouth and ill-seeming coverings" the spirits reminded their listeners.[34]

This sentiment informs the work of Epes Sargent, the Spiritualist author who first introduced actress Anna Cora Mowatt to mesmerism. Sargent studied and wrote about manifestations of negro spirits in his book *The Scientific Basis of Spiritualism* (in which he also described Mowatt's trance experiences). Referring to the spirits of those who had lacked power on earth he wrote, "God hath chosen the foolish things of the world to confound the wise; and God hath chosen the weak things of the world to confound the things which are mighty...."[35] Like Cora Richmond's biographer who marveled that "a little child should lead them," Sargent emphasized the heavenly subversion of earthly power relations which characterized so much of Spiritualist phenomena. Credence given the biblical injunction "first shall be last" certainly played a part in people's willingness to take inspiration or guidance from the spirits of traditionally weak or low status figures of *all* kinds, including women, children, blacks and native Americans.

From a practical point of view, the presumption that all these groups were more highly sensitive or susceptible to supernatural influences made it more likely that they would be conduits for spiritual communications. Ann Braude cites evidence of this with her anecdote about the Lieutenant in the Union army who was a Spiritualist, and told of a contraband slave he had encountered who was a medium. The union soldier concluded from his observations that the "negro character" was "intuitive, inspirational, religious and altogether mediumistic"; qualities also attributed to women, and which, it would have been assumed, made both groups susceptible to spirits.[36]

The earliest philosopher of Spiritualism, Andrew Jackson Davis, had connected blackness with femininity, and whiteness with masculinity.[37] This connection was made again by W. E. B. Du Bois in his 1903 work *The Souls of Black Folk*. Du Bois attributed the spirituality of negroes to the high degree of "double consciousness" they possessed, and associated it with the "feminine" in opposition to the masculine and material side of mainstream American culture.[38]

Du Bois used the concept of a double consciousness in blacks to refer to other issues, including the "internal conflict in the African-American individual between what was 'African' and what was 'American,'"[39] or a struggle between two competing identities. The manifestation of a double consciousness (or other personalities) in response to role conflict has been discussed in the case of Victorian women torn between incompatible ideals, as well as in cases of dissociative identity disorder. That negroes may have also experienced double consciousness, and for reasons related to internal conflict, proves another link between women and blacks in the nineteenth century, and one that can help explain the appearance of black spirits in female trance performances.

Perhaps because fewer examples of blacks' experiences overall were documented, there is apparently less evidence about black *trance performers* than there is about black *spirits* manifested by white mediums. The dearth of evidence of African American mediumship in the nineteenth century is nonetheless somewhat surprising, Robert Cox contends, given the inclusiveness of Spiritualism and the similarities between Spiritualist practices and West African religious rituals.[40] One example of black trance experience was reported by Charles Poyen, who introduced mesmerism to New England in the 1830s. He reported observing trances among the slaves who worked his parents' plantation in the West Indies. The similar gifts and faculties in the souls of diverse peoples "under whatever skin, black, red or white" indicated to him an equality among people which he saw as a justification for the abolition of slavery.[41]

Black activist Sojourner Truth converted to Spiritualism in her later years, although there seems to be no evidence that she had trance experiences. An article in the periodical the *New England Spiritualist* of May 26, 1855, mentioned an illiterate black girl in New Orleans who became a medium and was able in the trance state to write messages in Latin, Greek, Hebrew and Italian.[42] Another black medium was described in Emma Hardinge Britten's massive account of American spiritualists:

> In Macon, Georgia, a colored girl, who was an excellent physical medium, frequently exhibited the feat of thrusting her hand amongst the blazing pine logs, and removing it after some 60 seconds without the least injury. She always insisted, however, that she would only perform this feat when "Cousin Joe," whom she called her guardian spirit, was present and bid her to do it.[43]

The Georgia girl's "Cousin Joe" is reminiscent of the "Negro" manifested by the English housemaid Elizabeth O'Key in Dr. Elliotson's mesmeric experiments in London in the 1830s. Both these negro spirits were described as guardians or protectors, heroically intervening with almost superhuman strength or powers for the girls when they were physically challenged or threatened; forming an alliance of those who in their earthly lives, at least, had suffered a similar marginalization.

12

Spiritualism Crosses Over to England: Florence Cook and the Materialization Séance

Trance performances in London took a turn away from serious communications and political rhetoric towards sensational theatre in the spring of 1872, when a 17-year-old girl named Florence Cook began to manifest the spirit of an entity calling herself "Katie King"—with a fully formed "spirit body." Katie claimed to be the daughter of seventeenth-century English pirate Sir Henry Owen Morgan, who himself appeared under the name of "John King" through several other mediums. Observers were thrilled by this new spectacle. They had seen mediums entranced or possessed by the spirits before, but to see the bodies of spirits form right before their eyes, and feel their cold touch as they moved around darkened séance rooms was breath-taking. The materialized "Katie" was Florence Cook's "passport to success."[1] Cook's performance was soon emulated by other young women, who followed her example in introducing "new, thrilling, and daring phenomena and a theatrical style of mediumship which emphasized visual spectacle and display."[2] Among the "stars" who performed full form materializations were Mary Rosina Showers and the "Newcastle mediums," 18-year-old Miss Annie Fairlamb and 19-year-old Miss C. E. Wood. Miss Fairlamb and Miss Wood held séances in tandem and produced the spirits of "Pocha" (a childlike version of Pocahontas), and a mischievous little girl called "Cissie." The two child spirits played and frolicked together during séances, no doubt appealing to the Victorian audience's predilection for child performers and "infant phenomena" as Charles Dickens put it.

Before appearing in English séances, the first "full form materializations" of spirits had been seen in America as early as 1861. Kate Fox, who with her sister Maggie had been responsible for the first famous spirits rappings at Hydesville, was one of the first to manifest spirits with physical bodies. She "repeatedly conjured up the materialized form of the deceased wife of Charles Livermore, a wealthy New York banker."[3] Previously, in the 1850s, spirits had usually made themselves known through knocking, or moving furniture or other objects. Gradually they began to inhabit or possess their mediums, who would then physically enact their voices, gestures, and personalities. "Materialization" of a separate and distinct "body" of the spirit was the next logical step. A "spirit body" allowed a spirit to temporarily assume a body of its own, rather than to borrow the medium's body. This allowed sitters at the séance to physically touch and interact with the spirits as entities independent of the mediums. In theatrical terms, it was the *ne plus ultra* of Realism.

The public's increasing appetite for visual realism and visual stimulation was a major factor in the development of realistic spectacle in trance performance, as it was in theatre. Spiritualist phenomena began to gravitate towards more elaborate physical manifestations, and the first full form materializations began to appear as Realism was gaining ground in the theatre in the 1870s. These kinds of embodiments, as well as her personal star power, quickly made Florence Cook one of the most celebrated mediums in England.

The English had been quick to hop onto the bandwagon of Spiritualist phenomena when it crossed the pond with American mediums in the 1850s. This was partly because of the groundwork laid in Britain by a tradition of traveling mesmeric shows and medical exhibits of mesmerized subjects like Elizabeth O'Key in the 1830s. Dr. Elliotson, who had continued to experiment and write about mesmerism throughout the next two decades, eventually became a Spiritualist believer. Others who had been mesmeric trance subjects or performers in England became Spiritualist platform speakers or mediums when trance séances crossed over from America at mid century.[4]

The burgeoning Spiritualist practices of the English also had a precedent in their own radical religious revivals. As the ground in America had been made fertile for Spiritualism by the Great Awakenings, the English were primed by the experience of groups like the "Irvingites," trance-speaking followers of the charismatic Edward Irving, the Scottish Presbyterian minister with whom Elizabeth O'Key had been associated before becoming the subject of Dr. John Elliotson's mesmeric experiments.

Edward Irving's sermons began to attract attention in his small London church in the 1830s. To accommodate the growing crowds, which included members of the literary elite like Charles Lamb, William Hazlitt and Samuel Taylor Coleridge, who considered him a great orator, he had moved from his first small London church to a larger church in Regent Street which could hold 2,000. Irving had been censured by his Presbytery for his unorthodox theology, but his congregations loved him, and continued to flock to his services to listen to his riveting oratory. Even before he began his ministry in London there had been rumors of speaking in tongues and Biblical miracles among his parishioners back in Scotland. In July 1831, sudden manifestations of glossolalia broke out among both men and women in Irving's London church. The sensational outbursts, in which the subjects seemed to be in a state of trance, spread through the congregation, and caught the attention of the public.[5] Reports of the odd goings-on among the "Irvingites" filled newspapers, and were mostly treated with derision. At first the prophecies seemed to be in gibberish, or in unknown languages, but as they became more intelligible, it became clear that the ideas being communicated were radical and irreconcilable with existing church doctrines. Some suspected demonic possession. The manifestations divided the congregation, which dissolved, leaving Irving and a few loyal followers to search for a new location to hold their services. They were given use of a building owned by Robert Owen, the social philosopher and philanthropist who would, a few decades later, become a great supporter of the Spiritualist movement. Robert Owen was also the father of Robert Dale Owen, who would become embroiled in the Spiritualist "Katie King" scandal in America in the 1870s. The subversive performances of the Irvingites and of Elizabeth O'Key were a significant British precedent for the trance performances of Florence Cook and other young British mediums who sprang up on the Spiritualist stage in the 1870s.

Still, it was an American, Mrs. Hayden, who held the very first séances in London in 1852 and impressed some English observers as a dramatic new "prima donna." She had been given an enthusiastic send off by American Spiritualists, who were proud to be exporting the first emissary of the new movement to their backwards British cousins. An American daily paper referred, perhaps ironically, to the Spiritualists "sending a mission to benighted Europe," but this did not dampen American pride in the fact that the New World, not the Old, had been the first to receive spirit revelations. It was because, they believed, "here was greater political and religious freedom, and freer toleration of new ideas, than in any other quarter of the globe."[6]

When the medium Mrs. Hayden debuted in London, her sheer skill as a performer was remarked upon by Charles Dickens, who had long had an avid interest in both mesmerism and theatre, and was himself a riveting performer in staged readings of his own works. Spiritualist investigator Arthur Conan Doyle reported Dicken's assessment of Mrs. Hayden: "If ... the phenomena developed by her were attributed to art, she herself was the most perfect artist, as far as acting went, that had ever presented herself before the public."[7] It is not clear from Dicken's praise, or from Conan Doyle's account of it, what opinion the great novelist had of the *authenticity* of Mrs. Hayden's phenomena. But perhaps the literal truth of her performance was less important to Dickens than its artistry, and he was certainly qualified to judge both.

Mrs. Hayden did, however, convince at least one other public figure that her phenomena were genuine. Noted socialist philosopher and industrial entrepreneur Robert Owen, after numerous sittings with her, was impressed enough to convert to Spiritualism.[8] On the other hand, writer and philosopher G. H. Lewes, an early student of the psychology of acting, was skeptical, and after one sitting declared Mrs. Hayden a fraud.[9] Regardless of her ability to contact the spirits, Mrs. Hayden proved herself to be energetic and intelligent enough to construct a successful career for herself beyond Spiritualism. She later achieved a measure of success and respectability when she became a practicing medical doctor in America.

Scottish medium Daniel Dunglas Home followed Mrs. Hayden to London in 1855, and did much to popularize mediumship among the English upper classes. Home (or Hume) was an attractive and personable performer who easily worked his way into the confidence of society ladies with his gentlemanly persona. His performing abilities, in addition to his refined manners, made him the "perfect house guest" for hostesses seeking someone unusual to show off at parties. In addition to holding séances, he provided recitations, readings, and musical concerts.[10] Home was considered one of the most successful physical mediums of the age, known for remarkable séances in which he levitated heavy tables, played musical instruments, tossed objects around a darkened room, and altered himself physically by elongating and shortening his own body. His most spectacular feat was to levitate himself above the heads of the séance sitters, then float around the room and out the window, to re-enter moments later. His charm was considerable enough for him to be twice married to women with fortunes. Scandal resulted from his relationship with rich widow Mrs. Jane Lyon, who adopted Home and made him her sole heir. She later revoked her bequest, and sued to force Home to return her money. Elizabeth Barrett Browning was fascinated with Home, but her husband Robert Browning skewered mediums in general and very likely Home in particular in the scathing poem "Mr. Sludge."

Although apparently more common among the upper class and aristocracy at first (even Queen Victoria and Prince Albert were known to have tried "table tipping" at least one time),[11] mediumship and séance circles spread to British families of every class. For some, séances were a parlor game to pass the time, and for others, bereaved mourners, a way to contact the spirit of a lost loved one. Séances were held in both private and public settings. Many lower and working class Britons became interested in Spiritualism through lectures held at Mechanics' Institutes or Temperance Halls; in these cases trance performers often spoke on radical religious and social issues.[12] Emma Hardinge Britten reports that mediums spread among poorer classes through those who "sought aid at the Mesmeric infirmary."[13] Servants in upper class households were exposed to trance mediumship by observing the séances held by their employers, and some later became mediums themselves. There were reports of mediumistic circles in homes in America and Britain centering around a maid. The attraction of mediumship for the most marginalized member of the household is obvious, and there may have been slightly less opprobrium attached to the practice in a servant than for a higher class woman. It could be chancy for a servant at times, though. A servant girl in a New York family in 1855 was reported to have come under the control of spirits who enabled her to lift heavy objects, include a barrel of flour which she carried up a flight of stairs, and move a heavy table. She also exhibited clairvoyance and writing through the spirits (though she was thought to be illiterate). In this case, her employers were so unnerved by the display of these powers that they fired her.[14]

Spiritualism in Britain got another shot of respectability when Briton William Stainton Moses became interested. Stainton was a curate, an Oxford graduate, and a master at University College school. He wrote substantial scholarship on the subject of Spiritualism under the name M.A. Oxon. The spirit guides he manifested were suitably erudite, among them Plotinus (known as "Prudens"), Athenodorus (known as "Doctor") and St. Hippolytus (known as "Rector").[15]

Even as the English developed their own mediums, American mediums continued to tour and perform in England. Cora Richmond was a frequent visitor to Britain, and Kate Fox married an Englishman and lived and performed in England for a time. Mrs. Lenore Piper, who would later be the subject of extensive scientific scrutiny by William James, among other psychic investigators, also traveled to England. Mrs. Piper often manifested her spirit guide, a creole doctor named Dr. Phinuit, who

> gave his messages by speech, the medium being in a trance but not at all immobile. She would stand up and would put her thumbs, man-like where her waistcoat arm-holes would have been if she had had them.[16]

A pair of brothers from Buffalo, New York, Ira Erastus and William Henry Davenport, impressed both American and British audiences, even those who did not believe in the spirit appearances. J. N. Maskelyne, a famous magician, paid tribute to their technical skill, which greatly exceeded that of most other mediums. "The hole-and-corner séances of other media, where with darkness or semi-darkness, and a pliant, or frequently devoted assembly, manifestations are occasionally said to occur, cannot be compared with the Davenport exhibitions in their effect upon the public mind."[17] Seeming to consider them fellow professionals, Maskelyne admired their technique without weighing in on the question of the "truthfulness" of their manifestations.

Interestingly enough, the Davenports had made their first appearance in England at the home of one of the most successful men in nineteenth century theatre, Dion Boucicault. Boucicault was a melodramatist of Irish origin, whose plays were equally popular in Britain and America, and whose productions featured startlingly realistic scenic and special effects. Boucicault knew effective theatre when he saw it, and he evidently saw it in the performances of the Davenport brothers. On September 28, 1864, the Davenports, assisted by another medium, Mr. Fay, held a private séance for Boucicault and invited guests at his Regent Street residence. The combined celebrity of Boucicault, the Davenports, and the invited guests made this a news item, and it was reported in some detail by the *London Times*, the *Daily Telegraph*, and the *Morning Post*. *The Post* noted:

> The party invited to witness the manifestations last night consisted of some twelve or fourteen individuals, all of whom are admitted to be of considerable distinction in the various professions with which they are connected. The majority have never previously witnessed anything of the kind. All, however, were determined to detect and if possible expose any attempt at deception. The Brothers Davenport are slightly built, gentleman-like in appearance, and about the last persons in the world from whom any great muscular performances might be expected. Mr. Fay is apparently a few years older, and of more robust constitution.[18]

A couple of weeks later the performance was repeated for 24 distinguished witnesses, and described in detail by Boucicault in a letter to the *Daily News*.[19] The Davenports and Mr. Fay also began giving public séances that month, and began touring the provinces.

For mediums like the Davenports, who gave both private and public performances, and Mrs. Hayden, who charged for her services, the issue of professionalization was tricky. The respectability of female mediums in particular, like that of actresses, was especially threatened by taking money for any kind of public appearance. But despite the risks to reputation, mediumship, like acting, was a growing field of work for Victorian women. Numerous professional mediums advertised for work in the dozens of Spiritualist periodicals that had sprung up in response to readers' avid interest in the movement. By mid century, Ralph Waldo Emerson had included "medium" as a new profession in a list of American professions.[20] In 1860, a Mediums

Mutual Aid Society had been founded in Boston, to help develop, instruct and protect professional mediums. Average pay might be $5 for a sitting away from home and $1 for a sitting at home; this could be enough to provide a living.

The mother of an English medium wrote to the *Spiritual Magazine* about her distress over "fraudulent" mediums who were making it difficult for genuine mediums like her daughter to earn money. "I had hoped," she complained, "that this power in my daughter would have been the means of aiding, and honestly too, in the support of our family, for my husband is at times scarcely able to work for asthma."[21] A good living was no more guaranteed for mediums than it was for actresses, however, and only those who became "stars" in either line of work could count on financial success. Enough mediums "ended their careers as paupers to make one wonder whether expected monetary returns were the primary inducement to become a professional medium."[22] Emma Hardinge Britten made money publicly lecturing and writing about Spiritualism, and supported paying mediums for their work; but she defended herself against the charge of being mercenary by pointing out that she herself did not take money for séances or private sittings, and argued that

> if money or public applause were my object, I have two professions, — the stage and music, — in either of which I am a proficient, and could treble my present earnings, besides exchanging celebrity for notoriety, ease for fatigue, and adulation for ribaldry, scorn and persecution....[23]

Moreover, anyone receiving money for their mediumistic skills was more likely to be accused of fraud. Some Spiritualists, even some who were practicing mediums, were adamant about the necessity for mediums and trance performers to avoid any appearance of having a mercenary interest. For one thing, doing any kind of work for money was still considered vulgar among some members of society. And to charge for manifesting spirits, as if it were a theatrical entertainment, could undermine the seriousness of Spiritualist philosophy. An article in a Spiritualist periodical decried the fact that anyone purchasing the services of a medium had to beware of being "barnumed."

> If the manifestations of Spiritualism are a truth, as we know them from frequent personal observation to be, it becomes a duty to see that they are not Barnumed by mediums, or used fraudulently as money-making implements.[24]

In another article about the professionalization of mediumship in the May 1862 issue of the *Spiritual Magazine*, the author responds with a firm "no" to the rhetorical question "If doctors and lawyers are paid for their services, shouldn't mediums be paid as well?" No, he answers because mediumship is a free gift of God, and taking money both taints its practice and raises doubts about its authenticity. "If professional mediumship were discontinued and abandoned, Spiritualism would soon rise above the region of vulgar suspicion into a serener atmosphere...."[25]

Emma Hardinge Britten, not surprisingly, disagreed. She argued that the British prejudice in particular against paying Spiritualists to practice their "sacred" gifts was inconsistent with the custom of paying clergymen of all other denominations for their services.[26] And despite ethical considerations, for some women, mediumship and trance performance were not only one of the few options open for earning a living, but could also represent an opportunity for some emotional freedom and self expression. Judith Walkowitz argues that "humble female mediums with marital problems frequently looked to the Spiritualist lecture and séance circuit as a source of employment and refuge from unhappy homes."[27] A career as a trance speaker was certainly such a refuge for Cora Richmond, who remained largely self supporting through several failed marriages and widowhood.

Some female mediums could avoid the necessity of accepting direct payment from clients or sitters if they could attract generous patrons willing to give them a stipend to live on. Florence Cook, for instance, was supported for at time by a wealthy gentleman named Charles Blackburn, who paid her the equivalent of what a curate at the time might earn. Blackburn was an ardent believer in Spiritualism and the spirits — especially "Katie King," a provocative spirit who often elicited an ardent response from male sitters. The powerful effect of Katie's appearances through Florence Cook, and through other female mediums, provides one of the more interesting and peculiar stories in the history of nineteenth century trance performance.

Florence Cook

Florence Cook was born to a working class family in Hackney, London, and gave her birth date as 1856, although it may have been earlier. Around the age of 14 she began to fall into trances and show evidence of spiritualistic gifts. Claiming to be guided there by the spirits, she found her way to a local Spiritualist Circle, the Dalston Association of Inquirers into Spiritualism, where she learned how to develop and use her mediumistic powers.[28] Shortly afterwards she began a kind of apprenticeship with local mediums Frank Herne and Charles Williams. At that time Charles Williams was under the control of the spirit of the wife of John King (Sir Henry Morgan the pirate) and mother of the younger Katie King (Annie Morgan) who would soon began to control Florence. Frank Herne received financial support from Charles Blackburn, a wealthy Spiritualist from Manchester who was a member of the Dalston Spiritualist Association (the same gentleman who became Florence Cook's patron and protector, enabling her to practice her mediumship without having to charge a fee to the sitters of séance). Blackburn was also a supporter of the journal *The Spiritualist*, whose editor Mr. Harrison gave Florence endless free publicity and increased sales by writing numerous articles about her mediumship. Some joked that the paper should be renamed "Miss Florence Cook's Journal."

Florence's career clearly exemplifies the benefits of private patronage as well as the economic inducements for mediumship. The regular stipend Florence received from Blackburn was an important source of income for her parents and younger siblings. Her parents encouraged her mediumship, and her mother in particular seems to have done a lot to manage her career, and later on to manage Charles Blackburn. After Florence herself fell out of favor with Blackburn, her family maintained a close relationship with him, with her mother and sister moving in with Blackburn and eventually inheriting part of his property.

The exact circumstances of Florence's falling out with her patron are somewhat murky, but the rupture evidently had to do with her secret marriage to Frederick Corner, the son of family heavily involved in the Dalston Spiritualist Association. Another factor may have been her relationship with Dr. William Crookes who investigated her powers, as will be discussed later. By the time Blackburn was disenchanted enough with Florence to discontinue his stipend to her, Florence's younger sister Katie Selina had also become a medium, and Blackburn was convinced to resume support of the Cook family through his patronage of Katie Selina. He supported them until his death in 1891, when he left Mrs. Cook and Katie Selina the bulk of his estate in his will.

Florence's mediumship had meant a subtle upward movement for the family in terms of class. They were able to afford a home in a better neighborhood, and later move into Blackburn's own residences when he died. And Conan Doyle makes an interesting comment on the derivation of the spirit name "king" which suggests that the embodiment of that particular spirit also had a class connotation. Conan Doyle observed of the spirit called Katie King that "her earth name had been Morgan, and King was rather the general title of a certain class of spirits than an ordinary name."[29] And it should not be forgotten that Katie King's father John King, had, in his earthly manifestation as Captain Henry Morgan, been knighted by Charles II before passing into the spirit world. Florence Cook, by associating herself with a presumably higher, or at least upwardly mobile class of spirits, was attempting to re cast herself as a higher class woman in earthly society. And because the "class" of Florence as Katie was conferred by the spirit world, it could not be easily contested by that earthly society.

But whatever their "class," the spirits manifested by Florence Cook were distinctly mischievous if not downright provocative. One of the earliest séances Florence gave was at the home of Thomas Blyton, the secretary of the Dalston Spiritualist society, with only Blyton and Florence's mother and father in attendance. It was dramatic enough for Blyton to report it in a letter to the editor of the journal *The Spiritualist*, and gives a preview of the kind of improprieties that would characterize Florence's performances at the peak of her career. Thomas Blyton described how

> a chair was twice placed over my head, without its legs first touching me; then a portion of Miss Cook's dress was removed, and after being whisked in our faces, was thrown over my head, while a hassock was thrown into my lap, as well as a vulcanite necklace which Miss Cook had been wearing.[30]

In later séances, Blyton was once again the target of spirit high jinks. Alex Owen describes an incident in which the long suffering Blyton was "tied up by 'Katie King' during a séance, covered with a tablecloth, then an antimacassar, and made to sit still whilst a chair covered with various musical instruments was balanced on his head. The lights were then raised and much amusement afforded the other sitters."[31] Such tricks seemed to become more common in séances after the advent of the full form materialization of spirits. There were "numerous reports of unfavored sitters being beaten around the head, kicked, insulted, and robbed. Ladies were frisked and parts of their clothing removed. Gentlemen were teased and tickled."[32] The kind of intimate contact described in performances like these exceeded anything that could be found in even the most risqué theatre of the time.

Titillation does not explain the whole of the fascinations of Florence's manifestations of Katie King. As far as spirit phenomena, or theatrical characters, went, Katie had everything going for her. She had a notorious father who was literally a "pirate of the Caribbean," a sensational life story, a tragic death, and as her medium a beautiful golden haired young girl with considerable charms of her own. Florence's "Katie King" became as famous, or more so, than Cora Richmond's "Ouina." Katie King's story begins with her father, the notorious pirate Captain Morgan.

John and Katie King (Henry Owen and Annie Morgan)

The spirit Katie King/Annie Morgan came by her trouble-making personality naturally, as the daughter of John King/Henry Morgan, legendary pirate. According to the *Oxford Dictionary of National Biography*, the real Henry Morgan was born in Wales in 1635. He showed up in the Caribbean around 1658, sometime after the British capture of Jamaica from the Spaniards in 1655. Like other English adventurers at the time, Morgan probably came to take advantage of opportunities for trade or pirating. Although the war between England and Spain was officially over by 1660, the British government continued to turn a blind eye to, and even encourage the plundering and harassment of Spanish ships. Some British subjects, like Morgan, were granted a "privateering license" to lead raids against the Spanish, which Morgan did with spectacular success in the late 1660s and 1670s. Morgan married the daughter of the deputy governor of Port Royal, and in 1674 was knighted. He was appointed Lieutenant Governor of Jamaica, and later served as Governor for several years before his death in 1688, apparently of liver failure brought on by excessive drinking.[33]

Although Morgan never acknowledge himself to be a "buccaneer," he is known to have been responsible for some of the most savage acts of piracy on record. The ODNB notes that after capturing Panama from the Spanish in 1671, Morgan and his men hunted down survivors and "Spanish reports suggest that the privateers were unusually brutal in torturing captives to obtain information about hidden property and many died in the process."[34]

Morgan would have made a potentially thrilling villain, manifested in the dark quiet of a séance room, although by the time Morgan's spirit, now calling itself John King, began to appear in Victorian séances, the pirate was reformed, and his messages were often centered on repentance and forgiveness. These themes were especially stressed in the tale the spirit John King narrated to Dr. Henry Child in 1874.

Dr. Child, who described himself as the spirits' "amanuensis" took dictation and published John and Katie King's story under the title "Narratives of the Spirits of Sir Henry Morgan and his Daughter Annie, usually known as John and Katie King: Giving an Account of Their Earth Lives, and Their Experiences in Spirit Life for Nearly Two Hundred Years." In the book's Introduction, Dr. Child tells of how John King came to him in a séance with mediums Mr. and Mrs. Holmes in his home in Philadelphia, and asked Child to write his life story. The spirit of Katie appeared shortly afterward with the same request. So Child says he set aside an hour every day for the spirits to come to him so he could take dictation. In writing that the spirits "came to him in his study" Child could have meant that the spirits appeared in distinct "bodies" of their own, or that they appeared in the bodies of the two mediums, Mr. and Mrs. Holmes. Child's reference, and indeed most references to spirit apparitions after the advent of "full form materializations" are ambiguous. Accounts by Robert Dale Owen of séances during this period at Child's home make clear that Katie and John King appeared as independent entities separate from the mediums. Either way, Child's narrative is an intriguing account of spirit performance, and valuable for what it tells us about the background and traits of two popular and successful spirit characters.

The first chapter of Child's book, the John King narrative, conveys in essence the same figure of a daring, powerful and cruel leader that emerges from what is known about the real historical Sir Henry Morgan. However, John King's story of his earth experiences as Henry Morgan departs from the known facts and chronology of Morgan's life in several significant ways. For instance, John King/Morgan never mentions the real Morgan's marriage to the daughter of the Lieutenant Governor in Jamaica, but claims instead to have married a woman named Katie Lambert in London in 1659, during a brief period of domesticity before returning to pirating in the Caribbean. King also fails to mention the most extended and brutal period of Morgan's privateering in Jamaica, although acknowledging that he did, as Morgan, commit many barbaric acts in his lifetime. And while the historical Morgan never had children, John King's version of his life (both before and after death) prominently features his daughter Annie Morgan or Katie King.

As John King tells it, his crimes did not end immediately once he had departed the earth. In his first few years in the Spirit world, he continued his trouble making, intervening as a spirit in earthly affairs beginning soon after his death in 1688. He boasts that he had been involved in the supernatural events that precipitated the Salem witch trials, saying

> I was present and took an active part in certain manifestations which originated in western New York, and were soon transferred to Salem, Massachusetts, about the year 1690, which were continued until we discovered that they were causing too much suffering on account of the ignorance of the people....[35]

John King also brags (and name drops) about his role in the American Revolution, saying, "I knew Franklin, and was often with him and others in planning that war which resulted in your independence from the yoke of Great Britain. I took an active part in the war, for I had a good deal of fight in me then, and it has not all gone."[36] There seems to be no record of King repeating this boast when appearing in British circles through British mediums, although in these as well he comes across as the self-aggrandizing "braggart soldier" of ancient comedy. King also claims to have been the instigator of a number of manifestations of Native American spirits, including the raucous spirit theatricals produced by the Koons family in Athens County, Ohio, in the 1850s.

King began to regret his willful wickedness, however; and in the Spirit world he was allowed to learn from his mistakes, repent, and seek forgiveness. He takes the opportunity to enlighten Child, and through him the reader, about the true nature of Hell, which for him took the form of an agonized conscience and the painful "goadings of remorse" when he encountered his victims in the after life. Like Dicken's Jacob Marley, he is compelled to try to make amends. Although, as he acknowledges, "The orthodox world consigns such persons as myself to a lake of fire and brimstone," in the Spiritualist after life there was an opportunity to progress to a higher plane no matter how sinful one had been in life.

The spirit John King credits the spirit of his daughter Katie King, who had preceded him to the Spirit world, with setting him on the road to salvation. "...Katie, my darling Katie, was the charm of my life, the blessed ministering angel to me...." The Katie he describes is an idealized portrait of the angelic young child who sets her corrupt elders on the true path, her ability to influence him rivaling, it seems, that of God himself. "You may talk about God, and the power of great spirits to draw man up higher, but there is no other power that I have found which equals the love of a pure innocent child."[37]

This sweet angel, however, is hardly recognizable in the actual manifestations of the spirit of Katie, through either Mr. and Mrs. Holmes, or Florence Cook. The Katie manifested by Florence Cook, for instance, was often, to say the least, ill-behaved. Impertinent, naughty and at times seductive, the Katie most sitters saw was livelier, cheekier and a lot more fun (both for the medium and the audience) then one might have imagined given Child's narrative. Katie King certainly did, however, have a life worthy of a stage character, as we find out in the next chapter of Child's book, in which she takes over the narrative and describes her own life as a series of dramatic incidents and scenes suitable for a melodrama heroine.

Annie Morgan the pirate's daughter was born in London in 1660, to a drunken and abusive father and an apparently ineffectual mother. Her earliest recollection, from when she was about three and a half years old, was of a scene in which, as she says, her father "terribly abused my mother; indeed he almost killed her. I was dreadfully alarmed, and screamed until the neighbors rushed in to see what was the matter. The shock of the scene seriously injured my health..."[38] (Child 42).

Annie Morgan was also witness to the most significant historical event of her time. "I was in London when St. Paul's church was burned; that was at the great fire in 1666. Though I was then but six years old, I distinctly recollect that fearful conflagration."[39] As with John King, part of Katie's dramatic appeal was clearly her eyewitness accounts of great moments in history.

Katie tells of how her father deserted her and her mother for a number of years to travel back to the West Indies. She and her mother barely subsisted on their own until Katie was about 10 years old, when, as in a fairy tale, the father suddenly returned one day "with presents and the means of making us quite comfortable."[40] Katie remarks on the joyous, almost miraculous effect of his homecoming, making it seem even more like the wish-fulfillment climax of a melodrama plot. "Those only who have experienced such a change as this from abject poverty to a condition in which we had all our desires gratified, can realize what our enjoyment was at this time." But the good times were not to last; Katie reports that "Father, like many men under evil influences, resolved that he would amend; and for a short time, alas, too brief we were a happy family. His dissipated habits, however, recurred, and when he had squandered the means which he had brought home, he renewed his abuse of mother."[41]

The story then becomes a temperance play, when Henry Morgan, in a drunken rage, strikes his wife in the face, disfiguring her for life, before deserting the little family once again, this time permanently. Worse is to come, when the vulnerable young Annie, at the age of 17, meets a man who seduces and abandons her. She dies giving birth to a daughter who also dies. Looking back at her degraded life as Annie Morgan, Katie refers to this untimely death as a release from the "prison house of the body."[42]

In Child's narrative both John and Katie King exhibit a philosophical bent that is difficult to reconcile with their mischievous behavior when they actually manifested themselves in séances. Their narrative performances for Child, do, however, conform to Child's tastes and expectations. Child was a medical doctor, an educated and serious believer in the ideals of Spiritualism, and not a casual thrill seeker. The spirit performances, in both content and style, are appropriate for their audience.

Katie, for instance, tells Child that her ultimate and sacred purpose is to aid humanity in its spiritual evolution through her materializations and revelations. Part of her mission is to disabuse religious believers of some of their misconceptions about the nature of God — errors they cling to which hinder their spiritual progress. Notions of the gender of God, for instance have it all wrong. "Those systems of religion which recognize only a male God are exceedingly deficient and imperfect and have done much to retard the progress of the race."[43]

John King lectures on the uncivilized practice of capital punishment, arguing that it brings out the worst in people and in spirits, and impedes progress in both this life and the next:

> If mankind could realize the influence of capital punishment, not only upon the victim, but upon humanity and all those spirits who have any zest for such scenes they would abandon it at once. It is not only a relic of barbarism, but is great evidence of cowardice on the part of society to put forth its strong arm and pinion a helpless human being, and, after having him entirely within its control, to plunge him into this world....[44]

This speech, like much Spiritualist rhetoric, seems designed to appeal to an educated, humane and liberal audience.

Florence Cook's Performance of Katie King

In December of 1873, less than 2 years after beginning her performances of the fully materialized Katie King, an incident occurred which may have given Florence second thoughts about continuing her sensational manifestations. During a séance held on December 9, a man named William Volckman physically seized the spirit Katie in an attempt to prove that it was a dressed up Florence Cook, and that her mediumship was a fraud. Volckman was a Spiritualist and an investigator of séance phenomena, and had worked officially for the London Dialectical Society in 1869 to investigate séances. He was known to Thomas Blyton and had attended meetings of the Dalton Association of Spiritualists in the past. Supporters of Florence, including her future husband Elgie Corner, who were also in attendance at the séance, came to her rescue, pulling Volkman away and forcing him to leave. Her friends claimed later that Volkman was in cahoots with a rival medium named Mrs. Guppy who was trying to discredit the more popular and successful Florence Cook.[45]

The scandal was widely publicized, and may have helped put doubts in the mind of Florence's wealthy supporter Blackburn. Before the end of the next year, Blackburn had ceased to finance her. In the immediate aftermath of the scandal, Florence may have known that her stipend was in jeopardy. Shortly after, Florence went personally to the eminent scientist Dr. William Crookes, whom she had met socially two months before, and asked him to investigate her mediumship. Crookes, who would be knighted in 1897, was well known, a Fellow of the Royal Society, and had respectable credentials.

During a long and successful career as a chemist and physicist he was responsible, among other things, for discovering the element "thallium" and inventing the "cathode ray." Crookes had recently conducted a series of experiments with medium D. D. Home, and concluded that he was not a fraud. Florence was probably desperate at the time for similar validation from a prominent scientist. Crookes agreed, and before the end of December began a series of experiments with her that continued until April 1874.

Crookes brought Florence to his London home, where he had his laboratory, to conduct his investigations under controlled circumstances. Details of his experiments were published by Harrison in *The Spiritualist*. Crookes' study was composed of an outer room, with an inner room separated by a curtain. Crookes and fellow observers could sit in the outer room awaiting the appearance of the materialized spirits while Florence lay entranced on a sofa in the inner room. When the spirit Katie appeared to Crookes and the others, she was always dressed in a thin, filmy white garment with bare arms and feet. During one manifestation, Crookes was allowed to "feel" the spirit to see if it was wearing a corset,[46] which it was *not*. Its absence was apparently proof positive for Crookes that the spirit was genuine, as no *woman alive* would ever be caught without her corset. Florence stayed in the Crookes' home for up to a week at a time throughout late winter and early spring, until the final experiments were moved back to her home in Hackney. In later years, one of Crookes' daughters was reputed to have said that while staying with the family, Florence sometimes entertained the children by telling them harrowing tales of Katie's past adventures.

Crookes took 44 photographs of "Katie King," in some of which he, or Florence Cook appear along side her. He described in detail the physical differences between the spirit and her medium. The fact that some of these photographs, which still exist, show a Katie King who looks almost identical to Florence Cook calls Crookes' judgment, not to mention his veracity, into question. Skeptics at the time who were convinced that Florence was a fake thought that either Crookes was being completely hood-winked or that he had agreed to perpetrate the fraud with Florence. And the only explanation in either case had to be that Crookes was smitten with Florence — at the very least besotted with her and probably having an affair.

There is evidence from early on in their relationship that Crookes had warm feelings for Florence Cook. After only one experiment, the scientist seems to have already concluded that her manifestations were genuine. Apparently his gallantry had been aroused by the unchivalrous treatment of her at the séance with Volckman, and the ungentlemanly questioning of her veracity. In his first report on the experiments, published in *The Spiritualist* on

February 3, 1874, her wrote that he had undertaken the investigation in order to "assist in removing an unjust suspicion cast upon another." He felt under an honorable obligation to do this, moreover because "when this other person is a woman — young, sensitive and innocent — it becomes especially a duty for me to give the weight of my testimony in favor of her whom I believe to be unjustly accused."[47] His own words indicate that he had already decided Florence was "innocent."

No affair between Crookes and Cook was ever decisively proved, and Crookes maintained until the end of his life that Florence and her phenomena were genuine. It was not possible to believe, he insisted, that "an innocent schoolgirl of 15 should be able to conceive and then successfully carry out for three years so gigantic an imposture...."[48]

If this is in fact what Crookes believed, his relationship with Florence Cook demonstrated how the Victorian belief that women, especially pure and pretty young girls, were not strong or intelligent enough to plan and carry out an extended and skillful fraud (despite the contrary suspicion that any woman might be a natural liar or actress) laid otherwise educated and rational Victorian men like Crookes and Robert Dale Owen open to manipulation. Ironically it was educated and rational men themselves who had systematically perpetuated the beliefs and attitudes which rendered them vulnerable.

Crookes' experiments with Florence came to an end in April of 1874, not long after Florence's friend and fellow medium Mary Rosina Showers was exposed in a séance. Mrs. Showers, her mother, indignantly defended her daughter from the charges of fraud, on the grounds that such behavior was unthinkable in people of their class (Showers' family was firmly middle class, a step up from the Cook family's working class background).[49] By that time, Katie King had achieved a celebrity of her own, apart from that of the medium, and Florence announced a series of "farewell séances" so Katie's fans could say good bye to her.

These last séances, still ostensibly part of Crookes' scientific investigations, were moved from his home back to the Cook's home in Hackney. These experiments were "exhibitions" in which Crookes acted as the "impresario" for Katie. The last performance occurred on May 21, 1874, when Katie King appeared through Florence to her closest circle of English friends.

Florence continued her séance performances for the next 20 years or so after her last manifestation of Katie King. But she was less and less successful as her youth and her looks faded. She died poor in 1904 at the age of 48. Her husband Frederick then married the younger Cook sister Katie Selina, and lived on her inheritance from Charles Blackburn for the rest of his life. Years after William Crookes and Florence Cook died, two unrelated witnesses stated to members of the Society for Psychical Research that in later years Florence had told them that she and Crookes had in fact been lovers, and that he had covered for her in faking her manifestations of Katie King. One of these witnesses reported that Florence had also claimed that her sister Katie Selina was also a fraud, and had fooled Charles Blackburn into bequeathing his estate to her and Mrs. Cook. Florence may have been bitter because she was left out of this inheritance, and struggling financially late in her life.[50]

As the character often outlasts the actress, the spirit of Katie King continued to show up after the medium's career was essentially over. Shortly after Katie's last appearence through Forence Cook, it was clear that Katie King had not really left the Spiritualist theatre — she had just moved to a new venue. Even before having said good by to her English friends, Katie had taken the stage in Philadelphia, appearing through more than one medium. Her most sensational performances would be in séances with Dr. Child and the mediums Mr. and Mrs. Holmes.

13

"Katie King" and Robert Dale Owen

Robert Dale Owen, social reformer and abolitionist, was the eldest son of English reformer and entrepreneur Robert Owen. Robert Dale had first come to America with his father in 1825 to participate in the elder Owen's radical community of New Harmony in Indiana. Robert Dale become a trustee of the Nashoba community in Tennessee, which was founded to educate former slaves, and spent most of the rest of his life in America, becoming an American citizen and serving in the Indiana state legislature and the U.S. congress. His first encounters with Spiritualism in Italy in the 1850s had made him a firm believer, and he wrote several books on the subject, fascinated by the movement which provided, through observable spirit phenomena, a scientific basis for religious belief. By the time he first encountered the spirit of Katie King in Philadelphia, he had already written two books about spirit contact, *Footfalls on the Boundary of Another World* (1860) and *The Debatable Land Between this World and the Next* (1872).

Owen was in Boston in April of 1874 when he visited a medium named Mrs. Hardy through whom the spirits gave him a message indicating that he would experience a full form spirit materialization. According to his own account later published in the *Atlantic Monthly*, he was told "before you leave the earth, you shall see spectres (as you call them) walking about; and they will take you by the hand and converse with you.... You shall witness far more wonderful things than you have ever yet seen."[1] On May 29, Owen received a "startling summons," in the form of a letter from his acquaintance Dr. Henry Child of Philadelphia saying that the spirit of Katie King had manifested herself to Child during a sitting with mediums Mr. and Mrs. Holmes, and requested that Robert Dale Owen come to Philadelphia to see her. This was 9 days after Katie had made her last appearance in London through Florence Cook, and 8 days after John King/Henry Morgan had appeared to Dr. Child requesting that he write his autobiography. Child's letter mentioned that Katie had lately been seen in London during the experiments with medium Florence Cook by the prominent Dr. Crookes. Owen may not have known when the séances began that Florence Cook had known the Holmes's in London where all had worked as mediums a few years previously.[2]

Open-minded as always, Owen traveled to Philadelphia and had his first sitting with the Holmes's in their rooms in a small house on June 5. In the lengthy article written for the *Atlantic Monthly*, he described a set-up not unlike that which Crookes had arranged for Florence Cook in his London home. A small front room or parlor was connected to an inner room by one door. There was also in the parlor a large "spirit cabinet" of dark walnut with two openings, one of which apparently opened into the inner bedroom. Owen's first glimpse of Katie was of a "fair, thoughtful young face, a girl of eighteen apparently, by whom I was cordially welcomed in a low, pleasant voice." Owen seems to have reserved judgment about Katie the first few times he saw her, noting that she was clearly a "living, moving, thinking being"—but that "one of the mediums was out of our sight" and there was the matter of the door—"locked, padlocked, and otherwise effectually secured, it seemed, but yet a door—from the cabinet into the bedroom adjoining."[3]

The events which transpired over the next 40 sittings, however, were more than enough to convince Owen that Katie was a real spirit, and any objectivity he may have felt in June was clearly gone by the time the last séance took place that summer. The Katie King that appeared to Owen and Child and occasionally to a few other invited guests[4] seemed to be slightly more sedate, at least in the beginning, that the prankster that Florence Cook had often manifested. However, the substratum of eroticism that underlies the sittings is made even more potent by its subtlety and by Owen's seeming blindness to his own responses, even as he detailed his interactions with Katie.

At first, Katie only spoke or appeared to her sitters from the door of the dark cabinet. Gradually, as the séances progressed, she moved further away from the dark aperture to walk among them in her flowing white dress. In the June 7 sitting, Dr. Child was allowed to feel the spirit's pulse (72 per minute) and Owen was asked by another sitter present, a lady, to give Katie a ring. Owen lingers, in his account, on this first touch—marveling that the spirit's hand, "beautifully formed, was like that of a mortal woman, nearly of the same temperature as my own, and slightly moist. At the close of the sitting she advanced into the room, dropped a finger on my head, and touched several other persons."[5]

Owen's relationship with Katie seems to have grown closer in the séance of June 9, when he gave her a long chain of hair from Violet, a woman he had known long ago, in hopes that Katie could help him contact her in the spirit world. At the next sitting, Katie returned the chain of hair to Owen, saying, "Violet wishes you to keep this, in memory of her, until you are called to meet her in her spirit-home."[6]

Subsequent sittings revolved around standard séance phenomena such as relaying messages, both verbally and in writing, to sitters from absent or deceased friends, varied by the appearance of "three different faces ... one of a middle-aged man, one of a young lady, and another of a child."[7] The spirit of Katie remained the star attraction, however, a fact highlighted (literally) by a "brilliantly luminous hand" which appeared at the upper corner of the cabinet door and "pointed downward, sometimes waving, toward Katie" in the June 19 séance. This sitting was also notable for Katie's physical expression of affection for Owen. She beckoned him to approach her. "I did so," Owen recollects "extending my hand, which she pressed; then, as I bent my head toward her, she took it in both hands and kissed it, uttering her usual low and earnest 'God bless you, Mr. Owen.'"[8]

What Owen calls a "remarkable" sitting occurred on June 19, the details of which are bizarre enough to merit quoting at length from his account:

> First, we were surprised by a dusky face at one of the apertures. Soon after, the door opened and a girl at least two inches taller and rather stouter than Katie, with dark handsome Indian features, and a lither figure, arrayed in richly ornamented Indian dress, walked out to within two feet of us. She had a snow-white blanket over her head, which she held under her chin. This she waved toward us; it was very fine, thick, and soft to the touch. She came out three times, spoke to us, the last time quite distinctly, telling us that her name was Sauntee. "Good God!" cried Mrs. Holmes, in evident astonishment and alarm.[9]
>
> Next there issued from the cabinet the figure of a lad dressed in sailor-boy fashion; his bow and gestures awkward and jerky, his face frank and pleasant. He came out three times, and when we asked his name he answered, in hoarse and broken but audible tones; "Don't you know me? You've heard me speak often enough; I'm Dick."
>
> We had frequently heard of Dick, as one of the (alleged) operating and talking spirits in the dark circles for physical manifestations which Mrs. Holmes occasionally gave. Both he and the Indian girl presented themselves now for the first time.
>
> At last Katie herself appeared. When she stepped into the room, I asked permission to approach, and gave her a mother-of-pearl cross, with white silk braid attached, together with a small note, folded up, in which I had written: "I offer you this because, though it be simple, it is white and pure and beautiful, as you are." She took both, did not open the note, suspended the cross from her neck, kissed it and retreated to the cabinet, closing the door. In a minute or two she returned, the cross, shining as with phosphorescent luster, in one hand, and the folded note in the other; bent over me, and said, in her low, earnest voice and with her charming smile: "White and pure and beautiful like me — is it?" How did she read that note? The cabinet, with its closed door and its black-covered apertures, was, as I have often verified, quite dark. Ever after, when she appeared, she wore that cross on

her breast; reminding one of the well-known lines in Pope's Rape of the Lock.[10]

Owen appears by his own account to have become besotted with Katie King. He was writing love notes, giving her jewelry, and invoking poetry. Moreover, he seemed oblivious to the ambiguity of Katie's response when he compared her to the cross. "White and pure and beautiful like me — is it?" she replied with a question. Her words might be construed as mocking, provocative, or even as guilty, given later revelations. Whether he was conscious of it or not, clearly Owen's emotions were beginning to overcome his reason. He grew more protective of his Katie, and jealous of her honor as if she were a real woman. At the close of the next séance, one of the male sitters asked Katie for a kiss, and she demurred and hurriedly withdrew. Afterwards, Owen cornered Dr. Child to "remonstrate" against the man's lack of "decorum." Owen threatened to withdraw his presence and tacit support of the séances if there was any repetition of what he deemed disrespect and disregard of Katie's obvious wishes not to be interfered with (by anyone apart from Owen, evidently).

Katie took the opportunity to play on his sympathy. At the beginning of the next day's session, after "unusual delay" she beckoned for Owen to approach the aperture of the dark cabinet. He was ripe to become an actor in the play, rather than just an admiring spectator, and took on the role of a chivalrous Gallant to her imperiled Innocent. He described how her now familiar face, still beautiful but pale, "wore such a look of weary sorrow and deep depression that I was moved almost to tears when, in low and plaintive tones, she said: 'Mr. Owen, indeed, I cannot come out tonight unless I have assurance that my wishes shall be respected.'" He answered that as long as he was present, they would be. Not yet confident, she pressed him. "I want your promise ... when you touch me, it gives me strength; but when others, with whom I have no sympathy, are suffered to approach indiscriminately, it wearies me and exhausts me. I want your promise that no such overtures as that made last night shall be repeated." Owen vowed, "I will protect you, as I would my own daughter, from that and every other annoyance. No one shall approach you except with your express permission."[11] From then on, Katie referred to him as "Father Owen."

As one reads the article, Owen's blindness to what appears to be the increasingly audacious innuendo that he himself is reporting is almost painful. Not long after his declaration that he would defend Katie, she rewarded him with the offer of an unusual private sitting. Without irony Owen reports she also promised him "a good time." Owen's account of the next séance, at which only he and the two mediums were present, begins with an indulgent description of the clothing worn by Sauntee, the Indian spirit who sometimes preceded Katie as a kind of opening act. Owen writes for a paragraph about the "rich dark jacket of stuff resembling silk velvet, embroidered in white spangles, open over the bosom and showing an undergarment apparently of Indian-tanned buckskin" and the "black leggings and embroidered moccasins." His words are palpably sensual, as he details the look and feel of the spirit's garments, the "soft, light grey tissue covering her head and falling over her shoulders" and the lappets of the belt as "soft and thick as rich velvet."[12]

When Katie appeared, Owen showed her the mementos he had collected like love tokens during the course of the séances: a tiny lock of hair, a card upon which she had written his name, and a small nosegay, all preserved in a tortoise-shell box. Smiling at him, she promised, "I'll give you something better worth keeping." Going into the spirit closet, she retuned shortly with a pair of scissors, permitting him to cut from her hair "a beautiful ringlet, about four inches long, literally of a golden color, soft and fine."[13] The exchange of tokens continued in the next séance, when Katie selected several lilies from a bouquet in the room and gave them to Owen. She allowed him to touch her hair again, and then,

> once more — and for the last time that evening — she emerged from the cabinet, came quietly up to me, extending a hand. I passed my left arm gently around her, and sustained her left arm, bare from the elbow, in my right hand. To the touch her garments and her person were exactly like those of an earthly woman.[14]

The final few séances featured the eerie spectacle of Katie gradually appearing and disappearing, sometimes seeming to grow from a tiny spot of light, or hang in the air, or rise from the floor; and a luminescent lily which shone out from the dark. Katie's final gifts to Owen were pieces cut from the fabric of her dress and veil. Owen's "farewell séance" with Katie was on July 16, 1874. He called it a "sad and solemn leave-taking," and mentioned that the two ladies in attendance were both in tears.[15]

Before the article quoted above had even appeared in the *Atlantic Monthly* (which was publishing it as part of a serialized autobiography of Owen), Owen learned that an unidentified woman was claiming to have conspired with the Holmses to play the role of "Katie King" in the séances and dupe Owen, Child, and the other sitters. It was too late to stop the press, so Owen's *Atlantic* article appeared as written, accompanied by a disclaimer from the editor, William Dean Howells. The Holmses denied the fraud, and Henry Steele Olcott, who had been reporting for the *New York Daily Graphic* on trance manifestations by the Eddy brothers in Vermont, was invited to Philadelphia to investigate the situation.

Olcott, with Owen's support, arrived in Philadelphia in early January 1875 to interview the parties concerned and study relevant documents including letters to and from the Holmses, notes purportedly written by "Katie King," and the files of the city papers containing details of the scandalous exposé. Olcott quickly found his search for the truth mired in confusion, confessions of lies, recanted statements and conflicting testimony. Shortly after he had begun, an affidavit was produced and signed by a woman later revealed to be Eliza White, confirming that she had been paid by the mediums to impersonate the spirit of Katie King. Eliza White had been the landlady of the boarding house where the mediums stayed while in Philadelphia. When approached by the Holmses to act the part of Katie in the séances, Eliza, a widow and the sole support of her child and elderly mother, said in her confession, "I made up my mind to play the part for a short time, hoping that something better would turn up in my interest; in the meantime I would be earning my expenses and doing no one any harm."[16] After this public blow, and before Olcott was well in to the investigation, both Dr. Child and Owen publicly admitted that they had been the victims of fraud. The press pounced on the sensational announcements, and reported on them with, at times, less than perfect accuracy. A report in the *Eclectic* magazine stated that "Mr. Owen has published a card to admit that he was the victim of deception. A widow with two children has confirmed that she was paid to play the part, and to personate the materialized spirit."

In a book about spirit manifestations published later, Olcott discusses Eliza's confession, noting that after her success in playing Katie for the first few séances with Owen, "remorse entered the soul of the actress in this comedy of shame." He quotes her own protestations that

> after the first two or three nights my whole nature revolted at the idea of this gross deception.... The interest manifested by the people kept increasing, which only aggravated my sensitive nature ... I was often sick at heart; I felt that I was guilty of a great crime. Night after night was my pillow wet with tears; the heart would overflow with grief. I appeared to be surrounded with a cloud of sorrow from which there was no escape. Here was my helpless little boy, and frail, old mother looking to me for bread. In my troubled dreams I seemed to see their eyes riveted on me saying, "Our whole hope and dependence is on you."[17]

This outpouring of Eliza's reveals a strong dramatic flair. She portrays herself as that staple of melodrama, the fallen woman; her sins are grievous but prompted by maternal and filial obligations. Olcott wasn't so easily moved, however. Suspicious of the sob story and the entire confession, he decided to check into her background for himself.

Olcott found Eliza to be dishonest in several details. She was not a widow as she had claimed, but the wife of a man named Wilson B. "Bob" White. She had lived with him in Winsted, Connecticut, where he still resided, until leaving him following serious family disputes, and taking her son with her to Philadelphia in early 1874. Olcott found several people from her past who also testified to her questionable morals. Mrs. White was said to have worked as a prostitute during the Civil War while her husband's regiment was away at the front. She also appeared to have had theatrical experience prior to becoming involved in trance performance, as had Elizabeth O'Key. When Wilton B. White had returned from the war, he "traveled with a 'side-show' of natural curiosities and clog-dancers and ballad-singers, and Eliza took part in both singing and dancing."[18] Olcott quotes from an article published in the journal of a town near Winsted. It reported in detail on the scandal involving the former resident, including some history on "Katie King" alias Mrs. White's show business past.

> Some years ago her husband, familiarly known as "Bub" [sic] White, gave a sort of variety entertainment, under canvas, on the fair grounds in Litchfield, while the annual county cattle-show was in progress. The show consisted of a wild-cat "as ferocious and untamable as a South American hyena," a singing boy "with a voice like a mocking bird's," and "Bub," who was a violin player, composed the orchestra. Katie King made her debut on that occasion as a serio-comic vocalist, and as she was endowed with a good share of personal charms, and appeared in a bewitching costume, she took immensely, and the country swains poured out their "dime and a half" like water.[19]

Olcott found Eliza White completely untrustworthy, and her "confession" groundless. His investigations had turned up hints that she might have been bribed to say she had played the spirit and duped the séance sitters by persons keen to discredit Spiritualism and all its phenomena. With no evidence to convince him of trickery by the mediums, Olcott concluded that at least some of the Katie King materializations were genuine, in spite of the admissions from Dr. Child and Owen (too hasty, in Olcott's view) that they had been fooled.

Olcott was not the only one who continued to believe that the Katie King who appeared in the Philadelphia séances was real. J. M. Roberts, writing for the periodical *Mind and Matter*, depicted the whole attempt to discredit the séances and call into question the reality of Katie King as part of a larger "crusade against Spiritualism." In response to the argument that no spirit would have toyed so with Mr. Owen, and that only a real woman would have cheated him of valuable trinkets, not to mention his time and affection, J. M. Roberts insisted that it was only common sense that spirits, especially those of the weaker sex, would resume their earthly habits and defects when they were manifest by mediums. He said of Katie King, "What more natural than that she should manifest the same desire for admiration and personal adornment which marks the general female character in physical life?"

As for Mr. Owen, it was also natural that he would respond as gallantly to the spirit's charms as he would to those of a real woman. Roberts reveals an empathy, a sort of masculine solidarity, with Owen's situation and confusion, seeming to pity him most for having allowed himself to be persuaded that the Katie King he knew was *not* real. His view of both the masculine and feminine characters is less than original.

> Like many other strong and able men, Mr. Owen was highly susceptible to the too oft bewildering charms of female loveliness. He became infatuated with his celestial visitor, and sought to show his admiration to her by presenting her with material tokens of his sentiments. Katie, with a natural womanly weakness, was flattered by the admiration of so distinguished and influential a man, and accepted her gifts in the same spirit [sic!] with which they were given.[20]

Eliza White, a central figure, remains obscure. That she was "an actress in this comedy," as Olcott put it, is clear; but what role she played remains uncertain. She seems to have stuck to her story that she had played Katie King in the séances. Owen evidently met her at some later date, and she reportedly returned some of the gifts he had given her as Katie. Owen was so traumatized by the affair that he became mentally unbalanced and spent part of 1875 confined to an asylum.[21] But Owen was not like others, who, upon finding they had been fooled, turned quickly and bitterly on the Spiritualist movement, denouncing it and all its practitioners wholesale. Robert Dale Owen never gave up on Spiritualism. So strong was his will to believe that until his death in 1877, he was convinced that genuine mediums existed, and might still provide contact with the spirit world.

14

Materialization, Ectoplasm and Realism

Even after stating that the appearances of Katie King in the Philadelphia séances had been faked, Robert Dale Owen's desire to believe in spirit phenomena and, one assumes, his willingness to suspend his disbelief for future trance performances remained. For men and women like Owen, the emotional truth of the experience was more important than its credibility. Like the ideal Victorian theatre audience, they would surrender to the performer's spell, especially when this "spell" was accompanied by physical proofs. Their confidence that sensory evidence like sight, touch and hearing did not lie made it easier for them to accept the truths of the physical phenomena and spirit materializations of trance performances. When Robert Dale Owen had seen with his own eyes the bright smile and golden curls, and felt with his own hand the palpable warmth of the being calling itself "Katie King," he had believed that the spirit was real.

Other less "ideal" audiences for the materialization séances, with more rigorous views of what constituted "scientific proof" deplored the widespread fallacy of "seeing is believing." George Henry Lewes, whose analysis of the double consciousness of acting was one of the first attempts to apply psychological theory to performance, was one of these skeptics. He argued that while to *see* a thing might be to believe in its existence, people did not always judge correctly what it was they had actually *seen*, or whether they had seen it at all. Lewes might have been talking about Owen when he stated "when a man avers that he has 'seen a ghost,' he is passing far beyond the limits of visible fact, into that of inference. He saw something which he supposed to be a ghost." Lewes could not deny, however, the irrational strength of belief in the inference which seduced people into taking it for gospel. Lewes called Spiritualism an "ignoble and debasing superstition," and implied that it had more influence among those who lacked the strength of mind to resist its allure. "So strong is the fascination, and so delusive the fallacy, that scheming Americans and cunning girls are able to find fresh converts every day"—a dig at the American mediums who had introduced the Spiritualist contagion to England.[1]

However, Lewes' opinion did not change the basic dynamic, or imaginative contract between the trance performer and her audience. Sitters at a séance, like spectators at the play house, craved material and spectacular elements, and the pleasure of giving in to their appeal. And so trance performers, like theatrical producers, did their utmost to provide these. This had been true from early on in the Victorian period. In 1855, William Bodham Donne, the British examiner of plays, had deplored a similar trend in theatre, lamenting audiences' passivity and inability to use their imaginations. Increasingly, the only way to move the spectator was through physical embodiments:

> To touch our emotions, we need not the imaginatively true, but the physically real. The visions which our ancestors saw with the mind's eye, must be embodied for us in palpable forms ... all must be made palpable to sight, no less than to feeling: and this lack of imagination in the spectators affects equally both those who enact and those who construct the scene.[2]

Donne's description of theatre helps explain what was happening in trance performances in the 1870s and 1880s, and the increasing trend toward materializations. Some performers like Florence Cook and the Holmses, increasingly under pressure to produce bodies, may have done so by hiring actors to impersonate the spirits, or by resorting to elaborate and grotesque use of "ectoplasm."

Unlike trance performers of previous decades, who had produced spirits for their audiences by means of sounds, and by impersonating them through the instrument of their own voices and bodies, performers in the 1870s began to depend more on physical gimmicks like "spirit cabinets" through which materialized spirits could appear independently of the medium (in spite of the fact that these devices made the entire performance more vulnerable to exposure as a hoax).[3] Even though some spectators regarded these tricks as crude, and referred jokingly to the "spirit cabinets" through which faces or hands appeared like puppets, as "Punch and Judy" cabinets, such effects enjoyed great popularity for a few years.

In séances, as in the theatre, audiences still doted on charismatic "stars," but the primacy of the actor (and the telling of stories through words and characterizations) was weakening. People demanded not just spectacle, but *realistic* spectacle. And to be realistic in the theatre meant the palpably, physically real, such as solid scenery, props and live animals on stage. For the trance séance this necessity for realism resulted in need for some new substance out of which spirit bodies could be composed. At the height of the craze for the full form materialization of spirit bodies, that substance, called "ectoplasm," began to appear in séances.

Psychic investigators found themselves trying to understand and explain the ultimate in séance "realism," the ectoplasmic apparitions which sprang up like mushrooms at the turn of the century. Psychic investigators, working independently or as part of organizations like the British Society for Psychical Research (founded in 1882) conducted systematic studies of séance and trance phenomena even as these started to lose steam with regular sitters and audiences. These new psychic detectives were determined to discover, by close study and experimentation, the origins of the weird phenomena produced, whether these were spiritual or psychological. Two examples of mediums who produced ectoplasm in the waning years of the century were Eusapia Palladino and Elizabeth D'Esperance (Elizabeth Hope), two women, who, in other respects, could not have been more different.

Eusapia Palladino

One of the most studied trance performers at the end of the century was Eusapia Palladino who was born to a poor Italian family in 1845. Her mother died giving birth to her, and when she lost her father in 1866 (he was, by some accounts, killed by brigands) she was sent to work as a nursemaid for a family in Naples. There she began to exhibit peculiar qualities, claiming to see ghosts everywhere. She gained attention as a medium around Naples in the early 1870s, exhibiting her phenomena under the management of a Signor Ercole Damiana. In a somewhat tongue-in-cheek description, which also reveals a class bias, psychical researcher Alan Gauld characterized her as

> vulgar, earthy, and addicted to bad company. There were even hints that during the séances sitters' purses and other valuables were rather liable to dematerialize. It was clear that she was afflicted by a band of evil spirits, and British Spiritualists offered their advice to Signor Damiani in the columns of *The Spiritualist.* Miss Florence Cook of Hackney undertook a clairvoyant diagnosis of Eusapia's condition. Miss Cook perceived that Eusapia kept low company, and was followed by an undesirable man; and there is every indication that Miss Cook was right.[4]

Palladino was unreliable, even untrustworthy; nonetheless, her apparent psychic abilities were taken seriously enough to be thoroughly studied by an impressive roster of investigators, including Dr. Cesare Lombroso, the celebrated alienist, and the Nobel prize winning chemists Pierre and Marie Curie. Lombroso is better known for developing a pseudo-science of criminology based on the principals of physiognomy. He created a system whereby criminals, or potential criminals, could supposedly be identified by their facial features. His interest in the body's manifestation of internal truths was in line with a Victorian tendency to apply some version of the scientific method to every possible discipline. His work would have predisposed him to the investigation of trance and spirit phenomena of the physical variety, like that exhibited by Eusapia Palladino. And the series of experiments he did with Palladino beginning in 1891, assisted by 17 other researchers, helped make her a favorite subject for scientific investigation, much "sought after for her physical phenomena,"[5] as well as a celebrity on an international scale.

Researchers often referred to Eusapia's ignorance, or her peasant mentality. She did not lecture on abstract philosophical subjects like Cora Richmond, or tell stories of other worlds, or even amuse by singing and dancing. Her repertoire for the most part consisted of fairly standard physical phenomena such as levitating tables and other objects. These movements were sometimes achieved by what appeared to be phantom limbs, such as a third arm, which she produced out of her body, and which then dissolved or was reabsorbed. Some investigators referred to these as "ectoplasmic limbs." She also appeared to be able to produce outlines or portions, though never complete manifestations, of ectoplasmic bodies. Italian investigator Professor Chiaia recorded some of his observations in a letter to Cesar Lombroso when he was trying to convince the eminent scientist to come study her.

> The case I allude to is that of an invalid woman who belongs to the humblest class of society. She is nearly thirty years old and very ignorant; her look is neither fascinating nor endowed with the power which modern criminologists call irresistible; but when she wishes, be it by day or by night, she can divert a curious group for an hour or so with the most surprising phenomena. Either bound to a seat or firmly held by the hands of the curious, she attracts to her the articles of furniture which surround her, lifts them up, holds them suspended in the air like Mahomet's coffin, and makes them come down with adulatory movements, as if they were obeying her will… This woman rises in the air, no matter what hands tie her down. She seems to lie upon the empty air, as on a couch, contrary to all the laws of gravity.…[6]

This commentary suggests Eusapia's powerful ability to capture and hold the attention of her audience (the definition of "to entertain"). Her skill did not seem to depend substantially on her feminine beauty, or graceful manners. Eusapia, unlike other Victorian women trance performers, was seldom if ever described as being physically attractive, or possessing the innocent charm of a child. Her strength was not her personal charisma but her genius for riveting her sitters' attention on the physical phenomena she produced. Ruth Brandon attributed the medium's success in part to her ability to misdirect audiences by means of her sexuality. Reports of her séances often describe her spasmodic physical movements, writhing, groans and cries, and Brandon noted that these "orgasmic" fits often occurred just as phenomena were about to appear, diverting the audience's attention away from any likely means of faking them. Moreover, Brandon suggested that the male sitters' anticipation that she might sleep with them after the séance might also prevent them from focusing on the spirit phenomena at hand.[7] Many spirits hugged or kissed their sitters, but the spirits embodied by Eusapia often did them one better by "playfully biting" their loved one present at the séance. Lombroso explained this "vulgar" act by reasoning that even the most sedate spirit would take on some of the characteristics or idiosyncrasies of the medium (in this case Eusapia's coarse habit of biting to show affection), when obliged to materialize through her body.

The closer the focus on the female body — either that of the medium or that of the spirit — the more likely it was that eroticism would be a substantial undercurrent of the performance. This erotic subtext was inevitable, given the firmly entrenched Victorian assumption that any woman involved in an activity which invited the male gaze, such as acting, public speaking, or mediumship, might be assumed to be signaling her sexual availability. Actresses or dancers who showed more of their bodies had to deal with this perception, as well as with the suspicion that stage careers were used as cover for assignations, affairs or even prostitution. When, occasionally, one of these perceptions proved to be the case, it made it all the more difficult for the majority of women performers. Even today, performance remains "linked to sexuality because it is an *embodied* art ... Acting is a particularly acute case of the general phenomenon of woman being reduced to sexual object. The theatrical enterprise thus contains two divergent possibilities for women: transformation and objectification."[8] In looking back on cases of women's trance performance, it is often difficult to tell which possibility gained the upper hand.

Sexual activity was probably not what Professor Chiaia was referring to when he mentioned Eusapia Palladino's "surprising phenomena" in the letter to Lombroso. Even if he had observed overtly sexual behavior in the medium, he might not have considered it the kind of thing that would persuade Lombroso to undertake a serious scientific investigation of her. One thing does seem clear from the mass of descriptions of Palladino's performances, though. Unlike many Spiritualist speakers and mediums who preceded her, her performances depended less and less on an angelic image and inspiring words and more and more on the robust and earthy tricks and physicality.

Despite the lack of intellectual or spiritual inspiration in her performances, researchers were intrigued by Eusapia Palladino. Even though most of them discovered her practicing fraud at least once, and it was common knowledge that she would resort to tricks if necessary, most of those investigating her also concluded that *some* of her phenomena could not be explained by fakery, and had to be the product of spirit or psychic power. Even those few, like the Cambridge investigators in the 1895 tests, who found nothing convincing, acknowledged her cleverness in the production of phenomena, indicating that "Eusapia's trickery was of a skilful and practiced kind, and could not be attributed simply to her being in trance and not responsible for her acts."[9] They at least credited her with some will and agency, as well as talent for performance.

Partly as a result of the findings of the 1895 Cambridge investigation of Palladino, psychic researchers began to divide trance performers into two categories: "'mental' mediums, who write or speak automatically or see visions, and 'physical' mediums, who are responsible for physical effects."[10] Palladino, was, of course, one of the physical mediums, whereas the famous Lenore Piper, a subject of William James' study, was the most famous example of the mental medium. Piper's phenomena were confined to spirit communications, often with the voice and personality of the spirit, but, no other physical phenomena.

Buescher dates an uneasiness of serious Spiritualists with the grosser aspects of trance phenomena slightly earlier, beginning with the full-form materializations of the 1870s when a "growing preoccupation with phenomenal manifestations" drove some of the earliest Spiritualists like Andrew Jackson Davis away from the movement and "signaled a decline of sorts in the fortunes of spiritualism."[11]

This decline in spiritualism paralleled what many found to be a decline in theatre at the time. G. H. Lewes once again weighed in with his opinion — that theatre was becoming increasingly crude. He decried the appetite for "sensation pieces" and called the condition of theatre in the second half of the century "deplorable." He saw this in terms of the transformation of theatre from an art to an amusement, saying, "The drama is everywhere in Europe and America rapidly passing from an art into an amusement. ... those who love the drama cannot but regret the change, but all must fear that it is inevitable when they reflect that the stage is no longer the amusement of the cultured few, but the amusement of the uncultured and miscultured masses, and has to provide larger and lower appetites with food."[12]

The same class prejudice is evident from psychic investigator Frank Podmore's remarks about the direction taken by trance performance. Podmore, referring to the "excrescence" of "so-called physical phenomenon," noted that "at the best, whatever effect they may have had in advertising the movement with the vulgar, they seem to have exerted only a subsiding influence in inducing belief with more thoughtful men and women."[13]

Both statements reveal a bias, dating back to Aristotle, against spectacle. However effective it may be on weaker minds, spectacle is essentially vulgar. And consequently, those who produce it and enjoy it are vulgar. This attitude may explain the next shift in the direction of trance performances. As, increasingly, the audiences of thoughtful men and women that trance performers would have to prove themselves to were scientific investigators like Podmore, there would be a backlash against vulgar physical phenomena and a movement, in the early twentieth century, toward the more genteel mental and clairvoyant phenomena.

Trance performances and séances, which had developed along parallel lines with the Victorian theatre, began to lose viability towards the end of the era for the same reasons. A shift in emphasis from the persuasive acting of the medium to her manifestation of visual phenomena and physical bodies marked both a pinnacle and the beginning of the end of the form. The materialization séances of the 1870s were the height of trance performances, according to psychic researcher Frank Podmore. But one could argue that performers also rapidly brought on their own decline, as attempts to create the effects expected resulted in the practice and exposure of fraud. A similar process was occurring in the popular theatre, as attempts to satisfy the audience's ever growing Gargantuan appetite for realistic spectacle reached the limits of available theatrical techniques.

It was, paradoxically, the very proliferation and elaboration of special effects, and the attempts to convince audiences with material proofs that ultimately hurt more than helped both legitimate theatre and trance performances. The producers of both overreached themselves by thinking they could in fact reproduce reality. They seemed to fail to take into account that literal theatrical reality is impossible — the phrase is an oxymoron, like "spirit body." Not only is the complete replication of reality on stage impossible, but once attempted, anything that falls short is unconvincing in proportion to the amount of effort put into making it seem real.

One example of this is that one single absolutely genuine element on stage can make every other element or performance that is not *just as real* appear questionable or even ludicrous. Actors notoriously hate to perform with animals or small children, because the unassailable authenticity, the phenomenological reality of a dog or a baby, which is incapable of pretending, or acting a role, not only steals focus but throws into relief the utter artificiality of the actor's performance, and every element of the setting.

The limits and capabilities of live theatre, with its most sophisticated technology or effects, will be exceeded by striving too far to present a "slice of life" on stage as naturalist theory puts it. In the legitimate theatre, attempts to convincingly reproduce actual spectacular phenomena like fire, floods, or the wonders of the natural world, by material and physical means, even though audiences demand them, almost always fall short in the long run. Proof is the demise of spectacular productions of melodrama at the end of the nineteenth century. As Nicolas Vardac argues in his book *From Stage to Screen*, stage melodrama declined and was eventually replaced by cinema at the turn of the nineteenth century in part due to the fact that the audience's appetite and expectations for physical reality outgrew the possibilities of the art form.

Elizabeth D'Esperance

Not all the women studied by psychic investigators were clever peasants, however, nor did the physical nature of their performances necessarily deprive them of spiritual or psychic value or meaning. Lombroso also worked with a woman named Elizabeth D'Esperance, whom he called a "positive genius" in her normal state. She was born Elizabeth Hope in 1855, later taking on the pseudonym D'Esperance. She was able to produce fully formed spirit bodies from ectoplasm, but unlike most other mediums she possessed an unusual level of self awareness and was also able to remember what she did in the trance state. She wrote about her subjective experiences with precise detail. An example is her uncanny description of how an ectoplasmic body is produced.

> As soon as I have entered the mediumistic cabinet my first impression is of being covered with spider webs. Then I feel that the air is filled with substance, and a kind of white and vaporous mass, quasi-luminous, like the steam from a locomotive, is formed in front of the abdomen. After this mass has been tossed and agitated in every way for some minutes, sometimes even for half an hour, it suddenly stops, and then out of it is born a living being close to me.[14]

One of the spirits D'Esperance often formed a body for was Yolanda. Yolanda was an exotic 10-year-old Arabic girl with dusky skin and dark hair. She did not share her medium's cultivated nature, but was "semi-barbaric" and unfamiliar with everyday objects, such as chairs; she didn't know how to sit in one and fell off when she tried to perch on its back. She barely knew the alphabet (English or Arabic, one wonders?) but "knew at once the use of jewels" and craved constant attention and praise, according to Lombroso. Her ectoplasmic body was so "real, so carnally feminine, that a person who took her for a real woman attempted to offer her an indignity, resulting in profound injury to the medium."[15] This, then, was the highest proof that Yolanda's body was like a real woman's — it provoked an assault. The danger of interrupting the trance connection between a medium and her spirit was well known to observers and participants in trance séances. Some mediums were so traumatized by the experience, usually involving being grabbed by a man who was trying to prove that the spirit and the medium were the same, that they became physically ill and remained so for a long time afterwards. Elizabeth's description of this incident, which resulted in her suffering a severe hemorrhage of the lungs, is painfully vivid.

> All I knew was a horrible excruciating sensation of being doubled up and squeezed together, as I can imagine a hollow ...doll would feel, if it had sensation, when violently embraced by its baby owner. A sense of terror and agonizing pain came over me ...I felt I was sinking down, I knew not where. I tried to save myself, to grasp at something, but missed it; and then came a blank from which I awakened with shuddering horror and sense of being bruised to death.[16]

Little wonder the Elizabeth D'Esperance disliked many things about the process of materializing spirits. Moreover, she seemed to have little control over this or her other psychic powers such as automatic writing, drawing, and producing splendid "apports" of exotic flowers. Her abilities always fluctuated greatly, and often did not come when she wanted them or tried too hard, and sometime left her feeling ill and exhausted afterwards. Why then, one wonders, would she continue performing as a trance medium? Like the other women in this study, her motives were not singular, but one compelling reason was straightforward — when her husband died she depended on her trance performances for an income. Her later writing reflecting on her life and trance performances also shows that, eventually she began to understand her experiences, difficult as some of them were, as a means of gaining self knowledge and genuine spiritual enlightenment. It is also probable, as Alex Owen suggests, that after a troubled childhood, and at a low point in her life when her physical and mental health were suffering, mediumship was the only thing that helped. The same pattern can be seen in many female trance performers' stories.

Elizabeth D'Esperance's tendency towards depression was exacerbated by the social and emotional isolation and lack of stimulation she felt when she married at age 18. Her mental and physical health improved markedly as soon as she joined a Spiritualist society and began her trance mediumship. For her, despite its later hazards, trance performance proved more than a stop-gap coping mechanism, but became a long term source of solace, a way to keep going in a difficult world. The spirits were literally her "Nepenthes," the Greek word for the drug that can banish grief and trouble from a person's mind, and the name of the spirit she began to materialize in 1893. The spirit was a lovely Egyptian woman crowned with a glowing diadem. When she faded away after her first appearance, she left behind a note, written in Greek, which said, "I am Nepenthes thy friend; when thy soul is oppressed by too much pain, call on me, Nepenthes, and I will come at once to relieve thy trouble."[17]

Epilogue

Victorian women's trance performances varied widely in seriousness and significance, and it is difficult to generalize, either about the motives of the performers or about their influence on audiences. Large numbers of Spiritualists believed in the reality and wisdom of the spirits, but not all who performed or watched were believers.

Current scholars, like the Victorians, have suggested a variety of explanations for the trance performances, and brought a variety of beliefs to bear in their interpretations. Not only recent interpretations based on performance or psychological theories, but the psychic investigations and interpretations by Victorians themselves, help us understand the processes by which trance theatre was received and understood by its performers, audiences and critics.

Whether trance performers were actually channeling spirits, suffering from abnormal states of consciousness or dissociative identity disorder, or consciously acting spirit characters and presenting by theatrical means spirit phenomena is a question that may never be definitively answered. For any given performance by a medium, more than one explanation might have been in play. Some of Eusapia Palladino's testimony indicates that there were times when she faked phenomena, either consciously or unconsciously, which at other times she was able to actually produce. Proving or disproving the truth of spirit phenomena in particular is highly problematic since as in most matters involving faith or belief, there is little consensus as to what would constitute definitive "evidence" even if it were available. Certain explanations are favored over others depending on the cultural ideals and zeitgeist, and current understanding of science, psychology, philosophy and religion. The meaning of any individual spirit performance depends on its cultural context, as does theatre, and therefore may be better understood when interpreted as theatre and understood in terms of dramatic values and audience reception. An examination of trance performances in the context of a larger spectrum of Victorian popular theatre and theatricality, helps reveal why and how it worked, and what both spectators and performers had to gain from it.

Spirit representations, like Victorian theatre, could be Romantic or sensational. They could concern themselves with sentimental and domestic situations or with current social and political controversies; with timeless and universal truths, or with jokes, silliness and flirtation in real time. Spirit roles, like dramatic roles, ranged from tamed versions of the exotic, the foreign or the "Other," to characters like those of close family or neighbors. What trance performances, as a form of theatre, offered audiences, was some degree of entertainment or distraction, and very often real comfort, since even the most banal or amusing spirit communication could be considered evidence of life after death.

What it offered performers was perhaps even more complicated. For O'Key, trance performance provided a taste of excitement, a way to behave subversively, with impunity, at the center of attention. For Mowatt, it may well have been a crucial coping mechanism triggered by the role conflict she was experiencing in her personal life. For Spiritualist trance performers like Cora Richmond, trance performance represented opportunities for political and social expression, as well as therapeutic and economic benefits. For the stars of materialization séances like Florence Cook, it represented glamour and celebrity, at the very least, and an escape from the conventional limitations imposed on a Victorian girl. For some, trance performance was a compulsion, while for others it may ultimately have been a real source of comfort, insight and the elusive "Nepenthes" they sought.

The ideas and concerns, as well as the motives and responses revealed by these trance performances, lectures and séances illuminate for us some shadowy aspects of Victorian culture. They add to our understanding of how Victorians saw themselves, and created meaning for themselves a changing world. These stories also bring to light not only the varied experiences of the women at the heart of these spirit dramas, but the fundamental phenomenological power of the performances themselves. The very range of needs that might be met by these odd co-creations, or "remarkable exercises in group imagination," is one of their most compelling features.

Chapter Notes

Introduction

1. Bert O. States, *Great Reckonings in Little Rooms: On the Phenomenology of Theater* (Berkeley and Los Angeles: University of California Press, 1985), 158.
2. E. R. Dodds, *The Greeks and the Irrational* (Berkeley: University of California Press, 1951), 70.
3. Ibid., 73.
4. Joseph Fontenrose, *The Delphic Oracle* (Berkeley: University of California Press, 1978), 211.
5. Ibid., 255.
6. E. T. Kirby, *Ur-Drama: The Origins of Theatre* (New York: New York University Press, 1975), 2–3.
7. Ibid., 12.
8. Thomas Dempsey, *The Delphic Oracle: Its Early History, Influence and Fall* (New York: Benjamin Blom, 1972), 50–51.
9. William Ridgeway, *The Origin of Tragedy* (Cambridge: Cambridge University Press, 1910).
10. Victor Turner, *From Ritual to Theatre: The Human Seriousness of Play* (New York: PAJ, 1982).
11. See Judith Butler, *Gender Trouble: Feminism and the Subversion of Identity* (London & New York: Routledge, 1990) and Laurence Senelick, ed., *Gender in Performance: The Presentation of Difference in the Performing Arts* (Hanover and London: University Press of New England, 1992).

Chapter 1

1. See the introduction to Tracy C. Davis and Thomas Postlewait, eds., *Theatricality* (Cambridge: Cambridge University Press, 2003).
2. Martin Meisel, *Realizations: Narrative, Pictorial and Theatrical Arts of the Nineteenth Century* (Princeton: Princeton University Press, 1983).
3. George H. Lewes, *On Actors and the Art of Acting* (Leipzig: Bernhard Tauchnitz, 1875), 37–38.
4. Matthew G. (Monk) Lewis, *The Castle Spectre*, ii, iv.
5. Michael R. Booth, *English Melodrama* (London: Herbert Jenkins, 1965), 85.
6. Ibid., 2–3.
7. A. Nicholas Vardac, *Stage to Screen: Theatrical Origins of Early Film: David Garrick to D.W. Griffith* (1949; New York: Da Capo, 1987), 111.
8. Joseph Knight quoted in Vardac, 91.

Chapter 2

1. Dempsey, 55–56.
2. M. R. Booth, *Theatre in the Victorian Age* (Cambridge: Cambridge University Press, 1991), 3. Chapter One, *Theatre and Society*, contains other significant statistics about the rapid urbanization of Britain and its influence on theatre in the nineteenth century.
3. J. Arthur Hill, *Spiritualism: Its History, Phenomena and Doctrine* (New York: George H. Doran Co., 1919), 288.
4. Nina Auerbach, *Woman and the Demon: The Life of a Victorian Myth* (Cambridge, MA: Harvard University Press, 1982), 7.
5. Booth quoted in Judith Walkowitz, *City of Dreadful Delight: Narratives of Sexual Danger in Late-Victorian London* (Chicago: University of Chicago Press, 1992), 74.
6. Martin Meisel, "Perspectives on Victorian and Other Acting," *Victorian Studies* 6 (June 1963), 355.
7. Freud quoted in *The Divine Sarah: A Life of Sarah Bernhardt*, Arthur Gold and Robert Fizdale, eds. (New York: Random House, 1991), 4.
8. J. Ranken Towse quoted in *The American Theatre as Seen by Its Critics*, John Mason Brown and Montrose J. Moses, eds. (New York: W. W. Norton & Co., 1934), 104.
9. William Winter quoted in Brown and Moses, eds., 86.
10. James Gibbons Huneker quoted in Brown and Moses, eds., 153.
11. Adam Badeau quoted in *Kean and Booth and Their Contemporaries*, Laurence Hutton and Brander Matthews, eds. (Boston: L. C. Page & Co., 1900), 254.

12. Quoted in Hutton and Matthers eds., 248.
13. Anna Cora Mowatt Ritchie, *Mimic Life; or, Before and Behind the Curtain* (Boston: Ticknor and Fields, 1856), 126.
14. Louisa May Alcott, *Behind a Mask: The Unknown Thrillers of Louisa May Alcott*, ed. Madeleine Stern (New York: Willlam Morrow, 1975), xviii.
15. Ibid., xviii–xix.
16. Ibid., 7.
17. Olive Logan, *Before the Footlights and Behind the Scenes* (Philadelphia: Parmalee, 1870), 140.
18. Charlotte Brontë, *Villette* (Oxford: Clarendon Press, 1984), 369.
19. Ibid., 371.
20. Ibid., 197.
21. John Stokes, "Rachel's 'Terrible Beauty': An Actress Among the Novelists," *ELH* 51 (Winter 1984), 785.
22. Quoted in Nina Auerbach, *Romantic Imprisonment: Women and Other Glorified Outcasts* (New York: Columbia University Press, 1985), 248.
23. Jean-Jacques Rousseau. *Politics and the Arts, Letters to M. D'Alembert on the Theatre*, trans. Allan Bloom (Glencoe, IL: The Free Press, 1960), 47.
24. Quoted in Martha Vicinus, *A Widening Sphere: Changing Roles of Victorian Women* (Bloomington: Indiana University Press, 1977), 94.
25. Florence Nightingale, *Cassandra* (Old Westbury, NY: The Feminist Press, 1979), 41.
26. Ibid., 41.
27. Faye Dudden, *Women in the American Theatre: Actresses and Audiences, 1790–1870* (New Haven: Yale University Press, 1994), 2.
28. C. A. Somerset, *Crazy Jane: A Romantic Play in Three Acts* (London: J. Cumberland, 183?), 44.
29. John William Calcraft, *The Bride of Lammermoor: A Drama in Five Acts* (Edinburgh: London: Simpkin and Marshall, 1823), 54.
30. Ibid., 62.
31. Anna Jameson, *Shakespeare's Heroines: Characteristics of Women, Moral, Political and Historical* (London: George Bell and Sons, 1879), 58.
32. Ibid., 154.
33. George Farren, *Essays on the Varieties in Mania, Exhibited by the Characters of Hamlet, Ophelia, Lear and Edgar* (London: Dean and Munday, 1833), 59.
34. Elaine Showalter, "Representing Ophelia: Women, Madness, and the Responsibilities of Feminist Criticism," *Shakespeare and the Question of Theory*, Patricia Parker and Geoffrey Hartman, eds. (New York: Methuen, 1985), 80.
35. Georgina Weldon was an English medium who was also a playwright and opera singer. She narrowly escaped being confined to an insane asylum by her husband. Her story is told in Philip Treherne, *A Plaintiff in Person: Life of Mrs. Weldon* (London: Heinemann, 1923).

Chapter 3

1. The origins of animal magnetism, as it was initially called, are recorded in John C. Colqhuoun's *Isis Revelata; an Inquiry into the Origin, Progress and Present State of Animal Magnetism* (Edinburgh, 1836). For a thorough guide to early writing on the subject, see *Animal Magnetism, Early Hypnosis and Psychical Research, 1766–1925: An Annotated Bibliography*, ed. Adam Crabtree (1988).
2. In Dr. Elliotson's work with Elizabeth O'Key described in the next chapter, an almost total reliance on visual clues for diagnosis is evident.
3. Terry Parssinen, "Mesmeric Performers," *Victorian Studies* 21 (Autumn 1977), 89.
4. Robert Darnton, *Mesmerism and the End of the Enlightenment in France* (Cambridge, MA: Harvard University Press, 1968), 47.
5. Fred Kaplan, *Dickens and Mesmerism* (Princeton: Princeton University Press, 1975), 139.
6. Quoted in Jon Klimo, *Channeling: Investigations on Receiving Information from Paranormal Sources* (Los Angeles: Jeremy P. Tarcher, Inc., 1987), 220.
7. Maria Tatar, *Spellbound: Studies on Mesmerism and Literature* (Princeton: Princeton University Press, 1978), 4.
8. Tatar, 78. Short stories by Hoffman which deal with mesmerism include *The Agate Heart*, *The Magnetiser*, and *The Uncanny Guest*.
9. Kaplan, 77.
10. Ibid., 77.
11. L. Edward Purcell, "Trilby and Trilby-Mania," *Journal of Popular Culture* 11 (Summer 1977), 65.
12. See Daniel Pick, *Svengali's Web: The Alien Enchanter in Modern Culture* (New Haven: Yale University Press, 2000), 92 -93ff.
13. Quoted in Martha Noel Evans, *Fits and Starts: A Genealogy of Hysteria in Modern France* (Ithaca: Cornell University Press, 1992), 30.
14. In an address to the French Academy of Sciences, quoted in A.R.G. Owen, *Hysteria, Hypnosis and Healing: The Work of Jean-Martin Charcot* (London: Dennis Dobson, 1971), 187.
15. A. R. G. Owen, 189.
16. Michelle Perrot, ed., *A History of Private*

Life IV: From the Fires of Revolution to the Great War (Cambridge: Belknap Press — Harvard University Press, 1990), 679.

Chapter 4

1. British actress Fanny Kemble and American actress Anna Cora Mowatt both considered themselves in the emotional school of actors.
2. Owsei Temkin, *The Falling Sickness: A History of Epilepsy from the Greeks to the Beginnings of Modern Neurology* (Baltimore: The Johns Hopkins Press, 1971).
3. Janet Oppenheim, *"Shattered Nerves": Doctors, Patients, and Depression in Victorian England* (Oxford: Oxford University Press, 1991), 5–8.
4. Ibid., 181.
5. For more information on the conflation of these definitions, see E. M. Thornton, *Hypnotism, Hysteria and Epilepsy: An Historical Synthesis* (London: William Heinemann Medical Books Limited, 1976).
6. For more information on Irving, see Margaret Oliphant, *The Life of Edward Irving* 3d ed. rev. (London: Hurst and Blackett, 1864).
7. Kaplan, 36.
8. Page numbers of citations from articles or lectures published in *The Lancet* come from John Elliotson, *John Elliotson on Mesmerism*, ed. Fred Kaplan (New York: Da Capo Press, 1982).
9. Elliotson, 25.
10. Elliotson also describes an American woman who could preach entire sermons while mesmerized with "more than her waking eloquence." Quoted in Elliotson, 26.
11. Elliotson, 30.
12. Dr. Elliotson was, in fact, accused of scandalous conduct in an 1842 pamphlet entitled "Eyewitness, A Full Discovery of the Strange Practice of Dr. E. on the Bodies of His Female Patients" published anonymously in London.
13. Elliotson, 38.
14. Ibid., 34.
15. Ibid., 35.
16. Ibid., 36.
17. Ibid., 38.
18. Ibid., 38.
19. Richard Butsch, *The Making of American Audiences* (Cambridge: Cambridge University Press, 2000), 47.
20. Laurence Senelick, *Gender in Performance: The Presentation of Difference in the Performing Arts* (Hanover and London: University Press of New England, 1992), xi.
21. Victor Turner, *From Ritual to Theatre: The Human Seriousness of Play* (New York: PAJ Publications, 1982).
22. Ibid., 36.
23. Ibid., 39.
24. Ibid., 39.
25. Ibid., 44.
26. Ibid., 44.
27. Ibid., 44.
28. Ibid., 44.
29. Ibid., 45.
30. A common attitude of doctors at the time was that certain foods, especially meat, could cause excitement and even violence in some patients, and that their diets should be restricted to mild, harmless foods like bread and milk.
31. Elliotson, 50.
32. Ibid., 50-ff.
33. Ibid., 93.
34. Ibid., 93.
35. Ibid., 93.
36. Ibid., 93.
37. Ibid., 96.

Chapter 5

1. Samuel L. Mitchell, "A Double Consciousness, or a Duality of Persons in the Same Individual," *Medical Repository* 3 (1817), 185–186.
2. Dickson Bruce, "W.E.B. Du Bois and the Idea of Double-Consciousness," *American Literature* 64.2 (June 1992), 304.
3. John Elliotson, "Dual Consciousness," *Cornhill*, 27, 86–89.
4. Epes Sargent, *The Scientific Basis of Spiritualism* (Boston: Colby & Rich, 1891), 270.
5. Joseph Roach, *The Player's Passion: Studies in the Science of Acting* (Newark: University of Delaware Press, 1985), 45.
6. Roach, 41.
7. Kemble quoted in William Archer, *Masks or Faces?* in intro. Lee Strasberg, *The Paradox of Acting and Masks or Faces?* (New York: Hill and Wang, 1957), 213.
8. Frederic R. Marvin, *"The Philosophy of Spiritualism" and the "Pathology and Treatment of Mediomania": Two Lectures* (New York: A. K. Butts & Co., 1874).
9. J. Arthur Hill, *Spiritualism: Its History, Phenomena and Doctrine* (New York: George H. Doran Co., 1919), 210.
10. Laurence R. Moore, *In Search of White Crows: Spiritualism, Parapsychology and American Culture* (New York: Oxford University Press, 1977), 150.
11. Emma Hardinge, *Modern American Spiritualism* (New York, 1870; Elibron Classics Replica Edition, 2007), 50.
12. Archer, 185.
13. Lewes, 7.
14. The tangled connections and similarities

of trance states, hysteria, emotional acting and sheer sensibility remained strong well into the 20th century.
 15. Archer, 184.
 16. Ibid., 151.
 17. See J. O. Bearhs, "Co-consciousness: A Common Denominator in Hypnosis, Multiple Personality, and Normalcy," *American Journal of Clinical Hypnosis* 26 (1983–84), 100–113.
 18. Archer, 193.
 19. Henry Irving, Preface to Denis Diderot, *The Paradox of Acting* in intro. Lee Strasberg, *The Paradox of Acting and Masks or Faces?* (New York: Hill & Wang, 1857), 8.
 20. Roach, 181.
 21. Hock Guan Tjoa, *George Henry Lewes: A Victorian Mind* (Cambridge: Harvard University Press, 1977), 84.
 22. Quoted in Roach, 190.
 23. Lewes, 20.
 24. See Max Martersteig, *The Actor, an Artistic Problem* (1893).
 25. Roach, 180.
 26. Lorenz Kjerbuhl-Peterson, *Psychology of Acting: A Consideration of Its Principles as an Art*, trans. S. T. Barrows (Boston: Expression, 1935), 175.
 27. Imants Baruss, *Alterations of Consciousness: An Empirical Analysis for Social Scientists* (Washington: American Psychological Association, 2003), 108.
 28. Ibid., 110.
 29. Ibid., 124.
 30. Ibid., 149.
 31. Alan Read, "The Placebo of Performance: Psychoanalysis in Its Place," *Psychoanalysis and Performance*, Patrick Campbell and Adrian Kear, eds. (London: Routledge, 2001), 147.

Chapter 6

 1. Eric Wollencott Barnes, *The Lady of Fashion: The Life and Theatre of Anna Cora Mowatt* (New York: Scribner's, 1854), 70.
 2. Epes Sargent, *The Scientific Basis of Spiritualism* (Boston: Colby and Rich, 1887), 363.
 3. Theatre historian Garff B. Wilson identifies Mowatt as one of the original members of what he termed the "school of emotionalism" in American acting, in a group of actresses which included Laura Keene and Matilda Heron, among others. Garff B. Wilson, *Three Hundred Years of American Drama and Theatre* (Englewood Cliffs, NJ: Prentice-Hall, 1973), 172. Mowatt herself noted the necessity of intense emotion in her performances: "I never succeeded in stirring the hearts of others unless I was deeply affected myself," in Anna Cora Mowatt Ritchie, *Autobiography of an Actress; or Eight Years on the Stage* (Boston: Ticknor, Reed, and Fields, 1854), 244.
 4. Alex Owen, "The Other Voice: Women, Children and Nineteenth Century Spiritualism," in *Language, Gender and Childhood*, C. Steedman, C. Unwin, and V. Walkerdine, eds. (London: Routledge and Keagan Paul, 1985), 68.
 5. Alex Owen, *The Darkened Room: Women, Power and Spiritualism in Late Victorian England* (Philadelphia: University of Pennsylvania Press, 1990), iii.
 6. As Carroll Smith-Rosenberg has argued in *Disorderly Conduct: Visions of Gender in Victorian America*, "If we reject the view of women as passive victims, we face the need to identify the sources of power women used to act within a world determined to limit their power, ignore their talents, to belittle or condemn their actions" (17). Mesmerism was one of these "sources of power" for Mowatt.
 7. Johnson, 12.
 8. Carroll Smith-Rosenberg, "The Hysterical Woman: Sex Roles and Role Conflict in Nineteenth Century America," *Social Research* 39.4 (Winter 1972), 652–678.
 9. William Egginton, *How the World Became a Stage* (Albany: SUNY Press, 2003), 27.
 10. Quoted in Barnes, 72.
 11. Butsch, 68.
 12. Ibid., 66.
 13. Ritchie, 425.
 14. Catherine R. Burroughs, *Closet Stages: Joanna Baillie and the Theater Theory of British Romantic Women Writers* (Philadelphia: University of Pennsylvania Press, 1997), 34.
 15. Ibid., 48.
 16. This also partly explains the absence of "Gypsy" in Mowatt's *Autobiography*, since the manifestations of Gypsy clearly did not fit into the image of an ideal and normal woman she was trying to construct.
 17. Ritchie, 152–153.
 18. Ibid., 153.
 19. Ibid., 154.
 20. Described in Terry Parssinen, "Mesmeric Performers," *Victorian Studies* 21 (Autumn 1977), 89.
 21. See Robert C. Fuller, *Mesmerism and the American Cure of Souls* (Philadelphia: University of Pennsylvania Press, 1982), 21. Madeleine Stern also alludes to this point in her work on the phrenological movement in nineteenth century America. See *Heads and Headliners: The Phrenological Fowlers* (Norman: University of Oklahoma Press, 1971).
 22. Ritchie, 167.
 23. Alex Owen notes that many female mediums "disclaimed responsibility for their choice of career" by virtue of the fact that they spoke in a trance state. Alex Owen, "Other Voices," 39.

Ann Braude makes a similar argument throughout her study of nineteenth century female trance speakers in America who voiced socially and politically radical ideas. See Ann Braude, *Radical Spirits: Spiritualism and Women's Rights in Nineteenth Century America*, 2d ed. (Bloomington: Indiana University Press, 2001).
24. Ritchie, 167.
25. Ibid., 161.
26. Even the institutional use of mesmerism would raise suspicions. The most notorious case involved Dr. Charcot at Salpetriere in France in the 1870s and 1880s, when female hysterics mesmerized for medical scientific purposes were exhibited to the public in performances where, in the trance state, they re-enacted scenes from their own traumatic experiences, or sometimes "suggestions" from the doctors. For earlier instances, see the discussion of Dr. Elliotson and the O'Key sisters in London in the 1830s in Amy Lehman, *Theatricality, Madness and Mesmerism: Nineteenth Century Female Performers*. Diss. Indiana University, 1996.
27. Ritchie, 161.
28. Sargent, 217.
29. Ibid., 223.
30. Ibid., 224.
31. Ritchie, 72.
32. Review, *New York Times* (Jan. 23 1887).
33. Quoted in "Cushman, Charlotte," *The Concise Oxford Companion to the American Theatre*, Gerald Bordman, ed. (1987).
34. She did play the part of a harem girl in her first full-length serious play, *Gulzara, or the Persian Slave*, performed in 1840 for a private gathering of family and friends. Barnes: Chapter 5.
35. Deborah Epstein Nord, "Marks of Race: Gypsy Figures and Eccentric Femininity in Nineteenth Century Women's Writing," *Victorian Studies*, 41.2: 1.
36. Ibid., 2.
37. Ibid., 4.
38. Ibid., 4.
39. Sargent, 221. The ability of mesmerized patients to diagnose and prescribe for themselves was also seen in the case of Victor Race, mesmerized by Puysegur, a disciple of Mesmer, and also by Dr. Elliotson's patient Elizabeth O'Key, who, while in trance, gave frequent and impatient instructions to her doctors regarding her diet.
40. Ibid., 218.
41. Ibid., 218.
42. Ibid., 217.
43. Ritchie, 175-6.
44. Martha Noel Evans, *Fits and Starts: A Genealogy of Hysteria in Modern France* (Ithaca: Cornell University Press, 1992), 32.
45. Joseph Roach, among others, deals with the long history of moral disapproval of actors because of their skill in deceit and transformation in *The Player's Passion: Studies in the Science of Acting*.
46. Sargent, 219-220.
47. Ibid., 222.
48. Ibid., 221.
49. In *Radical Spirits*, Ann Braude includes a clear discussion of how the marriage of Swedenborgian notions with the phenomena of trance communications from the spirit world developed into American Spiritualism beginning in the late 1840s. Spirit communications purporting to come from Swedenborg himself or to espouse Swedenborg's ideas were common in the movement. Braude, Chapter 2.
50. Mowatt discusses the beginning of her conversion, and that of her husband James, to the doctrines of Swedenborg in Ritchie, 168 ff.
51. Sargent, 219-220.
52. Ibid., 223.
53. Alan Gauld, *A History of Hypnotism*, 363.
54. Sarbin's theories are outlined in Fred H. Frankel, *Hypnosis: Trance as a Coping Mechanism* (New York: Plenum, 1976), 16.
55. Spanos et al. quoted in Baruss, 117.
56. P. L. Harriman quoted in Reima Kampman and Reijo Hirvenoja, "Dynamic Relation of the Secondary Personality Induced by Hypnosis to the Present Personality," in *Hypnosis at Its Bicentennial*, Fred H. Frankel, ed. (New York: Plenum, 1976), 183.
57. Ibid., 187.
58. Owen, "The Other Voice," 48.
59. Gauld, 580.
60. Owen, "The Other Voice," 48.

Chapter 7

1. Emma Hardinge, *Modern American Spiritualism* (New York: 1870; Elibron Classics replica edition, 2007), 79.
2. Rev. J. L. Scott, *Scenes Beyond the Grave, Trance of Marietta Davis* (New York, 1854), n.p.
3. Uriah Clark, ed., *The Spiritualist Register for 1859* (Auburn, NY: U. Clark, 1859) 17. The context for this sentiment is the long history of conflict among American Protestant groups which had characterized religion in America since colonial times, and the competing and sometimes contradictory doctrines regarding how to achieve salvation. Those unable to profess unquestioning belief in church authorities could find themselves in serious trouble. An early example is the banishment of Anne Hutchinson from the Massachusetts Bay colony, a Puritan theocracy, for presuming to say she had received direct spiritual revelations from God. Although Hutchinson was not subject to

trances as far as we know, her insistence on the possibility of personal contact with a world of the Spirit makes her a precursor of nineteenth century female Spiritualists.

4. See Brett Caroll, *Spiritualism in Antebellum America* for more detail on Spiritualist organization and culture.

5. John B. Buescher, *The Other Side of Salvation* (Boston: Skinner House Books, 2004), 38.

6. Ibid., xii–xiii.

7. Ibid., 106.

8. S. B. Brittan, "Our Times," *Brittan's Quarterly Journal* (October 1873), 535.

9. Ibid., 537.

10. Ibid., 538.

11. Ibid., 539.

12. H. D. Barrett, *Life Works of Cora L. V. Richmond* (Chicago: Hack and Anderson, 1895), 3–4.

13. H. D. Barrett, 123.

14. Ibid.

15. Ann Douglas, *The Feminization of American Culture* (New York: Knopf, 1977), 117.

16. Eugene Taylor, *Shadow Culture: Psychology and Spirituality in America* (Washington, D.C.: Counterpoint, 1999), 131.

17. Mary Farrell Bednarowski, "Women in Occult America," *The Occult in America: New Historical Perspectives,* Howard Kerr and Charles L. Crow, eds., (Chicago: University of Illinois Press, 1983), 179.

18. Ibid., 183.

19. "Rev. of Miss Jay," *New England Spiritualist* (1855), 4.

20. Buescher, 77.

21. Nancy Rubin Stuart's *The Reluctant Spiritualist: The Life of Maggie Fox* is a fascinating and well-researched study of the medium. Barbara Weisberg's *Talking to the Dead* is another interesting account of the Fox sisters' lives and careers.

Chapter 8

1. Frances H. Green, *Biography of Samantha Mettler, the Clairvoyant* (New York: Harmonial Association, 1853), 103–104.

2. Lewes, 7.

3. George Taylor, *Players and Performances in the Victorian Theatre* (Manchester and New York: Manchester University Press), 30.

4. See Hans Robert Jauss, "Literary History as a Challenge to Literary Theory," *New Literary History* 2 (1970).

5. De Marinis, 158.

6. Ibid., 168.

7. Ibid., 168.

8. Ibid., 169.

9. Frank Podmore, *Mediums of the 19th Century,* vol. 2 (New Hyde Park, NY: University Books, 1963).

10. Podmore, *Mediums,* 8.

11. Ibid., 13.

12. See the work of Thomas Postlewait ("Autobiography and Theatre History" in *Interpreting the Theatrical Past*) and Mary Corbett ("'Artificial Natures': Class, Gender, and the Subjectivities of Victorian Actresses" in *Representing Femininity*) on actresses' attempts to construct their identities through their writing.

13. The table is on display at the national women's rights museum in Seneca Falls, New York.

14. Quoted in Eugene Taylor, *Shadow Culture: Psychology and Spirituality in America* (Washington, D.C.: Counterpoint, 1999), 138.

15. Emma Hardinge Britten, "How to Investigate Spiritualism."

16. Kenneth Silverman, *Houdini! The Career of Erich Weiss* (New York: Harper Collins, 1996), 39.

17. Houdin, *Les secrets de la Prestidigitation et de la magie,* qtd. in Silverman, 39.

18. "A Remarkable Poem," *The Spiritual Magazine* 2.4 (April 1861), 187.

19. H. D. Barrett, 555.

20. Alex Owen, *The Darkened Room,* 61.

21. Ruth Brandon, *The Spiritualists: The Passion for the Occult in the Nineteenth and the Twentieth Centuries* (New York: Alfred Knopf, 1983), 207.

22. John Buescher, "Singing with the Muse," from his website www.spirithistory.com/sngmuse.html.

23. "More from the Spirits in Buffalo," *The Spiritual Telegraph,* vol. 9., ed. S. B. Brittan (New York: Partridge and Brittan, 1854), 21.

24. Ibid., 22–23.

25. Ibid., 23.

26. Ibid., 24.

27. Laurence Moore, *In Search of White Crows* (New York: Oxford University Press, 1977), 111.

28. Adin Ballou, *An Exposition of Views ...* (Boston: Bela Marsh, 1852), 186, 187, 191.

29. Hardinge, 204.

30. "Strange Developments in a Family of Episcopalians," *The Spiritual Magazine* 4.1 (Jan. 1863), 74–76.

31. Baron Johan Liljencrants, *Spiritism and Religion* (New York: The Devin & Adair Co., 1918), 189–190.

32. Judge John Edmonds, *Letters and Tracts on Spiritualism: also Two Inspirational Orations by Cora L. V. Tappan* (London: J. Burns, 1875), 71ff.

33. Britten, *Modern American Spiritualism,* 208.

34. "Spiritualism and the Pantomimes," *The Spiritual Magazine* 2.2 (Feb. 1861), 59–60.

35. John S. Adams, *Rivulet from the Ocean of Truth* (Boston: Bela Marsh, 1854), 11.
36. Adams, 15.
37. Owen, *The Darkened Room*, 124.

Chapter 9

1. H. D. Barrett, 728.
2. *The Future Life: as Described and Portrayed by Spirits, through Mrs. Elizabeth Sweet*. 2d ed. (Boston: White & Co., 1869), 331, 333.
3. Britten, *Autobiography*, 111.
4. Ibid., 112.
5. Ibid., 114.
6. Ellen Ward, *Angels Messages* (Nashville: Wheeler, Marshall & Bruce, 1875), 301–302.
7. Quoted in Sarah Winter, "Mental Culture: Liberal Pedagogy and the Emergence of Ethnographic Knowledge," *Victorian Studies* 41.3 (Spring 1998), 427.
8. Katie Siegel, *Gender, Genre and Identity in Women's Travel Writing* (New York: Peter Lang, 2004), 125.
9. Slater Brown, *The Heyday of Spiritualism* (New York: Hawthorne Books, 1970), 48.
10. Ward, 307.
11. Sweet, 325.
12. *Strange Visitors: A Series of Original Papers. ... by the Spirits ... Dictated through a Clairvoyant* (New York: Carleton, 1869), 13.
13. Ibid., 14.
14. Ibid., 219.
15. Ibid., 167.
16. Ibid., 40.
17. Robert Cox, *Body and Soul: A Sympathetic History of American Spiritualism* (Charlottesville: University of Virginia Press, 2003), 69.
18. Ella Grace, "A Visit to Another World Described," *Planets and People* (Chicago, November 1895), 375–376. From http://www.spirithistory.com/grace.html.
19. C. G. Helleberg, compiler and arranger, *Spirit Communications, or a Book Written by the Spirits of the So-Called Dead* (Cincinnati: C. G. Helleberg, 1883), 46–47.
20. Ibid., 54–55.
21. Ibid., 106–107.
22. *Hafed, Prince of Persia* (Glasgow: Hay Nisbet & Co., 1896), 240.
23. Ibid., 235–236.
24. Liljencrants, 191–192.
25. Ward, 20.
26. Helleberg, 101–102.
27. Ibid., 103.
28. Ibid., 199.
29. Buescher, 95.
30. Ibid., 184–185.
31. Quoted in Cox, 136.
32. Buescher, 77.
33. William F. Barrett, *On the Threshold of the Unseen* (London: Kegan Paul, 1917), 124.

Chapter 10

1. H. D. Barrett, 34.
2. Ibid., 41.
3. Although neither is completely reliable, the only two contemporary biographical sources on Cora Hatch both relate this as the origin of her abilities. Besides Barrett's work, the other source is a sketch written by her first husband B. F. Hatch in the Introduction to *Mrs. Cora L. V. Hatch, Discourses on Religion, Morals, Philosophy and Metaphysics* (New York: B. F. Hatch, 1858).
4. Rev. Adin Ballou, *An Exposition of Views Respecting the Principal Facts, Causes and Peculiarities Involved in Spirit Manifestations: Together with Interesting Phenomenal Statements and Communications* (Boston: Bela Marsh, 1852), 11.
5. Ballou, 58ff.
6. Ibid., 215.
7. Ibid., 13.
8. Quoted in H. D. Barrett, 141.
9. Hardinge, *Modern American Spiritualism*, 156.
10. Quoted in H. D. Barrett, 275.
11. Ibid., 307.
12. H. D. Barrett, 479.
13. Ann Braude, "Cora Richmond," *American National Biography*, 1999.
14. Letter to the editor of the *Boston Daily Courier*, November 21, 1857. From "Making Sense of Cora Hatch," http://www.assumption.edu/whw/Hatch/Approaches.html.
15. Ibid.
16. Ibid.
17. Point 15 of "Divorce proceedings." From *Making Sense of Cora Hatch*. http://www.assumption.edu/whw/Hatch/Approaches.html.
18. H. D. Barrett, 270.
19. Ibid., 104.
20. Ibid., 301.
21. Quoted in ibid., 165.
22. Ibid., 271.
23. Ibid., 278.
24. Braude, *Radical Spirits*, 95.
25. *Making Sense of Cora Hatch*.
26. H. D. Barrett, 226.
27. Cora L.V. Daniels, *Letter to Amy Post*, 2 Jan. 1866. no. 1580. *Post Family Papers*.
28. Ibid.
29. Ibid.
30. Ibid.
31. Maragret Fox Kane, *Letter to Amy Post*, 11 April 1867. no. 1631. *Post Family Papers*.

32. Cora L. V. Daniels, *Letter to Amy Post*, 16 Feb. 1867. no. 1600. *Post Family Papers*.
33. Cora L. V. Daniels, *Letter to Amy Post*, 14 July 1867. no. 1652. *Post Family Papers*.
34. Buescher writes that "spiritualism was widely regarded as a threat in the South, 198.
35. Robert S. Cox, *Body and Soul: A Sympathetic History of American Spiritualism* (Charlottesville: University of Virginia Press, 2003), 170.

Chapter 11

1. S. B. Brittan, "Our Times," 538.
2. Quoted in Cox, 190.
3. Quoted in H. D. Barrett, 700.
4. Priscilla Sears, *A Pillar of Fire to Follow: American Indian Dramas 1808–1859* (Bowling Green, OH: Bowling Green University Popular Press, 1982), 35.
5. Ibid., 8.
6. Ibid., 5.
7. Review of *History of the Indian Tribes of North America, with Biographical Sketches and Anecdotes of the Principal Chiefs* in *Foreign Quarterly Review* reprinted in *The Eclectic Magazine* (Sept. 1846), 5.
8. Quoted in Robert S. Tilton, *Pocahontas: the Evolution of an American Narrative* (Cambridge: Cambridge University Press, 1994), 74.
9. H. D. Barrett, 85.
10. Ibid., 87–88.
11. Ibid., 90.
12. Ibid., 92.
13. Quoted in H. D. Barrett, 135.
14. William Howitt, "Gleanings in the Corn Fields of Spiritualism," *The Spiritual Magazine* 2.5 (May 1861), 194.
15. Helleberg, 196–196.
16. Quoted in Allen Putnam, "Spirit Works; Real but Not Miraculous," a lecture read at the City Hall in Roxbury, Mass., on the evening of September 21, 1853 (Boston: Bela Marsh, 1853), 33.
17. What sounds like an even more direct reference to Blake's poem is found in a line spoken by the heroine of the play *Oolaita or the Indian Heroine*, who protests, "Though Oolaita's skin were black as night, her soul is pure and spotless as the snow," qtd. in Sears, 44.
18. Cox, 206.
19. Jane M. Jackson, "The Indians," *The Banner of Light* (Oct. 3, 1868).
20. *Mind and Matter*, 2.4, 2.
21. Britten, *Autobiography*, 218.
22. "Boston Times Article," *New England Spiritualist* 1.2 (April 14, 1855).
23. Ibid.
24. Helleberg, 210.
25. Ibid., 217–218.
26. G. A. Redmon, *Mystic Hours: or Spiritual Experiences* (New York: Charles Partridge, 1859), 87.
27. Sweet, 222.
28. Fanny Green M'Dougal, "Souls and Scenes in Spirit Life," *Brittan's Quarterly Journal* 1.2 (April 1873), 223ff.
29. These remarks appeared in a letter Judge Edmonds wrote, they were extracted and published in the March 1861 issue of *The Spiritual Magazine*.
30. Helleberg, 192–193.
31. Ibid., 194–195.
32. Sweet, 200.
33. Ibid., 202.
34. Ibid., 24.
35. Epes Sargent, *The Scientific Basis of Spiritualism*, 5th ed. (Boston: Colby and Rich, 1887), 120.
36. Braude, *Radical Spirits*, 29.
37. Cox, 229.
38. Dickson Bruce, "W.E.B. Du Bois and the Idea of Double-Consciousness," *American Literature* 64.2 (June 1992), 300ff.
39. Ibid., 301.
40. Cox, 166.
41. Russ Castronovo, "The Antislavery Unconscious: Mesmerism, Vodun and 'Equality'," *Mississippi Quarterly* 53.1 (Winter 1999–2000), 41–45.
42. Untitled article, *New England Spiritualist* (May 26, 1855).
43. Britten, *Modern American Spiritualism*, 205.

Chapter 12

1. Owen, *Darkened Room*, 49.
2. Ibid., 41.
3. Alan Gauld, *The Founders of Psychic Research* (London: Routledge and Kegan Paul, 1968), 80.
4. Podmore, *From Mesmer to Christian Science*, 150 and Gauld, 193.
5. Arthur Conan Doyle, *The History of Spiritualism*, 2 vols. (New York: Arno Press, 1975), Chapter 2.
6. "Testimonial to Mrs. Hayden," *New England Spiritualist* (April 7, 1855).
7. Quoted in Arthur Conan Doyle, *The History of Spiritualism*, 2 vols. (New York: Arno Press, 1975) vol. 1, 148.
8. Conan Doyle, vol. 1, 162.
9. Gauld, *Founders*, 68.
10. Ibid., 71.

11. Ibid., 67.
12. Ibid., 75.
13. Emma Hardinge Britten, *Nineteenth Century Miracles or Spirits and Their Work in Every Country of This Earth* (New York: W. Britten, 1884), 151.
14. Article in *New England Spiritualist* 1.10 (June 9, 1855), 3.
15. A. W. Trethway, *The Controls of Stainton Moses* (London, n.d.) qtd. in Gauld, *Founders*, 78.
16. J. Arthur Hill, *Spiritualism: Its History, Phenomena and Doctrine* (New York: George H. Doran Co., 1919), 106.
17. Maskelyne quoted in Arthur Conan Doyle, *The History of Spiritualism*, vol. 1, 217.
18. Quoted in Conan Doyle, vol. 1, 218.
19. Conan Doyle, vol. 1, 219ff.
20. Moore, 104.
21. Quoted in Ruth Brandon, *The Spiritualists* (New York: Alfred Knopf, 1983), 45.
22. Moore, 109.
23. Hardinge, 254.
24. "Dr. Martin Van Buren Bly and the Times," *The Spiritual Magazine* 2.1 (Jan. 1861).
25. "Professional Mediumship," *The Spiritual Magazine* 3.5 (May 1862), 232.
26. Britten, *Nineteenth Century Miracles*, 152.
27. Judith Walkowitz, *City of Dreadful Delight: Narratives of Sexual Danger in Late-Victorian London* (Chicago: University of Chicago Press, 1992), 176.
28. Alex Owen, *Darkened Room*, 43–44.
29. Conan Doyle, vol. 1, 241.
30. Letter from Thomas Blyton to the editor of *The Spiritualist* magazine, rept. in Trevor H. Hall, *The Spiritualists*, American ed. (New York: Helix Press, Garrett publications, 1963).
31. Alex Owen, *Darkened Room*, 54.
32. Ibid., 54.
33. "Morgan, Sir Henry," *Oxford Dictionary of National Biography*, vol. 39, H.C.G. Matthew and Brian Harrison, eds. (Oxford: Oxford University Press, 2004).
34. Ibid., 125.
35. Henry T. Child, *Narratives of the Spirits of Sir Henry Morgan, and His Daughter Annie, Usually Known as John and Katie King* (Philadelphia: Hering, Pope & Co., 1874), 31.
36. Ibid., 31–32.
37. Ibid., 23.
38. Ibid., 42.
39. Ibid., 42.
40. Ibid., 42–43.
41. Ibid., 43.
42. Ibid., 44.
43. Ibid., 59.
44. Ibid., 29.
45. Alex Owen, *Darkened Room*, 67.
46. Hall, 55.
47. Quoted in ibid., 35.
48. Quoted in Conan Doyle, vol. 1, 240.
49. Alex Owen, *Darkened Room*, 71.
50. This seems to have been the belief of Trevor Hall, author of *The Spiritualists*.

Chapter 13

1. Robert Dale Owen, "Touching the Visitants From a Higher Life: A Chapter of Autobiography," *Atlantic Monthly* 35 (Jan. 1875), 57.
2. Alex Owen, *Darkened Room*, 66.
3. Robert Dale Owen, "Touching the Visitants," 58.
4. Owen mentioned that at one sitting, Mr. Oluf Sternersen, Swedish minister to the United States, was present. Robert Dale Owen, "Touching the Visitants," 59.
5. Robert Dale Owen, "Touching the Visitants," 58.
6. Ibid., 59.
7. Ibid., 59.
8. Ibid., 59.
9. The footnote reads, "She explained to me, after the sitting, that 'Sauntee' was the name of the (alleged) controlling spirit of Mrs. Fanny Young, an intimate friend of hers and a trance medium; and that … two months before this sitting Mrs. Young had died."
10. Robert Dale Owen, "Touching the Visitants," 60.
11. Ibid., 60–61.
12. Ibid., 61.
13. Ibid., 61.
14. Ibid., 61–62.
15. Ibid., 66.
16. Henry Olcott, *People from the Other World* (Rutland, VT: Charles E. Tuttle, 1972, rpt. from 1st ed. 1875), 433.
17. Ibid., 434.
18. Ibid., 439.
19. Ibid., 439
20. J. M. Roberts, "The Crusade Against Spiritualism: The Katie King Imbroglio," *Mind and Matter*, Chapt. III, vol. II, n. 45 (Oct. 2, 1877).
21. "Modern Sorcery," *Eclectic Magazine*, (Feb. 1876), 129.

Chapter 14

1. G. H. Lewes, "Seeing Is Believing," *Blackwood's Edinburgh Magazine* 88 (Oct. 1860), 381–382.
2. M. R. Booth, *Victorian Spectacular Theatre 1850–1910* (Boston: Routledge and Kegan Paul, 1981), 2.

3. Stuart, 283.
4. Gauld, *Founders,* 224.
5. John Beloff, *Parapsychology: A Concise History,* reprint (New York: Macmillan, 1997), 121.
6. Chiaia quoted in Conan Doyle, vol. 2, 14–15.
7. Brandon, *The Spiritualists,* 129–130.
8. Dudden, 2.
9. Gauld, *Founders,* 239.
10. Oppenheim, 246.
11. Buescher, 211, 206.
12. Lewes, 218.
13. Podmore, *Mediums of the Nineteenth Century* (New Hyde Park, NY: University Books, 1963), 182.
14. Quoted in Cesare Lombroso, *After Death—What?* (Boston: Small, Maynord & Co., 1909), 229–330.
15. Lombroso, 200.
16. survivalafterdeath.org.uk/mediums/desperance.htm.
17. Ibid.

Bibliography

Adams, John S. *Rivulet from the Ocean of Truth.* Boston: Bela Marsh, 1854.

Alcott, Louisa May. *Behind a Mask: The Unknown Thrillers of Louisa May Alcott.* Ed. Madeleine Stern. New York: William Morrow & Company, Inc., 1975.

Altick, Richard. *Victorian People and Ideas.* New York: W. W. Norton, 1973.

The American Theatre as Seen by Its Critics 1752–1934. Ed. Montrose J. Moses and John Mason Brown. New York: W. W. Norton & Co., 1934.

Animal Magnetism, Early Hypnotism, and Psychical Research, 1766–1925: An Annotated Bibliography. ed. Adam Crabtree. White Plains, N.Y.: Kraus International Publications, 1988.

Archer, William. *Masks or Faces?* Intro. Lee Strasberg, *The Paradox of Acting and Masks or Faces?* New York: Hill and Wang, 1957.

Auerbach, Nina. *Romantic Imprisonment: Women and Other Glorified Outcasts.* New York: Columbia University Press, 1985.

_____. *Woman and the Demon: The Life of a Victorian Myth.* Cambridge: Harvard University Press, 1982.

Baker, Michael. *The Rise of the Victorian Actor.* Totowa, N.J.: Rowman and Littlefield, 1978.

Barber, T. K., N. P. Spanos, and J. F. Chaves. *Hypnosis, Imagination and Human Potentialities.* New York: Pergamum Press, 1974.

Barish, Jonas. *The Antitheatrical Prejudice.* Berkeley and Los Angeles: University of California Press, 1981.

Barnes, Eric Wollencott. *The Lady of Fashion: The Life and the Theatre of Anna Cora Mowatt.* New York: Charles Scribner's Sons, 1954.

Barrett, H. D. *Life Work of Cora L. V. Richmond.* Chicago: Hack and Anderson, 1895.

Barrett, William F. *On the Threshold of the Unseen.* London: Kegan Paul, 1917.

Baruss, Imants. *Alterations of Consciousness: An Empirical Analysis for Social Scientists.* Washington: American Psychological Association, 2003.

Barzun, Jacques. *Berlioz and His Century: An Introduction to the Age of Romanticism.* New York: Meridian Books, 1956.

Basch, Françoise. *Relative Creatures: Victorian Women in Society and the Novel.* Trans. Anthony Rudolph. New York: Schocken, 1974.

Basham, Diana. *The Trial of Woman: Feminism and the Occult Sciences in Victorian Literature and Society.* New York: New York University Press, 1992.

Beahrs, J. O. "Co-consciousness: A Common Denominator in Hypnnosis, Multiple Personality and Normalcy." *American Journal of Clinical Hypnosis* 26 (1983–84): 100–112.

Bednarowski, Mary Farrell. "Women in Occult America." Howard Kerr and Charles L. Crow, eds. *The Occult in America: New Historical Perspectives.* Chicago: University of Illinois Press, 1983.

Beloff, John. *Parapsychology: A Concise History.* Reprint. New York: Macmillan, 1997.

Bennett, Bridget. "Sacred Theatres: Shakers, Spiritualists, Theatricality and the Indian in the 1830s and 1840s." *TDR* 49.3 (Fall 2005): 114–134.

Biography of the British Stage. London: Sherwood, Jones and Co., 1824.

Bjorlin, Joel. *Consulting Spirits: A Bibliography.* Westport, CT: Greenwood, 1998.

Booth, M. R. *Theatre in the Victorian Age.* Cambridge: Cambridge University Press, 1991.

———. *Victorian Spectacular Theatre 1850–1910*. Boston: Routledge and Kegan Paul, 1981.

Brandon, Ruth. *The Life and Many Deaths of Harry Houdini*. New York: Random House paperback, 2003.

———. *The Spiritualists: The Passion for the Occult in the Nineteenth and the Twentieth Centuries*. New York: Alfred Knopf, 1983.

Braude, Ann. "Cora Richmond." *American National Biography*, 1999.

———. *Radical Spirits: Spiritualism and Women's Rights in Nineteenth-Century America*. Boston: Beacon Press, 1989.

Britten, Emma Hardinge. *Autobiography*. Ed. and pub. Margaret Wilkinson, 1900. facsimile edition pub. by SNU Publications 1996, rpt. 1999.

———. *Nineteenth Century Miracles or Spirits and Their Work in Every Country of This Earth*. New York: W. Britten, 1884.

Brontë, Charlotte. *Villette*. Eds. Herbert Rosengarten and Margaret Smith. Oxford: Clarendon Press, 1984.

Bruce, Dickson. "W. E. B. Du Bois and the Idea of Double-Consciousness." *American Literature* 64.2 (June 1992): 299–309.

Buescher, John B. "Inducing Trance." http://www.spirithistory.com.

———. *The Other Side of Salvation: Spiritualism and Nineteenth-Century Religious Experience*. Boston: Skinner House Books, 2004.

———. "Singing with the Muse." http://www.spirithistory.com.

Bulwer-Lytton, Edward. *The Lady of Lyons*. *Nineteenth-Century British Drama*. Ed. Leonard R. N. Ashley. New York: Scott, Foresman and Company, 1967.

Burroughs, Catherine. *Closet Stages: Joanna Baillie and the Theater Theory of British Romantic Women Writers*. Philadelphia: University of Pennsylvania Press, 1997.

Butler, Judith. "Performative Acts and Gender Constitution: Phenomenology and Feminist Theory." *Gender Trouble: Feminism and the Subversion of Identity*. New York: Routledge, 1989.

Butsch, Richard. *The Making of American Audiences: from Stage to Television, 1750–1990*. Cambridge; New York: Cambridge University Press, 2000.

Calcraft, John William. *The Bride of Lammermoor: A Play in Five Acts*. Edinburgh and London: Simpkin and Marshall, 1823.

Camden, Carroll. "On Ophelia's Madness." *Shakespeare Quarterly* (1964): 247–255.

Cappello, Mary. "Alice James: Neither Dead nor Recovered." *American Imago* 45.2 (Summer 1988): 127–162.

Capron, Eliab Wilkinson. *Modern Spiritualism: Its Facts and Fanaticisms, Its Consistencies and Contradictions*. Boston: Bela Marsh, 1855.

Carlson, Marvin. *The French Stage in the Nineteenth Century*. Metuchen, N.J.: Scarecrow Press, 1972.

Castronovo, Russ. "The Antislavery Unconsious: Mesmerism, Vodun, and 'Equality.'" *Mississippi Quarterly* 53.1 (Winter 1999–2000): 41–56.

Chambers, Ross. *L'Ange et l'automate: variations sur le mythe de l'actrice de Nerval à Proust*. Paris: Archives de Lettres modernes, 1971.

Charney, Maurice, and Hanna Charney. "The Language of Madwomen in Shakespeare and his Fellow Dramatists." *Signs* 3 (1977): 451–460.

Child, Henry T. *Narratives of the Spirits of Sir Henry Morgan, and His Daughter Annie, Usually Known as John and Katie King*. Philadelphia: Hering, Pope & Co., 1874.

Conan Doyle, Sir Arthur. *The History of Spiritualism*. 2 vols. New York: Arno Press, 1975.

Cooter, Roger. *The Cultural Meaning of Popular Science: Phrenology and the Organization of Consent in Nineteenth-Century Britain*. Cambridge; New York: Cambridge University Press, 1984.

———. *Phrenology in the British Isles: An Annotated Historical Bibliography and Index*. Metuchen, N.J.: Scarecrow Press, 1989.

Corbett, Mary Jean. *Representing Femininity: Middle Class Subjectivities in Victorian and Edwardian Women's Autobiographies*. New York: Oxford University Press, 1992.

Cox, Robert S. *Body and Soul: A Sympathetic History of American Spiritualism*. Charlottesville: University of Virginia Press, 2003.

Crabtree, Adam. *From Mesmer to Freud: Magnetic Sleep and the Roots of Psycholog-

ical Healing. New Haven: Yale University Press, 1982.

Cunningham, Gail. *The New Woman and the Victorian Novel.* London: The Macmillan Press, Ltd., 1978.

Darnton, Robert. *Mesmerism and the End of the Enlightenment in France.* Cambridge: Harvard University Press, 1968.

Davies, Rev. Charles Maurice. *Mystic London; or Phases of Occult Life in the Metropolis.* London: Tinsley Brothers, 1875.

Davis, Tracy C. *Actresses as Working Women: Their Social Identity in Victorian Culture.* London; New York: Routledge, 1991.

———. "Does the Theatre Make for Good? Actresses' Purity and Temptation in the Victorian Era." *Q.Q.* 93: 33–49.

———, and Thomas Postlewait, eds. *Theatricality.* Cambridge: Cambridge University Press, 2003.

De Guistino, David. *Conquest of Mind: Phrenology and Victorian Social Thought.* London: Croom Helm; Totowa, N.J.: Rowman and Littlefield, 1975.

De Marinis, Marco. *The Semiotics of Performance.* Trans. Aine O'Healy. Bloomington: Indiana University Press, 1993.

Dempsey, Thomas. *The Delphic Oracle: Its Early History, Influence and Fall.* New York: Benjamin Blom, 1972.

Descotes, Maurice. *Le Drame Romantique et Ses Grands Créateurs (1827–1839).* Paris: Presses Universitaires de France, 1955.

Diamond, Elin. "Realism and Hysteria: Toward a Feminist Mimesis." *Discourse* 13.1 (Fall-Winter 1990–91): 59–92.

Diderot, Denis. "The Paradox of Acting." *The Paradox of Acting and Masks or Faces.* Intro. Lee Strasberg. New York: Hill & Wang, 1957.

Dingwall, Eric John, ed. *Abnormal Hypnotic Phenomena: A Survey of Nineteenth-Century Cases.* Vol. 4. USA, by Allan Angoff; Great Britain, by Eric Dingwall. London: J. A. Churchill, 1967–68.

Donohue, Joseph. "Women in the Victorian Theatre: Images, Illusions, Realities." *Gender in Performance: The Presentation of Difference in the Performing Arts.* ed. Lawrence Senelick. Hanover and London: University Press of New England, 1992.

Douglas, Ann. *The Feminization of American Culture.* New York: Knopf, 1977.

Dudden, Faye. *Women in the American Theatre: Actresses and Audiences, 1790–1870.* New Haven: Yale University Press, 1994.

Du Potet de Sennevoy, Jules Denis. *An Introduction to the Study of Animal Magnetism.* London: Saunders and Otley, 1838.

Eddison, Robert. "Souvenirs de Théâtre Anglais à Paris, 1827." *Theatre Notebook* 9 (1954–55): 99–103.

Edwards, Judge. *Letters and Tracts on Spiritualism: also Two Inspirational Orations by Cora L. V. Tappan.* London: J. Burns, 1875.

Egginton, William. *How the World Became a Stage: Presence, Theatricality, and the Question of Modernity.* Albany: State University of New York Press, 2003.

Elliotson, John. *John Elliotson on Mesmerism.* ed. Fred Kaplan. New York: Da Capo Press, 1982.

Evans, Martha Noel. *Fits and Starts: A Genealogy of Hysteria in Modern France.* Ithaca: Cornell University Press, 1992.

Farren, George. *Essays on the Varieties in Mania, Exhibited by the Characters of Hamlet, Ophelia, Lear and Edgar.* London: Dean and Munday, 1833.

Ferris, Lesley. *Acting Women: Images of Women in Theatre.* New York: New York University Press, 1989.

Fischer, Sandra K. "Hearing Ophelia: Gender and Tragic Discourse in *Hamlet.*" *Renaissance and Reformation* XXVI, 1 (1990): 1–10.

Fontenrose, Joseph. *The Delphic Oracle.* Berkeley: University of California Press, 1978.

Fornell, Earl Wesley. *The Unhappy Medium: Spiritualism and the Life of Margaret Fox.* Austin: University of Texas Press, 1964.

Frankel, Fred H. *Hypnosis: Trance as a Coping Mechanism.* New York: Plenum Medical Book Company, 1991.

Fuller, Robert C. *Mesmerism and the American Cure of Souls.* Philadelphia: University of Pennsylvania Press, 1982.

Gauld, Alan. *The Founders of Psychic Research.* London: Kegan Paul, 1968.

———. *A History of Hypnotism.* Cambridge, UK: Cambridge University Press, 1992.

Gay, Peter. *The Bourgeois Experience: Victo-*

ria to Freud. I, Education of the Senses. II, The Tender Passion. New York: Oxford University Press, 1984, 1986.

Gilbert, Sandra M., and Susan Gubar. The Madwoman in the Attic: The Woman Writer and the Nineteenth-Century Literary Imagination. New Haven, CT: Yale University Press, 1978.

Gilman, Sander L. The Faces of Madness: Hugh W. Diamond and the Origin of Psychiatric Photography. New York: Brunner/Mazel, 1976.

_____. Seeing the Insane. New York: J. Wiley: Bruner/Mazel Publishers, 1982.

Goffman, Erving. The Presentation of Self in Everyday Life. New York: Doubleday, 1959.

Gold, Arthur, and Robert Fizdale. The Divine Sarah: A Life of Sarah Bernhardt. New York: Random House, 1992.

Goldstein, Jan. Console and Classify: The French Psychiatric Profession in the Nineteenth Century. Cambridge: Cambridge University Press, 1987.

Green, Francis H. Biography of Mrs. Samantha Mettler, the Clairvoyant. New York: Harmonial Association, 1853.

Hafed Prince of Persia: His Experiences in Earth Life and Spirit Land ... Received through Mr. David Duguid, etc. Glasgow: Hay Nisbet & Co., 1896.

Hall, Trevor. The Spiritualists: The Story of Florence Cook and William Crookes. American ed. New York: Helix Press, Garrett Publications, 1963.

Hardinge, Emma. Modern American Spiritualism. New York, 1870. Elibron Classics replica edition, 2007.

Helleberg, C. G., compiler and arranger. Spirit Communications. or A Book Written by the Spirits of the So-Called Dead. Cincinnati: C. G. Helleberg, 1883.

Henahan, Donal. "Why They Were Crazy About Mad Scenes." New York Times, Sunday, Sept. 21, 1980.

Hilgard, E. R. Divided Consciousness: Multiple Controls in Human Thought and Action. New York: John Wiley, 1986.

Hill, J. Arthur. Spiritualism: Its History, Phenomena and Doctrine. New York: George H. Doran Co., 1919.

Home, D. D. Incidents in My Life. Secaucus, N. J., University Books, 1972.

Howarth, W. D. Sublime and Grotesque: A Study of French Romantic Drama. London: Harrap, 1975.

Hutton, Laurence and Brander Matthers, eds., Kean and Booth and Their Contemporaries Boston: L. C. Page & Co., 1900.

Ihrig, Grace Pauline. Heroines in French Drama of the Romantic Period 1829–1848. New York: King's Crown, Columbia University, 1950.

James, Henry. The Bostonians. New York: Dial Press, 1945.

Jameson, Anna. Shakespeare's Heroines: Characteristics of Women, Moral Political and Historical. London: George Bell and Sons, 1879.

Jones, Amanda T. A Psychic Autobiography. New York: Graves, 1910.

Kampman, Reimo, and Reijo Hirvenoja. "Dynamic Relation of the Secondary Personality Induced by Hypnosis to the Present Personality" in Hypnosis at Its Bicentennial, ed. Fred H. Frankel. New York: Plenum, 1976.

Kaplan, Fred. Dickens and Mesmerism. Princeton, N.J.: Princeton University Press, 1975.

Kerr, Howard. Mediums and Spirit Rappers and Roaring Radicals. Urbana: University of Illinois Press, 1972.

_____, and Charles L. Crow, eds. The Occult in America: New Historical Perspectives. Chicago: University of Illinois Press, 1983.

Kirby, E. T. Ur-Drama: The Origins of Theatre. New York: New York University Press, 1975.

Kjerbuhl-Peterson, Lorenz. Psychology of Acting: A Consideration of Its Principles as an Art. Trans. S. T. Barrows. Boston: Expression, 1935.

Klimo, Jon. Channeling: Investigations on Receiving Information from Paranormal Sources. Los Angeles: Jeremy P. Tarcher, Inc., 1987.

Knepler, Henry. The Gilded Stage: The Years of the Great International Actresses. New York: William Morrow and Company, 1968.

Leahey, Thomas Hardey, and Grace Evans Leahey. Psychology's Occult Doubles: Psychology and the Problem of Pseudoscience. Chicago: Nelson-Hall, 1983.

Lehman, Amy. "'Call Me Gypsy'— Anna Cora Mowatt and Mesmerism." Nine-

teenth Century Theatre and Film. 29.1 (Summer 2002): 49–65.
_____. Theatricality, Madness and Mesmerism: Nineteenth Century Female Performers. Diss. Indiana University, 1996. Ann Arbor: UMI, 1996.
Lewes, George Henry. On Actors and the Art of Acting. Leipzig: Bernard Tauchnitz, 1845.
Liljencrants, Baron Johan. Spiritism and Religon. New York: The Devin-Adair Co., 1918.
Litvak, Joseph. Caught in the Act: Theatricality in the Nineteenth-Century English Novel. Berkeley: University of California Press, 1992.
Logan, Olive. Apropos of Women and Theatres. New York: Carleton, Publisher, Madison Square; London: S. Low, Son & Co., 1869.
_____. Before the Footlights and Behind the Scenes. Philadelphia: Parmalee, 1870.
Lodge, Sir Oliver. The Survival of Man: A Study in Unrecognized Human Faculty. New York: George H. Doran Co., 1920.
Lombroso, Cesare. After Death—What? Trans. William Sloane Kennedy. Boston: Small, Maynard & Co., 1909.
Macready, William Charles. Macready's Reminiscences and Selections From His Diaries and Letters. ed. Sir Frederick Pollock. New York, 1875.
Marryat, Florence. There Is No Death. 5th ed. Griffith Farran & Co., Ltd., 1892.
Marvin, Frederic R. "Philosophy of Spiritualism" and the "Pathology and Treatment of Mediomania:" Two Lectures. New York: A. K. Butts & Co., 1874.
Maynard, Nettie Colburn. Was Abraham Lincoln a Spiritualist? or Curious Revelations from the Life of a Trance Medium. Philadelphia: Rufus C. Hartranft, 1891.
Meisel, Martin. "Perspectives on Victorian and Other Acting." Victorian Studies 6 (June 1963): 355–367.
_____. Realizations: Narrative, Pictorial and Theatrical Arts in Nineteenth Century England. Princeton: Princeton University Press, 1983.
Moers, Ellen. Literary Women: The Great Writers. New York: Doubleday, 1976: 173–210.
Moore, R. Laurence. In Search of White Crows: Spiritualism, Parapsychology and American Culture. New York: Oxford University Press, 1977.
"Morgan, Sir Henry" Oxford Dictionary of National Biography, vol. 39. Eds. H. C. G. Matthew and Brian Harrison. Oxford: Oxford University Press, 2004.
Mowatt, Anna Cora. Armand, or The Peer and the Peasant. London: W. Newberry, 1849.
_____. Fashion. Nineteenth Century American Plays. ed. Myron Matlaw. New York: Applause Theatrical Book Publishers, 1985.
Murray, Janet H. Strong-Minded Women: and Other Lost Voices from Nineteenth-Century England. New York: Pantheon, 1982.
Nelson, Geoffrey K. Spiritualism and Society. London: Routledge and Kegan Paul, 1969.
Nightingale, Florence. Cassandra. introduction by Myra Stark. Old Westbury, NY: The Feminist Press, 1979.
Nord, Deborah Epstein. "'Marks of Race': Gypsy Figures and Eccentric Femininity in Nineteenth-Century Women's Writing." Victorian Studies 41.2 (Winder 1998).
Olcott, Henry S. People from the Other World. Rutland, VT: Charles E. Tuttle Company, 1972 (reprt. from 1875 ed.).
Oliphant, Margaret. The Life of Edward Irving. 3d ed., rev. London: Hurst and Blackett, 1864.
Oppenheim, Janet. The Other World: Spiritualism and Psychical Research in England, 1850–1914. Cambridge: Cambridge University Press, 1985.
_____. "Shattered Nerves": Doctors, Patients, and Depression in Victorian England. New York, Oxford: Oxford Univeristy Press, 1991.
Owen, A.R.G. Hysteria, Hypnosis, and Healing: The Work of J.-M. Charcot. London: Dennis Dobson, 1971.
Owen, Alex. The Darkened Room: Women, Power and Spiritualism in Late Victorian England. Philadelphia: University of Pennsylvania Press, 1990.
Oxberry, William. Oxberry's Dramatic Biography and Historical Anecdotes. vol. II. London: George Virtue, 1825.
Palfreman, Jon. "Mesmerism and the English Medical Profession: A Study of

Conflict." *Ethics in Science and Medicine* 4 (1977): 51–66.

Parssinen, Terry. "Mesmeric Peformers." *Victorian Studies* 21 (Autumn 1977): 87–104.

———. "The Phrenology Movement in Early Victorian Britain." *Journal of Social History* (Fall 1974): 1–14.

———. "Professional Deviants and the History of Medicine: Medical Mesmerists in Victorian Britain." *Sociological Review Monographs* 27. 1979.

Perrot, Michelle, ed. *A History of Private Life IV: From the Fires of Revolution to the Great War*. Cambridge: The Belknap Press of Harvard University Press, 1990.

Peterson, M. Jeanne. *The Medical Profession in Mid-Victorian London*. Berkeley and Los Angeles: University of California Press, 1978.

A Phrenological Dictionary of Nineteenth-Century Americans. Compiled by Madeleine B. Stern. Westport, CT: Greenwood Press, 1982.

Pick, Daniel. *Svengali's Web: The Alien Enchanter in Modern Culture*. New Haven: Yale University Press, 2000.

Podmore, Frank. *From Mesmer to Christian Science: A Short History of Mental Healing*. New Hyde Park, NY: University Books, 1963.

———. *Mediums of the Nineteenth Century*. New Hyde Park, NY: University Books, 1963.

Poe, Edgar Allan. *Writings in the Broadway Journal: Non-Fictional Prose, Part I, The Text*. ed. Burton R. Pollin. New York: Gordian Press, 1986.

Poovey, Mary. *Uneven Developments: The Ideological Work of Gender in Mid-Victorian England*. Chicago: University of Chicago Press, 1988.

Postlewait, Thomas. "Autobiography and Theatre History." *Interpreting the Theatrical Past: Historiography of Performance*. Eds. Thomas Postlewait and Bruce A. McConachie. Iowa City: University of Iowa Press, 1989.

Purcell, L. Edward. "Trilby and Trilby-Mania." *Journal of Popular Culture* 11 (Summer 1977): 62–75.

Putnam, Allen. *Spirit Works: Real but Not Miraculous. A Lecture Read at the City Hall in Roxbury, Mass. on the Evening of September 21st 1853*. Boston: Bela Marsh, 1853.

Raby, Peter. *Fair Ophelia: Harriet Smithson Berlioz*. Cambridge: Cambridge University Press, 1982.

Read, Alan. "The Placebo of Performance: Psychoanalysis in Its Place." *Psychoanalysis and Performance*. Eds. Patrick Campbell & Adrian Kear. London: Routledge, 2001.

Redmon, G. A., M.D. *Mystic Hours: or Spiritual Experiences*. New York: Charles Partridge; Boston: Bela Marsh, 1859.

Ritchie, Anna Cora Mowatt. *Autobiography of an Actress; or Eight Years on the Stage*. Boston: Ticknor, Reed, and Fields, 1854.

———. *Mimic Life; or, Before and Behind the Curtain*. Boston: Ticknor and Fields, 1856.

Roach, Joseph. *The Player's Passion: Studies in the Scince of Acting*. Newark: University of Delaware Press, 1985.

Sargent, Epes. *The Scientific Basis of Spiritualism*. 5th ed. Boston: Colby and Rich, 1887.

Scheckel, Susan. "Domesticating the Drama of Conquest: Barker's Pocahontas on the Popular Stage." *ATQ* 10.3 (September 1996): 231–243.

Sears, Priscilla. *A Pillar of Fire to Follow: American Indian Dramas 1808–1859*. Bowling Green, OH: Bowling Green University Popular Press, 1982.

Senelick, Laurence, ed. *Gender in Performance: The Presentation of Difference in the Performing Arts*. Hanover and London: University Press of New England, 1992.

Showalter, Elaine. *The Female Malady: Women, Madness and English Culture, 1830–1980*. New York: Penguin Books, 1987.

———. "Hysteria, Feminism, and Gender." *Hysteria Beyond Freud*. Sander Gilman, et al. Berkeley: University of California Press, 1993.

———. "Representing Ophelia: Women, Madness, and the Responsibilities of Feminist Criticism." *Shakespeare and the Question of Theory*. ed. Patricia Parker and Geoffrey Hartman. New York: Methuen, 1985.

Siegel, Katie. *Gender, Genre and Identity in*

Women's Travel Writing. New York: Peter Lang, 2004.

Silverman, Kenneth. *Houdini! The Career of Erich Weiss.* New York: Harper Collins, 1996.

Smith-Rosenberg, Carroll. *Disorderly Conduct: Visions of Gender in Victorian America.* New York: Alfred A. Knopf, 1985.

_____. "The Hysterical Woman: Sex Roles and Role Conflict in Nineteenth-Century America." *Social Research* 39 (1972).

Somerset, C.A. *Crazy Jane: A Romantic Play in Three Acts.* London: J. Cumberland, 183?.

Spiegel, H., and D. Spiegel. *Trance and Treatment: Clinical Uses of Hypnosis.* New York: Basic Books, 1978.

States, Bert O. "The Actor's Presence: Three Phenomenal Modes." *Theatre Journal* 35 (October 1983): 359–75.

_____. *Great Reckonings in Little Rooms: On the Phenomenology of Theater.* Berkeley and Los Angeles: University of California Press, 1985.

Stern, Madeleine B. *Heads and Headliners: The Phrenological Fowlers.* Norman: University of Oklahoma Press, 1971.

Stokes, John. "Rachel's 'Terrible Beauty': An Actress Among the Novelists." *ELH* 51 (Winter 1984): 771–93.

_____, Michael R. Booth, and Susan Bassnett. *Bernhardt, Terry, Duse: The Actress in Her Time.* Cambridge: Cambridge University Press, 1988.

Strange Visitors: A Series of Original Papers ... by the Spirits ... Dictated through a Clairvoyant. New York: Carleton, 1869.

Stryk, Lydia. "Acting Hysteria: An Analysis of the Actress and Her Parts." Ph.D. Dissertation, CUNY, 1992.

Stuart, Nancy Rubin. *The Reluctant Spiritualist: The Life of Maggie Fox.* Orlando: Harcourt, Inc., 2005.

Sweet, Elizabeth. *The Future Life: As Described and Portrayed by the Spirits, through Mrs. Elizabeth Sweet.* Intro. by Judge John Edmonds. 2d ed. Boston: White & Co., 1869.

Tatar, Maria M. *Spellbound: Studies on Mesmerism and Literature.* Princeton: Princeton University Press, 1978.

Taylor, Eugene. *Shadow Culture: Psychology and Spirituality in America.* Washington, D.C.: Counterpoint, 1999.

Taylor, George. *Players and Performances in the Victorian Theatre.* Manchester and New York: Manchester University Press, 1989.

Temkin, Owsei. *The Falling Sickness: A History of Epilepsy from the Greeks to the Beginnings of Modern Neurology.* 2d ed., rev. Baltimore and London: The Johns Hopkins Press, 1971.

Thompson, F.M.L. *The Rise of Respectable Society, A Social History of Victorian Britain, 1830–1900.* Cambridge: Harvard University Press, 1988.

Thomson, Patricia. *The Victorian Heroine: A Changing Ideal 1837–1873.* London: Oxford University Press, 1956.

Thornton, E. M. *Hypnotism, Hysteria and Epilepsy: An Historical Synthesis.* London: William Heinemann Medical Books Limited, 1976.

Tilton, Robert S. *Pocahontas: The Evolution of an American Narrative.* Cambridge: Cambridge University Press, 1994.

Tjoa, Hock Guan. *George Henry Lewes: A Victorian Mind.* Cambridge: Harvard University Press, 1977.

The True Ophelia: And Other Studies of Shakespeare's Women. by an Actress. London; Toronto: Sidgwick & Jackson, Ltd., 1913.

Vardac, A. Nicholas. *Stage to Screen: Theatrical Origins of Early Film: David Garrick to D. W. Griffith.* (Da Capo paperback) Cambridge: Harvard University Press, 1949.

Vicinus, Martha, ed. *Suffer and Be Still: Women in the Victorian Age.* Bloomington: Indiana University Press, 1972.

_____, ed. *A Widening Sphere: Changing Roles of Victorian Women.* Bloomington: Indiana University Press, 1977.

Victorian Science and Victorian Values: Literary Perspectives. ed. James Paradis and Thomas Postlewait. New Brunswick, NJ: Rutgers University Press, 1985.

Walkowitz, Judith. *City of Dreadful Delight: Narratives of Sexual Danger in Late-Victorian London.* Chicago: University of Chicago Press, 1992.

Ward, Ellen. *Angels Messages, Through Mrs. Ellen Ward, as a Medium*. Nashville, TN: Wheeler, Marshall & Bruce, printers, 1875.

Weisberg, Barbara. *Talking to the Dead: Kate and Maggie Fox and the Rise of Spiritualism*. San Francisco, Harper Collins, 2004.

Winter, Alison. *Mesmerized: Powers of Mind in Victorian Britain*. Chicago: University of Chicago Press, 1998.

Winter, Sarah. "Mental Culture: Liberal Pedagogy and the Emergence of Ethnographic Knowledge." *Victorian Studies* 41.3 (Spring 1998): 427–454.

Woods, Leigh. "On Playing Shakespeare: Advice and Commentary from Actors and Actresses of the Past." *Contributions in Drama and Theatre Studies* 37. Westport, CT: Greenwood Press, 1991.

Nineteenth Century Periodical Literature

Ballou, Adin. *An Exposition of Views respecting the Princiapl Facts, Causes and Peculiarities involved in Spirit Manifestations: Together with Interesting Phenomenal Statements and Communications*. Boston: Bela Marsh, 1852.

"Boston Times Article." *New England Spiritualist* 1.2 (April 14, 1855).

Brittan, S. B. "Our Times." *Brittan's Quarterly Journal* 1.4 (October 1873): 535–540.

"Brown, Theocritus." "Animal Magnetism in London in 1837." *Blackwood's Edinburgh Magazine* 42: 384–393.

Clark, Uriah, ed. *The Spiritual Register for 1859*. Auburn NY: U. Clark; Boston: Bela Marsh; New York: S. T. Munson; Cincinnati: M. Bly; 1859.

"The Death-Blow of American Slavery from Spiritualism" (extracted from a letter from Judge Edmonds, Dec. 30, 1860). *The Spiritual Magazine* 11.3 (March 1861): 106–107.

"Dr. Martin Van Buren Bly and the *Times*." *The Spiritual Magazine* 2.1 (Jan. 1861): 29–32.

Howitt, William. "Gleanings in the Corn Fields of Spiritualism." *The Spiritual Magazine* 2.5 (May 1861): 193–206.

Jackson, Jane M. "The Indians." *Banner of Light* 24.3 (Oct. 3, 1868): 2.

Lewes, George Henry. "Seeing Is Believing." *Blackwood's Edinburgh Magazine* 88 (October 1860).

M'Dougal, Fanny Green. "Souls and Scenes in Spirit Life." *Brittan's Quarterly Journal* 1.2 (April 1873): 223–238.

"Miss Cora Hatch, the Eloquent Medium of the Spiritualists." *Frank Leslie's Illustrated Newspaper*. May 9, 1857.

"Modern Sorcery." *Eclectic Magazine*. (February 1876): 129.

"More from the Spirits in Buffalo." *The Spiritual Telegraph*, vol. 9. ed. S. B. Brittan. New York: Partridge and Brittan, 1854.

Owen, Robert Dale. "Touching the Visitants from a Higher Life: A Chapter of Autobiography." *Atlantic Monthly* 35 (Jan. 1875): 57–69.

"Professional Mediumship." *The Spiritual Magazine* 3.5 (May 1862): 232.

"A Remarkable Poem." *The Spiritual Magazine* 2.4 (April 1861): 187–188.

Roberts, J. M. "The Crusade Against Spiritualism: The Katie King Imbroglio" Chapt. III, *Mind and Matter*, vol. II, n. 45 (Oct. 2, 1877).

"Spiritualism and the Pantomimes." *The Spiritual Magazine* 2.2 (Feb. 1861): 59–60.

"Strange Developments in a Family of Episcopalians." *The Spiritual Magazine* 4.1 (Jan. 1863): 74–76.

"Testimonial to Mrs. Hayden." *New England Spiritualist* 1.1 (April 7, 1855).

"Visits to Dr. Elliotson's." *Chamber's Edinburgh Journal*. n. 396 (August 31, 1839): 249–250.

Unpublished Letters

Daniels, Cora L. V. *Letter to Amy Post*. 2 Jan. 1866. no. 1580. Post Family Papers. Department of Rare Books and Special Collections, University of Rochester Libraries, Rochester, New York.

———. *Letter to Amy Post*. 16 Feb. 1867. no. 1600. Post Family Papers.

———. *Letter to Amy Post*. 14 July 1867. no. 1652. Post Family Papers.

Kane, Margaret Fox. *Letter to Amy Post*. 11 April 1867. no. 1631. Post Family Papers.

Index

abolition movement 138
acting, conventions of 101; and the female body 172
"acting female" 26
African Americans 137–141; *see also* slaves
After Dark 14
Alcott, Louisa May 22
American Anti-Slavery Association 126
American Revolution 153; slaves fighting in 137
Anderson, John Henry 95
"Angel in the House" 18, 27
animal magnetism *see* mesmerism
Animal Magnetism (farce) 35
Antoine, Andre and the Theatre Libre 14
"apports" 94
Archer, William, on "double action of the brain" 59; *Masks and Faces* 58
Arctic, spirit travels to 104–105; *see also* Franklin, Sir John; Kane, Elisha Kent
Aristotle 6, 174–175; tragic hero 133
Arrowhead, Indian spirit 135
Astor Place Riot 130

Ballou, A.A. (Augustus) 116
Ballou, Adin 115–117
Barnum, P.T. 12–13, 81
Barrett, H.D. 83–85
Beerbohm, Max 15
Behind a Mask (Alcott) 22
Belasco, David 13, 15
The Bells 12
Bernhardt, Sarah 14, 19, 24; and Blanche Wittman 38
Bird, Isabella 106
Black Hawk, spirit of 133–134
black Spiritualists 125–126
Blackburn, Charles 149, 158
Blyton, Thomas 151
Booth, Edwin 19
Booth, John Wilkes 19
Booth, Junius Brutus 19
The Bostonians 96, 123
Boucicault, Dion 147
"Bowery B'hoys" 46, 130

box set 13
The Bride of Lammermoor 28
Brittan, S.B. 83–84
Britten, Emma Hardinge 57, 102; anxiety as speaker 58; and Indian guide 135; on mediumship 148–149; "Rules for the Spirit Circle" 93–94
Brontë, Charlotte 23–24
Brooks, Sarah, in seances with Cora Scott 117, 132
Browning, Elizabeth Barrett 145
Browning, Robert 145
the "Burned Over district" 79, 115
The Butchers 14

capital punishment 156
Cassandra (Nightingale) 26
The Castle Spectre 11–12
catharsis 6
Chandos, Leigh Hunt 101
Channing, Dr. William Francis 63, 68
Charcot, Dr. Jean-Martin 29, 30; as Svengali 36–37
Chiaia, Professor 171
Child, Dr. A.B. 100
Child, Dr. Henry 152–154, 160–163
childbirth, dangers of 111
cinema and realism 175
Civil War, as karma for slavery 137–138
Clark, Uriah 82; *Plain Guide to Spiritualism* 93
"closed performances" 90
Conan Doyle, Sir Arthur 144
consciousness, "discrete degrees" of 75–78; *see also* dissociative identity disorder; double consciousness
Cook, Florence 142–159
Cook, Katie Selina 150, 158
The Corsican Brothers 12
corsican trap 15
Crazy Jane 27
Crookes, Dr. William 156; affair with Florence Cook 158–159; investigation of Katie King 157–158

Index

The Curse of Cain 15
Cushman, Charlotte, as Meg Merrilies 70

Dalston Spiritualist circle 149–151
Daly, Augustin 13
Daniel Deronda 24
Daniels, Cora *see* Richmond, Cora
Daniels, Colonel W. 123
Darwin, darwinism 18, 83
Davenport, Ira 94, 146–147
Davenport, William 94, 146–147
Davis, Andrew Jackson, the "Poughkeepsie seer" 82, 106, 140
Davis, Marietta 81
The Dead Secret 15
De La Rue, Madame 35
Delphic oracle 4–5, 17
De Puysegur, Marquis 33
De Sennevoy, Baron Potet 41
D'Esperance, Elizabeth (Elizabeth Hope) 175–177; and Nepenthes 177; and Yolanda 175–176
Diamond, Dr. Hugh Welch 29
Dickens, Charles 35; *The Frozen Deep* 35; and mesmerism 35–36; on Mrs. Hayden 144–145
Diderot, Denis 25; *Paradox of Acting* 58
dissociative identity disorder 5, 61–62, 75–7
Dr. Jekyll and Mr Hyde 12
Doten, Lizzie 95
double consciousness 55–62
Dracula 12
Du Bois, W.E.B. 140
Ducrow, Andrew 60
Duguid, David 103
Du Maurier, George 3, 36–37
Duse, Eleanora 14

The Easiest Way 13
ectoplasm 16, 169–170
Edmonds, Justice John W. 99, 113
Edmonds, Laura 99
Ehrenborg, Madame Frederika 110
Elective Affinities (Goethe) 34
Eliot, George 24
Elliotson, Dr. John 39–54; on "dual consciousness" 55
Emerson, Ralph Waldo 147
epilepsy, confusion with hysteria 40
equality, gender 111
equality, racial 139–140
expectations, horizon of 89–91

Fairlamb, Annie 142
"fallen woman" 27
Fashion 63–64

Faucit, Helen 24
feminine roles 17–30
femininization of American culture 85
the Flying Dutchman 15
Forrest, Edwin 129–130
The Forrest Princess 129
Fox, Kate 79–81, 86–87, 142
Fox, Leah (Leah Fish) 80, 86
Fox, Maggie, affair with Kane 86
Fox sisters 79–81, 86; alcoholism of 87; recantation of 87
Foyt, Ada 123
Franklin, Benjamin (spirit of) 2
Franklin, Sir John 86, 104–105
Freud, Sigmund 19
Die Frieschutz 12
The Frozen Deep 35
"full form materializations" 142–143
Fuller, Margaret, spirit of 107

Garrison, William Lloyd, spirit of 138
Goethe, Johann Wolfgang von 34
Greeley, Horace 80
Green, Frances (Fanny) 88; and black spirits 137
Green, Mrs. Lizzie 108, 110, 112, 132–133; and Indian spirits 136–137
Guppy, Mrs. 156
gypsies 69; in literature 70
"Gypsy" (spirit) 64–78
The Gypsy Wanderer, or The Stolen Child 69

Hafed, Prince of Persia 103
Hatch, Benjamin Franklin 118–122
Hatch, Cora *see* Richmond, Cora
Hayden, Mrs. 144–145
Haymarket anarchists 126
Heaven, spheres of 112
Herne, Frank 149
Holmes, Mr. and Mrs., mediums 152, 160; see also Child, Dr. Henry
Holy Land, spirit travel to 103
Home, D.D. (Daniel Dunglas) 145
home theatricals 9
Hope, Elizabeth *see* D'Esperance, Elizabeth
Hopedale community 115–116
Houdin, Robert 95
Houdini, Harry 94; *A Magician Among the Spirits* 95
How I Escaped the Mad Doctors (Weldon) 30
Hutchinson Family singers (spirits) 96
hysteria 40, 72

Ibsen, Henrik 14
"Ideal Woman" *see* feminine roles

Index

Indian dramas 129–130
The Indian Princess or la Belle Sauvage 129
The Indian Prophecy 129
Indian Removal Act of 1830 130
Indians *see* Native Americans
Irene, ou le magnetisme 35
Irving, Henry 12, 14–15; and double consciousness 59

Jack the Ripper 12
Jackson, Andrew 130
Jackson, Jane M. 134
James, Henry: and *The Bostonians* 96, 123; on Swedenborg 107
James, William 146
Janet, Pierre 34, 77
Jay, Miss (medium) 85
"Jim Crow" 46–48
Jones, Amanda (medium) 112–113

Kane, Elisha Kent 86–87, 105
Kean, Edmund 21; Lewes on 60, 88
Kemble, Fanny 20, 57–58
King, John (spirit) 142, 150–156; on capital punishment 156
King, Katie (spirit) 142, 150–156; on religion 155–156; in seances with R.D. Owen 160–167
King Philip, spirit of Indian 134–135
Kotzebue, August von 35

Lady Audley's Secret 22
The Lady of Lyons (Mowatt) 21, 63
The Lancet 40–54
Lewes, George Henry: on acting theory 59–60; on alternating consciousness 60; on Mrs. Hayden 145; on Rachel 24; on "seeing is believing" 168
liminality 6
Lincoln, Abraham 85, 95, 137
Little Eva (*Uncle Tom's Cabin*) 13, 85
Livermore, Charles 142
Logan, Olive 22
Lombroso, Dr. Cesare 170
The Love Life of Dr. Kane 87
Lucia di Lammermoor 27

Macready, William Charles 35, 129–130
madwoman 27; *see also* Ophelia
A Magician Among the Spirits 95
magicians 94–95, 146–147
Mansfield, Richard 12
Mars, spirit travel to planet 110
Martersteig, Max, on "self-hypnosis" of actors 61–62
Martineau, Harriet 106

masculinity of antebellum American theatre 66
Maskelyne, J.N. 146–147
"mediomania" 57
Mediums Mutual Aid Society 14
mediumship, professional vs. private 18, 147–149
Meisel, Martin 10
melodrama 10; decline of 175
Mesmer, Franz Anton 31–36
Mesmerism 31–36; in America 63, 67; and Dickens 35–36; and Elliotson 39–54
Metamora 129
Mettler, Samantha 101
A Midsummer Night's Dream 15
Millerites and millenial frenzy 132
Miss Julie 14
Morgan, Annie Owen 154–156; *see also* King, Katie
Morgan, Sir Henry Owen 142, 152–156; *see also* King, John
Moses, William Stainton 146
Mowatt, Anna Cora 63–78
Mowatt, James 63, 65, 68, 74
multiple personalities 77
multiple personality disorder 5, 61; *see also* dissociative identity disorder
Myers, Frederic H. 57

National Spiritualist Association 126
Native Americans 126; as healers 135; spiritual qualities of 132; *see also* Indian dramas
naturalism 14
"neo-dissociation theory" 77
The New Age 35
Nightingale, Florence 26

The Octoroon 14
O'Key, Elizabeth 39–54
O'Key, Jane (sister of Elizabeth) 49–50
Olcott, Henry Steele 164–167
On the Threshold of the Unseen 113
Oolaita, or the Indian Heroine 131
Ophelia 27–30
oracle 1, 5
Ouina (spirit) 96, 127–132; *Ouina's Canoe and Christmas Offering* 128
Owen, Alex 64
Owen, Robert Dale, Jr. 130, 144; continuing belief in spirits 168; seances with Katie King 160–167
Owen, Robert, Sr. 144, 160

Paine, Thomas, spirit of 112
Palladino, Eusapia 170–175
pantomimes and spiritualism 100
Paradise, Marie-Therese von 33

Index

Paradox of Acting (Diderot) 58
Pepper's ghost 16
performing femininity 66
phrenology 11
Piper, Lenore 96, 173; and "Dr. Phinuit" 146
Plain Guide to Spiritualism 93
Pocahontas 128–130
Pocahontas: A Historical Drama 130
Podmore, Frank 91; on physical mediumship 173–174
Poe, Edgar Allan 95
Post, Amy 124–126
Post, Isaac 125
Poyen, Charles 141
Proteus 56
"Punch and Judy" cabinet 169
pythia *see* Delphic oracle

Race, Victor 33–34
Rachel (actress) 10, 22–23
realism on stage 13–16, 143, 169, 174–175
reception theory 89–91
repression 75–76
revivalism 79–81
Rice, T.D. (Jim Crow) 13, 46–48
Richmond, Cora L.V. 83, 115–126; death of husband and child 126; divorce 119; and politics 124–126; popularity in Britain 123; *see also* Ouina (spirit)
Richmond, William 126
Ritchie, Anna Cora Mowat *see* Mowatt, Anna Cora
Rousseau, Jean Jacques 25

Salem witch trials, John King's involvement in 153
Sargent, Epes 71; as Mowatt's mesmerist 63; *The Scientific Basis of Spiritualism* 69, 140
Schlegel, Friedrich 34–35
The Scientific Basis of Spiritualism 69, 140
Scribe, Eugene 10; *Irène, ou le magnétisme* 35
séance(s) 79, 88, 93; in Britain 145; materialization 119, 174; trickery in 94; unconventional manifestations in 97–101
"self hypnosis" of actors 61–62
shadow puppets (Indonesian) 4
shaman 1, 4–5
Showers, Mary Rosina 158
slavery, opposition to 113; spirit messages about 137–141
slaves, spirits of 139; spirituality of 140
"slice of life" theatre 13, 175
Smith, E.T. 14–15

Smith-Rosenberg, Carroll 65
Smithson, Harriet 29
"socio-cognitive theory" 76
somnambulism 43, 75
spectacle, appetite for 174
spectators, "ideal" 90
spirit cabinet 94
spirit travel 102–114
Spiritualism 79–87
splitting ("spaltung") as result of conflict 77
Stowe, Harriet Beecher 85; *see also* Little Eva
Strindberg, August 14
Svengali 3
Swedenborg, Emmanuel, and Swedenborgianism 74, 82, 106–107
Sweet, Mrs. Elizabeth 102, 139

table turning 92, 93
tableaux vivants 9, 124
Tappan, Cora *see* Richmond, Cora
Tappan, Col. Samuel F. 122, 126
Tecumseh, spirit of 132
theatricality 9; in Victorian culture 9–11
Trilby 3, 36–37
Trollope, Frances (Fanny) 106
Truth, Sojourner 124, 141
Turner, Victor 6, 48

utopias, spirit 108, 111

vampire trap 15
Vanderdecken (the Flying Dutchman) 15
Villette (Brontë) 23–24
Volckman, William 156

Wakley, Thomas 41
Ward, Ellen 105
Washington, George, spirit of 2, 113
Weldon, Georgina 30
well-made play 10, 13
White, Eliza 165–167
Wilberforce, William, spirit of 138
Wilcox, Mrs. Eliza (trance subject) 98
Williams, Charles 149
Wittman, Blanche 38
woman as angel 18
woman as demon 18
women's rights convention, Seneca Falls 92
Wood, C.E. 142

Zola, Emile 14

www.ingramcontent.com/pod-product-compliance
Ingram Content Group UK Ltd.
Pitfield, Milton Keynes, MK11 3LW, UK
UKHW042005140426
5217IPUK00015B/986